Praise for Ken Scholes and for
Long Walks, Last Flights & Other Strange Journeys

"Smart, savvy, poetic and the best damned thing you're likely to pick up for less than twenty bucks any time soon. Scholes can make words dance, and stories sing."
—Jonathan Strahan, *Locus* and *The Year's Best Science Fiction & Fantasy of the Year*

"*Long Walks* ought to ship with tissues. It didn't make me merely weep, it made me sob. Ken Scholes consistently delivers stories that are beautifully written and deeply moving."
—Mary Robinette Kowal, 2008 John W. Campbell Award Winner

"Whether it's gunfighters on the planetary frontier, mutant killer chimps on the moon, or Fearsome Jones and the three-eyed baby, Ken Scholes writes a wonderful, unique blend of science fiction and fantasy that blurs the boundaries between the genres. If you want strange journeys, here they are."
—James C. Glass, author of *Shanji* and *The Viper of Portello*

"This weird and wonderful first collection showcases stories born from a potent imagination and tamed with admirable skill by a natural storyteller. Ken Scholes embraces the wild pop culture abandon of Howard Waldrop and the seedy shadows of Joe Lansdale's trailer park nightmares without missing a beat, and without letting his influences override a truly original voice. Ken Scholes has the goods."
—Josh Rountree, author of *Can't Buy Me Faded Love*

"I thoroughly enjoyed *Long Walks, Last Flights, and Other Strange Journeys*. I can't remember another collection of short work that brought me such varied emotions. I laughed. I cried. I felt amazed, over and over, by Ken's wonderful imagination. In his hands, the short form transcends story to reach for the human soul. From bears with hearts to mechanical men steeped in grief, from the guy in the cube next to you to Hitler, Ken has no fear. He takes it all on, and he wins. Ken's writing has the brilliance of short story masters like Ray Bradbury and Harlan Ellison, and a voice fresh with the needs of the extraordinary times we are living in.
—Brenda Cooper, author of *Reading the Wind* and *The Silver Ship and the Sea*

"Here's the real joy in this collection: it's an 82,000 word long sampler, a teaser. Ken has novels on the way. He undoubtedly will do other collections. You have the rare privilege of getting in on the Ken Scholes ground floor. There's a lot more of Ken Scholes than appears in this wonderful collection."
—James Van Pelt, author of *Summer of the Apocalypse* and *Strangers and Beggars*

"Ken Scholes is a hot new voice to watch for on the interesting frontier between science fiction and fantasy. He has a keen eye for action and a keen ear for the sounds of the human heart. Grab on now, because he's going places."
—Harry Turtledove, author of *The Man With the Iron Heart*

"I've spent weeks trying to find the appropriate adjectives to describe how much I like Ken Scholes' stories. I finally figured it: Wow. That's it. Wow—just plain wow. Time spent reading Ken Scholes cannot be deducted from yr
—Ken Rand, author of *The*

"A Ken Scholes story will alternately ⋯ nake you think. Find every story of his you can ⋯ ming into the field."
—Dean Wesley Smith, aut

D1167177

"This is the golden age of fantasy, with a dozen masters doing their best work⋯ ⋯long comes Ken Scholes, with his amazing clarity, power, and invention, and shows us all how it's done."
—Orson Scott Card, author of *Ender's Game* and *Ender in Exile*

LONG WALKS, LAST FLIGHTS
& Other Strange Journeys

LONG WALKS, LAST FLIGHTS

& Other Strange Journeys

KEN SCHOLES

FAIRWOOD PRESS
Bonney Lake • Seattle

Long Walks, Last Flights & Other Strange Journeys
A Fairwood Press Book
December 2008
Copyright © 2008 by Kenneth G. Scholes

Fairwood Press
21528 104th Street Court East
Bonney Lake, WA 98391
www.fairwoodpress.com

Cover illustration & design by Paul Swenson
Book Design by Patrick Swenson

ISBN: 0-9820730-0-3
ISBN13: 978-0-9820730-0-1
First Fairwood Press Edition: December 2008
Printed in the United States of America

Dedication

For John Pitts, whose gracious eye upon these stories and upon my life
has made all the difference, again and again

and

For Joan Owens, English teacher extraordinaire, who left the party
before the punch was served

COPYRIGHTS

CONTENTS

SOMEDAY
Patrick Swenson

In the fall of 1995, with the help of friends and partners, I started
a small press magazine called *Talebones*. The magazine has been
a part of my life for a dozen years now, with 37 issues produced to
date. Some of the writers who've appeared in the magazine have
had good enough experiences that they've come back to me when
thinking about larger book projects. In 2000, I started Fairwood
Press to start publishing some of those larger projects. I've con-
templated folding *Talebones* on a number of occasions, but every
time I entertain that idea, I remember that 90% of my book projects
for Fairwood have come from *Talebones* alums. The magazine
seems to be a pretty good R&D department. Plus . . . people yell
and scream at me not to do it.

After starting the magazine, I also began teaching evening writing
classes. This is where Ken Scholes comes into the picture. Actually, he was already *in* the picture, submitting stories to *Talebones*
before I ever knew him personally. He sent me stories, and I would
reject them. And yet . . . I knew he was *close*.

Enclosed with one particular story rejection, I sent him a flyer
for the writing class. We still laugh about that: did I send it because
I thought he needed it, or what? Truth is, I sent the flyer to *all* local
writers, trying to drum up business. He'll say otherwise, but although he took the class, he probably didn't *need* to. He's since
sold most of the stories he submitted there. In the Winter of 2000, I
published his first short story, "The Taking Night," in *Talebones*
#18. Several more story acceptances followed, including the very
popular "Edward Bear and the Very Long Walk," about a brave
little bear who becomes a hero and longs to hear of "Someday."
And of course, Ken sold a lot of stories to other markets, including
those much bigger and more prestigious than *Talebones*.

It was just a matter of time before Ken's glimpse of Someday arrived. Seven years later, Ken had enough fabulous tales to gather into a collection. And then some. You can bet a second collection will follow on the heels of this one.

Here's what I like about Ken Scholes' fiction:

He tells great stories. Our humanity, the good and bad parts altogether, lives on every page, even when those stories don't directly involve humans. His prose simply bleeds with voice. It is distinct, unique, and always compelling. You're going to be both entertained and moved by a Ken Scholes story. In some cases, moved to tears. In some cases, you'll be snarfing up a lung with laughter. Ken's major multi-book deal for a huge fantasy series will catapult him onto the world-wide stage, and his marvelous writing is going to make him a star in the SF world. I can guarantee it now.

So you're getting into the action early on with this collection. I'm expecting big things from Ken, as I said, and although he'll say I helped him starting out, I knew he would find success on his own. I'm just hoping to grab a hold of his coattails from this point on.

Here's what I like about Ken Scholes, the human being:

He's genuine. He's warm, friendly, and doesn't have a big ego. He can talk with major writers and editors, he can talk to writers just starting out, and he can talk to them *all* with the same realness that embodies his personality. Along the way, as I got to know him through my publishing ventures, he became a good friend. We'd talked about having someone write a preface for this collection, and we'd decided the James Van Pelt introduction would be plenty. And then Ken changed his mind and said he wanted one. "But here's the kicker," he said. "I want *you* to write it." A half heart-beat later I said yes.

If you really want to get a sense of Ken the person, start at the back of this book with "Last Flight of the Goddess." That's where Ken lives. It's where his wonderful, lovely wife Jen lives, too, and Ken's total love of Jen is the cornerstone of that story. But all the way through, you'll see, embedded in that amazing voice, the Ken Scholes I know. You'll find him in all the stories here. You'll also find strange worlds, amazing team-ups of fictional and historical characters, expeditions into the heart, excursions into distant fantasy lands, and you'll find Truth.

Ken Scholes found his Truth. He found Someday. And now you can too.

INTRODUCTION
James Van Pelt

I'm almost sorry to say that my introduction to Ken was through one of the short stories in this book: "Edward Bear and the Very Long Walk," and the reason I'm *almost* sorry for that is that for a long time, Ken's story of a very, very brave toy doing the best he could for noble purpose is what I thought of when someone else mentioned his name, or I had a chance to make reference to him. That makes me sorry because it took me a while to discover Ken's writing is so much larger, varied and encompassing than that one story, because Ken is not a one-note flute. He commands the entire orchestra.

But I did discover Ken through that story. It provoked one of the first fan letters I'd written. "Edward Bear and the Very Long Walk" got to me through emotion, and that's what I told Ken in my note. I've been reading fiction for a long time, a good deal of that time as a teacher and writer myself, so when I read a story I'm often paying attention to the writer's craft, sort of like a dancer going to the ballet or a painter going to the gallery. I see the work differently now. When I was young, fiction always swept me away. Within a hundred words I'd forget that I was reading, and the author would have me. But growing up, reading a lot, becoming analytic, took the experience of reading for pure joy away.

I'm not totally sad about losing my joy in everything I read. I've gained some knowledge during that time. My writing is better for it, I hope, but I don't read much for recreation. Like Dorothy in *The Wizard of Oz*, I can't ignore the man behind the curtain. Mark Twain wrote about the effect of too much knowledge in *Life on the Mississippi*. About his first steamboat trip he said, "I stood like one bewitched. I drank it in, in a speechless rapture. The world was new to me, and I had never seen anything like this at home." That's how all reading struck me. Every book was beautiful. All words in a row mesmerized. Then, I studied structure and character and language rhythm. Like Twain, for me the river changed. He said, "Now when I had mastered the language of this water and had come to know every trifling feature that bordered the great river as familiarly as I knew the letters of the alphabet, I had made a valuable acquisition. But I had lost something, too. I had lost something which could never be restored to me while I lived. All the grace, the beauty, the poetry had gone out of the majestic river!"

Reading hasn't become *totally* without its charms for me, but the beautiful moment comes much more rarely. I got it when I read Connie Willis's *Passage*. It happened when I read Robert Holdstock's *Mythago Wood*. Neil Gaiman, Kelly Link and Ted Chiang can consistently make me forget that I'm reading. And it happened to me again when I read "Edward Bear and the Very Long Walk."

So I became a Ken Scholes fan. I think you will too.

My personal favorite in the collection is "Soon We Shall All be Saunders," with its surreal, cruel and funny look at corporate life. Well, it would be my favorite if it weren't for "Action Team-Ups Number Thirty-Seven," that made me laugh about superheroes, nursing homes, and archenemies at the end of days. Did I say "Action Team-Ups . . ."? I meant, "Of Metal Men and Scarlet Thread and Dancing with the Sunrise," which shows that Ken can blend fantasy, steampunk and political intrigue like nobody's business.

Okay, I can't pick a favorite, because as soon as I start trying I think of "Summer in Paris, Light from the Sky," that did the impossible of actually making me like Adolf Hitler, or I remember the twisted metaphysics of "Into the Blank Where Life Is Hurled."

Here's another problem in trying to pick a favorite from this collection: have you ever gotten into a discussion with a bunch of Stephen King fans? Eventually one of them will ask, "What is your favorite King novel?" They'll all think about it for a minute, and then the questioner will say, "Not counting *The Stand*, or course." The reason they eliminate *The Stand* is that not only is it an amazing story, but it's so much larger than the others. Comparing *The Stand* to the rest is like comparing a haiku to a sonnet. In this collection, the sonnet closes the book, the heart-rendingly funny and sad "The Last Flight of the Goddess."

I probably could pick a favorite as long as I don't count "The Last Flight of the Goddess," of course.

Here's the real joy in this collection: it's an 82,000 word long sampler, a teaser. Ken has novels on the way. He undoubtedly will do other collections. You have the rare privilege of getting in on the Ken Scholes ground floor. There's a lot more of Ken Scholes than appears in this wonderful collection.

Good thing you bought this volume! Put it on your bookshelf when you are done (where you can easily get to it for rereading and lending), but leave a lot of empty space to the right. That's where the *next* books from Ken will go. I know you are going to want them too.

LONG WALKS, LAST FLIGHTS

& Other Strange Journeys

THE MAN WITH GREAT
DESPAIR BEHIND HIS EYES

Meriwether Lewis stared down at the time-worn scrap of paper, holding it in his hands as if it were a rare butterfly too easily crushed. He'd been in one of his moods when the courier had summoned him two hours earlier. This time, he'd even loaded the pistol, placed it on the table near his chair and brandy. This time, he'd promised himself, he would follow through and be done with it. But now, sitting in Jefferson's study, curiosity pushed the darkness aside.

The President pushed back his chair, stood and turned away from the paper-strewn table to gaze out the window at the rain-soaked night. Lewis, glancing up briefly, thought he looked tired.

"Mr. President?"

"As you know, Meriwether, I'm not one given to fanciful flights. By God, I am a man of science and reason, but this shakes me to my very soul and confounds my sensibilities."

Lewis nodded, more to himself than not, remembering when this man — this intellectual Goliath — was his neighbor in Virginia. They'd spent hours talking together about plants and fossils and the expansive West. Thomas Jefferson was every part a scientist. He looked down at the green rectangle, wondered what tree this unlikely leaf fell from. He studied the face in the thumb-sized portrait and read the name again. "And you're certain it is him?"

"Yes. It's Jackson . . . that backwoods powder-keg. The years are heavy upon him in that likeness."

They were indeed, Lewis saw. Andrew Jackson, now a judge somewhere in Tennessee after a brief stint in the Senate, was in all actuality not much older than himself. But he wore twenty, maybe thirty years beyond in the small drawing.

Lewis turned the paper over, a wonder tinged with some form of fear lifted the hair on his neck and hands. Another picture, another name beneath it. "This is the President's House," he said in a hollow voice.

"Yes." Jefferson turned in from the window. "Yes it is."

"But — "

"But the President's House isn't nearly as old as the parchment. And it has never been called 'The White House.' At least not to my knowledge."

"And neither to mine." Lewis had spent a miserable winter in the unfinished, leaking shell of a house as laborers completed the work. "How did this come into your hands?"

Jefferson creaked into the wood chair and poured a glass of water from a ceramic pitcher. "A colleague at the Society purchased it at no small price from one of Gray's men. A sailor on the *Columbia* claims to have traded it away from a Chinook medicine-man." Captain Gray had named the river after his ship, Lewis remembered, and supposedly enjoyed several weeks of profitable trade among the West-coast natives. "The medicine-man claimed it held mystical properties, having come from a white holy man who lived deep in the forest north of the river's mouth . . . a teller of fortunes, the Indian claimed." Jefferson closed his mouth, pursing his lips in thought. "He should not be difficult to find, I would think."

Lewis looked up at his friend, his President. "You are proposing that I go?" An excitement gripped him; he had wanted to explore the West for longer than he could remember.

"Yes. Congress has approved the funding to outfit this Corps of Discovery." His brow furrowed. "But this is to be first and foremost a scientific and military expedition. The water route, the careful recording of flora and fauna, notation of any strategic import — these are all noble and legitimate endeavors. As written in the letter you shall shortly receive. This other matter is to be held in your strictest confidence." The President's jaw firmed.

"You shall have it, Sir."

Jefferson smiled, reached across the table to pat Lewis' hand. "I know I shall." He paused, looking even older and more tired. The strain between the French and the British had worn him down, Lewis knew, and factions from the States grumbled faintly of secession as anti-Federalist feelings grew. "If you find him, Meriwether, I have to know. I have to know, if he can tell us, whether this Union we have forged with our very blood and tears and sweat shall abide or perish still in its crib."

"Yes, Mr. President." Lewis turned the parchment over again. It masqueraded as United States currency — a twenty dollar note — and next to an illegible signature stood four small numbers that grew larger and larger in his widening eyes: 1971.

He handed it back to Jefferson, glad for the delicate butterfly to leave his fingers.

In the months Lewis traveled with him, Drouillard's anger often hid behind a placid face, but the half-breed suddenly spat into the mud, water running off his cap as he tipped his head. "Damn this rain," he said and the Fields brothers sniggered. Dark eyes flashing back at them, he cursed them first in French, then in a half-dozen tribal tongues.

Lewis smiled at his stalwart companion's outburst though today the darkness held him. It had followed Lewis across the continent, aloof but near enough to sense. Here, close to the end of their journey, it thrived.

Dark and bleak, the sky hung low with clouds when they could see it beyond the pine-ceiling. Still, the sky saw *them* and rained down its furious tears. The stink of ruined, rotting fur filled his nostrils and his ankles ached with every step. The damned rain pervaded everything, rotting even their clothes. The Pacific Coast, thus far, proved to be a wet and gray place.

Private Frazier sidled up to him. "Cap'n Lewis?" He turned to the lanky Virginian, but kept his feet shuffling forward through the loam that sucked at his moccasins. "Do you really think we'll find a ship? And whites?"

"That's what they said." Two weeks before, a handful of Indians in a canoe had told him and Clark what to expect at the mouth of the Columbia. And as they made their way down the river, more and more of the natives wore sailors' caps, carried rusted knives and cooked from copper pots. Last Thursday, they'd finally seen the ocean, distant on the edge of the horizon. Yesterday, Lewis and his small party had left Clark and the others to scout north of the wide river.

"Hell if I'm walking all the way back if there's a ship," Reuben Fields said.

"Hell if you ain't." Joseph Fields laughed. "Hell if we all ain't, if the Captains have their way."

The bushes ahead rustled and their dog bounded out, his black fur slick with rain. A small rabbit kicked its last in the Newfoundland's strong jaws. He's the only one who's truly happy here, Lewis thought. The rain didn't affect him, darken his outlook. Still, mood or no, they had their mission, and the Corps of Discovery was about its business regardless of the weather.

"We'll rest here a bit."

At his word, the men found trees to squat against, hiding from the downpour as best they could. Lewis leaned against an alder and Drouillard drew close. They spoke in low voices.

"Cap'n, I know it's none of my concern, but if I knew what we were looking for I could be more helpful."

Lewis looked at the dark man, nearly as tall as himself, and pursed his lips. "Even if I myself knew completely, I couldn't tell you."

Drouillard nodded. "The men are curious."

"Let them be."

The interpreter straightened. "Aye, sir."

Lewis closed his eyes and let the heaviness take him. Weariness is to be expected, he realized, after eighteen months of walking, paddling and riding the wilderness.

Still, what an adventure so far. There would be much to talk about and celebrate when they returned. *If* they returned. If the rain didn't wash the very skin from their bones.

They'd all celebrated when they glimpsed the broad, gray expanse of the Pacific. But the joy leaked out of him too soon. All his life it had, and for a brief moment Lewis craved death again. "This is the place to find it," he said, not realizing he spoke aloud.

"Captain?"

"Never mind," Lewis said. "Let's move."

At noon they broke into a clearing and an old Indian stood, leaning on a birch staff. Lewis nodded at Drouillard who stepped forward, hands signing their intent. The Indian waved him away. "We do not need to make the sign-talking," he said in thickly accented English. He pointed to Lewis. "The Man-from-the-River told me he dreamed of a red stork flying in the direction of the sinking sun."

The men mumbled and Lewis gave them a hard glance. They often called him 'Red Stork' when they thought he wasn't listening.

Lewis approached the old man. The Indian watched him through squinted, dark eyes buried in a sea of wrinkles. "Who are you? How do you come to speak English? Are you the Man-from-the-River?"

The native shook his head. "The Man-from-the-River sent me to bring you to him. He wishes to meet the great Red Stork." He motioned Lewis closer, out of ear-shot of the others. "He told me to show you this." For a brief instant, a ball of green paper lay exposed in his palm, then he curled his fingers around it again.

"You'll make camp here and await my return," Lewis said over his shoulder. "I'm going on alone." The old man turned and walked toward the clearing's edge. Lewis glanced at Drouillard to confirm his order, and the interpreter nodded, eyes narrow.

Lewis followed the old man, catching up as the brush swallowed them. "You didn't tell me your name."

The old man didn't break his stride. "I am called John Fitzgerald Kennedy."

The rain stopped.

They walked until twilight fell, pushing aside the gray overcast day for a deeper gloom. Many times, Lewis tried to engage his companion in conversation, hoping to draw out information from the old man. He merely answered the questions with questions.

"Why is he called the Man-from-the-River?"

"What would you call a man pulled from the waters?"

"Where do the green papers come from?"

"Who can know where powerful medicine comes from?"

"Why are you called John Kennedy?"

"Why am I called by any name?"

"Can he really see the future?"

"Why is seeing the future more wondrous than seeing today?"

Eventually, Lewis surrendered and settled into a morose silence. Now that the rain had let up, he knew he should check the powder in his rifle and pistols. But the woods seemed quiet and the old man walked them with a confident, comfortable step that spoke safety to Lewis' vigilant heart.

They broke from the woods into a clearing that hugged a sheer wall of rock topped thirty feet above with pines and moss and fern. A wooden lean-to nestled against the rock, a trickle of smoke leaking out from it.

"I must tell you he doesn't make much of the white-man talk anymore. I think he has forgotten how. He is old. Older than me." The Indian started for the shelter, then stopped as Lewis hesitated. "I will translate," John said.

Lewis nodded, a sudden apprehension twisting his stomach. "Very well."

As they approached, a faint chanting drifted to his ears, a mumbled litany that rose and fell like a song. It stopped as John lifted the weave of alder branches that served as a door. He hurriedly waved Lewis in, as if anxious to keep the moist evening air at bay.

Lewis unslung his rifle and stooped to look inside the dirt-floored lean-to.

The first thing he saw was a canopy of green paper, the bills hung from bone fish-hooks and dangling from the ceiling. It was the ceiling of a faded, soft forest that rustled as his shoulders brushed the lean-to's doorway. The second thing he saw was the old man.

The Man-from-the-River sat on a doe-skin rug, legs crossed, hands turned upward and held at shoulder height. Long white hair flowed over his head and cascaded to the floor, like spilled milk, hiding what clothing he wore, if any. Large ears poked out from the pale tangle. His skin, pulled tightly over the bones, was slightly olive — perhaps of Spanish or Moorish descent — and his eyes were hidden behind a strange pair of dark spectacles. A long pink scar ran out from his scalp like a river leaving a forest, disappearing behind the spectacles, above his left eye. A small fire guttered in a pit dug into the floor, near the rock face.

Leaning the short-barrel musket against the granite wall, just inside the door, Lewis squeezed himself through the narrow opening. The room was surprisingly warm and he wrestled out of the stinking buffalo robe and pushed it outside, the hide already a casualty of the region.

He sat down before the Man-from-the-River and waited for John. As the old Indian settled in, Lewis drew a peace medal from inside his shirt. "The Great White Father sends this token of his regard for the Man-from-the-River." He handed it across the fire and waited while John translated. Nodding, the faintest smile touched the old man's lips as he took the medal. He turned and put it behind him, mumbling something.

John looked at Lewis. "The Man-from-the-River thanks the

Red Stork for his generous gift and is glad that you have come seeking him."

"How did he get here?" Lewis watched, listening to the translation.

"He awoke in the great river and did not know himself. I pulled him to safety. Over time, my people realized he had much medicine and charged me to care for him, but far from our village. This was almost thirty summers ago."

Lewis pointed at the ceiling. "Ask him about the paper bills, about the pictures and words on them. Where did they come from?"

John shook his head. "It is not wise to ask such."

"Ask him."

The Indian asked the question quickly, gesturing impatiently at Lewis. Man-from-the-River nodded slowly, looked at Lewis, and shook his head as he spoke.

"They came with him out of the river and are a part of his medicine," John translated. "You should not be concerned with them."

"Tell him my Great Father believes that they are important and sent me to ask of them."

John did, listened to the reply, and paused, asking the old man a question with raised eyebrows. Man-from-the-River nodded, saying the words again more firmly. "These are not why you have come. You have come to swim the dream-waters with the Man-from-the-River."

Lewis tried to hide his frustration behind a smile. "No, I have come to know — "

The Man-from-the-River started speaking, and Lewis let him. "You are a man with great despair behind your eyes, Red Stork. You are a man of tremendous courage but a mighty sadness washes you like the tide washes a stone. You have come to swim the dream-waters and be healed of your darkness."

Lewis felt his temper stir as his patience faded. But he also felt something else stir. The simultaneous hope and fear of being known by this strange old man. His thumb nervously tapped the butt of one pistol and he held his tongue. Finally, he said, "I have no need of healing." The lie rolled easily from him.

"Then we will eat," the Man-from-the-River said through his interpreter.

At that, he produced a bowl of dried fruit and two smoked salmon from a recess in the stone wall. They ate in silence.

When they finished, Lewis tried again. "My Great Father is a knowledgeable man. He has worked very hard to build a strong and just home for his children. He watches them and worries for their well-being. He hears that Man-from-the-River has much medicine and can tell the future. He sees Man-from-the-River's green paper and wonders what it is and where it comes from." If he hadn't held the parchment himself, hadn't seen the thousands of them that hung suspended above his head, he would have felt alarmed for Jefferson's mental state. His voice raised an octave. "Your servant, John Fitzgerald Kennedy, showed me one of these papers so I would come here with him. Now you tell me nothing about them. My Great Father will be unhappy if you do not send me home to him with answers for his questions." He sat back and waited.

Man-from-the-River's response was simple: "If your Great Father wished to ask questions of me, he would have come himself." Silence settled over them. He spoke again, quietly. "But perhaps when swimming the dream-waters you will find answers for him. Many have powerful visions, for Man-from-the-River's medicine is strong and sometimes his dreams are also shown when he gazes upon your own."

"Very well, I will swim the dream-waters." Lewis had participated in other tribal rites, finding them quaint and pointless however meaningful to these simple savages. And, he reasoned to himself, even the white man had his own, albeit superior, rites — baptism, communion, and the like. "But I am ignorant of such ways for my people no longer swim the dream-waters."

Man-from-the-River nodded, smiling, and pulled off the dark spectacles to reveal his eyes. He spoke to John, who also nodded.

"Man-from-the-River is glad to swim with you and hopes you will find the healing of your sorrow in the waters."

Lewis didn't know what to say. All his life, he'd wrestled with his moods but in public, particularly since the formation of the Corps, he'd bent his will to concealing the gripping melancholy. Certainly Clark knew — they'd been friends long enough — and on more than one occasion Jefferson had asked after his heart, but they, too, had years under the belt. Was it possible this man could see past his resolve in so short a time?

Lewis said nothing.

John half-stood. "I will return in the morning. You will need no further interpretation." He lifted the door to leave.

"I'd rather you stayed," Lewis said.

"It is not the way." He left, replacing the woven screen of branches. Lewis turned back to the old man.

Grunting in satisfaction, Man-from-the-River stretched a gnarled hand above his head and plucked a crisp green parchment. Laying it on a flat, smooth stone he reached behind and drew a bone knife. He duck-walked to Lewis and tugged at his pack, pointing at his bedroll and then at the corner of the hovel. Lewis unrolled it and stripped out of his jacket.

The old man ran the knife along his hand, not breaking the skin, to show Lewis his intentions. Familiar with the bonding ritual, Lewis nodded and winced as the blade sliced through his offered hand. A line of crimson beaded up and he watched it. Man-from-the-River cut his own hand and pressed their wounds together, chanting in a low voice.

After about five minutes, Man-from-the-River pulled away and drew a squirrel-skin sack from beneath his own bedroll. He carefully untied its strings, folded the green parchment in half lengthwise and sprinkled a mixture of herb and powder into the valley it created. Then, he rolled the paper around it as if it were a cigar and ran his tongue around it to hold it shut. He twisted the ends and grinned up at Lewis with raised eyebrows.

Lewis smiled back, inwardly wondering what the contents of the medicine bag were and what effect they may have on his physiology.

Man-from-the-River dug a stick out of the fire and held it to one end while he puffed at the other. The room filled with a scent of old paper mingled with alfalfa. After drawing in a lungful, he grunted and passed it to Lewis.

He filled his lungs and burst into a fit of coughing. The smoke tasted sweet with just a hint of licorice. Man-from-the-River laughed and motioned for him to try again. He did.

They passed it back and forth for half an hour, each lungful stretching at Lewis' perceptions. The room began to vibrate slightly. It pulsated like a great beating heart. He could hear the rasp of his beard growing, could see the blood racing beneath Man-from-the-River's skin. Each time he moved, his surroundings moved with him. Finally, when the cigar was nothing but a glowing stub, Man-from-the-River re-opened their wounds, mingled their blood again, and waved Lewis to the bedroll.

He fell into it like it was the deepest of rivers.

Then, he swam.

*

Images crowded his eyes, fleeting pictures that moved across a window set in the side of an ornate wooden box. He heard sounds, too, but they were far away. He sat in a strange chair, reclined in front of the box, drinking a weak beer from a light but somehow metal can.

WHOMP.

He saw a low black carriage without horses, surrounded by strangely dressed men. A man sitting in back with a woman suddenly jerked then slumped over.

WHOMP.

He saw a large metal box-like something that settled down from the sky. Men holding strange rifles, wearing green uniforms and helmets, scrambled from it into a jungle.

WHOMP.

He saw a man-shaped creature jump from a ladder onto a dusty, barren landscape, heard a crackling voice talk about small steps and giant leaps.

WHOMP.

He saw the flag of the United States, burning in the hands of a wild-haired, wild-eyed youth, and realized the handful of stars had become a crowded field.

WHOMP.

Suddenly, Lewis was somewhere else — a room crowded with young people dressed strangely. He stood behind a lectern, a stick of chalk held tightly in his hand. In front of him lay an open book. His own face stared back at him from one of the pages. Clark's face looked out from the other.

WHOMP.

The scene changed again to the comfortable chair and the window-box.

A black man in a suit led a mob of other blacks on a march through streets that looked vaguely familiar.

WHOMP.

"Miss, you'd better look at that note," he heard himself say in a voice not his own. "I have a bomb." He sat in a less comfortable, narrow seat with a briefcase on his lap. He opened it slightly, showing the indecently dressed woman a bundle of red sticks and wires. He sat in a tunnel-like corridor with humming in his ears. The other chairs around him, row on row from one end of the tube to another, were nearly empty. When he saw the windows, he looked out the one closest.

The first thing he saw was his reflection, also not his own. Instead, Man-from-the-River, thirty years younger, with short dark hair and dark skin, eyes hidden behind dark glasses.

The second thing he saw was the ocean of darkness above and below. He was flying.

WHOMP.

Now, weighed down by a pack and satchel, he stood by an open door and stairs leading down into the sky. Wind howled and tore at him. Outside, nothing but darkness and cold awaited him. A disembodied voice crackled near him: "Is everything okay back there, Mr. Cooper?"

"No," he said and jumped into the storm.

He fell faster and faster, eyes forced open, until something snapped and billowed. Something like the hand of an almighty, saving god jerked him upward, threatening to rip him asunder. A moment of pain, then he floated on the air. Lightning flashed. Frozen rain pelted. Above him, a metal bird rumbled away.

Below him, somewhere lost in a November night, a river awaited. Time opened its mouth and swallowed him whole.

Lewis slept.

"I was a teacher, before."

Lewis opened his eyes, forced them wide against the room's threatened collapse. A sharp pain lanced the front of his head and his mouth tasted like dry ashes. Man-from-the-River sat slouched in the corner, dark glasses bouncing back the flickering fire.

Lewis stretched and sat up as quickly as his head allowed. "You speak English?"

The old man chuckled. "Sometimes. How do you think JFK learned it?" JFK . . . John Fitzgerald Kennedy, Lewis realized. "Now *that* was a goddamn shame," Man-from-the-River said. "Oswald could have never pulled it off alone."

Lewis didn't know what to say. A dozen questions danced in his brain.

"Yes," the old man continued, "Teaching history, you see the unlikely, accidental heroes and the true ones. You were a true one, Meriwether Lewis, and one of my favorites. The tragedy is that you never saw it. And me? Well, I was never a hero . . . just a guy who wanted to be part of history, a guy tired of talking about it all the time." He nodded at the green papers overhead. "I suppose somewhere up there people still talk about both of us, too. Movies, books . . . God knows what else." He laughed and it became a wet cough.

Lewis shifted uncomfortably. "I don't know what you mean."

Man-from-the-River waved a hand and his outstretched fingers caught the smoke and dispersed it in gray tendrils. "You don't have to, Captain Lewis."

"Where do you come from?"

The old man coughed again. "Someplace I'll never see again." He pulled off the spectacles. He chuckled and then sang in a quiet voice: "We've all come to look for America."

Lewis leaned forward. "The United States of America? Tell me, I beg you, what you know?"

"Jefferson sent you. Your Great Father, right?"

He nodded. "Yes. The scrip . . . it's from our future, isn't it?" Lewis swallowed back a sudden queasiness in his stomach. "You . . . you are from our future, too."

Man-from-the-River smiled. "What do you really want to know Meriwether? You've seen everything in the dream-waters. You know the Union shall prevail. Oh, they'll kill Abraham, Martin and John. Bobby, too. There will be wars and rumors of war. There will be peace and rumors of peace." He paused. "What do you really want to know, Meriwether?"

Sadness sprung into his throat. Water pried at his eyes. He'd held it back long enough, denied it long enough. Whatever squeezed his heart also muttered that his one moment of true honesty was upon him here in this lean-to, thousands of miles from home. Lewis choked, his voice a whisper. "But," he asked, "Will I prevail?"
Man-from-the-River looked away. "I am an old man. My remaining days are few and I have waited years for your arrival. Stay with me and I will teach you to swim the dream-waters alone. In time they will wash your sorrows as they have washed mine and those who came before me."

Yes, he thought. For years he'd wrestled his demon. He *could* stay; he *could* find some kind of peace here, away from the world.

There truly was medicine in this place, with this old man. But duty nudged him. "Sir, I can not." Lewis's voice shook. "And you have not answered my question."

Man-from-the-River looked at him. Their eyes locked. "You will survive your expedition. You will be hailed a hero."

Lewis held his stare. "That is not what I mean."

"You are no coward. You are strong and hard to die. Remember those words well."

"And my melancholia?" A tear leaked out. "I fear sometimes it may be the end of me."

Man-from-the-River said nothing. Lewis waited but knew he had his answer. The knowing somehow gentled him. Hours crawled and Lewis drifted off again. He awoke with John Fitzgerald Kennedy gently shaking him.

The native pointed to a still, slumped figure. "He swims the deepest dream-waters now."

Lewis stayed to help build the pyre. Man-from-the-River had left detailed instructions with John and they carried them out. He resisted the strong urge to snatch one of the green papers, the scrip of a far-away time. Instead, they packed them into a battered satchel and placed them onto Man-from-the-River's naked chest.

Not Man-from-the-River, Lewis thought, but Man-from-the-Sky . . . Man-from-Tomorrow.

John Fitzgerald Kennedy lit the pyre and the kindling crackled to life despite the fine morning rain. "He wished for you to stay. He spoke often of you. He waited for your coming with great anticipation."

Lewis nodded, lost in thought. Soon, he would head south and find his small group of men. They would meet up with Clark and the others on the Columbia, wait out the winter on that western shore and eventually turn homeward. What would he tell his President and friend? How would he tell this part of his journey? Or should he tell it at all?

The fire grew and ashes lifted from the burning satchel like gray butterflies suddenly freed.

Lewis sipped his brandy and watched the dancing flames in Jefferson's hearth. Every flame now a pyre. Every ash, a question he knew he could not answer honestly.

"Missouri will suit you well," the President said with a smile.

"*Governor* Lewis." He raised his glass and Lewis did the same.

"Thank you, Sir."

"Anything for a hero of the Republic."

There was an endless march of parades and speeches and parties. Attentions from the highest of society and huzzahs from the basest. Lewis lived in a whirlwind frenzy.

Jefferson stood and went to a high shelf. He reached for a large book, opened it, and removed the familiar green scrap of paper from its pages. He held it in his hands. "What of our other matter, Meriwether?" the President asked.

Lewis had thought long on what to say. He'd waited politely for weeks, expecting the question to come at any time. He cleared his voice.

"I . . . I found nothing, Mr. President."

Jefferson remained silent, waiting for Lewis to elaborate.

"I did inquire. This medicine man – Man-from-the-River they called him – he died a year earlier of the pox, I'm afraid."

Jefferson sighed, turning the scrip over again. "Perhaps a clever hoax then," he said. "Still, wouldn't it be something to know. To really *know*."

Lewis closed his eyes. The brandy, the warm fire, wrapped him tight. Behind his eyes, despair lay at arm's length, appeased for now. "To know what, Sir?"

Jefferson placed the scrip in the book, closed it and replaced it on the shelf. He smiled, his voice suddenly merry. "How it all turns out, of course. Our great experiment in Democracy."

Lewis opened his mouth to speak, shut it, opened it again. "But . . . "

"Yes?"

His words tumbled like the waters in a hundred rivers he had crossed over the past few years. "But if we could know, Sir, exactly how it would all come out. If we could know for certain that we either would or would not prevail in whatever task we had set our hands to do . . . would it change anything? If we knew success was guaranteed, could that not lead to risks that might undo our own future?" Jefferson studied Lewis, caught in his words. "And if we knew that our failure was certain, wouldn't we still do what needs doing? In faith and in hope for something better?" He leaned forward now, feeling the heat in his face. The darkness stirred inside of him at the question, a cold lover rolling over in her sleep. "If you knew that you would fail, Sir, wouldn't you still try?"

Jefferson laughed. "Of course." He clapped Lewis's shoulder. "My old friend, I think perhaps you're a bit drunk."

Lewis smiled. "Perhaps a bit."

"I'll find us coffee."

Lewis again closed his eyes as his friend and President left the room. Sleep fell over him like a canopy of green paper bills. Images flashed against the inside of his eyelids. A door opening onto the sky. This time, no storm clawed and no darkness blinded him, but somewhere up ahead both waited. One day, he knew, they would take him. But not now. Instead, a clear, warm night met his leap. He spread his arms in supplication. Below, a river wound its way west throwing back moonlight and starshine, calling him towards some rendezvous he could not name. Once again, time swallowed him.

And he dreamed he was flying.

ACTION TEAM-UPS
NUMBER THIRTY-SEVEN

Thursday, 3:32 P.M.

The dentures I lost on reconnaissance last week have come back to haunt me. Cavanaugh made a big show of it, waving them beneath my nose in the cafeteria line. Smug bastard. If I were ten years younger or if he were forty years older, I'd have shown him completely new uses for tapioca pudding. Regardless, I have my teeth back and that made lunch slightly more tolerable.

Saw the new guy today. I nearly choked on my meatloaf. The line of his jaw, the jutting ears, the arch of the eyebrows. Even his bulbous nose was broken in all the right places. I couldn't help but smile at the memories of my fists connecting time and time again. He'd always been easy to hit. I leaned over to Mrs. Derkins. I just had to ask.

"Who's the new guy?" I pointed with my fork and when her eyes followed, I swapped my skim milk for her chocolate.

Phlegm rattled before she spoke. "Why, I don't believe I've seen him before, Mr. Carlson. He's a handsome fellow."

"If you like the criminal type," I said. I don't think Mrs. Derkins heard me, though. She was too busy squinting at her milk carton. I'll find out more tonight.

Friday, 3:32 A.M.

After the unfortunate events surrounding my dentures, I've had to significantly limit patrols. It was a mistake letting men into the nursing profession. Cavanaugh and his goons were everywhere and he'd made it pretty clear that he knew I was up to something. Usually it's safe after two o'clock. I slipped out, the wheels on my chair silent. I use the chair for patrol . . . it gives me an extra hour or two of stamina.

The nurse's station stood empty, but the door to the day room hung open a crack. Blue light flickered, soft moans oozed, the up-beat whoop of porno music eased itself out into the sterile hallway. No one ever asked where the videotapes came from. Forty years on the street and a guy has his sources. My particular source made sure a new tape showed up every week.

It didn't always work. *Good Bi Guys 3: Backdoor-O-Rama* had actually kept me stuck in my room until *Driving Missy Daisy* redeemed my nights a long week later.

Tonight was Stanley. He'd be in there for another two hours.

I let myself into the Administrator's office with a paperclip and found the most recent admission papers in her outbox. Of course, it couldn't be simple. He wouldn't be going by the name I'd known. No. Now he went by Dirk Derringer. But at least I knew.

My old arch-nemesis was here. My unfinished business follow-ing me home like a mangy stray dog.

Saturday, 8:47 A.M.

Not much to report. Nurse Jamison had no panty-lines beneath her tight skirt. Deciding to investigate, I tipped myself over in front of her twice and dropped my pencil three times, but to no avail. At least I stayed busy.

Sunday, 12:13 P.M.

I arranged steak for supper today. It accomplished two things: everyone ate, and it took most of the old farts three times longer to chew it. It's good that the dot-com bomb didn't get all of my assets. Naturally, I took advantage of this time to search Mr. Derringer's room. I moved quickly. Well, as quickly as I could. I *am* pushing ninety.

In the end, I found an old scrapbook in the bottom of his bureau. There were pictures of Derringer as a young man. Pictures of him with people like Mary Marionette AKA the Puppetress, and Jay

Jacob Jackson AKA the Laughing Londoner. I also found a picture of me in there. One of those rare shots of the Night Marauder that someone had sold to Life back during the war.

This was all I needed. And I knew better than to go it alone. Time I pulled some strings.

Monday, 2:46 P.M.

Kid Sling Shot finally showed up after my fourteenth call. Of course, he wasn't a kid anymore . . . close to seventy by now, I think. He had retired years ago and made a killing in the tire business.

He sat in my room on the edge of my bed. "Nice place, Cal."

"It's a shit-hole," I told him.

He shrugged. "Another few years and I may be joining you here."

I laughed but it sounded more like a bark. "Ann would never allow it." I often though about Ann. She'd been something else back in her Night-Girl days.

He laughed too, then went serious. "What's so urgent, Cal?"

"I need you to get the gang together. Call Colonel Patriot and have him rally the troops."

He laughed even louder. "What on earth for?"

"Lunatic the Clown. He's here. And if he's here . . . well, you figure it out. The others will follow."

"Cal, Lunatic's dead. Died years ago in prison. Remember?"

I did remember something along those lines, but it seemed so long ago and out of reach. What I'd seen here was closer. "I'm telling you, Jimmy, he's here. Goes by the name Derringer now."

He patted my hand. Actually *patted* my hand. I nearly came across the room at him. But arthritis kept me in check and cooler heads prevailed.

I can't remember the rest of the visit. I think we talked a bit about the old times. When he left, I knew I was on my own.

Fuck sidekicks. Fuck them all sideways and starboard.

Tuesday, 11:26 A.M.

I think Nurse Martinez went bra-less today. I was formulating my strategy for investigation when someone poked me in the rib.

"You been sneaking around again, Carlson?" Cavanaugh asked. A smug-looking Dirk Derringer stood behind him.

I glanced back at Nurse Martinez's jiggling chest. "Not me, Mr. Cavanaugh."

He leaned in close. "Well, Mr. Derringer here seems to think you were in his room the other day. Can you tell me anything about *that?*"

I ran my tongue over my teeth just to be sure they were there. "I have no idea what you could possibly be talking about. Sunday was *steak day*. For the love of Pete, I'd *never* miss that."

He leaned in even closer. "No one said anything about it being Sunday."

I pretended to faint. When I opened my eyes two dusky orbs of flesh danced in front of them as Nurse Martinez checked my vitals. Cavanaugh had moved on. Derringer just smiled knowingly.

Thursday, 1:11 A.M.

I opened one eye and saw him sitting by my bed, his red nose glowing like blood by moonlight. "You." I couldn't get up the mucus to spit.

"Nice to see you, NM. Miss me?" He wore a shaving cream mask around his eyes and bright green pajamas accented with little yellow bananas. A white sheet substituted for a cape.

"What do you want, fiend?"

He lowered his voice. "Did you know that Nurse Jamison goes *commando* at least twice a week?"

"I did. And Nurse Martinez — "

" — goes bra-less every other day," he interrupted. Lunatic laughed and slapped his knee. "I know, I know. That was brilliant earlier. Absolutely brilliant."

He kept laughing. No longer the wailing maniacal laugh I remembered from years gone by. The marvels of modern medicine, I later learned. Still, his laughter was contagious. I joined in until we were shushing each other and wiping tears from our eyes. He'd smeared his shaving cream mask all to hell.

Our laughing settled into a chuckle and became an uncomfortable pause. "What do you miss most," he finally asked, "about the good old days?"

I thought for a moment. "Purpose," I said.

"Yeah. Me, too." He stood. "You know, I got a look at the Administrator's computer. She's got a T-1 connection. Very fast. You know what that means?"

I'd lost my millions on high tech; I hadn't made them there. "No, I don't know what that means."

"Porn," he said.

I waved him off. "I get it delivered every week. Keeps our jailers busy."

"Still," he said. "Something to do."

He let himself out.

Sunday, 3:32 A.M.

We fly, Lunatic and me, sailing around corners. He rides the back of my chair scattering Jello and Skittles in our wake.

Stanley tries to catch us, but only manages to snag my cape before the lime-flavored dessert brings him down hard on the tile.

I've lost my teeth again but I'm having too much fun to care.

Tomorrow should be Commando Day for Nurse Jamison, and those web cams I ordered should be in any day now.

I can't wait to see what's next.

SOON WE SHALL
ALL BE SAUNDERS

Soon we shall all be Saunders with his greasy hair and his sweaty hands and his stink of onions and menthol shaving cream. We'll all wear stained white shirts and our bellies will push and pucker at the buttons and we'll leave our jacket opened because it could never make the stretch to be otherwise, especially sitting at our gray desks in our gray cubicles underneath those gray lights. Our shoes will be scuffed and the hem of our pants will ride just a few inches too high and on weekends, at the grocery store, we'll stoop and fix shopping cart wheels gone wrong and give the manager our cards.

I wonder if it will hurt?

I wonder if my wife will still recognize some part of me when Saunders walks in the door at the end of the day? I don't think she's met 'Phil from Inside Sales.' Maybe she'll scream at the stranger in her home in those brief moments before she becomes Saunders, too. Or maybe Saunders won't go home to my house. Maybe all the Saunders in the world will go back to that apartment that smells like cat litter and vanilla-scented Glade Plug-ins, spilling over into the hallways, into the street, into the neighborhood, into the city. Hundreds — no, wait, thousands — no, wait, *millions* — of Saunders lining up across the world, just wanting to go home.

The epidemic started just after lunch and spread quickly.

Saunders hit his monthly numbers today — Tuesday — just two weeks into June. Was it a coincidence that today was the day for the Big Announcement? Bob the VeePee called us all into the lunch room. We packed ourselves in and felt the temperature rising with the pressure to perform.

Bob gave Phil Saunders the Special Parking Place. He gave Phil Saunders the Plaque of Appreciation. He gave Phil Saunders a round of applause and we joined in with feigned enthusiasm. Then, he gave us the Encouraging Speech.

"You should all watch what Saunders does," Bob said. "This man is a selling machine. You would all do well to be more like him. Andrews Merchandising Supply and Bag Manufacturing could use a dozen — no wait — a hundred more like him."

"Why stop at a hundred?" Larry from Accounting said just loud enough for some of us to hear. "Imagine a whole world of Saunders."

And suddenly, Larry *was* Saunders with his big class ring and his chewed-down nails and his glasses smudged from greasy fingers pushing them up his pock-marked nose. Bob looked up, surprised, and then he changed, too.

I ran from the room, waving my arms.

"Where's Bill off to?" a half-dozen Saunders asked behind me.

I'm fortunate. At our office, I'm always the last to catch the various bugs that go around. Maybe I'd be the last to catch this bug, too. I raced past Madeline at the front desk.

"What's wrong, Bill?" she asked from behind her headset, finger poised above a button on her phone.

"Saunders," I said.

"Employee of the month again?" She smiled. "Don't take it personally, Bill. We can't all be Saunders."

But oh yes we can, I thought. Soon we shall all be Saunders. Saunders who specializes in the personal touch, the plastic bag logo design by fax, the over-the-phone label gun repair tips, the never ending stream of cash register paper to customers who just keep coming, coming, coming back.

"Leave while you still can," I told her as I left the office.

I doubt she listened to me. Now, she's Saunders, too.

I was afraid to go home. I called instead.

"Sarah?" I asked when she answered.

"Yes Bill?"

"Pack a bag, take the baby, drive to your Mother's."

"Bill, my Mother's in Michigan."

"I know," I said. "Trust me. Something bad is happening."

Sarah sighed. "Did you start drinking again?"

"No," I lied. I was calling from the bar.

"Bill, someone from your office called. They're worried about you. They say you just up and ran out in the middle of a staff meeting."

I closed my eyes. "Who called?"

"Phil," she said. "Phil Saunders." She paused. "He seemed like such a nice guy."

"If he comes over," I said, "Don't let him in."

"Why would he come over?"

But I hung up the phone when Saunders walked into the bar.

"It's not bad being me," he said over drinks. Saunders drank cheap light beer and didn't mind at all if I smoked. Saunders smiled and his crooked teeth looked slightly green in the hazy light.

I waited. Waited for my clothes to tighten, waited for the beer and pretzel cravings to grab me, waited for the sudden impulse to ask the bartender what model of cash register he used or where he currently purchased his merchandising supplies. Nothing happened.

So Saunders and I talked in quiet tones and one by one, the people changed around us and drifted over.

"Hi, I'm Phil," they kept saying to me and to one another.

I learned about his ex-girlfriend, Paula in Shipping, who he'd only slept with the one time after the Christmas party last year. I learned about his cat, Frisky, and his collection of Batman action figures. I learned about his father, the war hero who never came home, and his mother (the twinkle in her little boy's eyes) who lived in the apartment upstairs and had him up for spaghetti every Friday night.

While he droned on, I pondered my immunity. Which would be worse, I wondered? Being Saunders or being *with* Saunders? And I imagined going home, unlocking the door, walking inside and seeing the whole house full of Saunders, imagined going to the crib and looking down at the tiny little Saunders with his greasy hair and his sweaty hands. I swallowed my scream along with my bourbon.

He kept droning on even after the drinks stopped coming because the bartender — now also Saunders — drifted over to join the growing crowd. Eventually, I left my money on the counter and walked out into streets crowded with blue slacks and brown jackets, white stained shirts and green-striped ties. Shaving cream and onions all around.

"Hi, I'm Phil," someone said when they jostled me.

*

I walked into the pawn shop and put four hundred dollar bills on the counter. "I need a gun," I told the man who stood there watching.

Behind him, on the news, pandemonium and madness spread out from the city.

"There's a three day wait," he said.

"I don't have three days," I answered. I put another five hundred dollar bills down. He stared at me in disgust until I added another three.

He pulled out a .38 special and set it on the glass.

"Bullets?" I asked.

He shrugged. "I don't sell those."

I brushed past Saunders on my way out the door.

I sat in the park and stared at the empty revolver. Saunders stopped by and sat on the bench.

"Hi Bill," he said.

I looked at him. "Hi Phil."

"What are you doing with that gun?"

I didn't say anything.

"Are things really so bad?" he asked.

I still didn't say anything.

A dozen more Saunders joined us in the park. Saunders with his gray raincoat in the summer and his silly, crooked smile and his thick, hairy ear-lobes. "Is that thing loaded?"

I shook my head. "Any idea where I could find a bullet?"

Saunders put his hand on my shoulder. "Listen Bill, maybe you should reconsider. I'm really not sure that gun's the answer for you."

I stared at him.

Saunders stood. He reached into his pocket. He pulled out a carefully folded plastic sack and handed it to me. "Have you ever considered the possibility of plastic? Less mess. No bullets required."

I took it. I dropped the pistol in it. "I'll think about it, Phil."

He smiled. Then all of them walked away to give me time to think.

I sat for a long while. Sat until long after dark, until long after the streets emptied as a city full of Saunders went to bed in their cotton pajamas with their orange tabby cats.

I must have drifted off myself. I dreamed about ham and onion sandwiches. I dreamed about big-boned Paula sweating on top of me with a vacant expression in her eyes. I dreamed about my mother's spaghetti and my new parking place at work.

Soon we shall all be Saunders, I thought, when I opened my eyes.

A homeless man pushing a shopping cart full of his life passed by. He was the first person I'd seen who *wasn't* Saunders. One of the cart's wheels made that grinding noise that sounded like music to my ears and I stood up.

I smiled at him. "Let me fix that for you," I told him.

A GOOD HAIR DAY
IN ANARCHY

E d the Barber looked up from his newspaper when the kid walked in, and as usual, he noticed the hair first. It was long, blond and tied back with a leather thong, underneath a white stetson. Good hair — the best he'd seen since the last transport from Houston Prime three months ago.

The second thing he noticed was the gun-belt and the fifteen notches burned into the leather.

"Heya, Pops. What about a haircut?"

Ed stood, still eyeing the belt. Pearl handles jutted out of holsters on each hip. He waved to the single chair.

"Hop in." The kid tossed his hat onto the low, magazine-strewn table, and climbed into the seat. "Sure those won't get tangled up?" Ed nodded to the pistols.

The kid patted a handle, grinning. "They're fine. I always keep 'em close." Winking: "You can't be too careful in these parts."

Ed nodded, draping the sheet around his first customer of the day. Anarchy was a small mining town, an island of life in an otherwise desolate waste, home to both bandit and beast. "What'll it be, fella?" He spun the chair so the kid could see himself in the mirror.

"Take it down real short," he said.

"You sure?" It took a good two years to get hair like this; best to be safe now rather than sorry later. Still, his fingers itched for the scissors, hoping he'd heard right.

"Yep. Real short."

Ed shrugged and untied the thong, letting the hair cascade down over the white-sheeted shoulders. Then, he took up the shears and set them to snickering over the thick golden strands. Now it was time for the other part of his job — the small talk. "So, you new in town?" Of course he was, but Ed asked anyway.

"Passing through, tending to business."

"Oh? What do you do?"

The kid stared blankly into the mirror, locking eyes with the barber's reflection. "You don't know?"

Ed shook his head. "Nope. Sorry."

"I'm a hunter." Ed dropped the scissors, then stooped to recover them with shaking hands while he mumbled an apology. The kid grinned, then chuckled. "Don't be scared, old man. Just do a good job on my head, see?" Again, he winked.

Hunters were the last line of justice in the Frontier System — an easy job to get but a hard one to keep. New Texas, vast as it was, boasted only seven hunters still on the register. There might have been two or three on New Wyoming and New Colorado, the neighboring two planets. Ed reached back in his brain for a statistic he'd once heard: Only one in five made it through the first hunt. Only two in five, their second. The odds didn't get much better beyond that, keeping the field exclusive. Nearly a decade had passed since a hunter had come to Anarchy.

Ed went back to his work, his mouth suddenly dry. He needed to call Marshal Brady, let him know about the kid. Across the room, the vid-screen's single, wide eye stared back at him. He didn't want to ask, but he did it anyway, knowing the answer. "So, who are you after?"

"Slope Dobbins."

Ed paused, his stomach knotting. "The gunslinger?" He swallowed, then went on cutting. "Haven't heard that name in years."

"The same. What do you know about him?" The kid's wary eyes followed Ed's movements in the mirror.

"A bit, I reckon." The clippers buzzed and shook to life. "He's known throughout the System, especially here on New Texas. Heard he was dead, though. Died in the desert, alone, gut-shot."

"That's what they say. I happen to know he's here, in Anarchy." Again Ed stopped, straightening and moving around the chair carefully. "That's why you're cutting my hair." The kid bristled at his questioning look. "I'm Kid Jackson. You know, the hair?"

The scissors went back to work, threads of gold drifting to the floor with every metallic whisper. "I'm sorry, Kid. I don't know who you are. News travels slow around here."

Ed felt the shoulders tighten up, saw the impatience firming up the jaw-line. "I grow my hair long while I hunt. Once I find my prey,

I get it cut. Then . . ." He raised his hand from beneath the sheet and made a pistol with his forefinger and thumb. As the thumb-hammer fell, he clicked his tongue. "It's my . . . trademark, my calling card."

"Oh. I didn't know. Sorry." The tenseness leaked out and the shoulders softened.

"It's okay."

"Slope Dobbins, eh? Here in Anarchy?" Just the name made Ed's stomach hurt.

"Yessiree," the Kid said. "Hell, I wasn't even born when he was in his prime." He grinned at Ed, slightly inclining his head. The barber gripped his temples firmly between thumb and forefinger to stop the movement. "But you probably *remember* the sonofabitch. You look around his age."

"Sure. I remember." He set the scissors down and picked up the antique electric clippers, checking the guard. "Came to New Texas from the Sol System — that's what they say, anyway. He was on one of the last ships before the Waygate cut out. He was a teacher, wasn't he? Then one day someone — "

The Kid interrupted. "Lightning Jeb Walker. Dobbins spilled his beer on him at the Independence Day parade and Walker challenged him." The Kid's eyes came to life and Ed let him finish the story. He didn't mind.

"They stood on Main Street, Dobbins with a borrowed gun, and when the mayor's hat hit the ground, both gun-hands scrambled. Walker was faster, but his fat head got in the way. He started to say 'slowpoke,' but by the time he said 'slope,' his brain figured out there was a hole in his throat. That's the first man Slope Dobbins killed. That's what started it all."

Ed nodded, remembering the first time he heard the story. God, I was young back then — younger even than the Kid, he thought. "I heard that was just a story – that the name came from a pronounced forehead and receding hairline . . . "

"Nope. Maybe it was a fluke — real lucky shot and all, but still a true story," the Kid said. "Everyone came after him, then, and he had to learn. Had to somehow live up to the legend. He became the best."

"He'd be pretty old, now, if he's still alive. What makes you think he's here, in Anarchy?"

"Old drunk up Yuma-way told me. Said he knew him. Said a

couple of Aboriginals found him in the desert and brought him here to swap him for liquor. Said he stayed on, decided to tame Anarchy, eventually settled down and had a family."

"Said all that, did he?" Ed tried to hide his shock and failed. "Anarchy's a small town. I'd think we'd know if Slope Dobbins was around."

The Kid nodded, eyes narrowing with suspicion. "He said that, too. Said you all knew."

Ed managed to keep the clippers in his hand, but they betrayed him, taking a deep bite of hair from the back of the Kid's neck. Licking his lips, he finished up in silence and rubbed the menthol-scented hair tonic onto the neck and scalp. With a flourish he spun the chair and waited for the Kid's approving nod. Then, Ed snapped the sheet away.

The Kid handed over a ten mark bill. "Good work, Pops."

"Glad to help, but I was wondering . . . " The Kid paused in the doorway, and turned, the New Texas sun glaring off his hat. "You said you get your hair cut when you've found your man." Ed waited. "Don't you think maybe you're a bit . . . premature?"

Hands hitched in his gun belt, the Kid winked. "Not at all, Pops. Where can I find Marshal Obadiah Brady?"

"He's asking after you. Asking about Slope Dobbins."

The face on the vid-screen sobered. "How long ago?" Brady looked tired, Ed thought, his leathery skin a field of scars and wrinkles, his eyes buried in crow's feet. His silver hair needed a trim, Ed noticed.

"He just left. I sent him to the saloon. Figured you could meet him there."

"Kid Jackson, you say? Out of New Colorado? Let me look him up." His face turned to the side and his fingers clacked quickly. "Hmmm. Kid is right — I don't remember ever being his age. How'd he find out?"

"Charlie Greenbaum. Guess he's up in Yuma nowadays."

The marshal stood, face then chest sliding up and off the screen. "Hank's out checking into some trouble on the Reservation — some Ab stole Ike Martin's skipper or something. I'm gonna need a hand, I reckon, with this Kid."

"But I — "

"Ed, you and I both know I can make a call up to Brailey, get a lifter of rangers down here. But with that goddamned 'gate reopening it could be a while."

In all the excitement, Ed had forgotten about the Anarchy Gazette's headline. Since its first collapse thirty years ago, the Arbuckle Waygate had guttered to life three times, never for longer than a week. And each time, the System spiraled into chaos as disillusioned settlers swapped out with starry-eyed romantics, both looking for a better life. Ed started, suddenly aware that Brady still spoke. "Besides, I like to keep Anarchy business right here in Anarchy. We just don't need the publicity."

Ed nodded and watched Brady's gnarled hands work the buckle of a gun-belt. There were no notches carved into it. Some men looked dangerous without props.

Brady bent and pushed his face close to the screen. "So meet me at Susie's, Ed. Bring your gun. You are forth-with deputized."

"Great." The barber swallowed and absently scratched himself. "I'll see you there."

The screen went white, then shut itself off, and he sat down, hard, in the barber chair. He lifted a hand and watched it tremble. Then, he slowly stood, reached into his cabinet and pulled out a tarnished pistol. Shoving it into his belt, Ed the Barber locked his shop and headed west on Main.

Overhead, the sky was crisply blue and its solitary yellow eye glared down, swollen and angry. On the horizon, a line of jub-jub trees marked the meandering Mud River that cut through the wastes. Anarchy's dirt streets were quiet — a handful of skippers tied haphazardly in front of a half-dozen storefronts, their bug-eyes wide and unblinking, rear-legs rubbing music into the air as they waited for their owners. A few schooners were mixed in, rust-flecked, glass-chipped, parked with three tires up on the make-shift sidewalk, three on the ground. Their solar engines hummed as they fueled themselves for their next run. As he looked at the dilapidated equipment and giant insects, Ed found it hard to believe that thirty years ago he'd bought into the marketing ploy like so many others. There was nothing quaint or romantic about the New Wild West. All it took to see *that* was the sudden collapse of an intergalactic highway that no one understood. The sudden descent of silence on a vast, dark ocean. Of course, Ed thought, he could've left like so many others. But it was home now.

Wiping sweating palms onto his pants, he moved with short, deliberate steps. He stopped outside Li'l Susie's and waited.

Marshal Brady was a big man, taking long, confident strides. He gave Ed a grim smile and shifted the plasma rifle to his shoulder so he could shake his hand. "Good to see you, Ed. Ready?"

"No."

Brady pushed through the doors, leveling the plasma rifle as he did. Ed followed, hand on the butt of his antique blaster. They waited in the doorway as their eyes adjusted to the dimly lit room.

A few frightened Abs, tall and spindly, moved for the back door, nostrils flaring. "Much going now," one said to Susie as he flipped a coin to her. Susie's fat arm jiggled as she snatched the five-mark from the air, her angry eyes on Ed and Brady.

Brady cocked his head at her, ignoring her glare. "Where's the Kid . . . the hunter?"

A voice from the street, familiar to Ed: "Behind you, Slope Dobbins."

They both turned slowly to look out the open door. Kid Jackson stood, face painted with self-importance, both guns drawn and powered up.

Ed wondered how fast he could get to the blaster, knew it would never be fast enough, and glanced nervously at the marshal for direction. Nausea made his bowels gurgle, watery with the moment.

"I don't know what you're talking about." Brady's voice was calm. "But if we could sit down and have ourselves a drink together, maybe we could sort this whole thing out."

The Kid spat in the dirt. "I don't need to sort anything out, Dobbins."

Brady chuckled. "You think if I was Slope Dobbins I'd walk into an ambush like *this?*" He shook his head. "Son, let's have that drink. I'll tell you all about Slope Dobbins and his life here in Anarchy, if you really want to know."

"But Charlie Greenbaum — "

"Charlie Greenbaum's a drunken bum. Only in town a month before I ran him out for the card-cheat he is. Must have one helluva grudge to sic a hunter on my ass." Brady slowly lowered his rifle, then leaned it against the door-jam. "Susie, let's have a bottle." Ed watched uncertainty wash over the Kid's face. Then, he heard Brady gasp with surprise and pleasure. "Say, aren't you Kid Jackson?"

The uncertainty swelled into pride. "Yes," he said. "Yes I am."

Ed smiled inwardly. Brady always knew the tunes folks would dance to.

"I hear you're one quick sonofabitch. Hear you took out Jake Reilly on New Colorado — your first time out, no less." New Colorado was the greenest of the three worlds that made up the Frontier System.

The Kid nodded, grin widening. "New Colorado tamed up fast after that. Thought I'd try my hand here." He looked them over and then slipped the guns back into their holsters. Then, he pulled out a slim metal cylinder. "Do you mind? I just want to be sure." It was a bloodhound — a small one.

Brady shrugged. "If you need proof. Ed?"

Ed's scissors, always in his pocket, had become a local joke. Always ready for the job, they laughed, just in case someone needed an emergency trim. He stepped up and snipped a single silver wire from Brady's receding hairline.

Kid Jackson unscrewed one end of the cylinder and held it to the barber. Carefully, Ed dropped the hair into the bloodhound. As soon as he screwed the lid in place, the machine buzzed to life. "Got a speck of blood," the Kid said. "It's twenty-some years old. Some woman — governor's daughter, no less — kept his bloody shirt after a shoot-out in Neo Abilene. Started out a hostage, ended up in the sack with him. She wanted a souvenir, she said, something to remember that night." The machine blinked a red light. "Looks like you're right, Marshal."

"Of course I am. Now what about that drink?"

"So I tell him, 'Bull*shit* you ain't Tommy Cross,' and I shoot him in the head." The Kid broke into laughter, pounding the table with his fist. "You should've seen the look on his face!"

They'd been drinking the better part of the day, Ed occasionally glancing up to the clock. The saloon had filled up as miners drifted in from their shifts. In the corner, a group of Abs sat brooding over cards, their sand-gray skin and wide black eyes flat in the fluorescent light. Li'l Susie had changed into her evening wear, a see-through dress that a woman her size had no business wearing.

Ed took Brady's cue and joined in the laughter. Then, the Kid's face went as serious as a drunk man's could. "So you said you'd tell me about Dobbins and Anarchy, Marshal. He *was* here, wasn't he?" His voice slurred around the question.

Brady wiped his eyes as his laughter faded. Then, he poured another drink for the Kid. "Yep. Sure was."

"So?"

"Just like the story goes — some Abs found him out in the wastes, close to death, and brought him here. I traded them two bottles of Earth whiskey and doctored Slope up. I always intended to turn him in — quite a reward for the bastard back then — but I couldn't . . . "

Disgust filled the Kid's voice. "You were afraid."

"No." Brady laughed. "Not at all. Slope Dobbins wasn't a man who inspired fear. Legends are different from life, Kid."

The Kid turned on Ed. "What about you? Did he scare you?"

"Terrified me." Ed's voice was quiet in the noisy room. He'd been drinking a lot and the whiskey had burned away his queasiness.

The Kid grinned. "Yeah. That's more like it. Anyway?"

"Anyway, that was a long time ago. You look all over Anarchy, Son, but you won't find the legendary Slope Dobbins around these parts. Not one man matching his description."

"So he's dead, or moved on?"

The Marshal didn't answer. Ed poured another drink, stared at the amber fluid, then tipped his head back and took it in. Then, Brady reached for the bottle but the Kid grabbed it away.

"Well?"

Ed cleared his voice and leaned in, toward the Kid. "What if it's neither?"

Eyes wide, then angry, turning on Brady. "But you said — "

"No one said he wasn't here." Ed raised his eyebrows in Brady's direction and smiled.

"Ed," the Marshal started but was cut off.

"Well where is he, Godammit?" A fist slammed into the table, making the glasses jump, while the other hand fumbled for a pistol.

"What if he decided to stay?" Ed asked. Brady shot him a warning glance and slowly lowered his hands beneath the table. Ignoring Brady, the barber leaned in even closer and lowered his voice. "What if the very thought of killing suddenly sickened him and he hated what he'd become, what the stories made him?" His face was near enough now to smell the whiskey on the Kid's breath, mingled with

hair tonic and sweat. "What if every time he heard his name or saw
a gun his stomach knotted up and went to water? What if he
dreamed at night, not just about the men he killed, but their wives
and children and mothers and fathers, too?" Jackson's face hung
somewhere between a smile and frown as Ed continued. "What if
he decided to change? To be someone else? Maybe settle down,
start a family, even open a business . . . say, a barber-shop?" He
gave a tight-lipped smile and sat back, hands folded across his white
barber's smock, eyebrows raised. There was a moment of silence,
thick as a quilt.

Then, the Kid bellowed laughter like a lifting cruiser spouted
smoke, and every head in the saloon turned as voices died mid-
sentence. "*You? Slope Dobbins?*" Again, he guffawed, leaning in,
himself, eyes shifting around the room. "You know what *I* think?"
He licked his lips.

"What?" Ed's face split into a broad grin, on the edge of laughter, himself. The warmth of the liquor in his belly felt good.

"*I* think you're drunk."

"I am, at that."

"I'd have to agree," Brady said, shaking his head in disbelief.

"Slope Dobbins!" The Kid chuckled and Brady's grim look gradually melted into a smile as his hands slipped back up to the table,
unnoticed. Throughout the room, voices resurrected conversations.

"Only one way to find out," Ed said, pulling out his scissors. He
snipped a pinch of gray from above his ear and extended it to the
hunter.

"You're serious?"

"Why not? Can't barbers be notorious gunslingers?"

Shrugging, the Kid pulled out the cylinder, opened it, and dropped
the hair in. When the light flashed red, he started laughing again.
"You're a real card."

Then, he stood. "I'm off, then, fellas. Guess my trademark's
shot to hell now." He ran a hand through his bristling scalp before
settling the hat in place.

"It's good hair," Ed said. "It'll grow back fast."

"Hopefully before I find Dobbins — hate to lose my reputation."

"Hopefully." Brady stood, and Ed climbed to his wobbly legs.

"Thanks for the drink . . . and the laugh."

"Don't mention it."

Kid Jackson, quite drunk, swaggered out into the night.

*

The clippers hummed over Brady's silver hair. Outside, Anarchy had started its day.

The newspaper and streets were full. The governor declared a holiday to celebrate the Waygate reopening. Twelve years of mail glutted the Skipper Express. Shiploads of merchandise moved through customs into the grasping hands shopkeepers and farmers. Eighteen of the town's children bundled off to distant relatives and fancy schools eight hundred light years away. Four families, new settlers with fresh faces and bright eyes, replaced them. All was truly right in the world.

Ed felt puffy, his skull pounding and his breath sour from last night's whiskey.

"That was close yesterday," Brady said. "Ouch!"

"Sorry. I'm pretty hungover." He'd actually thought about closing up the shop today — something he hadn't done in twenty years of barbering — but midweek holidays meant good business and good business was rare in Anarchy.

"Thought that damned bloodhound would do you in. You never told me about the governor's daughter."

Ed grinned weakly into the mirror. "There was no governor's daughter. I don't know whose shirt he got ahold of, but it isn't mine. Another story, just like that whole name thing."

Brady snorted. "I still don't know why you didn't just shoot him, Slope."

Ed's eyes softened, feeling the lurch in his stomach. "I just couldn't. You know that, Brady."

"Why not, dammit? He was a threat, and there you were, sloppy drunk, spilling your soul to him — just inviting trouble. You know I would've covered for you. Could've just put a plasma charge through his head — ow, Godammit!"

That time, it was deliberate. He'd found it was the best way, by far, to make his point nowadays. "That's not my life, anymore, Brady. I'm just a barber now." Ed Dobbins paused, inhaled the scent of electricity and oil from the humming clippers. "Damn, that Kid had good hair, too. The kind that makes me love my work."

Brady snorted, then yelped again as the clippers fed.

INTO THE BLANK
WHERE LIFE IS HURLED

A sudden, sharp increase in the room's temperature signaled the Fallen's arrival, and William scrambled to the floor to prostrate himself. He averted his eyes, hearing the door the open, and waited as the sweat trickled down his sides. Soft footfalls passed his desk and he risked a glance up. The Fallen strode through the office, arrogant and nude, the stubs on its back twitching as if with memories of flight. William held his breath as it opened Fisk's door and slipped inside. Then, he waited to a count of twenty and returned to his desk.

The un-crowded newsroom remained silent though a hundred questions begged for asking. *The Fallen . . . here? Why? Did you see its eyes? No . . . never, never the eyes.* The temperature dropped a hair and William went back to the paper he'd been doodling.

He'd intended it to be a poem. The words rarely came to him but when they did, his fingers looked for release to no avail. In this place, pencil leads broke, words ran together, ink faded and all lines of literary endeavor bled into a meaningless puddle of bits and blotches. The only stories he wrote now . . . the only stories he was *allowed* to write . . . were the meaningless drivel the Gazette required of him.

Long ago, before the War that brought him here, he remembered a blossoming career as a novelist. Tales of the fantastic and supernatural. Now, words haunted him like unrequited love.

For five minutes longer, he fiddled with the paper. The temperature shot up as Fisk's door opened again and William joined the others on the floor. The Fallen rarely traveled to this ring and to his knowledge, they'd never visited this building before today. This was the second he'd ever encountered.

He waited, listening to the footfalls, heard them stop at his desk, and forced his eyes open to confront the bare feet before him. The Fallen hissed, then continued on its way. As it left the building, the scattered collection of reporters and support staff released held breath and the temperature returned to normal.

"Hodgson . . . my office. Now."

William climbed slowly to his feet and let them carry him to toward Vernon Fisk's voice. The others looked at him, faces still pale.

"Be a good chap and close the door," Fisk said from behind his desk, waving half of a cigar at an empty chair. William pulled it shut and sat down. "Still taking stabs at your passion, eh?"

Surprised, William realized that he still held the pencil and scrap of paper tightly in his fist. "I'm sorry, sir."

"No need, no need." Fisk leaned forward. He was a fat man, his face pocked and perpetually slick with sweat. "I was a brewer you know. Brewed great beers. Even won an award. Of course, down here it comes to nothing. I tried for years before giving up."

William nodded.

"Well, enough of the past. On to the future." He nodded towards the door. "You're probably wondering what that was about. Special assignment . . . from the top, or from the bottom if you prefer." He snorted at his own joke. "Story of the century for us, it is."

The Gazette printed little that was news. During his time with the paper, William had interviewed new arrivals, promoted local gossip, and churned out propaganda on demand.

"Sir?"

Fisk stubbed out his cigar. "Story of the century. Somewhat of a celebrity I'm told, too. I guess you know him; he was after my time."

"Who, sir?"

"Why . . . Harry Houdini, that's who. Just arrived and already at it."

William's mind lurched him back to the turn of the century in a different life. A Blackburn stage, an angry mob, an arrogant showman and the equally arrogant young man William had once been. He could still hear the clinking of the shackles.

"Smug bastard," William said in a low voice. "I'm not surprised."

Fisk looked up. "Yes, *it* said you'd met before. I trust it wasn't a favorable encounter?"

"I was young. He made a challenge; I took him up on it. Went over two hours, he did, but in the end he got out of it." William chuckled. "Of course, I didn't see it. Afraid of the mob. I fled the scene and hid out."

"Well, you've got the story. *They* insisted."

"An interview then, sir?" Dread crept into him . . . this was the last person he wanted to sit down with, even for half an hour in one of Hell's more tolerable rings.

Fisk belly-laughed. "More than that, Hodgson. It seems Mr. Houdini has announced his run for the Ear. You're to accompany him, chronicle the journey, and return with the story." Fisk paused. "Well, no guarantees on returning. It *is* the Ear, of course."

William knew little about the Ear. Somewhere on some abandoned edge, it supposedly stood alone. Whispered legends traveled the rumor circuit: Few had seen it, few had spoken into its cool, crystal surface. Some believed Michelangelo had carved it on some great Assignment of Grace from Above, guarded by angels as he worked tirelessly. William believed it was most likely bunk.

"But sir, I'm not sure I'm the best — "

Fisk interrupted. "You're *not* the best. But They want you. And who am I to deny Them?"

William swallowed. "He'll take one look at me and that'll be that, with all due respect."

"How long's it been since you met him?"

Time was hard to count here. He did the best math he could. "Over twenty years."

Fisk grunted. "I'll book you passage on the *Titanic*. You'll leave at dawn for Hellsmouth. Two weeks . . . enough time for you to grow out that beard of yours, I should think. I don't think he'll know you, Hodgson."

William stood. A heaviness fell over him. Two ghosts rattling their chains from his past. Houdini and the sea. It couldn't get much worse.

William re-slung his sea-bag at the tavern door. He'd waited a full five minutes, his brain racing ahead to scout out the possibilities. Would Houdini recognize him? During his two weeks on the black, oily sea his beard had itched its way to fullness, but would that be enough? And if he were recognized, what did it really matter? The night he had bound the swaggering showman was long buried in the past. But William had not forgotten; he doubted Houdini had either.

Opening the door, he pushed his way inside. The tavern was crowded with a scattering of damned souls that drank in small groups talking in low voices.

Houdini was not hard to spot; all new arrivals carried an otherworldly quality and Houdini transcended even that. He seemed the only unbroken man in the room, sitting alone at a table in the back corner. He looked up, his face an inverted triangle beneath tangled hair. He'd aged from the young stage-hound he'd once been but his eyes still held their brightness. He smiled as William approached.

"You're the reporter then?" Houdini extended his hand.

The grip was strong and William returned it. "Yes. Bill Hopewell, Graytown Gazette."

"Englishman?"

William nodded and sat. Houdini waved to the bartender, a misshapen, one-eyed dwarf in a stained apron. The dwarf dried off his hands with a towel and moved sluggishly towards them.

"I spent a great deal of time in England," Houdini said. "Great country, great people."

"Thank you, Mr. Houdini."

The bartender reached their table, his one eye soaking in his newest customer. "What'll it be, gov?"

William nodded towards Houdini's empty glass. "The same."

Houdini chuckled. "Water then, Bulsby." He leaned in towards William as the dwarf moved away. "And call me Ehrich, William. Houdini was a stage name and there is no stage here."

They sat in silence, the low voices from other tables providing a static buzz. The dwarf returned with two glasses of slightly brown water and Houdini laid a small, carved stick on the table. Most used coins here but some few elite carried the badge of a Fallen patron. Curiosity and dread danced slowly behind William's eyes. A patron. For Houdini.

The dwarf nodded. "On the house, of course."

"Good man," Houdini said. He put the stick in his pocket. "These come in handy."

William pulled a travel-stained notebook and pencil from his jacket pocket and placed them before him on the table. He sipped

the tepid water, grimacing as the slight taste of sulfur hit his tongue.
"May I ask you some questions, Mr. Houdini?"

Houdini looked up. "Please. And again, call me Ehrich."

William forced a weak smile. "Very well. Ehrich." He paused.
This was always the uncomfortable bit, the question he never wanted
to ask. To him, it implied rudeness and a lack of compassion. Still,
he had to ask: the inquiring minds clamored to know. "What brings
you to Hell?"

Houdini barked a short laugh. "Direct, aren't you, Bill?" He
folded his hands and his eyes shone in the dimly lit tavern. "A burst
appendix and an inflated ego." William scribbled this down. "How
about you, Bill?"

The question caught him off guard. No one asked, at least not
in polite company. He felt an embarrassed flush rise to his face like
an unexpected house-guest six o'clock of a Sunday morning. He
cleared his voice, eyes focused on the paper before him. "The war.
Artillery shell I think."

"The Great War?"

"There are no great wars." Suddenly his ears were full with
the crash of rifles and the screams of dying men. His nose was
filled with the stink of blood and smoke. He ventured a glance at
Houdini. Sympathy etched the older man's features.

"Sorry, Bill. You're absolutely correct." Houdini grinned a weak
grin. "If it helps at all, we won you know."

"I know. It doesn't." He paused, took another drink. "You were
a showman before." It was a statement, not a question.

"Of sorts. A magician. An escape artist. A de-bunker of pho-
nies. But that's not important anymore."

"And you intend to run for the Ear?"

"Yes. You and I, Bill." The light came alive in Houdini's eyes.
His face shone. "Know anything about the Ear?"

"Michelangelo. Assignment of Grace. Those who speak into it,
speak to . . . well, speak to . . . it's bunk. Rubbish."

Houdini nodded slowly. "Perhaps. But it is out there, waiting, at
the edge of Hell itself. And I intend to say my bit into it."

William forgot his note-taking and looked up. "Why in Hell would
you do such a thing? Have you any idea what lives in those Wastelands? Have you — "

Houdini interrupted him with a wave of his hand. "I made a
promise, Bill. I will keep that promise."

"You . . . *we* . . . may never reach it. And if we do, it may be for nothing. And, regardless, we may never return to tell anyone." He felt fear now and agitation, hungry hands grabbing at him.

"It doesn't matter if I return." Houdini's eyes hardened. "It only matters that I go." He raised his glass to his mouth and gulped. He stood, somehow towering larger than life despite his lack of height. "There will be much time for questions on the way. We leave at dawn."

Deliberate in his step, Houdini strode from the room. And William sat for a long time after he left.

It took nearly a week to reach the Wasteland's edge. The film crew waited for them there, a scattering of tents, two large trucks and a bullet-riddled biplane. Over the days and nights of walking, William had found an unexpected depth in his traveling companion along with answers to the questions. At night, in his tent, he scribbled his notes by candlelight, shaping a story that came so close to fiction that his spelling faltered and his pencils broke. Still, he pressed on, filling half of his notebook.

Surprisingly, he'd found similarities between them and that identification led to the beginnings of admiration. He himself had been the son of an Anglican priest; Houdini was the son of a rabbi. Both had committed themselves to a life of physical exercise. Both had written strange tales of fancy. At first, it had unsettled him, recalling that night long ago and the contempt they'd had for one another. But with time, that bled away.

Now, they stood on a rise, the film crew camped immediately below and the Wasteland stretching out towards a line of broken-toothed mountains. William raised a questioning eyebrow at Houdini's smile. "What's this about, Ehrich?"

Houdini chuckled. "I arranged it with His Lordship. It was really more of a suggestion but the old bugger jumped on it. Did you know that in all of Hell there are but three aeroplanes?"

William was not surprised. He hadn't seen one since the War.

"I thought it would do nicely to capture the moment for posterity's sake."

A man in khaki saw them, barked orders, and waved. He walked quickly up the hill towards them, out of breath as he arrived.

"Ah," he said. "There you are." He ignored William, shoving his hand into Houdini's and pumping it furiously. "Albert Maxwell the third."

"Ehrich Weiss. And William Hopewell of the Gazette."

The director glanced at William briefly, then shifted his attention back to his star. "No need for modesty. You are Harry Houdini."

Houdini shrugged. "Are you ready?"

"Yes. We've all the necessary precautions. We'll follow behind in the trucks, out of the way of course. We'll use the plane to hop ahead, shoot the scenes, and back to camp before nightfall."

"Precautions?" William knew a little about the Wastelands. The nights there belonged to the Shriekers and Howlers . . . the days belonged to the Abandoned.

"I'll show you." Maxwell turned and started down the hill. Shouldering their packs, the two travelers followed.

A mixed crew awaited. Several Hindis, a few Arabs and a scattering of Irish-looking scrawny men. Maxwell was American. The men looked up as they approached, then went back to their work. They were disassembling a vast array of vaccuum tubes and unhooking wires from a gas generator.

Shock grabbed William as his memories played out the past. An electric pentacle, he realized. Something his imagination had cooked up for stories he'd written long ago. "Where did you get this?"

Maxwell shrugged. "It was provided. Along with these." He uncovered a tarp on one of the trucks, then pried open a long wooden crate. It contained a dozen Enfield rifles. He opened another box and dug out a handful of shells. "Blessed by some Damned priest in Graytown." He lowered his voice. "Doesn't mean much, but it should be enough to stop a Howler."

He saw the look that must have been on William's face. Houdini saw it, too. "Not for us, Bill. Part of the contract, I'm afraid." He offered a reassuring, sympathetic smile. "We'll be fine without them. Trust me."

They spent the remainder of the day in camp, Houdini and Maxwell off to the side excitedly discussing logistics and filming techniques. They pitched their one-man tents on the edge of the Wasteland, struggling to sleep as the night desert came alive with unbearable noise.

In the morning, after a brief session in front of the camera, they set out alone.

*

True to his word, Maxwell and the cameraman flew ahead in the two-seater, landing, shooting film, leaving, returning and departing again as the sky grayed towards night. William lost track of how many trips were made, and gradually lost track of how many days had passed in this dead, shattered place. Somewhere behind, the caravan crawled slowly along. Some nights, he could see it glowing miles back.

Twilights, as they stopped to make camp, Houdini always drew away, mouth working silently as he etched signs and symbols into the hard-packed ground. William avoided asking where he'd learned the protective ward-making. The first night, he'd lain awake terrified as the screaming pummeled his ears and shook the tent. But the wards had held each night and the days had passed without incident or encounter.

Eventually, the mountains loomed above them, casting long shadows that overtook them as they trudged along. They could just make out the smallest speck of a gated cave when they encountered their first Abandoned. Only they didn't know it at first.

A speck became a figure became a child, sitting alone with its head in its hands. The little boy looked up as they approached. His eyes were red from crying. He wore a tattered overcoat and knickers.

"Papa?"

Houdini took a step forward; William caught his arm. "Careful, Ehrich."

He shot William an angry glance. "It's a child, Bill." Houdini moved closer and knelt before the boy.

William felt danger but didn't know what to do with it. "It can't be. No child could survive out here alone." He swallowed, tasting the dust. "It's bait. Or worse."

Houdini ignored him and stretched a hand out to the boy. "What's your name? What are you doing here?"

The child's lip trembled. "I'm . . . lost." William saw something, a darkly intelligent light, behind the child's eyes. "My name is Mayer Weiss."

William saw Houdini flinch and then tense. "Mayer?"

The child began to change. Its mouth stretched and elongated, jagged teeth filling a gaping hole. The eyes became black and it lunged forward with a deep growl. It tackled Houdini, its claws grappling for a hold.

William couldn't move. He willed himself to act but his rebellious legs held fast. Houdini rolled in the sand, yelling, pushing and kicking at the creature.

Even in the burning Wasteland, he felt the temperature shift upwards. There was a dark flash and suddenly Ehrich lay still and alone. The creature had flown thirty feet to land heavily in the sand. Another flash and it began to shriek. Flash after flash, the Abandoned was torn apart and strewn onto the desert floor.

Fascinated, William forgot to prostrate himself. When it had finished, the Fallen glared at them, hissed disgust, and vanished.

William went to Houdini and offered him a hand up. "Are you okay?"

Houdini nodded, shaken, staring at the pieces of meat. "I wondered . . ." The words drifted off. He brushed off his clothes. "I *thought* it had been too easy."

William watched him without a word. A knot of dread grew in his stomach.

"They're protecting us," Houdini muttered. "As if They want us to succeed."

Yes, William thought. And he knew that no good could come of it.

The carved words above the gate were Latin.

"Broken dreams, eh?" Houdini said, smiling. "It's not far now, Bill. Not far at all." He pointed to the dark opening. "Just beyond the caves." He turned and smiled to the camera, giving a thumbs-up sign.

Maxwell nodded excitedly. "We'll see you on the other side boys." He'd briefed them that morning. The caravan would stop here and they would make several trips flying gear over the mountains to set up a small camp. There would even be champagne.

Houdini handed Bill an electric torch. He clicked it on and its tongue of light probed the cave. The hair on his neck stood up. With a firm clap on the back, his companion brushed past and into the cave. William followed.

The difference in temperature was uncanny. Outside, the desert baked. Inside, coolness prevailed. The cavern stretched deep into the mountain, straight and wide enough for three to go abreast. They walked side by side, Houdini whistling a circus tune as they went.

Behind them, the iris of light gradually closed as they made their way.

"No broken dreams as yet," Houdini said.

William shrugged. He thought back to the relative ease of the wasteland crossing and the Fallen's intervention. "Maybe They've come ahead of us."

"Maybe." Houdini paused. "Did you hear that?"

William stopped as well and leaned forward. "No."

An hour later, the straight, broad cavern spilled into a massive room. Easily two dozen openings marked the opposite wall. Houdini rubbed his chin. "I *thought* it was too easy."

A drowsy fog settled onto William.

Then Houdini's eyes went wide. "Papa?" He moved towards one of the openings.

William caught his arm. "Ehrich?"

Panic laced Houdini's voice. "Surely you heard that?"

He shook his head. He'd heard nothing. At first.

Then he heard the crying from another opening at the far end of the room. He turned towards it, the voice familiar. He opened and closed his mouth, then turned back to where Houdini had stood. Houdini was already disappearing into the opening, following a voice that William could not hear.

"Oh, William, why?" the distant voice said between sobs. He turned away from his companion.

"Mother?" He broke into a trot.

"Oh, William."

He ran blindly, the light bouncing over the narrowing walls as he followed the twisting and turning passageway. After what felt like hours, he stumbled into a small chamber. His mother knelt in the center, hands folded imploringly, clutching a crumpled letter.

"Oh, my boy. My precious boy."

"Mother?" He stopped and crouched beside her, reaching for her. "I'm here." Somewhere in the back of his mind a nagging tickle tried to tell him that this could not be his mother. But he could see her, hear her voice, smell the lavender soap from her skin.

She looked up at him. "You can't be here. You're dead."

As he reached for her, she pulled away. "Mother, I'm here.

She thrust the letter under his nose. "No. Dead. It's all right here. You couldn't leave well enough alone, could you?" She sneered and then spat at him, the warm, dry phlegm splattering his cheek. Frustration tightened his throat in preparation for tears. "No Mother. I'm . . ." Another voice, further away, called to him and something outside of himself forced him to his feet.

"My Lord," the voice said, "Why have you forsaken me?"

"Father?"

"He's dead too," the old woman spat. "Dead and in Hell, God Damn him."

As he raced from the chamber, she cackled wordlessly after him.

He found his father in another room, trying to drink dust from a hollow in the floor. "Son? Is that you?"

"Father, what are you doing here?"

The old man looked up. His clergy collar hung open at the neck of his ripped black shirt. "You could've saved me."

William moved closer but another voice caught him. The frustration became despair and the despair vented itself in his cry. "No."

The voice was that of his wife. Then another joined it. And another. Until it seemed that a multitude surrounded him. The voices coalesced into a litany of his misdeeds and good intentions gone wrong, every dream or hope another had attached to him, every disappointed expectation. He fell onto his side and clutched his head.

One more voice joined the choir. A voice like nails on slate. "Enough."

He sucked in hot air and fought to control his breathing. He could not force his eyes open.

The voice spoke again. "You are the one called Hodgson."

The heat became unbearable. A rough hand grabbed at his arm and tore it away from his face.

"You will speak."

William finally looked. The Fallen stood over him glaring down, its black eyes burning into him. "Y-yes," he whispered. "I am Hodgson."

The creature nodded. "Your time is nearly come. On the third day you will bind the one called Houdini. Is the meaning of this clear?"

William sat up, cowering. Memories of that stage long ago leaped back to him. The Fallen anticipated his question.

"This binding will hold. This is what Hell has chosen for him."

He swallowed. He wanted to say no, wanted to strike back, to cry out to some God for deliverance and bring down this demon. He swallowed again, trembling with fear.

The Fallen dropped a small black box. It landed with a thud and the creature turned its back. "When you have bound him, this will be yours."

William took the box and fumbled it open. The pen inside was blindingly beautiful, even in the dim cave. It shone with a sharp clarity like nothing he'd ever seen in this place and he knew in a moment that it was not *of* this place. He stroked it, feeling its power, and knew that with this pen his curse would be lifted. With this pen, Hell could become Heaven for him.

"Close the box. I can not bear the blasphemy it contains."

He closed it and the Fallen turned, scooping it up.

"Is the meaning of this clear?"

William licked his lips and nodded. He closed his eyes. When he opened them again he sat alone and the caves were silent but for Houdini's sobs somewhere far ahead.

They saw the camp first, three tents pitched near the bi-plane. Two figures worked at connecting the electric pentacle. Twilight was not far off.

William had found Houdini and dragged him from the caves two days before. Neither man spoke of what they had encountered, but Houdini showed it in his eyes. They had been bright and dauntless before. Now, loss swam in them from time to time. Silence settled between the two more frequently as they neared the end of their journey.

Now with the camp in sight, Houdini grinned. They stopped, catching their breath. "There it is, Bill. By God, there it is." He pointed.

The desert became scrub and then transformed into a patch of bright green. Centered in the lawn, a large object sparkled and threw back light.

The horizon stood close here at the edge of the Ring. Behind them, the mountains crawled upward. Ahead of them, the Wasteland evaporated into a sheet of blank gray just past the Ear. This, William knew, was the edge of Hell itself.

He couldn't share Houdini's joy. Tomorrow would be the third day and since the caves, he'd realized exactly why their journey had been so easy.

They entered the camp and the small crew applauded as the camera rolled on. Maxwell broke out a case of champagne and they drank it warm from the bottles.

Houdini raised his bottle in the direction of the lawn and its large crystalline ear. The light had already gone but they'd seen it, massive and shining, set into the ground and leaning slightly so that one could climb into it and whisper homeward. "Tomorrow at first light," he said loudly.

Always the showman, William thought. Somehow it made him feel better about what he must do.

He slept fitfully, awakening again and again in the tent. At dawn, he climbed into his clothes to meet Houdini and the camera crew outside. The filming commenced without a word and Houdini turned towards the grassy plain. The Ear, perhaps thirty feet in diameter, caught pink light and winked at them from the center of the plain.

It's beautiful, William thought. He believed the stories now. The sight of it easily persuaded him.

Houdini started towards the grass, then stopped. A large stake had been driven into the desert floor. Near it, the Fallen stood grinning. Houdini took a step back and in a flash, the Fallen had gripped his arms, holding him tightly.

"Bind him, Hodgson." Its voice was a hiss.

Houdini struggled, then recognized the name. "Hodgson?" He twisted, his face going red with fury and effort. His eyes locked on William's and went cold. "*You.*"

Someone shoved chains into his hands and the Fallen dragged Houdini to the stake. William began binding him just as he had done on that Blackburn Stage so many years before. Houdini spat and bit, writhing and kicking.

"I should've known. Hodgson, you bastard."

William said nothing and did his best to avoid the showman's eyes. The accusations they shouted were louder than Houdini's words. In ten minutes, the strong man was bound, facing the grass and the Ear. Maxwell grinned, the crew laughed and pointed. The camera rolled on.

Houdini howled.

The Fallen dropped the box at William's feet. He picked it up, turned his back on them all, and returned to the tent.

He wrote all day and into the night, nearly oblivious to Houdini's cries. Gradually, the cursing had become pleading. At one point, William could have sworn he'd invoked the faith of both their fathers, but then the pen grabbed him and dragged him back into his passion.

The stories and poems unfolded like magic onto the page, flowing out in ways they never had during his life. He wrote until the cramping of his hand forced him to stop, and then, he read what he had written.

The stories and poems weaved a tapestry that blended into one monumental message that Hell could not contain, and William's heart could not contain it either. He broke into tears and threw the pen away from him. He grabbed up the strewn papers from his notebook in fistfuls and shredded them.

He stood, grabbed up the pen, and strode into the early morning. He could feel determination and rage hardening his face and stiffening his limbs as he walked towards the Ear.

Houdini hung limply by his chains. He raised his head weakly. "It's okay, Bill."

William ignored him. The Fallen stood nearby. Clutching the pen, William approached. "I've changed my mind," William said.

It hissed. "Take that obscenity from my sight," it said, waving the pen away, eyes squinting to avoid the golden glare of light from its surface.

Without a word, William sprung forward, bringing the pen up and plunging it into the Fallen's white chest. It shrieked as the sliver of heaven slid into its skin and black filth plumed out like a swarm of gnats. The Fallen clutched at it and William kept his grip as he came down on top of the demon.

Behind him, Houdini's voice took on new life. "The grass, Bill, by God in Heaven, the grass!"

William's body translated the words before his mind could. Hand firmly on the pen, driving it deeper, arms locked around the Fallen, he scrambled with his feet to drag the creature onto the lawn. It screamed and bucked against him, then melted into dust. William lay still, panting, feeling the cool of the grass enfold him.

He sat up. Maxwell and his crew stood in silence. Standing, he picked up the golden pen.

"I could use that," Houdini said with a tired grin.

He took it to him and crouched beside him while the escape artist did his trick. He watched as Ehrich took the pen apart by touch, stripping it down to its basic parts before selecting the piece best suited for picking the locks that held him.

The film crew continued shooting.

When Houdini finished, he stood, rubbing his wrists. He winked at William. "I'm glad you figured it out, Bill."

William nodded. The tapestry within the stories and poems he'd written. "It was never about the Ear."

"No."

Maxwell stepped forward. His face looked pale. Before he could speak, Houdini pounced and spun him into a human shield. "The rifles?" he asked.

At last they approached the Ear. Now armed, William and Ehrich cautiously watched the lone cameraman that followed. They had tied the others up.

"It's too big of news to not film it," Houdini had said, giving in to Maxwell's pleas despite William's misgivings.

The Ear stood before them now and Houdini leaned his rifle against its base. Then, he leapt into the air and caught the rim, pulling himself up and onto the crystalline lobe. He climbed a bit, then looked down. "I think this is it," he said. His voice carried perfectly.

William put his attention back on the cameraman while Houdini spoke slowly above him.

"The message I want to sent back to my wife is . . ." Houdini paused, then spoke clearly and firmly: "Rosabelle. Answer. Tell. Pray. Answer. Look. Tell. Answer. Answer. Tell."

He climbed down. The tears ran freely down his face. "You're sure you have nothing to say?"

William nodded. "I'm sure."

They left the cameraman untied and climbed into the waiting plane.

"Now for my last escape." Houdini released the brake and the sent them bouncing towards the expanse of gray ahead. William heard Maxwell shouting for the single man standing to keep shooting and then the voice was lost in the roar of the engine.

They lifted into the air and were swallowed by nothingness.

They flew in silence, flew on for hours long after the fuel became vapor. A random line of verse from his past floated to the surface of William's mind. *Into the blank where life is hurled.* He didn't realize he'd said it aloud until Houdini asked.

"Something I wrote a long time ago," he shouted.

Now the engine coughed and sputtered. Now the plane shuddered and bucked in the wind. Now the gray around them took on tinges of blue. Now a green cliff soared ahead of them and two waiting figures waved. A rabbi and a priest, he knew, watching their prodigal sons come Home.

Houdini laughed. William laughed with him.

THE SANTAMAN CYCLE

M uscles tire. Words fail. Faith fades. Fear falls. In the Sixteenth Year of the Sixteen Princes the world came to an end
when the dragon's back gave out. Poetry died first followed by
faith. One by one the world-strands burst and bled until ash snowed
down as huddled masses whimpered in the cold.

The Santaman came reeking of love into this place and we did
not know him.

This is his story.

This is our story, too.

The Breaking of the Dragon's Back

Muscles tire. It's all we really knew. The dragon's back held up
the world. The poetry and faith of the Singing Literocrats held up the
dragon by the will of the Sixteen Princes. One Literocrat fell to the
sword, another to plague, a third to famine. Halved in this way, the
choir faltered in its song and the dragon caved in on its spindly legs. The
Sixteen Princes had no time to act, to change the course of this sudden, sweeping end. They drank wine and spoke of lemon trees instead.

We sat in the cold until the Santaman came.

The Coming of the Santaman

Myth became life. No one really believed in the Santaman until
he came with his tattered red robe and his dripping red sword. No

one really believed in his undying love until he burst into our direst need to carve us a new home from the bones of the world.

We looked up at the whistle of his wolf-stallion. "Why do you weep and whimper?" the Santaman asked from the back of his mount.

"We whimper for the end of our world," one of us said. "We weep for the fall of the Singing Literocrats and the Breaking of the Dragon's Back."

The Santaman grinned and shook his sword. Blood rained down from it, mixing with the ashes. "Weep also for the Sixteen Princes who have failed you."

"Why, Lord?" someone asked.

The Santaman spun his mount. "For I have avenged you in the Name Above All and they are no more."

We did not waver in our weeping. There was no lull in our lament.

The Ending Rest of the Sixteen Princes

The Santaman drew a head from his pouch, held it high by its golden hair. Its eyes and mouth worked open and the Fourth Literocrat sang us the song of the Ending Rest of the Sixteen Princes:

Muscles tire. Words fail. Faith fades. Fear falls. Love avenges. Hope births.

The Santaman heard the faltering song and felt the faltering faith of the Half Dozen Choir. The Santaman saw the breaking of the dragon's back and knew from his Seeing Pool the inaction of the Sixteen Princes. He rode out in rage reeking of love. He roared his vengeance at the darkening sky. Click-clack went the claws of his wolf-stallion on the Purple Palace's marble floors. Snick-snack went the blade of his singing sword as sixteen heads came tumbling down amid spilled wine, spilled blood and lemon blossoms.

He burned their summer palace into the ground with stone-fire and rode East to seek the last of the literocrats.

*

The Last of the Literocrats

Dust rose from the West as the Santaman approached. The wolf-stallion growled and tore sod and the last of the Literocrats lay down their lyres by the Murmuring Stream as the dragon's eye faltered above them.

"Take up your tools and lift your song," the Santaman cried.

"We are halved," the Fourth Literocrat said. "Our song is lost. The world ends. The dragon's back, already broken."

The sword licked out, then pointed North. The Murmuring Stream ran pink. "Sing a new home," the Santaman cried again. "Beyond the ether at the Edge of the World."

Two voices rose and fell in song. A third burbled in the stream. Scooping the golden-haired head from the water, the Santaman came seeking us to tell us of our new carved home.

The Ether at the Edge of the World

"North of the faraway beyond the ether at the Edge of the World" the head sang and died. The Santaman cast it aside.

"The way is too hard," we told the Santaman. "And we are afraid."

He sheathed his sword and climbed down among us. He cast open his arms, his red robes hung like bleeding meat. "Do not be afraid. I walk with you."

North, he walked his wolf-stallion and we followed after. In twilight, we walked and as the ruined cities fell behind us, others joined our ragged band.

Lost also behind us, the last of the literocrats sang sunrise and sunset, sang muscles and sinew, sang bones and teeth.

Death crabs scuttled and scavenged. Snick-snack went the sword.

Black Drawlers shrieked and savaged. Snick-snack went the sword.

Some of us fell. Some of us faltered. All of us hoped.

The faraway wrapped us and the ash snows fell away.

Sunlight bathed us and we swam out into the ether at the Edge of the World.

Swam towards our new carved home.

Our New Carved Home

Motes swim. Light diffuses. Home rises.

We see it through a smoky glass. We watch it twitch and meep with each note of the framing song.

The Santaman laughs and beats his sword against his thigh: "Ho, ho, ho."

We few remaining weep and set our feet on emerald grass. We smell the reek of love upon the wind. We wipe our eyes. We wipe our eyes and look again.

Ahead a dragon.

Upon his back a world.

HIBAKUSHA DREAMING IN THE SHADOWY LAND OF DEATH

Some of us started getting together for Group Psychotherapy after the war ended. I think it was Peach Boy's idea. He'd seen a flier, written in English, nailed to a post at the market and thought it might be a good way to practice the new language. He rallied up me, Golden Boy, One Inch Boy, and Urashima Taro, and we went down together to meet with the American psychiatrist, Amanda Fullbright Hampton, at her new office in a former Imperial Army officer's quarters in Tokyo.

We shuffled in each Tuesday with nothing better to do and sat in a circle, our hands wrapped around cups of steaming tea. Outside, American soldiers swaggered past Dr. Hampton's window, their pink faces shining and their white teeth flashing smiles. Each Tuesday, she made a great show of her annoyance and shut the blinds but I could tell she welcomed their looks. I found myself wondering if she didn't sometimes put on stockings and a shorter dress and high heeled shoes and go to the places where the soldiers drank in order to find one she could take home from time to time. Then, I wondered if maybe she might like to take me home sometime. Usually, I wondered this during our meetings. Apart from the fantasizing about Dr. Hampton, I found the Group Psychotherapy rather useless.

"What do you think about Kintaro's story?" Dr. Hampton asked me. She smiled and shifted her skirts.

I shrugged. "I'm sorry."

She leaned in and I tried not to look down her shirt. "He was talking about his mother."

I shrugged again. "We all know she was an ogress." When the psychiatrist frowned, I continued. "Well," I said, "she was."

The true nature of this was lost on her. She was looking for something underneath it, some kind of meaning. But we'd all learned the hard way that there wasn't any meaning left in the world. Most of the gods left a long while ago. Those who couldn't leave simply forgot who they were. Some of us who weren't quite gods didn't have that luxury. Of course, we couldn't tell her that.

Kintaro the Golden Boy cleared his voice. "Regardless," he said. "I saw a woman who could have been her twin down at the market and suddenly I felt — "

Issun-Boshi, the One Inch Boy interrupted. "You know who I saw the other day?"

"Who?" Momotaro the Peach Boy asked.

Kintaro looked stunned by the developing side conversation. He was used to getting more attention than the rest of us. He shifted his gaze from Peach Boy to One Inch Boy to me.

Dr. Hampton sighed. I started wondering if she were better in bed than she was at Group Psychotherapy and I was beginning to realize that she simply had to be.

I grinned at her and sipped my tea before turning to One Inch Boy. "Who did you see?"

"One of the Forty Seven," he said. Even Kintaro's eyebrows raised at this. Dr. Hampton tapped her pencil on her clipboard.

"I thought they were all dead by now," I said.

Peach Boy snorted. "That doesn't mean anything. Look at us. We're living proof of the Karmic Cycle." He grinned.

Only I wasn't so sure of this. Of course, I was also the only one of us who didn't know who he was.

Kintaro the Golden Boy remembered his past life as the heroic foster son of an Ogress. He could talk for days about wandering around with the regent warrior Minamoto no Yorimitsu and his Four Guardian Kings, fighting bandits and Spider Gods.

And Momotaro was quick to remind everyone that he distinctly recalled the smell and texture of the giant peach that he arrived in, and cried openly when he spoke of that childless old woman and her husband who found him, *Heaven's gift of a son* in his own words. Next up was Urashima Taro, a fisherman who saved a turtle, visited the undersea Dragon's Palace and returned home to find that three hundred years had passed. "Imagine my surprise," he told us all that first day we met.

And there was Issun-Boshi, who insisted — despite his presently Sumo-sized self — that he spent part of his life in miniature because his own mother had wished to have a boy "even if he were only one inch tall." A skilled samurai, he killed an Oni with a sewing needle and won the heart of a princess who wished him to normal size . . . and then some, it seems.

Fact is, everyone knew themselves but me.

"And who are you?" Dr. Hampton asked me the same day she asked the rest of us.

"I'm hoping you can help me sort that out," I told her with a smile. She shifted uncomfortably and it was the first time I wondered what she might look like without her clothes. It was easier to think of that than it was to think of that unexpected and sudden end to the war, the piercing sunrise that swallowed two cities.

That was two years ago. Today, we were talking about our mothers (again) until One Inch Boy brought up the ronin and everything changed.

Kintaro leaned forward in his chair. "Where did you see him?"

One Inch Boy glanced at Dr. Hampton as if asking for permission to continue the digression. She said nothing. "At the G.I. Bar," he said, "on the water-side of the Dai-Ichi Seimei Building." He paused. "He'd been drinking sake for days." He paused again. "Well fed, too."

I knew the bar, down by Allied Command, but I'd never been there.

"Perhaps," Dr. Hampton said, "Kintaro would like to finish what he was saying?" She smiled; there was sweet sadness in it.

Momotaro stroked his thin mustache. "It sounds like he's done well for himself. I wonder what he's been up to?"

One Inch Boy shrugged. "I asked. He wouldn't say."

"Probably no good," Kintaro said. "Why, I wouldn't — "

But this time, Dr. Hampton did the interrupting. When she did, she uncrossed her legs and I saw a bit of creamy white calf. "Time's up," she said. "Please take a cookie with you when you go."

And we did, because like everyone, we were so hungry that even the Gaijin sweets appealed to us.

"I'm not sure about this," I told Peach Boy outside the bar.

"What's not to be sure about?" he said, smiling. "Maybe there's work to be had. Good money, easy money."

"But what about the Americans?"

One Inch Boy spoke up now. "Giving birth to a baby is easier than worrying about it."

I scowled. "What's that supposed to mean?"

Kintaro pushed past me. "Come on," he said. "It's fine."

We slipped in. There were uniformed soldiers everywhere, drinking and listening to loud music, talking even louder. I could smell their sweat. The four of us stopped and looked around the room. One Inch Boy pointed, then picked his away across the room to an old man at the far corner of the bar.

The ronin looked up at us and smiled, showing the gaps where many of his teeth had been. "Boys," he said, "it's good to see you."

He stank of sake and sweat and he wore cast-off American clothes. I thought I should recognize him but I did not, though the others did.

"What have you been up to?" Kintaro asked, clapping the old man on the back.

The old man chortled. "A little of this and a little of that. You?"

Golden Boy shrugged. "We're trying American Group Psychotherapy for free cookies, hot tea and English lessons."

"And the psychiatrist has shapely legs," I added.

"Well," he said, "I can drink to that." And he did.

One Inch Boy leaned towards him, lowering his voice. "You're doing very well for yourself. Are you working?"

The ronin flinched. "A bit," he said.

"We need work," Peach Boy said. "Maybe you can help us out."

The old man shook his head. "I don't think I can." He drained his sake and belched.

"And *I* don't think you work," Kintaro said. His eyes narrowed. "You drink too much to work."

The ronin shook his head and wagged a finger at the Golden Boy. "For my work, I drink just enough."

Kintaro still retained a great deal of his superhuman strength though he didn't look it. He'd traded the round, boyish features for the defeated look of a middle-aged man who'd watch his people rise and fall. But when his hand came down on the ronin's shoulder, I heard the old man's bones groan beneath the power of Kintaro's grip.

I pushed myself between them and scowled at Kintaro. "There's no need for this," I said.

Kintaro sneered. "He doesn't smell right." He looked around the bar. "He smells like *them*. Hell, he looks like *them*."

I wondered if this was how it was meant to be now. Our gods had moved on. Only a few of us remained from those olden times and we lived quietly and wondered if the American bomb and boot might be the end of us. I wondered if perhaps waking up on the edge of that blasted ruin of a city was simply an illusion. Perhaps I was in Yomi, the land of the dead. And perhaps my companions were dead, too, and we were all wandering towards the edges of what might be life without ever truly finding it.

I put my hand on Kintaro's arm and brushed it off the old man. I was surprised at my own strength. "There is no need for this," I said again. Then I turned to the ronin. "I'm sorry for my friend," I told him.

He smiled but the light went out in his eyes. "Be sorry for all of us," he said with a quiet voice.

I looked at the others. All but Kintaro had looks of profound sadness on their faces. Kintaro still looked angry.

He spat on the floor. "Be sorry for yourself, old man," he said to the old man. Kintaro glared at the rest of us and stormed out of the bar. I noticed a few of the soldiers watching him as he went.

While Peach Boy and the others apologized for our friend, I slipped out behind him into a sullen, gray evening.

I caught up to him near the water. "Why are you so angry?"

Kintaro's voice was louder than was proper. "Why I am so angry? Why are you *not* angry? Look around you." He cast his arm about, encompassing the jeeps and soldiers moving freely among our people, freely upon our island. "We are hungry. Are they? We are broken. Are they? And that old man — once a hero to his people — bends and takes every inch they'll give him. He's up to something. I know he is."

"But Kintaro," I said, "if we had prevailed would it be any different for them beneath *our* flag?" I swallowed, feeling myself tremble as memory washed me. "If we had their bomb wouldn't we have done the same?" Then, I let my voice become gentle. "Besides, each week we go to see the American Dr. Amanda Fullbright Hampton. We drink her tea and eat her cookies and speak her language. If the old man has found a way live in this hell who are we to judge him?"

His voice was sharp. "What do you know?"

And he was right. I knew little. I couldn't remember any of the war. Or anything before that. Nor any of my past incarnations. I woke up in a ditch on the edge of a blasted city, Peach Boy's tattered shoe prodding me. I woke up with no knowledge of myself, my skin nearly as pink as a Gaijin, my vision blurred, and my hair burned away. Within a week, my skin had darkened to its appropriate tone, I could see just fine and I needed a haircut. They said it was how they knew I was one of them after all.

By the time I opened my mouth to reply, Kintaro had walked away. It was the last time I saw him alive.

Kintaro the Golden Boy was killed the night before our next session with Dr. Hampton. We learned the news from the woman he rented a sleeping mat from in an Army warehouse that had been converted to sleeping quarters for low income workers.

"What happened?" Peach Boy asked her.

"He killed Americans. Fifteen of them."

"But why?" Issun-Boshi asked.

She shrugged. "Ask the old man."

We went to the bar but the old man was not there so we wandered about that part of the city, learning what we could without drawing too much attention to ourselves. Gradually we pieced together the end of Golden Boy.

Kintaro had stormed an American barracks with a katana and a rusty revolver he had found in a culvert. Some said he'd been shot over thirty times before he fell. Others said he'd not been shot at all. But many had seen the bodies pulled out from the building. The streets whispered the story to us but to my knowledge it was never reported in the American news. A thousand years of heroics and his last battle went unremembered by his foes, despite the price he extracted from them.

We still met at Dr. Hampton's office for our session. She pointed to the teapot and we served ourselves. "What would you like to talk about today?" she asked.

"Kintaro is dead," Issun-Boshi said. His voice sounded hollow to me and his eyes were red. "I would like to talk about that."

"Maybe we're all dead," I whispered. But no one heard me.

Dr. Hampton looked surprised and, for a moment, ambushed by

our sudden honesty. Her eyes went wide for a moment, then she regained her composure. "What happened?"

We filled in the details as best we could. When we were finished, she let out her breath. "I'm sorry," she said. And suddenly, I realized she was crying and that there was greater beauty in her tears than there could ever be in her legs or breasts. For that hour, I did not wonder at all about how she was in bed. For that hour, her Group Psychotherapy was as mighty as old magic, as crafty as any dragon. She simply put down her clipboard and laughed with us, cried with us, as we talked about our fallen friend. As his story was told, her eyes became alive and her skin flushed, her breath caught easily in her throat. When we finished, she came around to each of us and hugged us. It felt improper even though her hair smelled as good as I had imagined it might and her body felt as warm.

"I'm afraid," she said as we stood to leave, "that this will be our last session together."

We looked at her blankly and Peach Boy spoke first. "What do you mean? We need you now more than ever."

She looked out the window and I realized that her face was not lined with sadness just from our loss but from some other loss inside of her. Then she recovered. "I don't think I can help you." She paused and chose her words carefully. "I'm not sure you need help." Then she paused again. "Besides," she said, "I have to return to America."

So one by one we filed out of her office, cookies clenched in our fists and stuffed into our pockets. Each stopped at the door and gave her a slight bow. She hugged each of us again.

I let the others go first. "I'll catch up," I told them.

I shifted on my feet before her, holding my hat in my hands. "I was wondering . . . " My eyes met hers for a brief second. They were blue with flecks of green in them and they were an ocean that could drown me. I lost my words and shifted again.

"Yes?"

I saw the curve of her breast beneath the white silk of her blouse. I followed the line of her neck to her tiny ears. "I was wondering now that I'm not your patient if you'd like to take me home with you sometime?"

She laughed and I felt the heat rise on my cheeks as I looked away. But her hand reached out and touched my arm and I knew then that her laugh was all nervousness and intoxication. She was

drunk on the legend of us, or at least of my friends and their memories of Kintaro, and her smile told me her answer before she gave
it.

"I would like that very much," she said. "Meet me here at nine."

Bowing again, I fled into the rain to find my waiting friends.

We went back to the bar, hoping the old man would be there to
tell us why Kintaro had attacked the Americans. His corner was
empty so we took it and talked in low voices over cheap beer.

We talked about Kintaro for a while, then talked of the future.

"What will we do?" Issun-Boshi the One Inch Boy asked.

Momotaro the Peach Boy shrugged. "I have a cousin in America.
He works in orchards in a desert near the Pacific. He's offered me
work and will help me get on my feet there." He sipped his beer. "I
think I will go there and start over again."

"You think they will let you go to America?" I asked. This sounded
off to me.

He shrugged and grinned. "I am Momotaro. I will find a way."

One Inch Boy turned to me next. "What about you? Are you
going to America, too?"

I shook my head. "I don't think so."

"Then what will you do?"

"It's hard to know what to do when you don't know who you
are," I said.

"Me," Urashima Taro said, "I'm going back to the ocean." He
saw our puzzled looks. "The here and now holds nothing for me.
Perhaps the queen of the Dragon Palace will have me back." He
sighed. "Otohime and her twenty maids in waiting. And this time, I'll
let a thousand years pass before I return. And I will hope that our
people — that all people — have learned a better way."

We raised our glasses and drank to that.

Peach Boy turned to One Inch Boy. "What about you?"

Issun-Boshi smiled. "I had a dream last night," he said, "of a
monster rising from the waters. I think it would make a fine movie
but I need to find a writer for it."

"Why don't you write it yourself?" I asked.

"I tried," he said.

"And?"

"And," he said, "I think I'm better at being in stories than I am at writing them."

We all laughed, we all raised our glasses again, and we fell into silence for a while. Then, one by one my friends stood and filed out. I stayed because I didn't want to tell them I was going back to Dr. Hampton's in an hour.

The old ronin slipped in across from me as soon as they had gone. He was sober now and there was steel in his eyes. "It's not too late," he told me. "You can start over."

I stared at him blankly. His Gaijin clothing was gone now and he was dressed simply in black. His face was shaved, his hair combed. "What happened to Kintaro?" I asked him.

"It was never for Kintaro," he said. "But he asked. I should have kept silent. I should have found you."

I blinked. "What was never for Kintaro?"

He pulled a scrap of paper from his pocket and pushed it into my hands, then he folded his fingers over my hands and clenched them tightly. "*Amanonuhoko*," the ronin said and I remembered it.

It was called the Halberd of the Heavenly Marsh. It had made the world, or at least the beginnings of it. The memory jarred me after so long without recollection. A sea churned, an island formed. Creation.

The old ronin was speaking rapidly now. "I found it," he said. "My work. I've done terrible things." His eyes darted to the left and right. "They pay well for our artifacts," he said, "and I took their money like a whore and drank it away."

He withdrew his hands from mine and I looked down at the writing on the paper. It was a name and address in the United States, in a place called Michigan.

"I tried to tell Kintaro but he wouldn't listen. It had already been shipped. And even if it hadn't, he couldn't have used it. It wasn't for him."

Then he stood and turned to leave. My mouth opened and closed but I couldn't find the words. I had questions, but there were too many and I could not find the right one to ask.

Standing before me, he bowed deeply. "I beg your forgiveness, lord," he said. "I did not recognize you at first."

Then he left as quickly as he arrived.

*

When I tapped lightly on Dr. Hampton's office door, she opened it and ushered me inside quickly, looking up and down the street, her eyes moving with practiced precision.

She wore a shorter dress and silk stockings. Her bustline was tighter than the other dresses I had seen. It revealed the downward slope of her breasts, the secret shadow of her cleavage. Her brown hair was down now, covering her ears, and she did not smile at me.

Instead, taking my hand, she led me up a narrow flight of stairs and took me into her bedroom. She closed the door and turned down the lights.

I stood still, not knowing what to do. After two years of imagination and fantasy, the moment was upon me and I felt shame. A match flared and I saw her face in the glow of it. It bore resolve, not desire.

"I've watched you watching me," she said as she touched the match to the stub of a candle.

I didn't know what to say. "I'm sorry."

She turned around, pulling her hair up off her neck. "Unzip me?"

My hands shook as I worked the small zipper down. She waited there, the white horizontal line of her bra's back strap stark against her pale skin. When I saw that she wasn't moving, I reached up with my hands and parted her dress, pushing it over her shoulders as she released her hair and dropped her arms to her sides. The sleek fabric slid over her; I heard the sound of it rustling her skin before it fell crumpled to the floor.

Slowly, she turned and pressed herself against me. "Do you think this will help you?" Her right hand moved to the zipper of my trousers.

I swallowed and nodded.

"Do you want to know why I'm doing this?"

I nodded again.

She leaned forward and kissed me on the corner of my mouth. "All of your friends know who they are. In the midst of this death, they are alive." She kissed me again. "Maybe," she said, "if you feel alive you will know who you are."

I gasped at her hand's movement and another memory gripped me. Another beautiful woman in another time.

I felt something stirring but I did not know if it was life. She tugged at my clothing as she pulled me into her narrow bed and I let my mouth and hands wander her until we were both naked. Then, in the moment when I rolled onto her, fear seized me and I lunged out of the bed to extinguish the candle.

"What are you doing?" she asked. "What's wrong?"

But how could I tell her that suddenly I remembered another time, another lover, and knew that I dare not see her for who she truly was in this underworld we occupied? How did I tell her that if I saw her, like that lover long ago, she might haunt me all my days in the wrath of her own lifelessness?

Instead, I took her silently and in the dark.

When we finished, we lay close together and smoked American cigarettes. "I want to tell you the truth," she said.

"Yes?"

"It may hurt you."

I shrugged and smiled. "I've been hurt before."

"I think I am carrying Kintaro's baby," she said in a quiet voice.

"Oh," I said. I wasn't angry. I don't think I was even hurt by it. I may have even felt proud for my friend in that moment of revelation.

She continued. "I wasn't sure. I'm still not. But it *could* be his." She crushed out her cigarette. "I've decided I'm not a very good psychiatrist after all. I will go home and have my baby."

I wanted to tell her that I could come with her, that I could be a father to Kintaro's child — if it were indeed Kintaro's son — and raise him as my own. But when I opened my mouth to say the words, I felt a fist close over my heart.

"It was never for Kintaro," the old ronin said. I thought about the scrap of paper in my pocket and the address in Michigan where the Heavenly Halberd of the Marsh had been shipped.

I closed my mouth.

A match popped and she lit another cigarette, offering it to me. I took it and dragged on it, feeling the smoke fill my lungs.

"What are you thinking?" she asked me.

I leaned in and kissed her forehead. "I am thinking that you are a very good psychiatrist."

After she fell asleep, I dressed and slipped out into the night.

I felt differently, I realized, and it took me a moment to place the feeling. When it hit me, I smiled and wept at the same time because I knew it suddenly for what it was.

I felt alive.

*

Later that night, I went back to the bar but discovered it was closed. Military Police moved in and out of the building, barking orders, and I slipped back into the shadows and walked down to the waterfront.

I stood there for a long while, watching the water and wondering about Kintaro the Golden Boy, and Dr. Amanda Fullbright Hampton, and my other friends. I thought about the memories, just out of reach, that teased me now. Especially the memory of blinding heat and light, a wind of heaven that blasted down buildings and left only shadows to mark what had once been men.

The power of it forced me to sit.

I did not hear the man approach until he spoke to me.

"Good evening," he said in bad Japanese.

I looked up. Dirty light from the streetlamps painted a tall, slender American — middle-aged and wearing a trenchcoat and hat. "Good evening," I said in careful English as I stood.

He nodded towards bar down the street. "Bad business, that," he said. Soldiers were carrying a stretcher out draped in a blood-stained, white sheet.

"What happened?"

He pursed his lips. "An old man in the bar killed himself with a sword."

I was not surprised. "It is called seppuku," I told him. "I think you know it as hara-kiri."

The American nodded. "I think he recited a poem first. But I couldn't understand it."

Yes, I thought, he would do that. "It is the ritual to restore honor for a fallen or failed warrior."

"There are already too many deaths," he said. The man extended his hand to me and I took it. "My name is Ed Deming."

We shook hands. "I do not know my name or I would tell you."

He smiled and I saw sympathy in it. "These are hard times," he said.

"Yes."

"May I sit with you?"

I nodded and sat back down. He joined me. After a minute, I spoke. "You are not a soldier," I said.

Deming shook his head. "No. A statistician." My blank look conveyed my lack understanding. "I work with numbers," he said. "Probabilities and such."

"Ah. I see."

"I'm here to help with the census." Then as an afterthought, he added, "I'm from Iowa."

I looked at him. "Iowa?"

"It's part of the United States. Near the middle."

I pondered this for a moment. "Do you know of a place called Michigan?"

Deming smiled. "I know it. It's not far from Iowa. What about you? Are you from Tokyo?"

I shrugged. "I'm here now. I think I'm from Nagasaki. I'm — " I paused, trying to find the word " — I am hibakusha." It was a new word. *Explosion-affected person.*

A sadness washed the American's face. "I'm sorry," he said.

I shrugged again. "Nothing can be done for it."

"But you're okay? You're healthy?"

I nodded. "And my memory is coming back."

"Well, that's a blessing."

Perhaps, I thought. "So what do you think of our country?"

He smiled. "I think it's beautiful." And when he said it, I was reminded of the beauty in Dr. Hampton's tears when we first told her Kintaro had been killed, when she had joined us in our pain. Of course, I didn't know then that it had been her pain, too, because some part of her had loved Kintaro. "And," he continued, "I'm impressed with the resolve of your people to come back from this terrible, tragic war."

I snorted. "You think we will come back from this?"

"I really do."

I studied him now. There was confidence in his jaw line and the wrinkles in the corners of his eyes spoke of wisdom and humor.

"What makes you think such a thing?"

"Because everything you've done so far, you've done all the way." His face lit up. "Think about it. If that tenacity were applied to being the best you could be, to providing the best quality of goods and services, you could have the world's wealth without firing a shot." His hands moved now as he talked and I felt something like hope growing inside of me. "If you have superior quality — both in your product and producers, your workforce and your managers —

your productivity will climb and your expenses will fall. I really believe it."

"And you're a statistician?"

He nodded. "I am."

But in my heart, I knew he was a wizard, a sorcerer from old whose words were full of power and whose eyes were full of the future. I found myself wanting to believe him.

"How would we do such a thing?" I asked him.

He raised one finger, pointing it towards heaven as he extended it towards me. "First," he said, "transform the individual. That transformed individual will see himself differently, see the world in a new way. He will see the interdependency of it all and will bring about change." And in his next words, I *saw* the interdependency as he echoed the ronin's words. "It's never too late," Ed Deming said. "You can start over here."

We sat in silence for five minutes. Then I looked up at him. "I think you are a very wise man who will help my country very much," I told him.

He chuckled. "I don't know about that." He stood slowly and I heard his bones and joints creak. "But I do know it's late and I should be getting back." I stood, too, and when he bowed to me slightly, I returned the bow. Then we shook hands.

"I hope you remember who you are," Deming said.

"Thank you," I said. "I hope you enjoy your time in our country."

With a smile and a tip of his hat, the American Ed Deming turned and strolled away to leave me with my thoughts.

After he'd gone, I walked out onto the pier and found a place to sit in the deeper shadows. At some point, I fell asleep and I dreamed.

My people's automobiles were on every highway in the world. Japanese radios were in every home. Our goods went out from our tiny island and the wealth of the world came back to us. There were no more ronin riding their solitary wave, no more hibakusha with their souls burned to ash, and Nomi, that shadowy land of death, was a distant memory. Its gates were sundered and its captives free and alive again.

And I saw Ed Deming in my dream, speaking to my country's leaders, offering a new way to conquer and build our empire.

*

When I woke up, I knew who I was and I knew what I must do. I would go to America, to Michigan. I would take back what had been given to me so very long ago and I would climb once more to that bridge between heaven and earth, thrust the blade of *Amanonuhoko* deep into the sea and shake out its droplets over my land. I would recreate what I had created once before and the re-creation would drive out the shadows and spirits that had kept my people hungry and without hope.

I would do these things. But how?

"First," Deming's voice echoed inside of me, "transform the individual."

A declaration formed within me and I said the words to myself, silently. Then I spoke the words aloud to the empty night. "I am Izanagi," I said. "I will find a way."

And when I said it, I heard splashing in the water below and I opened my eyes. The moon had come out from behind the clouds and in its silver light, I saw my friend Urashima Taro on the back of an enormous, ancient turtle. He had two beautiful women with him and he grinned up at me.

"Have you decided yet what you will do?" he shouted.

"Yes," I told him. "Will your friend carry me to California?"

Urashima Taro bent in close to the turtle's great head and whispered something in its ear. He listened for a moment, winking at one of the pretty girls who giggled and blushed. "He says that he will carry you anywhere, Lord Izanagi, until you remember how to fly."

I bowed deeply to the old turtle and to my friend and his female companions. I stepped out of my broken shoes and peeled off my tattered socks. I removed my shirt and trousers, folded them, left them neatly on the pier.

Then laughing with joy and shaking with hope, I leaped into the cold waters of Tokyo Bay.

ONE SMALL STEP

We realized things had gone too far on the moon when Anderson's chimps killed him, shaved themselves, and democratically elected one of their own to put on his lab-coat and demand a meeting with the rest of us.

Of course, Anderson started this whole goddamn mess, and he deserved what he got. Even Gable and Tennyson agreed on that point, and those two never agreed on anything.

I met Dr. Roger Anderson after a paper he delivered at the World Economic Development Conference in Thailand. Now everyone knows it as *Tomorrow's Labor Force: Inter-species Collaboration for a Better Future*. It's the paper that got him the funding to move his lab to the moon and start training his chimps to do their part in the New Economy.

Of course, the Bible people didn't mind. The way they saw it, chimps were just dumb animals like oxen or horses; disbelieving evolution has advantages. The animal rights people got pretty uptight until the Helen Dialogue.

I got involved just after that. But I remember watching it on TV.

It's a fixed camera in the corner of a room, focused on a small table and two chairs. There is a puzzle on the table. There are other toys strewn about.

Helen ambles in and sits at the table. Her chart says she's been signing since infancy and has been on the treatments for nearly six months. She's come the farthest of them all.

Anderson enters and sits across from her, balancing his clipboard on his knees. "Make the puzzle for me, Helen," he says while signing to her. The microphone is also on the wall so his voice is muffled.

"Cookie?" Helen signs.

"Puzzle first; cookie after," Anderson signs back.

Helen sucks her thumb for a moment, grins, and puts the puzzle together quickly. She claps her paws and hoots. "Cookie," she signs.

Anderson spills the puzzle pieces out. "Again."

Helen shakes her head. "Cookie." Then she makes a rude gesture.

Anderson points at the puzzle. His voice is shaking a little. "No."

She howls, bounces from wall to wall, scattering the puzzle pieces. Then, she stops suddenly, stands up as tall as she can and pokes Anderson in the chest with a hairy knuckle before signing with jerky movements: "I'll make the shitting puzzle if you give me a cookie. Puzzle for cookie, you shit."

The rest you know. That incident started a six hour dialogue. At one point, a psychologist was called in. The animal rights people had a hard time protesting from then on.

The chimps wanted it.

Later that year, funding came through for a new lab and training area to simulate conditions for their new line of work. That's when I was recruited.

I was a high school English teacher.

But after meeting with Anderson and his research staff — and interviewing with Helen and her pack — I suddenly found myself teaching chimpanzees how to read and type.

Eventually, when the new facility was ready, my classroom moved to the moon.

Helen's brother Chuckles was the fastest to pick up one-handed touch-typing. The U.S. military invested a large chunk of change in a keyboard that strapped to a forearm. They even designed a keyboard that would work over the top of a pressure suit.

We practiced, he in his suit and me behind a monitor. "Hi Chuckles," I said into the microphone.

His fingers flew as the computer synthesized the characters in an electronic voice. "Hi Mike. How are you today?"

"Fine thanks. Are you ready to start?"

He nodded. "Yes."

"Fine," I said. "Let's play twenty questions."

He bounced a bit. All of them loved the game. They loved to talk about themselves. And they loved to know about us.

I settled into my chair. "I'll start. What color are my eyes?"

Chuckles leaned forward. "Your eyes are blue."

"Correct. Your turn."

"Einstein has funny hair," he typed, waving at the picture behind me.

"Yes, but that is not a question."

"Why does Einstein have funny hair?"

Chuckles is the one they democratically elected a year later.

"We've killed and eaten Dr. Anderson," Chuckles typed when we were all in the room. It sounded monotone as the computer pronounced the words — like a passionless act. He had scabs all over from cutting himself with the razor and the blood stained lab-coat hung to the floor. "I helped kill him and eat him."

I knew the answer to my next question but I had to ask it anyway. "Why?"

His fingers started to fly then paused, tapped delete several times and continued. "Because of Helen."

"Helen was in an accident, Chuckles. You know what. You were there." We'd all watched the wall collapse. And while Anderson tried to talk them through the rescue, Tennyson and I had raced to the airlock, scrambled into our suits and gone into the mine. By the time we arrived, the chimps were hyperventilating in their suits. We pulled Helen's broken body out of the debris and buried her outside the lab.

He howled, pounded the floor, and straightened upright. "Anderson — " he paused, looking for the vocabulary " — made it happen."

I wanted to argue with him. I opened my mouth but closed it because I just wasn't sure.

I'd seen the last tape Anderson made with Helen the night before her death.

I had to break into his desk to find it.

*

This is a better camera, sharper image, less warble. It is fixed in the corner of the room and it's a better room. Cleaner. No toys or puzzles — Anderson's apes had put away childish things. A porthole in the corner of the room offers a barren exterior view of the moon and the training site.

Helen waits at the table, her hands folded over her lap. She's wearing the keyboard, but she only uses it half the time. Anderson walks in and sits across from her.

"Hello, Helen," he says while signing out the words.

"Hi, Doctor Anderson." She types the greeting, signing his name.

"Chuckles said you wanted to see me."

Helen nods. "I want to play twenty questions."

The back of Anderson's head moves. "Okay. What color are my eyes?"

She shakes her head. "I want to ask the questions."

Anderson leans forward. Anyone who knew him knows that this is Roger's posture of intrigue. "What would you like to ask, Helen?"

"Are you — " she pauses, shakes her head a bit as if clearing it — "Are you the god?" She types the word because she doesn't know the sign for it.

"Excuse me?"

"Are you . . . the god?"

"I'm not sure I understand."

"The one in the book. Do you make us like you?"

"Which book?"

"The black book."

"Do you mean the Bible?" His voice sounds surprised now. She nods.

"Where did you get a Bible?"

She makes a shrill noise, she clicks her tongue at him, she waves her hands. "We took it."

Now he seems perplexed. "You took a book?"

"Yes."

"Why?"

"To be like you."

Anderson pauses. He runs his hands through his hair and sighs. "How many books, Helen?"

"I'll ask the shitting questions," she signs.

He turns off the tape here. Whatever else was said is lost. But we know that after the tape, he made a note on his desk to have us inventory our books and determine what else was missing. Next to the note, he'd scribbled *Morris*, underlined, with a question mark.

I looked at his bookshelf when I saw that note. Of course I knew what book to look for. I looked for the gap where *The Naked Ape* might've been but they were too clever to leave gaps.

The next morning, after the corporate trainers left for a four day re-supply at Armstrong City, Anderson ordered Helen and the others into the mine, ordered her down to the deeper parts while the others stood by.

In the hours after our meeting, the chimps were quiet.

Locked in the control room, we tried to radio out. Twenty questions came back to haunt us:

"What is that?" Chuckles had signed three months ago.

"An antenna," I had told him. "What color are my eyes?" Tennyson and Gable whispered behind me. They were talking about the tranquilizer rifle locked in the veterinary supply cabinet.

We'd let them run freely through most of the facility for most of a year. We'd wanted them to know how to work the hatches, the suits, the equipment. Affordable labor, acceptable risk, and adequate skills with appropriate supervision. That was the executive summary in a nutshell.

I wasn't much of a biologist, I hadn't followed much beyond basic science in college. But I remembered evolution's full house slapped onto the table, all chips shoved recklessly in — the naked, hunting ape. The thinking monkey that went to the moon.

"What do you want?" I had asked Chuckles from the doorway, at the end of our meeting.

His eyes narrowed. He blew spittle at me. "We want clothing. We want all books. We want Helen back."

"I'll see what I can do," I told him.

Tennyson tried to get the rifle. There were only ten of them — nine with Helen gone. Plenty to post guards at the facility's intersections.

They bludgeoned him to death with pipe wrenches and hammers and moon rocks we didn't even know they'd smuggled in.

This time they didn't dismantle the camera first. Gable reached out to turn off the camera; for some reason, I grabbed his hand and stopped him. I don't know why.

After that, Chuckles asked to meet with me again. The first time, he'd used his suit radio. This time, he used the intercom, holding the keyboard's speaker close to the microphone.

"We don't need to meet," I told him. "Helen is gone. Help yourself to the books and clothing."

They ransacked our quarters. I watched them on the cameras, though from time to time a chimp looked up and a camera went to static.

Locked in that crowded, cluttered room, lit by the light of a dozen monitors, we slipped into sleep.

When I woke up, there was a note from Gable.

I had to try, it said.

The movie was a bad joke. "Hey, Pops, I'm going to the moon to teach chimpanzees how to mine on Mars." What else could a boy's father do? He wrapped the movie up and presented it to me at my going away party.

"Get your paws off me," he said when I tried to hug him goodbye. "You damned dirty English teacher."

Everyone laughed at his bad Charlton Heston impersonation. I hadn't even taken off the cellophane.

Chuckles didn't struggle with it at all.

They were all in the lounge watching *Planet of the Apes* on our flat screen television. Gable was naked, bruised and bloody, stretched out on the floor like a scientist-skin rug. I think he was dead; I hope he was.

I don't know if he had tried to escape, tried for the gun or tried to reason with them.

No answer would be the right one.

While they hooted and howled at the movie, I made my way to the airlock. I was suiting up when Chuckles and two of his thugs approached quietly.

He tilted his head to the side. "Where are you going?"

"I'm going to get Helen for you," I said, not bothering to sign.

"You said Helen is gone."

"I lied."

His fingers danced, clackety-clack. "What is *lied?*"

"I said something that was not true."

"I'll go, too."

I shrugged, putting on the rest of my suit. "Fine by me, Chuckles." I checked my straps, I checked my boots, I pulled on my helmet and tugged on the gloves.

He went to his locker and suited up.

Together, we went out into the light of the earth. He brought his pipe wrench for good measure.

It wasn't hard at all. It's easy to forget the one small step between us and them.

I jump-walked to Helen's shallow grave. I fell onto it, crying out, careful to catch myself on my hands and ease myself slowly to the ground.

When Chuckles shook me, I moaned.

When he poked me with his wrench, I stirred.

When he rolled me over, I brought up a rock the size of a cantaloupe and smashed out his faceplate.

After that, it wasn't hard to use his wrench to pop open the supply shed. We didn't use much in the way of explosives when it came to training.

I didn't need much.

After setting the charges and watching them go one by one by one, I sat on a ridge and watched to make sure no suited figures emerged. I watched the air vent out, white and cold, like the last sigh of a dangerous dream.

Then I watched my watch, watched my oxygen gauge, watched the horizon for the returning supply truck.

Africa hung above me in the sky. That cradle of life tipped its face away from me, ashamed.

OF METAL MEN AND SCARLET THREAD
AND DANCING WITH THE SUNRISE

Rudolfo's Gypsy Scouts found the metal man sobbing in an impact crater deep in the roiling smoke and glowing ruins of Windwir. He crouched over a pile of blackened bones, his shoulders chugging and his bellows wheezing, his helmet-like head shaking in his large metal hands. They approached him silently, ghosts in a city of ghosts, but the metal man still heard and looked up.

Gouts of steam shot from his exhaust grate. Boiling water leaked from his glassy jeweled eyes. Nearby lay a mangled metal leg.

"Lla meht dellik ev'I," the metal man said.

The Gypsies drug him to Rudolfo because he could not stand on his own and refused to be supported. Rudolfo, from his tents outside the ruins, watched them return just like the message bird had promised.

They dragged the metal man into the clearing and released him, dropping the leg as well. Their bright colored tunics, cloaks and breeches were gray with ash and black from charcoal. The metal man gleamed in the afternoon sun.

They bowed and waited for Rudolfo to speak. "So this is all that's left of the Great City of Windwir?"

To a man, they nodded. Slow, deliberate nods.

"And the Androfrancine Library?"

One of the Gypsy Scouts stepped forward. "It burned first and fastest, Lord." The scout stepped back quickly, head bowed.

Rudolfo turned to the metal man. "And what do we have here?" He'd seen mechanicals before. Small ones, though, nothing quite so elaborate as a man. "Can you speak?"

"Llew etiuq kaeps nac I," the metal man said.

Rudolfo looked again to his Gypsy Scouts. The same scout

who'd spoken earlier looked up. "He's been talking since we found him, Lord. It's no language we've ever heard."

Rudolfo smiled. "Actually, it is." He turned back to the metal man. "Sdrawkcab kaeps," he told him.

A pop, a clunk, a gout of steam. The metal man looked up at Rudolfo, at the smoke-filled sky and the blackened horizon that was once the world's largest city. He shook and shuddered. When he spoke, his voice carried a depth of lament that Rudolfo had only heard twice before. "What have I done?" the metal man asked, his breast ringing as he beat it with his metal fist. "Oh, what have I done?"

Rudolfo reclined on silk cushions and drank sweet pear wine, watching the sunset wash the metal man red. His own personal armorer bent over the mechanical in the fading light, wiping sweat from his brow while working to re-attach the mangled leg.

"It's no use, Lord," the metal man said.

The armorer grunted. "It's nowhere close to good but it will serve." He pushed himself back, glancing up at Rudolfo.

Rudolfo nodded. "Stand on it, metal man."

The metal man used his hands to push himself up. The mangled leg would not bend. It sparked and popped but held as he stood.

Rudolfo waved. "Walk about."

The metal man did, jerking and twitching, using the leg more as a prop.

Rudolfo sipped his wine and waved the armorer away. "I suppose now I should worry about escape?"

The metal man kept walking, each step becoming more steady. "You wish to escape, Lord? You have aided me. Perhaps I may aid you?"

Rudolfo chuckled. "I meant *you*, metal man."

"I will not escape." The metal man hung his head. "I intend to pay fully for my crimes."

Rudolfo raised his eyebrows. "What crimes are those exactly?" Then, remembering his manners but not sure if they extended to mechanicals, he pointed to a nearby stool. "Sit down. Please."

The metal man sat. "I am responsible for the razing of Windwir and the genocide of the Androfrancines, Lord. I do not expect a trial. I do not expect mercy. I expect justice."

"What is your name?"

The metal man's golden lids flickered over his jeweled eyes in surprise. "Lord?"

"Your name. What is your name?"

"I am Mechoservitor Number Three, catalog and translations section."

"That's no name. I am Rudolfo. Lord Rudolfo of the Ninefold Forest Houses to some. General Rudolfo of the Wandering Army to others. That Damned Rudolfo to those I've bested in battle or in bed."

The metal man stared at him. His mouth-shutters clicked open and closed.

"Very well," Rudolfo finally said. "I will call you Isaak." He thought about it for a moment, nodded, sipped more wine. "Isaak. Tell me how exactly you managed to raze the Knowledgable City of Windwir and single-handedly wipe out the Androfrancine Order?"

"By careless words, Lord, I committed these crimes."

Rudolfo refilled his glass. "Go on."

"Are you familiar, Lord, with the Wizard Xhum Y'zir?"

Rudolfo was. He nodded.

"The Androfrancines found a cache of parchments in the Eastern Rises. They bore a striking resemblance to Y'zir's later work including his particular blend of Middle Landlish and Upper V'Ral. Even the handwriting matched."

Rudolfo leaned forward, one hand stroking his long mustache. "These weren't copies?"

The metal man shook his head. "Originals, Lord. Naturally, they were brought back to the library. They assigned the translation and cataloging to me."

Rudolfo picked a honeyed date out of a silver bowl and popped it into his mouth. He chewed around the pit, spitting it into a silk napkin. "You worked in the library."

"Yes, Lord."

"Continue."

"One of the parchments contained the missing text for Xhum Y'zir's Seven Cacophonic Deaths — "

Here Rudolfo's breath rushed out. He felt the blood flee so quickly from his face that he tingled. He raised his hand and fell back into the cushions. "Gods, a moment."

The metal man, Isaak, waited.

Rudolfo sat back up, drained off the last of his wine in one swallow and refilled the glass. "The Seven Cacophonic Deaths? You're sure?"

The metal man shook in one great sob. "I am now, Lord."

A hundred questions flooded Rudolfo. Each shouted to be asked. He opened his mouth to ask the first but closed it when Gregoric, the First Captain of his Gypsy Scouts, slipped into the tent with a worried expression on his face.

"Yes?" he asked.

"General Rudolfo, we've just received word that Overseer Sethbert of the Entrolusian City States approaches."

Rudolfo felt anger rise. "*Just?*"

Gregoric paled. "Their scouts are magicked, Lord."

Rudolfo leaped to his feet, reaching for his thin, long sword. "Bring the camp to Third Alarm," he shouted. He turned on the metal man. "Isaak, you will wait here."

Isaak nodded.

Then General Rudolfo of the Wandering Army, Lord of the Nine-fold Forest Houses, raced from the tent bellowing for his armor and horse.

Battlefields, Rudolfo thought, should not require etiquette nor be considered affairs of state.

He remained mounted at the head of his army while his captains parleyed with the Overseer's captains in a moonlit field between the two camps. On the horizon, Windwir smoldered and stank. At last, they broke from parley and his captains returned.

"Well?" he asked.

"They also received the birds and came to offer assistance."

He sneered. "Came to peck the corpses clean more likely." Rudolfo had no love for the City States, hunkered like obese carrion birds at the delta of the Three Rivers, imposing their tariffs and taxes as if they owned those broad, flat waters and the sea they spilled into. He looked at Gregoric. "And did they share with you why they broke treaty and magicked their scouts at time of peace?"

Gregoric cleared his throat. "They thought that perhaps we had ridden against Windwir and were honoring their kin-clave. I took the liberty of reminding them of our own kin-clave with the Androfrancines."

Rudolfo nodded. "So when do I meet with the tremendous sack of moist runt droppings?"

His other captains laughed quietly behind their hands. Gregoric scowled at them. "They will send a bird requesting that you dine with the Overseer and his Lady."

Rudolfo's eyebrows rose. "His Lady?"

Perhaps, he thought, it would not be so ponderous after all.

He dressed in rainbow colors, each hue declaring one of his houses. He did it himself, waving away assistance but motioning for wine. Isaak sat, unspeaking and unmoving, while Rudolfo wrapped himself in silk robes and scarves and sashes and turban.

"I have a few moments," he told the metal man. "Tell more of your story."

Light deep in those jeweled eyes sparked and caught. "Very well, Lord." A click, a clack, a whir. "The parchment containing the missing text of Xhum Y'zir's Seven Cacophonic Deaths came to me for cataloging and translation, naturally."

"Naturally," Rudolfo said.

"I worked under the most careful of circumstances. We kept the new text isolated in a secure location with no danger of the missing words being added to complete the incantation. I was the only mechoservitor to work with the parchment and all knowledge of my previous work with prior fragments was carefully removed."

Rudolfo nodded. "Removed how?"

The metal man tapped his head. "It's . . . complex. I do not fully understand it myself. But the Androfrancines write metal scrolls and those metal scrolls determine our capacity, our actions, our in-actions, our memories." Isaak shrugged.

Rudolfo studied three different pairs of soft slipper. "Go on."

The metal man sighed. "There is not much more to tell. I cata-logued, translated and copied the missing text. I spent three days and three nights with it, calculating and re-calculating my work. In the end, I returned to Brother Charles to have the memory of my work expunged."

A sudden thought struck him and Rudolfo raised a hand, unsure why he was so polite with the mechanical. "Is memory of your work always removed?"

"Seldom, actually. Only when the work is of a sensitive or dangerous nature."

"Remind me to come back to this question later," Rudolfo said. "Meanwhile, continue. I must leave soon."

"I put the parchment in its safe, left the catalog room and watched the Androfrancine Gray Guard lock it behind me. I returned to Brother Charles but his study was locked. I waited." The metal man whirred and clicked.

Rudolfo selected a sword in an intricate scabbard, thrusting it through his sash. "And?"

The metal man began to shake. Steam poured out of his exhaust grate. His eyes rolled and a high pitched whine emanated from somewhere deep inside.

"And?" Rudolfo said, sharpness creeping into his voice.

"And all went blank for a moment. My next memory was standing in the city square, shouting the words of the Seven Cacophonic Deaths — all of the words — into the morning sky. I tried to stop the utterance." He sobbed again, his metal body shuddering and groaning. "I could not stop. I tried but could not stop."

Rudolfo felt the mechanical's grief, sharp and twisting, in his stomach. He stood at the flap of his tent, needing to leave and not knowing what to say.

The metal man continued. "Finally, I reversed my language scroll. But it was too late. The Death Golems came. The Plague Spiders scuttled. Fire fell from sulfur clouds. All seven deaths." He sobbed again.

Rudolfo stroked his beard. "And why do you think this happened?"

The metal man looked up, shaking his head. "I don't know, Lord. Malfunction, perhaps."

"Or malfeasance," Rudolfo said. He clapped and Gregoric appeared, slipping out of the night to stand by his side. "I want Isaak here under guard at all times. No one talks to him but me. Do you understand?"

Gregoric nodded. "I understand, General."

Rudolfo turned to the metal man. "Do you understand as well?"

"Yes, Lord."

Rudolfo leaned over the metal man to speak quietly in his ear.

"Take courage," he said. "It is possible that you were but the tool of someone else's ill-will."

Isaak's words, quoted from the Whymer Bible, surprised him. "Even the plow holds love for splitting the ground; and the sword grief for spilling the blood."

Rudolfo's fingers lightly brushed a polished shoulder. "We'll talk more when I return."

Outside, the sky grayed in readiness for morning. Rudolfo felt weariness creeping behind his eyes and in the tips of his fingers. He had stolen naps here and there but hadn't slept a full night since the message bird's arrival five days before, calling him and his Wandering Army south and west. After the meal, he told himself. He would sleep then.

His eyes lingered on the ruined city painted purple in the pre-dawn light.

"Gods," he whispered. "What an unexpected weapon."

Sethbert did not meet him at the edge of his army; instead, Rudolfo rode in escort to the massive round tent. He snapped and waved and flashed hand-signs to his Gypsy Scouts, who slipped off to take up positions around the tent.

Sethbert rose when he entered, a tired smile pulling at his long mustache and pock-marked jowls. His Lady rose, too, tall and slim, draped in green riding silks. Her red hair shown like the sunrise. Her blue eyes flashed an amused challenge and she smiled.

"Lord Rudolfo of the Ninefold Forest Houses," the squire at the door announced. "General of the Wandering Army."

He entered, handing his long sword to the squire. "I come in peace to break bread," he said.

"We receive you in peace and offer the wine of gladness to be so well met," Sethbert replied.

Rudolfo nodded and approached the table.

Sethbert clapped him on the back. "Rudolfo, it is good to see you. How long has it been?"

Not long enough, he thought. "Too long," he said. "How are the cities?"

Sethbert shrugged. "The same. We've had a bit of trouble with smugglers but it seems to have sorted itself out."

Rudolfo turned to the lady. She stood a few inches taller than him.

"Yes. My consort, the Lady Jin Li Tam of House Li Tam." Sethbert stressed the word consort and Rudolfo watched her eyes narrow slightly when he said it.

"Lady Tam," Rudolfo said. He took her offered hand and kissed it, his eyes never leaving hers.

She smiled. "Lord Rudolfo."

They all sat and Sethbert clapped three times. Rudolfo heard a clunk and a whir from behind a hanging tapestry. A metal man walked out, carrying a tray with glasses and a carafe of wine. This one was older than Isaak, his edges more box-like and his coloring more copper.

"Fascinating, isn't he?" Sethbert said while the metal man poured wine. He clapped again. "Servitor, I wish the chilled peach wine tonight."

The machine gave a high pitched whistle. "Deepest apologies, Lord Sethbert, but we have no chilled peach wine."

Sethbert grinned, then raised his voice in false anger. "What! No peach wine? That is inexcusable, servitor."

More whistling and a series of clicks. A gout of steam shot out of the exhaust grate. "Deepest apologies, Lord Sethbert — "

Sethbert clapped again. "Your answer is unacceptable. You will find me chilled peach wine even if you must walk all the way to Sadryl and back with it. Do you understand?"

Rudolfo watched. The Lady Jin Li Tam did not. She fidgeted and worked hard to hide the embarrassment in the redness of her cheeks, the spark of anger in her eyes.

The servitor set down the tray and carafe. "Yes, Lord Sethbert." It moved towards the tent flap.

Sethbert chuckled and nudged the lady with his elbow. "You could take lessons there," he said. She offered a weak smile as false as his earlier anger.

Then Sethbert clapped and whistled. "Servitor, I've changed my mind. The cherry wine will suffice."

The metal man poured the wine and left for the kitchen tent to check on the first course.

"What a fabulous device," Rudolfo said.

Sethbert beamed. "Splendid, isn't it?"

"However did you come by it?"

"It was . . . a gift," Sethbert said. "From the Androfrancines."

The look on Jin Li Tam's face said otherwise.

"I thought they were highly guarded regarding their magicks and machines?" Rudolfo said, raising his glass.

Sethbert raised his own. "Perhaps they are," he said, "with *some*."

Rudolfo ignored the subtle insult. The metal man returned with a tray of soup bowls full of steaming crab stew. He positioned the bowls in front of each of them. Rudolfo watched the careful precision. "Truly fabulous," he said.

"And you can get them to do most anything . . . if you know how," Sethbert said.

"Really?"

The Overseer clapped. "Servitor, run scroll seven three five."

Something clicked and clanked. Suddenly, the metal man spread his arms and broke into song, his feet moving lightly in a bawdy dance step while he sang "My father and my mother were both Androfrancine brothers or so my Aunty Abbot likes to say . . . ." The song went from raunchy to worse. When it finished, the metal man bowed deeply.

The Lady Jin Li Tam blushed. "Given the circumstances of our meeting," she said, "I think that was in poor taste."

Sethbert shot her a withering glare, then smiled at Rudolfo. "Forgive my consort. She lacks any appreciation for humor."

Rudolfo watched her hands white-knuckling a napkin, his brain suddenly playing out potentials that were coming together. "It does seem odd that the Androfrancines would teach their servitors a song of such . . . color."

She looked up at him. Her eyes held a plea for rescue. Her mouth drew tight.

"Oh, they didn't teach it that song. I did. Well, my man did."

"Your man can create scripts for this magnificent metal man?"

Sethbert spooned stew into his mouth, spilling it onto his shirt. He spoke with his mouth full. "Certainly. We've torn this toy of mine apart a dozen times over. We know it inside and out."

Rudolfo took a bite of his own stew, nearly gagging on the strong sea flavor that flooded his mouth, and pushed the bowl aside. "Perhaps," he said, "you'll loan your man to me for a bit."

Sethbert's eyes narrowed. "Whatever for, Rudolfo?"

Rudolfo drained his wine glass, trying to rid his mouth of the briny taste. "Well, I seem to have inherited a metal man of my own. I should like to teach him new tricks."

Sethbert's face paled slightly, then went red. "Really? A metal man of your own?"

"Absolutely. The sole survivor of Windwir, I'm told." Rudolfo clapped his hands and leaped to his feet. "But enough talk of toys. There is a beautiful woman here in need of a dance. And Rudolfo shall offer her such if you'll be so kind as to have your metal man sing something more apropos."

She stood despite Sethbert's glare. "In the interest of state relations," she said, "I would be honored."

They swirled and leaped around the tent as the metal man sang an upbeat number, banging on his metal chest like a drum. Rudolfo's eyes carefully traveled his partner, stealing glances where he could. She had a slim neck and slim ankles. Her breasts sloped up rather than down, pushing against her silk robe, jiggling just ever so slightly as she moved with practiced grace and utter confidence. She was living art and he knew he must have her.

As the song drew to a close, Rudolfo seized her wrist and tapped a quick message into it. *A sunrise such as you belongs in the East with me; and I would never call you consort.*

She blushed, cast down her eyes, and tapped back a response that did not surprise him at all. *Sethbert destroyed the Androfrancines; he means you harm as well.*

He nodded, smiled a tight smile, and released her. "Thank you, Lady."

Sethbert looked at Rudolfo differently but Rudolfo made a point from that moment forward of looking at the Overseer's Lady. Dinner passed with excruciating slowness while banter fell like a city-dweller's footfall on the hunt. Rudolfo noticed that at no point did Sethbert bring up the destruction of Windwir or the metal man his Gypsy Scouts had found.

Sethbert's lack of words spoke loudest of all.

Rudolfo wondered if his own did the same.

Rudolfo slept for two hours in the back of a supply wagon, dreaming of the red-headed Lady, before Third Alarm woke him. He leaped from the pile of empty sacks, drawing his sword and dropping lightly to the ground.

He raced past mustering soldiers and stopped at his own tent.

He'd long ago learned the value of not using his own bed or tent in the field. Gregoric stood waiting.

"Well?" Rudolfo asked.

Gregoric grinned. "You were correct, Lord. Entrolusian scouts. Magicked."

"Did they see what they came to see?"

Gregoric nodded. "And left quickly when I called the alarm."

"Very good. That will give them cause to scamper quickly home. And our own scouts?"

"Also magicked and right behind them."

Magicked scouts were nearly impossible to spot when you did not expect them. But Rudolfo *had* expected them. They had come. They had seen Isaak. They had left. And five of his best and bravest Gypsy Scouts had followed after.

"Very well. I will want to hear their report personally."

"Yes, Lord."

Rudolfo turned and entered the tent. The metal man's eyes glowed softly in the dark. "Isaak, are you well?"

The metal man whirred to life. The eyes blinked rapidly. "Yes, Lord."

Rudolfo walked over to him and squatted down. "I do not believe you are responsible for the devastation of Windwir."

"You indicated that may be the case. I only know what I remember."

Rudolfo thought about this for a moment. "What you *don't* remember is possibly more relevant. The missing time between seeking Brother Charles and finding yourself in the streets uttering Xhum Y'zir's spell." He looked at his sword, watched the light from Isaak's eyes play out on its burnished surface. "I do not think it was a malfunction. Sethbert — the Overseer of the Entrolusian City States — has a man who knows how to write those metal scrolls. He even has a metal man of his own."

"I do not understand. The Androfrancines and their Gray Guard are so careful — "

"Guards can be purchased. Gates can be slipped. Keys can be stolen." Rudolfo patted the metal man's knee. "You are quite a wondrous spectacle, my friend, but I suspect you understand little the capacity we humans have for good or ill."

"I've read about it," the metal man said with a sigh. "But you're right; I do not understand it."

"I hope you never do," Rudolfo said. "But on to other things. I have questions for you."

"I will answer truthfully, Lord."

Rudolfo nodded. "Good. How were you damaged?"

Isaak's metal eyelids flashed surprise. "Why, your men attacked me, Lord. I thought you knew this."

"My men found you in a crater and brought you to me straightaway."

"No, the first ones."

Rudolfo stroked his beard. "Tell me more."

"The fire had fallen, the lightning had blasted, and I returned to the library seeking Brother Charles or someone who could terminate me for my crimes. Nothing remained but ash and charred stone. I began calling for help and your men came for me with nets and chains. I sought to evade and they attacked me. I fell into the crater. Then the other men came and brought me to you."

Rudolfo offered a grim smile. "I wondered. Now I know more. By morning, I will know all."

Isaak looked up. "Lord, you bid me remind you to return to your question about the removal of my work-related memories."

"Ah, that." Rudolfo stood. "Perhaps it will come to nothing. Perhaps tomorrow, we will go down an altogether different path." He extended his hand to the metal man, who took it. The metal fingers were cool to his touch. "But if the winds of fate allow it, I would have work for you in my forest manor, Isaak."

"Work, Lord?"

Rudolfo smiled. "Yes. The greatest treasure in the world lies between your metal ears. I would have you write it all down for me."

Isaak released his hand. His eyes went hot and steam shot out from him. "I will not, Lord. I will not be anyone's weapon again."

For a brief moment, Rudolfo tasted fear in his mouth. A *metallic* taste. "No, no, no." He reached out, took up the hand again. "Never that, Isaak. But the other bits. The poetry, the plays, the histories, the philosophies, the mythologies, the maps. Everything the Androfrancine library protected and preserved . . . at least what bits you know. I would not have these pass from our world because of a buffoon's ambition."

"That is a monumental task, Lord, for a single servitor."

"I believe," Rudolfo said, "that you *may* have some help."

*

The magicked Gypsy Scouts returned from the Entrolusian camp before dawn. They carried a bound, gagged, hooded man between them, deposited him in a chair and removed his hood. Another scout put a large leather pouch on the table.

Servers laid breakfast to the table — oranges, pomegranates, cakes made with nuts and honey, berries with liquored syrup — while Rudolfo studied their guest. He was a smallish man with delicate fingers and a broad face. His eyes bulged and veins stood out on his neck and forehead.

Isaak stared. Rudolfo patted his arm. "He looks familiar to you?"

The metal man clicked. "He does, Lord. He was Brother Charles' apprentice."

Rudolfo nodded. He sat at the head of the table and nibbled at a cake, washing it down with chilled peach wine.

The Gypsy Scouts gave their report; it was brief.

"So how many do they have?"

"Thirteen in total, Lord," the chief scout answered. "They are in a tent near the center of his camp. We found him sleeping among them."

"Thirteen," Rudolfo said, stroking his beard. "How many mechoservitors did the Androfrancines have, Isaak?"

"That is all of them, Lord."

Rudolfo pondered for a moment why they'd been spared in Y'zir's spell but the realization struck him quickly. The ancient desert mage would have known nothing of such scientific wonders. If they'd stayed out of the way, huddled in their stalls beneath the library . . .

He waved to the nearest Scout. "Remove his gag."

The man blustered and flushed, his eyes wild and his mouth working like a landed trout. He started to speak but Rudolfo shushed him.

Rudolfo stabbed a slice of orange with a small silver fork. "I will ask you questions; you will answer them. Otherwise you will not speak."

The man nodded.

Rudolfo pointed at Isaak with his fork. "Do you recognize this metal man?"

The man nodded again, his face now pale.

"Did you change this mechoservitor's script on the orders of Overseer Sethbert of the Entrolusian City States?"

"I . . . I did. Overseer Sethbert — "

Rudolfo snapped his fingers. A scout drew a slim dagger, placing its tip at the man's throat. "Just yes or no for now."

The man swallowed. "Yes."

The knife eased up.

Rudolfo selected another slice of orange and popped it into his mouth. "Did you do this terrible thing for money?"

The man's eyes filled with tears. His jaw tensed. Slowly, he nodded again.

Rudolfo leaned forward. "And do you understand exactly what you did?"

The Androfrancine apprentice sobbed. When he didn't nod right away, the scout refocused him on Rudolfo's question with a point of the blade. "Y-yes, Lord."

Rudolfo chewed a bit of pomegranate. He kept his voice level and low. "Do you wish mercy for this terrible crime?"

The sobbing escalated. A low whine rose to a howl so full of misery, so full of despair that it lay heavy on the air.

"Do you," Rudolfo said again, his voice even quieter, "want mercy for your terrible crime?"

"I didn't know it would work, Lord. I swear to you. And none of us thought that if it *did* work it be so . . . so *utterly*, so . . . "

Rudolfo raised his hand and his eyebrows. The man stopped. "How could you know? How could anyone know? Xhum Y'zir has been dead five thousand years. And his so-called Age of Laughing Madness has long passed." Rudolfo carefully selected another honey-eyed cake, nibbling at its corners. "So my question remains: Do you wish mercy?"

The man nodded.

"Very well. You have one opportunity and only one. I can not say the same for your liege." Rudolfo looked over at the metal man. His eyes flashed and a slight trail of steam leaked from the corners of his mouth. "In a few moments, I am going to leave you here with my best Gypsy Scouts and my metallic friend, Isaak. I want you to very slowly, very clearly and in great detail, explain everything you know about scripting, maintaining and repairing Androfrancine mechoservitors." Rudolfo stood. "You only have one chance and you only have a few hours. If you do not satisfy me, you will spend the rest of your natural days in chains, on Tormentors Row for all the known world to see, while my Physicians of Penitent Torture peel away your skin with salted knives and wait for it to grow back." He tossed back the rest of his wine. "You will spend the rest of your days in urine and feces and blood, with the screams of young children in your ears and the genocide of a city on your soul."

The man vomited now, choking foul-smelling bile onto his tunic.

Rudolfo smiled. "I'm so glad you understand me." He paused at the tent flap. "Isaak, pay careful attention to the man."

Outside, he waved for Gregoric. "Bring me a bird."

He wrote the message himself. It was a simple, one-word question. After he wrote it, he tied it to the bird's foot with the green thread of peace but it felt like a lie. He whispered a destination to the bird and pressed his lips briefly to its small, soft head. Then he threw it at the sky and the sky caught it, sent it flapping south to the Entrolusian camp.

He whispered the question he had written. It sounded empty but he whispered it again. "Why?"

It took less than two hours. When Rudolfo returned to his tent, the metal man sat at the table, sifting through the pouch of tools and scrolls and the man was gone.

"Do you know enough?" Rudolfo asked.

Isaak looked up. "Yes, Lord."

"Do you want to kill him yourself?"

Isaak's eyelids fluttered, his metal ears tilted and bent. He shook his head. "No, Lord."

Rudolfo nodded and shot Gregoric a look. Gregoric returned the nod grimly and left in silence.

The bird had returned in less than an hour. His question had gone unanswered. Sethbert's reply had been terse: *Return to me the man you took. Surrender the servitor that destroyed Windwir.*

He'd had an hour to ponder the why. Ambition? Greed? Fear? The Androfrancines could have ruled the world with their magicks and mechanicals and yet they hid in their city, sent out their archeologists and scholars to dig and to learn, to understand the present through the past . . . and to protect that past for the future. In the end, he found it didn't matter so much *why* the City States and their mad Overseer had ended that work. What mattered was that it never happen again.

"Are you okay, Isaak?"

"I grieve, Lord. And I rage."

"Aye. Me too."

A Scout cleared his voice outside. "Lord Rudolfo? We've taken a prisoner at the edge of camp."

He looked up. "Yes?"

"A woman, Lord. She came magicked and asking for your protection under the Providence of Kin-Clave."

He smiled but there was no satisfaction in it. Maybe later, when all of this unpleasantness had passed. "Very well. Prepare her for travel."

"Lord?"

"She is to be escorted to the seventh manor. You leave within the hour. The metal man goes with her. Select and magick a half-squad to assist you."

"Yes, Lord."

"And fetch me my raven." Rudolfo fell back into the cushions, exhaustion washing over him.

"Lord Rudolfo?" The metal man struggled to his feet, his damaged leg sparking. "Am I leaving you?"

"Yes, Isaak, for a bit." He rubbed his eyes. "I wish for you to start that work we spoke of. When I am finished here, I will bring you help."

"Is there anything I can do here?"

The realization fell on him. I could ask him, Rudolfo thought. I could ask him and maybe he would go for me now. I could send him south and west, following the Three Rivers until he reached the walled cities at their deltas, speaking his words and bringing down death. But the thought fled as quickly as it arrived. "I'd be no better than Sethbert."

"Lord?"

He rubbed his eyes again and yawned. "Pack your tools, Isaak. You're leaving soon."

The metal man packed, then swung the heavy pouch over his shoulder. Rudolfo climbed to his feet.

"The woman you will be traveling with is Jin Li Tam of House Li Tam. I would have you bear a message to her."

Isaak said nothing, waiting.

"Tell her she chose well and that I will come to her when I am finished here."

"Yes, Lord."

Rudolfo followed Isaak out of the tent. His raven awaited, its feathers glossy and dark as a wooded midnight. He took it from the scout's steady hands.

"When you reach the seventh manor," he told his scout, "tell my steward there that Isaak — the metal man — bears my grace."

The scout nodded once and left. Isaak looked at Rudolfo. His mouth opened and closed; no words came out.

Rudolfo held the raven close, stroking its back with his finger. "I will see you soon, Isaak. Start your work. I'll send the others when I've freed them. You've a library to re-build."

"Thank you," the metal man finally said.

Rudolfo nodded. The scout and the metal man left. Gregoric returned, wiping the apprentice's blood from his hands.

"Sethbert wants his man back," Rudolfo said.

"I've already seen to it, Lord."

Somewhere on the edge of camp, Rudolfo thought, a stolen pony ambled its way home bearing a cloth-wrapped burden. "Very well. Magick the rest of your Gypsy Scouts."

"I've seen to that as well, Lord."

He looked at Gregoric and felt a pride that burned brighter than his grief or his rage. "You're a good man."

Rudolfo pulled a thread from the sleeve of his rainbow robe. This time, no other message. This time, no question. He tied the scarlet thread of war to the foot of his darkest angel. When he finished, he whispered no words and he did not fling his messenger at the sky. It leaped from his hands on its own and sped away like a black arrow. He watched it fly until he realized Gregoric had spoken.

"Gregoric?" he asked.

"You should rest, Lord," the chief of his Gypsy Scouts said again. "We can handle this first battle without you."

"Yes, I should," Rudolfo said. But he knew there would be time enough for rest — perhaps even a life-time of rest — after he won the war.

SO SANG THE GIRL
WHO HAD NO NAME

The mind is its own place, and in itself
Can make a Heaven of Hell, a Hell of Heaven.
John Milton, *Paradise Lost*

utside, the shriekers and howlers rode a hot night wind. Inside, Jeb Donner drained a warm Corona and prayed to Ashtarte that the wards he'd purchased in Graytown, carefully spoken over his eighteen wheeler, would hold.

"Another?" The bartender, a small gnollish figure, swiped a soiled towel over the oak counter, the cloth drinking up the moisture-bead rings.

"Please." He grinned. "It's hot as hell tonight."

The ugly little man laughed at the joke. "Go figure." Another bottle materialized and Jeb took it, the temperature of the glass matching that of his hand. "Where you headed, Driver."

Donner took a pull, swished the suds around the inside of his mouth. "Mesquite."

The bartender's eyes rolled. "Thought they had plague in Mesquite."

"Nope. Not yet."

Nodding, the keeper of The Last Leg Saloon moved down the counter, his rag darting out to capture each spot of spilled beer. "You're the second one today, then."

Donner's eyebrows arched even as his body tensed. "Second driver?" It would be like that devil Gruentorgle to double up, just to make sure the shipment got through. His way of kissing ass.

"No," the bartender said, shaking his head. "Second one bound for Mesquite."

Relief settled into his shoulders, relaxing them. He drained off the last of the tepid beer and clinked the bottle down on the counter. Mesquite was an out of the way town, squatting on the edge of the Eighth Ring, secluded from the rest of the desmesne by the Kuorouac Mountains.

A shrieker, safely outside the circle of protection, blasted the wall, its wail rattling the glasses that stood like a smudged, empty army along the shelf. Down the line of the bar, a shit-miner shook his head. "Out in force tonight," he said to no one in particular.

Winter nights meant shriekers and howlers through-out the Ring. Up north, along the inner edge, they called them shredders — their voice could flay a man, twist metal, unless protected by ward or sanctuary. Donner had seen their work and come close to being their work one too many times. He'd pulled in to The Last Leg well before sundown, spending a solid hour checking and re-checking his spells and his rig.

"You'll want a room then?"

He nodded. "Private, if you got it." At the little toad's scowl, he reached deep into his pocket and bypassed the gold coins for the carved stick. He held it out to the bartender, who blanched as he recognized the marks.

"Gruentorgle, eh? Yeah, private's fine. No problem." He scribbled the name down on a credit-slip and produced a key with the carbon copy. "Got my last one. Check-out's at ten."

"I'm gone once they shut up." He nodded at the wall, which rattled again in answer as the noise outside reached a crescendo. He needed to hit Jessolm Pass just after dawn to be in Mesquite before dark. Then, spend a night in luxury at one of those fancy hotels they boasted, and make his delivery next morning before heading back. A shame, but a job's a job.

He stood and stretched out the road-knots that bound his legs and arms. A dull ache in the small of his back urged him toward the stairs, knowing a bed was near. "Well, I'll catch you on my way back through."

The bartender winked. "Not like there's much choice."

That's when Donner saw the girl for the first time and wondered how he'd missed her before. She sat in the corner, quietly sipping a Merlot, watching him. Beside her stood a battered mountain bike and a backpack. He smiled and she smiled back.

Why not, he thought. Ignoring exhaustion, Donner picked his

way through the uncrowded bar. The dim light hit her in a way that made her pale skin glow, and as her head turned to follow his approach, candle-light glinted off her long dark hair. She had a nose-ring, gold and very subtle. He liked it.

"'Lo," she said.

"Howdy." He nodded at the bike. "You ride that in?"

Her smile broadened, showing teeth. Her eyes, deep and gray, flashed in amusement. "Yeah."

His own grin grew. "Liar."

Her eyes, now suddenly blue, widened and he could see she fought not to smile as she faked insult. "I never lie."

Donner leaned in. "You just did. Name's Jeb. Jeb Donner." He stuck out a hand and she took it, her grip cool and firm. He waited a moment, not wanting to release her. "And you are?"

She shrugged. "When I know, I'll tell you."

New arrival, then, maybe. Or just playing games.

"Can I buy you a drink?" Standing over her he could see down the neck of her shirt, see the two perfect globes of white disappearing too soon into her sports bra.

"Already have one."

"Can I sit down?"

She raised her eyebrows expectantly. "Sure. I was just leaving."

"Leaving? So soon?"

She stood, stretching, arms up over her head. Nearly as tall as he was, she stood near him, the smell of her sweat a perfume to his nose. The air around her seemed cooler and it washed over him. His eyes followed her long legs, the line of her neck, the curve of her ears. Easily half his age, he realized. She brushed by him to grab her pack. "'Night, Driver," she said as her hip lingered, pressed into his groin. Then, she slipped up the stairs.

Something rooted him where he stood, mouth-open, memory of her touch alive on him, running the length of his body.

"Goodnight," he said. But she was already gone. Behind him, the bartender and the others at the bar laughed.

The bartender laughed loudest. "Don't you think we already tried?"

*

His eardrums told him when the bedlam outside died out, and he crawled to wakefulness reluctantly. Pulling on his Levis, Jeb Donner thought about the girl with no name. She'd intruded into his dreams and they'd swum together in a deep, cold lake, naked beneath a night sky that was safe and speckled with stars, their noses filled with the scent of pine needles. Their ears filled with music. A nice dream, and the only one he could remember . . . ever. He wanted to see her again.

He stepped into his boots and headed down the stairs, his shirt unbuttoned and hanging open. The temperature had already climbed, despite the darkness that wrapped the saloon. When he saw the empty room and the lights out in the kitchen Donner cursed himself for forgetting to have his thermos filled the night before. It would be a long haul without coffee.

Someone had already unbarred the door, he saw, and another glance revealed the missing bike. Already gone, wherever it was she rode, crazy kid. Beautiful. But crazy.

He stepped out beneath the beginnings of a gray sky, pulling the door shut behind him. His Kenworth stood isolated in the asphalt lot, just this side of the safe-mark. Chips and dents stood out down the long, black tanker-trailer where the night-things had tried their best but the runes, painted in florescent green, had held. Grinning, he circled the truck twice to be sure and climbed into the cab.

He fired her up, the engine's roar sending shudders through him. Once she purred, he hit the switch and watched his gas gauge climb. Half his trailer was fuel, half cargo space; it was the only way to travel the wastes. While the truck warmed, he twisted and thrust himself half into the disused sleeper behind the seats. Rummaging around, his hand closed around an unopened Coke. He popped the top and poured the caramel-colored liquid into his mouth, feeling its aluminum-tinted warmth on his tongue. He checked his short-barreled Remington pump and his road map. Time to fly.

He gave the horn a farewell blast and rumbled out of the parking lot, onto the Eastbound highway. Beneath his headlights the road stretched out, rutted, strewn with sand and tumbleweeds. Gruentorgle had told him it was clear; he never lied about the road — he lacked scruples in some areas, but the shipment to Mesquite was paramount. They were one of the last plague-free townships on the Ring's edge, and Baal wanted the delivery through pronto.

The first hour crept by, the sun slipping upwards in a brilliant scarlet ball that swallowed the western sky behind him. Its light poured out thick over the scrub and rock-strewn wasteland, glinting back from the twisted, shredded metal of burned-out cars out too late.

Watching the sun in his mirrors, Jeb didn't see the bike until he was nearly on top of it —

— and he locked up the brakes, his lap scalded by the hot coffee and his throat suddenly seized with panic.

Oh fuck oh shit oh fuck, he thought as the neighborhood slipped by in slow motion and the little girl on the pink bike grew closer and closer. He spun the wheel and the rig turned in its skid, tires screaming. He heard the metallic crunch, the wet thud beneath the tractor —

— and the bike disappeared with a clatter, bouncing out behind the trailer. He wrestled the Kenworth to a stop and fumbled the door open, falling onto the hot asphalt. His body shook uncontrollably with the sudden memory and he lay there, body coated in a sheen of suddenly cold sweat, mouth filled with the taste of gun-oil and carbon.

A pair of bare legs appeared in his line of sight and he followed them up, past the shorts, traveled over the small breasts jutting out from a cotton T-shirt, climbed the long, slender neck and finally settled on a mouth that didn't know whether to smile or frown.

"Looks like you wrecked my bike, Driver," the girl who had no name said with her hands on her hips. "Guess you're my ride to Mesquite, now."

It felt alien, her there in the truck beside him, hugging her knees to herself and looking out the passenger window. Donner found himself constantly willing his eyes back onto the road, occasionally treating himself to a sideways glance.

He held the rig at ninety, watching the line of mountains disappearing behind them in the mirrors. The sun stood over them now, filling the canopy of the sky with shimmering heat that penetrated the metal with an oppressive brutality. Waves distorted the highway and desert, casting the illusion of water puddles just beyond reach.

They'd rode in silence the better part of the trip over the pass. Now on a straight shot for Mesquite, Donner felt more conversational. "I'm sorry about your bike."

"Yeah. Doesn't matter. I shouldn't have left it in the middle of the road." The bike was a tangled ruin of aluminum and rubber; they left it on the shoulder. She shrugged and he caught it from the corner of his eye. "I had to pee. Should've taken it with me."

"You really ride it all that ways?" It made no sense to him — seven hundred miles lay between The Last Leg and the closest city. And a good hundred miles between the saloon and where he'd hit her bike. The math made no sense.

"Yeah. I left around midnight. It's cooler then." She said it with a matter-of-fact voice as if it were no big deal. "Got about twenty miles per hour."

Midnight. No way. He looked over at her, eyes narrow. Twenty miles per hour? Maybe; she looked strong. "You're kidding, right? You hitched or something."

She shook her head. "No. I rode."

"But the shriekers?" She didn't answer. After a minute slipped by he decided to change the subject. "So what's in Mesquite for you?"

"Not sure. I just know I need to go there." He stole a look; she stared at the horizon, eyes seeming far away. Like a lost child, he thought. "What about you, Driver?"

"Delivery."

"Delivering what?"

A delicate question. He didn't know how much to say, particularly in the light of her newness to this Ring. And she seemed so young. How did he explain Baal's peculiar means of widening his sphere of lordship? He decided to take the direct route. "Plague."

"Plague?" Disgust and surprise flavored her voice. "Why?"

"I just drive it there," he told her. "I don't ask questions."

"Maybe you should."

He looked back to the road, avoiding her penetrating stare. Her eyes flashing and amber. "It's just how it works. It's my job. I deliver the goods. A month, maybe two months later they're ready to bargain."

"Bargain?"

"Yeah. Ready to do whatever it takes to get the vaccine." He risked a glance back to her. She sat frozen, eyes locked onto him.

"Look," he said, "don't kill the delivery-driver if you don't like the package."

"You're a monster."

"You ever have the plague?" Meanness rode his voice, twisting his mouth into a sneer. She shook her head. "Well, I have. It isn't pretty. You itch, then you break open in sores. The stink is awful and you lay there in the pus and blood while your skin cracks and cracks and the worms twist themselves out of you." Her eyes went wild and her mouth suddenly bulged, a small hand coming up to press her lips shut. He cursed and slid the truck to a halt, waited while she threw up out of the open door, then started them rolling again.

"Sorry," he said. "Sometimes the job just gets to me. Sometimes —
— *shit just happens as casual as a cup of McDonald's coffee spilling in your lap and a little girl going underneath your truck. You're only doing forty but it's enough. And she lays there, twitching and calling for her Mommy or her Daddy or her Sissy to save her, to help her, to take her home and everything fucking falls apart around you* —

" — I just kind of snap." He shook his head, swallowing the acrid taste in his mouth. Again, the intrusion, like a fist, left him disillusioned. Foreign memories. *His* memories. Twice in one day.

"You okay?"

Donner realized he hadn't accelerated, hadn't shifted. Just let his foot off the pedal. The truck lurched to a halt. He looked at her. "No. Guess not."

This time, he threw up, his stomach twisted around the memories of a time before this.

Three hundred miles out of Mesquite the temperature gauge shot into the red and Donner pulled to the side. The girl lay curled in the sleeper, eyes closed, lips moving. "Better wake up," he said. "We've got trouble."

The sun hung dangerously low and already the wind whipped across the desert floor. He dropped lightly to the road and went to the front of the rig, climbing onto the bumper to pop the massive hood with one hand. He smelled the antifreeze burning on the engine block and traced the radiator hose to the point where it had burst. A quick fix.

The girl climbed out of the truck. "We okay?"

"Will be." He brushed past her, reaching under his seat for his tool kit. Inside, he found the duct tape. He'd started out with a spare hose, but had traded it to another trucker for a half-case of Valvoline three days before. He climbed back under the hood and wrapped the hole, burning his fingers and forearms in the process. Then, he unclamped a water-can from the side of the rig and up-ended the contents into the steaming radiator. "Time to go." His watch showed less than ten minutes lost, but what had been a com-fortable cushion of time was now whittled away. The tape wouldn't hold at the speeds he'd counted on.

They made fifty miles before the tape gave out and he re-wrapped, this time using twice the amount. The sun squatted on the horizon ahead of them and his eyes went from it to the odometer. "We're not going to make it."

Night settled on them and he fired up the headlights. The en-gine ran hot and Donner kept the speed under sixty now; the roll of tape looked suspiciously thin after two more stops. A knot grew in his stomach and he glanced at the girl. Her face, limned in the dashboard glow, rested against the passenger window, eyes open and dreaming. As the wind picked up, a keening wail came to his ears from far away, answered by another, closer shriek. He looked back to the road. They came, relentlessly, and he wished he'd never traded that hose away.

Suddenly, the cab filled with hot dry air and the outside noise slapped him harder. She'd rolled the window down.

"What the fuck are you doing?"

She looked at him, a strange light in her eyes. A smile played at the corners of her mouth and it opened, round and inviting. He waited for her to speak, but she didn't. She sang instead.

The song sounded familiar but he couldn't place it. From a long time ago, he realized, a song about love and bridges laying down and silver girls sailing on, shining in their time. A song about night and dark-ness falling and pain all around, so sang the girl who had no name. The quietness of her voice ran fingers along his arms and he shuddered, blinking through tears. "What . . . what song is that? What does it mean?" She didn't answer, just kept pouring the melody past her lips.

That's when he realized that the keening outside had stopped entirely. And that the road before them had taken on a surreal glow.

"You're doing this?" She nodded, smiling. Just like in the song, he felt the easing of his mind.

*

She pointed at a turn-out just ten miles from Mesquite's closed gates and Donner down-shifted to a stop. She still sang, and in a daze, he followed her as she left the truck. He walked close behind her, watching the world change around them as they followed a path into a desert that slowly unfolded into forest. The sand became lush green grass and she stretched a hand back to clasp his and draw him up beside her. Then, she stopped singing and the silence wrapped them as completely as the grove of pines. His breath caught in his throat when he saw the lake.

"There now," she said. "It should hold until morning."

"You . . ." He didn't know how to finish the sentence.

"Me." She stifled a giggle. Then, she peeled away her T-shirt and shrugged out of her bra. The denim shorts fell to the ground and she came into his arms, kicking off her shoes awkwardly. She was cool to touch, soft and smooth. Her mouth sought his, her tongue slipping past the guard of his teeth. She tasted like cinnamon, and he resisted at first when she pulled away. "Last one in is a loser," she said and raced for the water.

Pulling off his clothes, he followed.

"It wasn't Mesquite I was looking for," she said. "It was you."

They lay naked in the grass, staring up at a star-scattered sky that grayed toward dawn. They'd made love all night, in the water, on the ground, moving to the rhythm of an unsung, remembered melody. They'd finished two hours ago and lain in one another's arms, silently drinking in the cool air.

Donner propped himself up on an elbow and looked at her. She suddenly seemed so far away. "Me?" She nodded, her hand absently tracing its way up his thigh, across the fuzz of his stomach. He shivered. "I don't understand."

"How did you come here, Jeb? Do you remember?"

He swallowed. Again, the taste of gun oil filled his mouth, the distant memory of wrapping his mouth around a cold, nickel plated barrel. His stomach lurched. "I . . . I killed a girl," he said. "With my truck. A long time ago." He considered saying more, then stopped and changed the subject. "What about you? Do you remember?"

"Yes," she said. Her hands paused their slow crawl over him. "I came here for you. To tell you Hell doesn't have to be what it's been for you."

He opened his mouth, but she stopped his question with a hand, then a kiss. She rolled onto him, pinned him down with her light, cool body. "Let's do it again," she said against his neck.

They did, and she lay on top of him for a long while afterward. Donner fell toward sleep, her body a blanket over his own. How long had it been since he'd needed a blanket? How long since he'd swum in ice-cold water or made love underneath the stars? Some part of him remembered that he had, long ago. But the memories hid in shadows too thick to penetrate. Drowsiness pulled at him, his breathing matching hers as his hands slipped from her waist. Bending her face to his ear, she whispered, barely discernible: "She was my sister. Her name was Hope."

He awoke in the desert, not far from his truck, naked and alone.

Stiff, sore and shaken he dressed, climbed into the cab and rolled that last ten miles into Mesquite. Then, he bought a radiator hose, put it on, and left without making his delivery. He dumped the trailer at the summit of Jessolm Pass and nudged it over the edge with the nose of his tractor, watching it bounce and turn and tumble as it fell. His truck-driving days would be over now. Baal's first lieutenant, Gruentorgle, would send him back to the Ninth Ring, but it didn't matter any more.

He reached The Last Leg just past dark and left his truck unwarded and unlocked. Ignoring the noise-storm that grew on the night air, he pushed through the double doors and looked in the corner where she'd sat. Empty. But he'd known it would be. She didn't belong here. She'd come for him, eased his mind with her song, moved on. Back home now in a place of cool lakes and bright stars, he thought, with her message delivered. Hell would never be same.

The bartender grinned at him from behind the counter. "Wanna beer? Corona, right?" The bottle clinked onto the counter as the gnollish man winked at him and ran a hand across his brow. "Hot as hell tonight, eh, Driver?" Chuckling, he moved up the bar, rag suck-ing up the moisture like a demon drinking souls.

Donner didn't laugh, simply took a pull of the warm beer. The joke didn't seem funny anymore, and he opened his mouth to say so. Instead, he started to sing the girl's song in a rich baritone voice he didn't remember having. Inside, the temperature dropped. Outside, a small part of Hell became silent and still.

EDWARD BEAR
AND THE VERY LONG WALK

He was a bear, and his name was Edward, and he lay twitching in the corner of a room that smelled of death. He didn't exactly know what Death smelled like, but he knew that's what he smelled. Because Something Very Bad had happened here. He just couldn't remember what.

A small boy in short pants flickered over him, smiling. "Hello Bear. It's about time you woke up."

Edward sniffed and stirred. "Hello. Are you — ?"

"No. I'm not. I am the Funplay Holographic Nursery Brain."

"Oh." Edward stood. "It's just that you look like, I mean I thought you might be, well, you know . . . "

"No. I'm not."

Edward reached out a paw to touch the boy's arm. It passed through. "Oh. I see."

"Do you know what's happened to the children?"

Edward swallowed. Suddenly, he wanted to cry. "Yes. They're . . . sleeping?" He hoped and hoped and hoped and hoped, grimacing as he did. He looked around.

Makeshift beds lined the room. Small hands gripped blankets, small eyes stared at the ceiling.

"No." The boy frowned. "They've died."

"Because of Something Very Bad?"

"Yes. And I need you to be a Very Brave Bear. Can you do that?"

Edward nodded once, twice, three times, and blinked.

"Good. I need you to leave the Nursery and find Someone. Tell them about the children."

Edward heard a squeaking sound and knew he made it. He felt a Tremendous Fear growing in him. "Why can't you go? I can't leave the Nursery . . . I've never left the Nursery alone." The boy hissed and his image warbled, then came back into focus. "Yes you can. You must. I can't leave . . . I'm not real. *You* must go, Bear. But first you have to open the door."

Edward shuffled out of the corner. The room was stifling, heavy with rottenness and a buzzing dance of flies. He tried to remember the last time he'd played with the children, but couldn't. He squinted, trying to conjure up any memories of the Something Very Bad.

He faintly remembered his birthday, waking up surrounded by laughter, in the midst of the Nursery. And distorted tales from the children about traveling Very Far to Find a New Home. They had such bright and shining faces, and they were all so smart. Whenever he couldn't understand what they told him, they called him "Silly Old Bear" and "Bear of Little Brain."

He also carried vague recollections of the grown-ups, pausing in the Nursery door or sitting with their children. They were even smarter than the children. And they never talked to the toys.

He was a bear, and his name was Edward, and he was a toy. He remembered being told this on his birthday when he woke up after a Very Long Sleep. It was as if he'd gone to sleep in his comfortable house in the Wood (under the name of Sanders) and woke up here. He had hoped for cakes and cream and possibly honey and candles to blow out when he first opened his eyes. Instead, he led the children in a song and then a dance.

A few weeks later there was no one left to play with.

Edward simply went to sleep.

"Over here, Bear," the boy said. The boy stood by the door, pointing to a flat button in the wall. "Push this." With a static pop, the boy disappeared.

Edward's fur paws whispered over the vinyl floor. He reached the door and stretched as tall as he could. The button was an arm's length out of reach. "Bother."

He looked over each shoulder, spotting an oblong plastic box. He waddled to it, picked it up easily, and lay it against the door. "This should work quite nicely," he said to no one in particular. He climbed and stretched and reached. "Bother."

Edward hopped down and began pacing the narrow aisle between beds, trying hard not to notice the white, stretched skin and puffy, staring eyes. Pillows, he thought.

Moving from bed to bed, holding his breath and squeezing his eyes shut at each, he carefully wriggled four pillows free. He placed them against the door and scrambled up, striking the flat button just as he tumbled to the floor.

Nothing happened.

"Drat and Bother. Chris — I mean, Holo-what's-it Nurserious Brain?"

No answer.

"Are you there? Hallo?"

Silence.

Edward sat, head in his paws, and thought. And thought. And thought. Then, he sighed.

His stomach growled, even though he knew he didn't *need* to eat exactly. He could go long periods of time without food. Still, mouths were for eating and bellies for filling and a bit of something would be nice. But not in this room. So how to leave? That was his Question of the Moment. And he had to find Someone and tell them about the children.

The hairs in his ears tickled to a faint sound above. He sniffed.

"Air," he said, leaping to his feet. "Air . . . but from *where?*" A grill set high in the wall grinned down at him when he looked up.

Edward paced the floor, thought of a song that went nicely with his Difficult Situation, hummed it through a few times and then thought of A Plan.

The grill was too high to reach.

There was no one to ask for help.

He would try the button *again*.

With a whisper and a groan (and a thud as he fell down) the door hushed open — just a bit. Squeezing through, his gurgling stomach protesting the pressure, he padded into the hall to find Someone.

Edward heard the crying long before he saw the girl. She sat in a large room wrapped in fading stars, holding her head in her hands.

"Hello?"

The girl looked up and sniffed. She stared at him.

"I mean . . . er . . . I hope I'm not interrupting." Edward entered the room. "I really wouldn't want to bother you but I seem to be very lost and you seem to be very sad."

She stood and flickered as she moved.

"I'm looking for a grown-up." Edward used his most confidential and important tone.

The girl started crying again. "They're all gone," she said through her tears.

"Oh." Edward shifted uncomfortably from left to right.

"I killed them all," the girl whispered. Her eyes widened. "All of them."

Edward backed up a step. "Oh. Well. In that case perhaps it would be best if I were — "

The girl suddenly began to stretch upward, her legs, arms and torso extending themselves like taffy, her hair spilling down around her shoulders like milk. Her eyes grew faraway pale and her skin pulled then sagged.

"It was an accident," the old woman said. "A terrible accident." And she pointed at a console as the stars disappeared. She flickered again.

Edward followed the line of her finger to a dangling cord.

The children called them their "Jack-in-the-necks" — a small hole that helped them know things when they plugged wires into it. Edward himself had a "Jack-in-the-belly" so he could play with other toys.

"Plug in," she said.

Edward plugged in and suddenly found his head full to the point of bursting, as if hands tugged at his ears and snout, pushing and pulling at once. "Oh," he said and sat heavily on the floor.

Her name, Edward knew, was the *Nancy Bell*; she was a starship, the first of five to hastily leave a dying home. Earth. A place he couldn't remember well but now understood was once green and blue and full of life. The old woman who had been a little girl was a manifestation of the ship's brain and she was dying, trickling away with the moments.

After nearly a century of travel she'd reached her goal and awakened her cargo — three hundred men, women and children. But there was a flaw . . . a minute tear in her program that gradually became a gaping hole. Critical EM shields had malfunctioned, the comm-array burned off in an unforeseen asteroid belt, air-tanks ruptured. It was all she could do to launch her comm-sat.

The *Nancy Bell* crash-landed on an otherwise quiet Tuesday, using the southern hemisphere's tepid ocean to break her fall. She dragged herself onto the wooded beach to die, a massive diseased whale of charred metal. The virus awaited and systematically executed the survivors.

"We worked so hard."

Edward looked up from the floor at the sound of her voice. *Nancy Bell* still stood in the center of the room, staring at nothing.

"We did?"

"Yes. For a vaccine."

"Oh." Another burst of data, white light collapsing his field of vision. He saw blood cells and antibodies in a kaleidoscope, twisting and turning on themselves.

"We found it," he heard her somewhere outside of himself. "But it was too late."

Yes, he realized. The grown-ups had programmed the necessary information into the ship, dying before the *Nancy Bell* had gotten results. The formula, the cure, lay in so many sparks of electricity in a dying ship's mind. Life for four other vessels, en route and unsuspecting.

"You must help me save them."

"Me?" Edward's voice was more a squeak than anything else and having been somewhat unsure of it, he repeated himself. "Me?"

"You're all that's left." She changed again, shrinking into a boy in short-pants that immediately filled his heart with hope. "You are going to go on a very long walk to climb a very tall mountain."

"I am?"

"Yes. I need you to be a Very Brave Bear. Can you do that?"

Edward thought for a moment. "Y-yes."

Another blast and the room spun; he closed his eyes. He saw the communications satellite turning in slow orbit, dish tilted toward a green-blue haze, thirsty like a sponge for water. He saw the muted ship, unable to answer the repeated blip of questions. And he saw the portable transmitter lying in the great ship's belly and the red hover-wagon near the airlock. Then geography swept at him, over him, like a rushing beast.

He knew his minuscule toy brain, designed for telling stories, singing and playing with the children, couldn't contain the flood of information. He knew he'd begin forgetting Everything as soon as he unplugged.

He also knew the ship didn't have the strength to tell him again. But he would remember the most important parts: The wagon. The pack. The walk. The mountain. And the Big Green Button.

Edward Bear unplugged and stood up. The boy smiled at him, then flickered and began to fade.

"Silly old bear," he said. "I know you can do it."

Edward Bear left the ship on a quiet Friday, his muzzle still wet with something quite like (but not) condensed milk and his paws still sticky with something quite like (but again not) honey. His send-off party, launching his great *Expotition*, had been a smashing success. There had been plenty to eat for Everyone — which was especially important, him being the only Someone in attendance.

He stepped through the yawning hatchway giving the wagon a tug. It buzzed noisily behind him and he looked back. It bobbed up against the lip of the door. With the slightest lift it cleared and floated easily. Edward couldn't remember exactly what the Something strapped to the wagon did — already most of what the *Nancy Bell* told him had leaked away. But he knew it was Important and that he had to take it up the mountain.

And press the Green Button. He mustn't forget that.

Bear trudged across the sand, head turning side to side, nose working the wind. The air was heavy, a thick salt smell. A breeze cut across the massive ship, whipping up the sand and bending the brush that grew behind a line of driftwood. A golden sun in a blue sky. Behind him, he could hear waves rushing the beach with tiny, deep-down-inside roars followed by satisfactory sighs. When he reached the driftwood he climbed onto a log and watched the ocean for a while. He'd heard the boy in short-pants talk about the ocean a long time ago. It was bigger than Anything.

Nancy Bell lay half-submerged. Scattered around her lay the remnants of camp. Canopies, stacked boxes, a line of clothes dry now for weeks that no one would wear. Toys nearly buried by the shifting sand, toys that no one would play with ever again.

Edward sniffed back a tear. He looked the other way now, back to the forest. Trees stretched thin and tall, reaching for the sky, blossoming like green balloons. Beyond them, purple hills rolled up and over like a rumpled quilt and, looming behind the hills, a mound of stone, white and enticing as vanilla ice cream. His mountain. He climbed down from the log and followed the line of wood until he came to a trail that disappeared into the forest. Dragging his red wagon, he waved goodbye to the ship.

The woodland swallowed him and at first it reminded him of Home. Only none of his friends seemed to be about. He'd always loved the Wood, and this one was not so different. Certainly the ferns were larger and the berries had an unfamiliar gray hue. Some of the trees stood straight and thin and very, very tall with branches that swept out and down covered with small dark needles. But the branches began too far up for convenient honey-gathering climbs.

Once, about two hours into his walk, Edward heard a buzzing louder than his wagon and his heart jumped. He spun round and round, finally seeing the bearer of glad tidings. The biggest bee he had ever seen zipped past his nose.

"Bees mean honey," he said out loud. His stomach rumbled its agreement.

At four hours he came across a small hole. He poked his head inside, shouted "Hallo," and then thought better of it and moved on. Once, forever ago it seemed, he'd found himself stuck in a hole very much like it.

At six hours into his Very Long Walk, Edward Bear decided that this forest wasn't anything at all like Home. The sun disappeared somewhere behind him, leaving the wood painted in charcoal shadow.

At six-and-one-half hours into his Very Long Walk, the noises started up and the light gave out altogether and Edward decided that it was actually the Wrong Sort of forest for Small Animals Entirely On Their Own.

He parked his wagon and hid in the hollow between two large stones. Edward tried to sleep but didn't for a long while. Unfamiliar sounds and smells troubled him. At last, he slept fitfully.

In the morning, he met the Parrotishes.

They were standing around his wagon, poking it with long sticks. Thin and tall, like the trees, they hooted as he crawled out from his makeshift bed. There were five of them, all wearing bits of skin around their waists. Their brown, bark-like skin blended with the forest and their wide black eyes shone like pools of oil. The tallest wore a vine around his forehead hung with feathers, leaves and twigs.

"Hello," Bear said in a quiet sort of voice. He felt a little afraid.

They jumped, looked at him, and backed away slowly.

He jumped, too, and wondered if he could edge himself back into his bed and start over again after having a bit more sleep and a bit less company.

They studied him carefully and suddenly self-conscious, Edward patted himself down, raising a small cloud of dust. "I'm a bit of a mess. I'm on an Expotition, you know."

The four shorter Parrotishes looked at what seemed to be their leader. It stepped forward.

Edward saw no time like the present to make introductions. "Good morning. I'm Edward Bear. Pleased to meet you." He moved closer and stuck out his paw.

The leader sprung back, hooting and whistling. The followers hooted and whistled, too. Then, clearing it's voice, the leader shuffled cautiously closer to Edward and stuck out its own three-fingered hand. "Good morning," it said. "I'm Edward Bear. Pleased to meet you."

Edward blinked, dropped his paw. "You are?"

A pause. "You are?"

"*I* am. Who are *you?*"

"I am. Who are you?"

"I'm Edward Bear." Edward shifted uncomfortably.

"I'm Edward Bear." The leader imitated his shift. Then, the others behind him did the same.

"I'm Edward Bear," four voices said.

Edward nodded enthusiastically. Just like parrots, he realized. And so he called them Parrotishes.

They were still nodding enthusiastically when he grabbed up the handle of his floating wagon and continued down the trail.

The Parrotishes shadowed him through the forest for three days, always disappearing at dusk, always reappearing at dawn. They moved apart and silent, occasionally whistling or hooting or proclaiming themselves to be Edward Bear.

On the third day, he made up a Song for Bears on Very Long Walks. He called it "Edward Bear and the Very Long Walk" and found himself suddenly part of a choir. Around the forest, thin and reedy voices parroted back his words. He tried to conduct them but gave up in the end; they wouldn't sing their bits properly and no harmony could be found. He began to whistle instead.

On the fourth day he found a beehive that no one seemed to care much for. He declared a holiday and helped himself. If honey *could* be sweeter and stickier, this honey was. The Parrotishes watched from a distance, imitating his "Oh My's" along with the wet smacking noises.

As he walked, the terrain changed. The trail gave out but so did the choked foliage. The trees began to thin and long purple blades of grass took over. At the forest's end, a bright blanket of rolling prairie met his eyes. Looming over him, the brilliant mountain shone against an azure sky.

Leaving the forest meant leaving its shade. For half a day Edward moved across the prairie, feeling the heat through his fur. The wagon whispered along behind him, occasionally sputtering over a rock or hissing reluctance as he tugged uphill, cresting rolls and ridges. He paused several times to look for his troupe of emaciated echoes, but they were no where to be seen, as if owned by the shadows of the wood. Overhead, large birds zipped between spherical clouds, riding a wind he couldn't feel. As the sun set, the air chilled and the sky became a painting gently fading into gray. He spent his first night in the open, curled into a tight ball on a bed of grass.

The next morning, he took a few steps toward the mountain before he realized his wagon was gone.

At first, he looked about frantically, his head moving quickly, his nose sniffing the air as if he might catch the scent. Nothing.

For a few hours, he sat down and cried. He had failed. His Expotition had ended.

The sky choked with clouds that suddenly cut loose and water sliced the air around him, soaking him completely and turning the prairie into purple sponge. Lifting his snout to the darkened sky, Edward howled.

A howl answered him and he looked up into the black eyes of a single Parrotish. "I'm Edward Bear," the Parrotish said, and motioned for him to follow.

Belligerently, Edward trudged behind the Parrotish. The rain let up as they entered the forest at a point someplace other than where he left it the day before. Once, the Parrotish broke out into "Edward Bear and the Very Long Walk," but Edward didn't feel like singing. An anger settled over him, mixed with sadness. His thoughts kept wandering back to the children's hollow eyes, fixed on nothing ever again, shining for No One. He couldn't remember how many other children were coming, or when, or even how, but he knew their eyes would be empty, too, now that he'd lost his wagon.

A hoot and whistle stopped his little brain. He looked up to see that his guide had joined the four others, the leader among them. It held a length of wood in its slender fingers and it pointed to a round, dark mouth in the side of a low hill. His guide prodded him and Edward turned.

The Parrotish pantomimed dragging something and then pointed to the hole. "I'm Edward Bear," it said. The others chimed in eager but low voices.

Edward moved toward the hole. Some dreadful stench that smelled very much like Death leaked out of it. He felt afraid and his hackles rose. "Oh. In there?"

"Oh. In there?" they echoed.

"Uh. Well." He shifted. "Oh bother."

They echoed him, then backed away and motioned at the hole. He looked back and forth, between them and the dark opening. Then, he made what he believed was a Very Brave Decision. "Well, then," he said in as cheerful a voice as he could, "let's just go and have a look." He marched to the hole and paused as the leader touched his shoulder. When he turned, the leader thrust the stick into his paws.

It was a spear, he realized.

The dirt walls gave off a damp smell that mingled with the odor from deeper within. As his eyes adjusted to the dark, Edward saw that the tunnel stretched gradually down. His ears picked up various sounds: water dripping, gentle snoring, soft whimpering and an electric buzz that he at first mistook for bees. Clutching his spear as best he could, sharpened point thrust before him, he made his way downward until the tunnel widened into a larger den. He felt something like wet wood shifting beneath his feet and as he moved them the smell grew worse.

In the center of the room, near two mounds of breathing hair, his wagon hummed while lights flickering off and on along the pack it supported. In the far corner, thin, small figures cowered.

Edward tip-toed toward the wagon, listening carefully to each snore. He shifted the spear to one paw and stretched the other toward the wagon's handle. He could leave quietly, he knew, without waking them. And he should, so he could climb the mountain. To Save the Children, he told himself.

The softest hoot and whistle came to him from the shivering forms across the den. He looked at the wagon, then to the mounds of hair, then to the corner. He picked his way past them and went to the three small Parrotishes huddled together. They were children. Their hands were tied and as he turned the first around to bite at the tough vines one of the mounds snorted and barked. Edward put down his spear and went to work, tooth and claw, finally severing the bonds. The free Parrotish began untying its neighbor while Edward went to the last. Quietly, he led them out of the cave.

Outside, the five Grown Up Parrotishes surrounded the children, clutching them as well as Edward in tight embraces while they whistled their pleasure. When they turned to leave the clearing, beckoning him to follow, Edward hesitated. "Uh . . . Excuse me please?"

They stopped. "Uh . . . Excuse me please?" the leader said.

"Let me just fetch my wagon." He turned back to the cave. He plunged back into the darkness, spear held loosely. Softly padding to the wagon, he lifted its handle and tugged. A growl rose up behind him and he spun around, dropping the handle with a clang.

"Uh. Terribly sorry to have awakened you. I think I'll just slip out now. Please, go back to sleep."

The hair mound became a creature nearly twice his size, short back legs supporting a massive torso and long arms. A horn slowly sprouted from the head and saliva splattered the floor from a wide, tooth-lined mouth. The other stirred now, as well, and Edward tried another approach.

"This," he said with a squeak, "is just a dream you're having. It will be over soon enough so — "

The first beast sprang, tumbling Edward to the ground. He rolled himself into a ball as best he could.

Edward knew he should run but his paws closed over the spear. He couldn't leave without the wagon. He managed what he thought was a fierce growl and leaped to his feet. The creature barked loudly, scooping up a large, heavy-looking stick. Swinging the club, the monster charged and Edward thrust the spear forward with all his strength, feeling it hesitate against skin before breaking through the beast's shoulder. It shrieked in pain, dropped the club, and lashed out with a long arm.

Hidden talons tore into the side of Edward's face, dropping him to the floor. He kept his tentative hold on the spear and dragged it down with him, opening a larger gash in the beast. Out of the corner of his eye, Edward saw its companion watching the fight for an opportunity to jump in.

The wounded creature pounced, fastening its mouth on the top of Edward's head while its talons raked his torso and belly. The spear broke beneath the weight with a loud snap.

Edward heard a low murmur that crescendoed to a loud shriek. He knew, in a distant way, it was himself. His paws scrambled over the stinking, matted hair as he tried to roll over and away. Fire flashed its way deep into each wound and bits of fur and toy-gel stung his eyes. His paw closed over the sharpened end of his broken spear and, in a panic, he gripped it and thrust it upward into the soft throat of his adversary.

It howled, talons working fiercely, mouth opening and closing on Edward's head. Then it went limp.

Edward struggled free, rose shakily to his feet, and roared. The other beast slammed into him before he could turn to face it. He went down hard. He vaguely heard angry hoots and whistles racing down the tunnel before cotton filled his ears. He vaguely saw five forms burst into the den, rocks clutched tight in small fists. When the lights stopped flashing in his head, a muddled darkness descended.

He awoke to sunlight and pleasant smells and eight faces staring down at him. He tried to sit up but gentle hands pushed him down.

"I'm a bit of a mess," the Parrotish leader said, mouth working carefully around the words. "I'm on an Expotition, you know." It sounded hollow and far away.

Edward noticed that one of his ears, stained yellow with crusty toy-gel, now decorated the leader's headband. He also noticed the lacerations on its arms and chest. The others crowded around him, too, and he could see they fared no better. Two of them held horns that dripped blood. Another held a steaming handful of something that looked like mud. It began dabbing the mud on Edward's head.

Turning his head slowly, he took in his surroundings. He lay in the clearing outside the cave. Nearby, the red wagon hummed and bobbed on air. An owl swooped down and perched at his feet.

"Oh, it's you." Edward tried to smile but couldn't find the strength.

"You'd better hurry," the owl said. "You haven't much Time."

Edward nodded.

"Oh, it's you," the Parrotish leader said.

Edward slept.

The pain licked him and chewed him in his dreams, ever in the background.

Large metal whales swam across the night while children slept safe inside. A pig and a bear went round and round a bush. A spinning top moved in slow motion around a blue-green marble. A bear and a rabbit sat down for cakes and milk. Eyes stared empty at the ceiling, hands clutched blankets.

"Tell them about the children." The boy became an old woman who became an empty balloon discarded in the sand.

He awakened to movement. Somehow they'd tied him to a bed of ferns on top of the pack and he rode the wagon as they took turns pulling.

"Hello?" They stopped and looked down at him. His head pounded and his arm felt like jelly as he raised his paw. The mountain could be seen looming above the tree-line, squatting in its purple nest. "There. I need to go there."

The Parrotishes paused, huddled, and a lively debate ensued. Edward tried to make up dialogue to go with their gibberish but gave up. It hurt too much to think.

After a few minutes, they turned and broke from the cover of the forest. Edward lay back and closed his eyes.

Time rushed like a brook over pebbles, daylight fading into dusk, dusk giving way to dark and dark becoming dawn. The Parrotishes only stopped to force water or honey into his mouth. He spat most of it onto his chest, unable to hold it down. At one point, one of the children gave him a doll made from the purple prairie grass. It looked something like a bear, and he clutched it with his good arm as best he could.

Gradually, it grew cold, but even when Edward saw his breath he still felt like he was on fire. A cold bit of mud to roll in would be quite nice, he thought.

As they climbed, he saw a pig throwing snowballs at a baby kangaroo. They both paused to wave at him; he waved back. Later, a tiger bounced over and kept pace with him long enough to ask how he felt. The tiger bounced away before he could say "Terrible, thanks."

At some point, two of the Parrotishes came around to his feet and pushed the wagon while two pulled. The three children and one of the others, Edward realized, weren't with them any longer. In the fog of his fever they had left the Expotition and he hadn't noticed. Tirelessly, they pushed on. With one last shove and yank, the wagon skipped across the slightly rounded summit and came to a halt. Edward began tugging at the vines that held him in place and the Parrotish leader helped untie him, but when Edward tried to stand he wobbled. They crowded in to steady him and he sat heavily in the loose-packed snow. "Bother," he said.

His right arm didn't work and neither did his left leg. And the missing ear had bobbed in front of him every time the Parrotish leader leaned over to check on him during the journey.

From where he sat, he waved to the pack and then pointed to the highest point of the summit. They unstrapped it and carried it over, propping it up in the snow. When he tried to stand again, they caught him up beneath the arms and carried him to it.

His left paw lingered over the green button. He felt he should say Something Quite Clever. He closed his eyes and sighed. "For the children."

The chorus rang out around him: "For the children."

Then he pushed the button and sagged back against his friends.

He was a bear, and his name was Edward, and he lay against a snow-clad rock watching the ocean swallow the sun far away. A pink flash of fading light on metal caught his eye below where the gray water met the white beach. He tried to make up a song about the *Nancy Bell* but couldn't. His friends, the Parrotishes, stood aloof and talked in low tones. They had tried a half dozen times to load him into the empty wagon. He'd waved them off and finally had snapped at one them, growling as he did.

He finally felt cool, but weariness soaked him through like bread in condensed milk.

"Hello, Bear!" The boy sat down beside him.

"Oh. Are you here now?"

"No. Neither are they." The boy waved to a line of animals that stood at a respectable distance. Tears ran down the pig's face.

"Well then. I'm afraid I don't quite — I mean, if you're *not* here now, then exactly *who* is talking to me right now?"

"No one. You're talking to yourself."

Edward thought about this. "I see," he said, but didn't really see at all. He tried to twist his head back to the pack. With his good ear he could hear it twittering and bleeping into the sky. "Did I finish the Expotition?"

The boy smiled. "You did. You're a Very Brave Bear."

He sighed, the words making him quite comfortably warm. "Well," he said in a satisfied sort of voice, "I suppose I am Somewhat of a Somebody now." He coughed violently.

"Yes you are. You're a Hero, Bear." The boy packed a snow ball and sent it flying out over the rim of the mountain. "Someday Everyone Who Is Anyone will know all about Edward Bear and how he saved the children. Someday there'll be statues of you and stories and — "

" — And pomes and songs?"

He laughed. "And *poems* and songs."

Edward smiled. "I especially like songs about honey."

There was an uncomfortable silence before the boy spoke again. "Do you understand what's happening to you?"

Edward couldn't help it; the sob escaped him before he could grab it and hold it in. "I-I'm *broken.*"

"Yes."

"That's why all of you are here now but Not Here."

"Yes. We're a part of your sub-brain. For Comfort and for Calm in Times of Great Distress."

He waited, watching as the last sliver of sun fell into the sea. He felt a tear slip out. "Am I *dying?*"

The boy nodded twice slowly.

"And there's Nothing To Do for it?"

"I'm sorry, Bear."

Edward heard the sound of crunching snow and turned his head. The Parrotish leader squatted next to him. It untied the decorated headband and then re-tied it around Edward's head. "I'm Edward Bear." The leader then handed him the purple doll.

Edward took it and nodded. The leader turned and re-joined the group. Tugging the wagon, they trudged away, disappearing downward.

"So this is the End of Me?" He felt something heavy squeezing inside him and he choked back another sob.

The boy nodded. "It is. For *this* you, anyway."

"But I was Brave?"

"Yes. Very."

"And a Hero?"

"A Hero, yes."

He smiled and closed his eyes. "I'm very tired."

"Then go to sleep."

"I will but . . . " He peeked at the boy.

"But what?"

"Will you stay with me and hold my hand and tell me about Someday again, only very slowly, until I fall asleep?"

The boy looked at him and Edward saw that his eyes sparkled with love and tears. "Silly old bear, of course I will."

As the boy talked quietly about statues and stories and poems, the familiar sound of a song drifted up to Edward Bear from somewhere down below.

THAT OLD-TIME RELIGION

R everend J. Junius Beech preached his new god for the first time at the Wednesday prayer meeting of the Holiness Gospel Tabernacle in Stafford, Mississippi about three weeks back. I know because I heard it, sitting with my wife in the fourth row.

He stood up behind his pulpit. He looked out over the un-crowded room, smiling a weak smile. His skin looked a bit yellow and his eyes were red and ringed with dark circles. A gasp worked its way through the sanctuary when he drew the new god out from behind the pulpit and set it in the place he usually set his big, battered Bible.

"Folks," he said to us. "I've got some new stuff to talk about."

Now don't get me wrong. I'm not a regular at the Tabernacle by any means. I went to stop my wife from nagging me. Hell, eigh-teen years ago I was beating Jimmy-June Beech up, calling him faggot and pussy, with the rest of Stafford High School. And fifteen years ago, his wife and I were losing our virginity in the back of my Dad's Plymouth out at Goose Holler. Brenda Hamilton, cheerleader and all-around in-girl, had not met Jesus yet so I reckon it was all right.

Now, Brenda *Beech*, director of the Sunday School Program and Women's Missionary Movement, sat in the front row, watching her husband and pretending that she didn't know I was two pews behind her.

"What is *that?*" I whispered to my wife.

She shushed me.

"No, Sue, I'm serious. What *is* it?"

It looked like it was made of dark iron or stone. The new god stood about eight inches high and from here it looked like something from a horror movie. A large apelike head, tentacles, a fish tail, the body of a wolf and very well-hung. I know it wasn't really moving, but it sure seemed like it was. And it seemed to drink light.

Sue leaned in. "I don't know, Billy. Just listen. Maybe it'll do you some good."

A few gray or balding heads turned our way, stern faces sending off a damnation warning.

"This," Reverend Beech said, "is my new god. His name is Glim." Now those gray and balding heads turned on him. He smiled. "It's okay, folks," he said. "He doesn't need to be your god, too. Just mine."

Someone behind me whispered something about the Reverend's cheese finally sliding off the cracker.

Up on the platform, Beech stroked the little god's head, gazing down on the statue with more love and wonder than I had ever seen on a person's face before that day. His eyes came up, narrowed, took in the scattered church-folk. "My own personal god to give me the desire of my heart."

One couple stood to leave. Deacon Frank Duke shook a finger at the minister. "I don't know what you're playing, Parson, but the board's gonna hear about this."

The Reverend shrugged and went back to adoring Glim. "Do what you need to, Frank. But the proof's in the pudding." He put on his magic smile. "When I was a young boy, I promised to love my God and preach the gospel and bring revival to a lost world in need of happiness and hope. I didn't know how hopeless and unhappy I was myself. And how badly I needed a personal answer to my prayers for everyone else. Because," now he leaned on the pulpit, "you can't understand empty if you've never been full."

Then, he picked up his new god and sat back down.

After service, he stood at the back next to his wife. He kept the little god nestled in the crook of his arm, shaking hands with those folks that hadn't already left or hadn't brushed past him glowering at his blasphemy.

"Where'd you find it?" Annie Mae was asking him as we approached.

The Reverend shrugged. "He found me, I guess. I was prayer-walking the woods behind the parsonage and there he was. He told me that if I'd worship him, he'd give me the desires of my heart."

"I think it's lovely," she said, moving on. Annie Mae had a thing for the preacher going back to grade school. Everyone in town knew it.

"Hope it all works out, Reverend," I said, shaking Beech's hand. I smiled at his wife. "Brenda. How are you?"

She went a bit pale but stayed proper. "Fine, Billy. You?" I tried hard not to remember her warm, soft skin up against me, her moans, her mouth on mine. I wondered if she tried hard not to remember the same.

I tried to keep my eyes on hers but they kept drifting down. "Can't complain."

"Can I touch it?" Sue asked the Reverend. He nodded and she reached out a finger to pet the little god. I watched gooseflesh jump up her arms. Her eyes even rolled slightly up and the breath came out of her. "Oh."

"Maybe you'll want one of your own," Reverend Beech said.

She stood there trembling. Finally, I put my arm around her shoulders and steered her towards the car.

"Things are gonna get bad, Stevie," a voice said. "They're gonna get *real* bad."

I looked around the parking lot, then I looked at Sue. "Did you say something?"

She shook her head slightly, gazing over her shoulder at the Reverend and his new god.

Sue brought her own god home the next week. She said his name was Rud. He had two penises, a dog's head, a lion's body and big wings. He had a snake for a tongue.

"It sure is ugly," I said.

"Goddamn it, Billy," she said, throwing a *People* magazine at me. "Show some respect."

I grabbed a beer and headed back to the living room.

Sue's personal god never left her side. She set it in the kitchen window sill when she cooked, drove it around with her in the car when she ran errands and placed it on top of the television in our bedroom at night when she slept. Fact is, at first I didn't mind, though I thought it was a bit odd. She seemed happy, and her being happy meant I could drink more beer and not go to church.

Three nights later we were laying in the shadow of her new

god when Sue rolled over and kissed me, hard on the mouth, like she hadn't done for some time now.

"Guess what?" she said.

"You're horny?"

She punched me in the arm just hard enough to show she meant it. Then she giggled. "No."

I sighed. "Didn't think so."

She nuzzled in close, her lips brushing my earlobe. "I'm pregnant, Billy."

I felt a hundred things at once. First, of course, being surprise. I sat up. "You're what?"

She sat up, too, grinning. "Pregnant."

"That's not possible. You know that. I took the test. You were there when the doctor — "

She put a finger over my mouth. "I know what the doctor said."

Now I started doing math in my head. My surprise was turning into anger and I shoved her finger away. "But we haven't . . . I mean, we . . . " Realization came crawling home like a drunk without his keys. She hadn't wanted any from me for at least six months. I could feel my scalp tingling. "Who was it, Sue?" A parade of men marched across my imagination.

She crawled out of bed, the nightgown bunching and pulling here and there to reveal her skinny legs and round breasts. She went the television, took down Rud and brought him to bed. She petted him while I stared at her. Finally, she looked up at me. "Didn't you want a baby, too?"

I didn't know what say or do. I climbed to my feet and grabbed my pillow. "Not like this."

I tossed and turned on the couch for an hour, expecting to hear her crying in the other room. She wasn't. She was crooning and singing and speaking in tongues to her new god. I got up, grabbed a beer and went to the porch.

The moon hung high. Frogs croaked. The night air fell on me like a hot, wet wool blanket.

"Hell of a mess, Stevie," the voice said.

I looked around. "Who's there?"

"You know who it is, Stevie."

I looked around some more. "And why do you keep calling me Stevie?"

A pause. "I call everyone Stevie."

I bent over and looked under the porch swing. "Why?"

Another pause. "It's easier to remember that way. You all have so many different names."

I settled back into the swing. "What's *your* name then?"

"Unimportant."

"Your name is Unimportant? What kind of parent names their kid Unimportant?"

"I don't have parents."

"Oh. Right," I said. "Disembodied voices wouldn't need parents, would they?"

"You're pretty smart for a guy who works in a tire factory."

I cracked open my beer and took a drink. "Thanks."

"I suppose," the voice said, "you're wondering why I called you out here?"

"You didn't call me. I couldn't sleep. And my wife's — "

"Listen up, Stevie. It's gonna get real bad."

"Why are you telling me this?" I asked.

"Because you're listening."

"Not by choice," I said. "Head voices aren't really a matter of choice."

The voice chuckled. "That's true. But at least you haven't popped off to Doc Rawlings for a little yellow pill to make it go away."

I shrugged. "Night's young yet."

Now the voice laughed. "I think those of you with senses of humor have always been my favorites."

"Some folks around here would just say I'm a smart-ass."

"You should've met Moses," the voice said. "Now *he* was a smart-ass."

"I thought you said you had trouble remembering names?"

"I was just kidding. Memory like an elephant." A short, barking laugh. "I used to call *him* Stevie, too."

"Great," I said. "I think I see where *this* is going."

"I expect you do. So you'd better get some sleep."

And right then, I dropped my beer, fell over on the swing, and slept sound as a redneck at a Felini film festival.

*

I woke up to the smell of pancakes and bacon. I kicked my beer can off the porch and walked inside. Sue stood naked in the kitchen, rubbing her stomach with one hand while she worked the griddle with the other. She was completely oblivious to me or to the popping grease that speckled her skin. She was too busy singing to her god.

I stood there in the doorway watching for a few minutes. She looked thinner, almost bony. The line of her jaw had that skull-like angle to it. Paper yellow skin pulled tight over bones. But her stomach bulged just a bit. She set down the spatula.

"Morning, Billy," she said over her shoulder. "Are you still mad?"

I grunted, reaching for a mug.

"It's not unheard of, you know," she said. "Miracles, I mean."

I poured coffee. "Your sleeping around ain't quite a miracle, Sue." I thought about this for a second. "It's close. But not quite."

She blanched, her lower lip quivering. "That's what you think? You think *that?*" I could run it like a countdown. She always moved from surprise to anger in about ten seconds. Her eyes, red and dark-circled, went narrow and her lips pulled back into a sneer. She grabbed the closest thing handy — the spatula — and started whipping it through the air. I stepped back, sloshing coffee onto myself. She started screaming. I couldn't tell what exactly. With my free hand, I caught her wrist as the spatula flashed past my face. I gave a little twist, not enough to hurt her too bad, and she dropped the spatula.

"That's about enough," I said. "What's got into you? You tell me you're pregnant. We both know I fire blanks. And *you're* all riled up about it?" I looked her dead in the eye. "How'd you *think* I'd feel?"

Now her lip quivered again. Tears worked at the corners of her eyes. "I don't know, Billy. I thought you'd be happy." She glanced over at her god, there on the window sill. "It's my heart's desire."

"Are you listening to yourself, Sue?"

She nodded. "It's true, Billy, I swear to Rud."

"Rud?" All that anger hunkering down in me started rattling my ribcage. "You swear to *Rud?*"

I pushed past her, scooped up the little statue and cocked back my arm, aiming for the brick fireplace.

"No, Billy!" she screamed.

I opened my mouth to shout back and suddenly felt fire shooting up my arm from my fingers. I dropped the statue. It ran out of the kitchen and scuttled under the couch, a bit of my finger still in its little mouth. "Holy shit, Sue, that bastard bit me."

She laughed. It was a cold sound. "Serves you right."

She coaxed the little god into the open and packed her bags while I cleaned and bandaged my finger. I heard her whispering to it while she slammed closets and drawers around. I sat on the couch in silence while she showered and dressed.

She paused at the door. "I just can't be with anyone who doesn't respect my faith."

I nodded, glowering at the statue poking out of her purse.

"Maybe you should talk to Reverend Beech," she said. "Maybe he could help you find one of your very own."

"If you're going," I said, "then go."

She slammed the door, rattling the glass.

I put my head in my hands and listened to her car grumble to life and chew up gravel.

"You did the right thing, Stevie," the voice said. "I'm proud of you."

"Go to hell."

"Blasphemer," the voice said. After that, it stayed silent for some time. I found myself a beer and started working out the details of what my life had suddenly become.

I called in sick for about a week, then finally forced myself back to work. I eased my pickup into a nearly empty parking lot, looking for some sign of life in the factory.

The foreman, Gus Shooper, stopped me at the door. "We're closed down, Billy."

"Closed down?"

He scratched himself. "Yep. No work."

"Why?"

"Where you been, Billy? Don't you watch the news?"

I shook my head.

Gus squinted at me from beneath his ball-cap. "Doesn't matter, I reckon. News is off now, too."

I felt something roll over in my belly. "What's happening, Gus?"

"The world's done changed, Billy." His eyes had craziness in them I'd never seen before. "It's changed something fierce."

I left him there and drove into town. A few scattered people walked, humming to the little gods they carried or pushed in strollers. Most of the stores stood dark and empty, signs in the windows and doors wide open. *Help yourselves*, one sign read, *I don't give a shit no more.*

I drove around the block three times before I stopped at Reverend Beech's house. I rang the doorbell and when no one answered, I started pounding. Brenda answered, her face pale.

She looked surprised to see me. "Billy?"

I pushed past her. "Where's my wife, Brenda?" I looked around the living room. I'm not sure why I thought she'd be here, but it seemed as good a guess as any. Her folks had passed on some years back and the Tabernacle had always been more of a family to her.

"She's not here," Brenda said. Now I looked at her more closely. Her eyes were red and dark-circled but it looked more like she'd been sleepless and crying.

"Where's Jimmy-June, then?"

"At the temple, I expect," she said.

"The temple? They changed the name again?"

She glanced outside, making sure no one was nearby, then closed the door. "Not the tabernacle. It's closed. The temple. Out towards Aimsville."

"Brenda, what's going on?"

A tear let loose. Then another. She fell into my arms, sobbing. My hands went around her, feeling her warm skin through the thin dress she wore. She cried into my chest and I hoped she didn't feel what was happening to me below the belt.

I just held her like that for maybe five or ten minutes. Then, I eased her back and looked into her eyes. "What's going on?" I asked again.

"I don't know. Something bad, I think."

"Something really bad, Stevie," the voice said. I ignored it.

She filled me in then, telling me about the radio sermons and then the local television, about the network vans and the satellite broadcasts, about the people discarding their lives, their wives, their jobs, their businesses, their children as new gods made their dreams come true. "All around the world," she told me. "They're just everywhere now, Billy."

Of course, the Pope had spoken out. Theologians and skeptics, too. But the proof was, as the Reverend has said, in the pudding. Soon enough they became quiet. They called them the Many or they called them the New Gods. Or they didn't call them anything at all, just gave their hearts over without needing to hang a name on it.

In towns and cities all around the world, roadside temples and living room shrines arose. You could hear the singing for miles.

"And that's where my wife is?"

Brenda nodded. "With my husband."

Something in the way she said it didn't sit right. "*With* him?"

She nodded again, this time slowly.

"I have to go." I stood up from the couch where we'd sat talking for the last hour.

She caught my hand. "Don't go. Stay with me."

I shook off her hand. "I'd like to, Brenda, but I can't."

She jumped up, pressing herself to me. I felt her breast brush my arm. Her mouth moved over my neck. I felt the stir. I wanted to kiss her, but I knew it would be an angry kiss, a kiss that was more like a slap for her husband and my wife than any good thing for Brenda and me.

"I can't," I said.

Her shoulders slouched. "What are you going to do?"

"I'm going to end this. If I can."

"You can't, Stevie," the voice said.

My voice rose an octave. "I have to try, don't I?"

The voice said nothing. Brenda thought I was talking to her.

"Will you come back for me when you're finished?"

I looked at her. I remembered her naked skin, her nervous, fumbling hands working my button fly jeans, the smell of bubblegum and the sound of Rush's "Tom Sawyer" distant on the radio.

"Why would you want me to, Brenda Hamilton?"

"Because," she said, "for the last three weeks — maybe even for all my life — I've heard nothing except how unhappy and hopeless I am." Her lips brushed mine. "If I have to be that way while the world comes down around us, I'd rather not be unhappy and hopeless alone."

"I'll come back."

I kissed her. Then I left.

The voice waited for me in the truck. "Now you're coveting your neighbor's wife, Stevie."

I started it up and backed into the street. "No, I'm not."

"And bearing false witness," it added.

"Well, at least I'm not an idolater," I said.

"That's true. And she's right, you know."

"About the Reverend and my wife?"

The voice laughed. "No. Well, not the baby anyway. The baby really is Rud's. And there are about four hundred or so thousand other babies on their way, too. The dawning of Nephilim once again. Completely inexcusable." The voice paused to let it all soak in but I had no idea what the hell it was talking about. "What she's right about is the world coming down around you."

"Really?" I turned onto Main Street and pointed my truck towards Chuck's Hardware Store.

"It's always a hard decision, but I really do like that old time religion best."

I watched the empty businesses slide by. "What's that mean?"

"Stevie, you know what that means."

"No, I don't. Really."

"You went to Sunday School."

"A long time ago."

"Why do you think I forbid idolatry?"

"Because believing in one God is ridiculous enough without believing in a whole pack of them?"

The voice laughed. "Good one, Stevie." He paused. "No. It's simple really. Stretch back your mind you'll remember the verse."

I thought I did but it had never made much sense to me. "You're a jealous God?"

I parked in front of Chuck's and climbed out. I put a rock through the plate glass door and let myself in. An alarm went off.

"I am indeed. That's why I'm not too upset about what you're doing. You think your wife is being unfaithful. You mean to do bodily harm to the man you suspect. I'd do the same."

I walked to the gun case, used the same rock to smash it. I helped myself to a few pistols and a few boxes of shells. "I'm glad you see it my way."

"But you don't have much time. I've made my decision."

I left the store, climbed back into the truck. "What decision is that?"

"How to destroy the world a second time."

A memory from Sunday School leaped to mind. "I thought the rainbow was all about you promising not to do that?"

"Actually," the voice said, "I promised not to use water. This time, it'll rain fire for forty days and forty nights. Ever see any of those movies about the end of the world?"

I had. They were my favorites, especially the one about the leather-clad cop and the suped-up car. "Great."

"Don't worry; I plan on sparing you. And a few others."

I turned the truck around and caught the highway for Aimsville. "I appreciate that." I studied the sky. It was yellow with black clouds. "Before you do that, though, I have an idea of my own."

"What's that?"

"This all started with Jimmy-June and his new god. What was it he said?" The voice didn't help me out any. I remembered it on my own. "These new gods — they give people the desires of their heart, right?"

"Well, Stevie, heart's desires are highly subjective and can often — "

I interrupted. "I know that. But what was it James Junius Beech wanted? What was the desire of *his* heart?"

The voice became excited. "Oh. I know this one."

I said it first: "A revival that would sweep the world. He said so that night."

"I don't think it's going to work, Stevie."

"But if it does, will you spare the world?"

"Hmmm." The voice went quiet for a moment. "This sounds familiar. I think it had something to do with finding one righteous man someplace. A long time ago."

I saw the temple ahead. It had gone up fast and stood half finished in Jerry David' cotton field. Cars and bicycles lay strewn around it. "Well?"

"Okay. But honestly, I don't think it's going to work."

"I have to try."

"But why? What's in it for you?"

I shrugged. "I'm not sure. Does there have to be something in it for me?"

"Actually," the voice said, "it usually means the most when there isn't."

I pulled in and parked, pointing the truck back towards town. I left it running. Sounds of singing, moaning and babbling filled the late morning air.

I loaded the pistols and shoved them into the back of my jeans, pulling my wife-beater out of my pants to cover the butts. I walked up to the large double doors and let myself in.

Most folks were naked, young and old alike. They lay or knelt or crouched or sat scattered around the room like a vast human carpet. They'd built shelves into the walls — the sort you'd see holding knick-knacks in your grandmother's house — and had placed their little gods all around the massive room. I'd never seen any sight quite like the one before me, not even at those movies that showed in the old theater across town. I felt a strange anger, a strange urge to just start shooting or to maybe ground up those little gods in a blender and make folks drink them down with unsweetened Kool-Aid.

No one noticed me. They were all too busy with their sinning and singing. At the front of the temple, up on a platform, stood an altar made of black stone. The Reverend and my wife lay in the shadow of that altar.

I picked my way through the crowd. Chuck, whose store I'd just raided, looked up from some girl I seemed to recall worked for him. He smiled at me, his yellow skin saggy and his eyes red. "Here to worship, too, Billy?"

I didn't say anything. I kept walking. Finally, when I got to the front, I climbed onto the altar and drew the first pistol. I didn't know if anyone saw me raise it. I didn't say anything by way of announcement. I aimed at a little god on a nearby shelf and pulled the trigger. The gun roared over the noise in the room. I didn't wait to see what they did. I kept aiming and firing, aiming and firing. I hit some. I missed most. Those I hit exploded like clay pigeons. Those I missed leaped down and scrambled among their worshippers.

"Billy!" My wife, Sue, crawled to her feet below me, disentangling herself from the Reverend. "What are you doing?"

"I'm ending this, Sue. It's an abomination."

The Reverend stood up, snarling. "You'll end nothing." He moved toward me and I drew the other pistol, leveling it at his bare chest.

"I wouldn't if I were you, Jimmy-June."

"Billy, this is insane. You can't just bust into church in the middle of worship," Sue said. She took a step forward. She'd gotten even skinnier in three days, except her belly. It was swollen, laced with purple stretch marks like thick veins.

"You shut the hell up," I told her, waving the other pistol at her.

The people in the sanctuary were scrambling, trying to find and soothe their little gods. The few whose little gods I'd managed to hit sat rocking and keening low, guttural sounds.

"You defile the House of the Many," the Reverend said. He had a different fire in his eyes now. Something old and dark and terrible.

I don't know where the words came from. They just showed up when I needed them. "What did this people unto thee, that thou hast brought so great a sin upon them?" I said.

That fire in his eyes flickered, as if he remembered those words from a life he'd forsaken for his heart's desire. His god, now larger than the other ones, clutched at his leg and glared up at me.

"Listen to me," I said to the room. And more words poured out, things I'd never heard or read. I shouted, I stomped, I raged against their idolatry. I railed for at least thirty minutes, waving my pistols anytime someone moved towards me. Somewhere in the midst of it, someone started singing. Another started crooning. A few naked bodies slithered back together. Even the new gods ignored me, climbing back onto their shelves to look down on me with satisfied smirks.

The Reverend laughed. Sue followed his lead and laughed, too. "That was a good try, Billy," Jimmy-June said. "But it's far too late for that. They're everywhere now. You can't stop them."

"I hope you're wrong," I said. "And I'm truly sorry for what I'm about to do if you're not." Then I shot him. And then I shot his little god, too. I paused, waiting to see if I'd saved the world.

I hadn't.

Pandemonium ensued. New gods poured down the walls howling as they rushed me. I grabbed Sue but she bit and scratched and kicked at me, screaming and covered with blood. A mob formed up. I saw familiar faces — sheriffs and deputies, judges and councilmen, even the mayor. Of course, they were all naked and unarmed. I pushed my wife at them.

"You're all going to burn," I shouted.

When I left out the back door, I looked to the sky. It was growing closer to orange now. The clouds like charcoal briquettes gone gray with just a tinge of red. "I told you it wouldn't work, Stevie," the voice said. "And now you're a murderer on top of everything else."

I jogged to my waiting truck, watching for all hell to break open behind me. It didn't.

I wanted to cry. I wanted to be sick. Instead, I climbed in and punched the gas down hard with my foot. "Yeah, but I did it for you, and that makes it okay."

"They *always* say that," the voice said.

"Yes, we do," I agreed. "Maybe it makes it easier to do what's got to be done."

"And does it?" the voice asked me.

I paused. I watched the temple shrinking in my rear-view mirror. I wondered about my wife and James Junius Beech. I wondered how much had started between them before this whole god business. I wondered if her baby would've come out twisted and horrible all at once or if it would've had time to be an innocent and grow into evil like a new pair of shoes. I wondered if Sue was sitting there on the floor holding her dead preacher's head in her lap and crooning to her little god while its son kicked in her belly. I thought of all of this before answering the voice. Easier?

"No," I said. "Not really."

Now we're loading the pickup, me and Brenda. She's wearing a tank top and a pair of cut-offs — her first immodest outfit since Jimmy-June asked her to the prom and she asked Jesus to save her soul from the likes of me. She looks damn fine.

Brenda can't hear the voice, but I can. It says there's a mountain we can crawl under up in Kentucky somewhere. It says there's a Remnant, whatever that means, so we won't be alone. Other mountains to fall on what's left of us all around the world, other hills to cover us, so that something is left to build from when the Big God's jealousy is sated. It also says we've got about a day before fire starts falling from the sky, burning clean what's gone dirty and wrong.

She keeps asking me about her husband and what happened. I keep dodging the questions because I'm pretty sure she won't want to be with me if I tell her the truth. And I need her to be with me not just tonight but for whatever nights are left.

She said it about herself, but I think it holds true for everyone. All our lives we hear how unhappy and hopeless we are. And if I have to be that way while the world comes down around me, I'd just as soon not be alone.

Now we're in the truck and heading north. Brenda sits close to me even though the temperature is climbing.

Now we're crossing into Kentucky and the voice has been silent for a long time. And I don't know if I'm more worried that I never heard it at all or that I'll never hear it again.

Now a mountain looms ahead and we drive for it, smelling sulfur on the wind. Hands waving us in. Haggard, sleepless faces gray with grief and fear.

The sky is boiling above.

Soon, it will be falling.

EAST OF EDEN
AND JUST A LITTLE BIT SOUTH

I was in line at the supermarket, fixing to buy me some beer, when I decided to tell my story. I'd just seen the headlines on the papers saying JFK had been successfully cloned by alien tax professionals and Elvis was living his life as a woman named Loretta Stills in New Jersey. Way I figure, a bit more truth can't hurt:

My name is Cain. The Good Book is flat-out wrong about me.

Most folks ask two questions about me. They want to know why I killed my brother. They think it was about sacrificing unto the Lord and such. My brother, Abel, with sheep; me with vegetables. Fact is, the Lord Almighty His Own Self is a meat *and* greens man. I should know. I had supper with him often.

No, that is not how it happened at all. And furthermore, I did not kill my brother. Not exactly anyways.

And the second question: Where did I find my wife?

Now I'm gonna tell you.

It started with supper, of course.

Ma and Pa were bitching about the good old days when the Lord banged on the trailer door. Yes, we lived in a trailer. Matter of fact, before the Big Flood, we *all* lived in trailers. The whole world was a bit like some parts of Mississippi.

"What's for supper?" the Lord His Own Self asked and then sneezed mightily.

"Meat," said Abel.

"Greens," said I.

"Beer," said Pa.

"Not you again," said Ma. She didn't care much for the Lord in those days on account of her menstruation and childbearing.

Me and Abel set to gathering up and putting the cats out what with the Lord being allergic and all. Yes, the Lord God is allergic to cats. Possums, kangaroos and armadillos, too, if you must know.

Pa handed the Lord a beer. He cracked it and sucked down some suds. He sighed contentedly.

"Sure is hot," he said.

"Yep." Pa gave Ma a hard look and she set another place at the table. We all sat down. The Lord sneezed again.

We ate quiet, me and Abel, listening to the grown-ups talk. I was sixteen or so then; my baby brother was fourteen I think, though we never put much truck in age back then.

The Lord helped himself to more meat and greens and smacked his lips. Ma glared. Pa just sat looking sorry. Then, the Lord spoke.

"You two need to get busy." He put down his fork for a moment to look at Ma and Pa.

"We're plenty busy *now*," Pa said. "What with that damn snake and you evicting us."

"That's not the kind of busy I mean. Babies. That's what I mean."

Ma looked perturbed. Pa looked hopeful. The Lord continued. "This whole world's waiting on you two. Room for a whole lot of trailers, way I see it."

Ma mumbled something, her face a bit pink.

"Now, I know," the Lord said in His Most Understanding Voice, "That this is not a simple task. But I reckon a few more ought to do it."

Ma had enough. "A few more?" Her voice rose the same way it did when Pa went past his nightly six pack. "A few *more?* I think not."

The Lord got real quiet and just watched.

"It mightn't be so terrible bad," Pa said. "We'd have more help around here."

She shook her head. "I think not."

Me and Abel, we saw the storm brewing. I could see in his eyes that he was thinking the same thing: Time to go outside and throw rocks at shit.

"But," Pa said and then everything else got lost as Ma banged her glass on the table, spilling Yoo-hoo every place. Yes, we had Yoo-hoo back in those days.

"I," she said in her most serious voice, "Think not."

"But what about your boys?" The Lord pointed to us each.

"Fine, strong boys. Almost men. They're gonna need wives soon so as they can do their part."

Ma's voice became very cultured all of a sudden. "So you are suggesting that I have more babies so my boys can marry up with their sisters?"

The Lord shrugged. "Ain't no law against it. Yet."

My stomach hurt from this. Abel looked like he was going to throw up all that good meat and greens right there in the Presence of the Lord Most High. Part of me wanted to run away. Another part was curious.

But the decision was made for us. "Why don't you two boys go throw rocks at shit or something," Pa said. So we hightailed it out of there.

Abel looked squeamishly at me while we threw rocks. "You reckon he really means it? That bit about sisters and babies?"

"I reckon he does," I said, lobbing a rock at a beer can on the fence post. I knocked it down with ease.

"Gross." Abel set the can back up.

"Yep."

He hucked his rock, missing by a long shot. "That dog won't hunt," he said. "That dog won't hunt for a damn sight."

So we decided to take matters into our own hands.

Boys is curious. They were then, they are now. I can't count how many times we asked about stuff. All the way back, I remember pointing to my belly button and then pointing to where Pa's should've been. Sometimes, if he'd past his nightly six pack, he'd talk about how it used to be.

One night when we were very young he even talked about how he met Mama. "I just went to sleep," he'd say. "Woke up and I was married." Then he'd lean in, looking around to make sure Ma wasn't near. "Stay awake, boys. Stay awake."

Of course, he had a big scar when he woke up too, but he didn't know exactly why on account of him being asleep when it happened.

Me and Abel, we started to thinking about this. Seemed a nap and a scar weren't near so bad as copulating with our yet-to-be-born sisters.

But we didn't know where to start. We *did* have some idea as to who we could ask. But that was tricky.

In the end, near as we could figure, all we needed was a goat's head, a fat dead rat and a six pack.

We headed west and just a bit north. Most of you all know that the Lord put an angel and a big fiery sword in the way of the Garden. What you most likely didn't know was that the angel's name was Bubba and he was bad-ass.

He was also dumb as wood.

He was stretched out napping in the sun when we got to him.

"Hey fellas," he said with a yawn. It was a powerful hot day.

"Hey Bubba," we both said. Then we offered him the six pack. He grinned.

Then we commenced to kicking that goat's head around while Bubba drank beer.

Every so often, Abel would kick the head up and over Bubba and it would land in the Garden.

Bubba'd go fetch it for us.

After a while, though, Bubba got tired of chasing the goat's head. Finally, he waved to us. "Get it your own damn self. Just mind the sword."

So we did. We made a great show of looking about for the head, all the while watching Bubba, who settled back down to snoring.

Now that fiery sword was big and noisy. It whistled and whizzed about but mostly stayed more to the middle of the Garden. We knew what we wanted wouldn't be there.

We spent all morning turning over rocks and talking to every snake we found. Mostly, they just hissed at us.

Then, just as we were like to give up, we found a big one. It was all orange and yellow and pink and blue and it had little stubs where it used to have feet. It lay under a big rock . . . one that took both of us to roll.

"Hiss," the snake said in a bored voice.

"Howdy," Abel said.

"Hello," I said.

"Hiss." It moved away, looking unhappy with us disturbing its rock and its rest.

"We came to talk to you." Abel had a way with words so I let him do the talking.

"Snakes don't talk," it said.

"You just did."

I'd never seen a snake shrug before, but this one did. "Hiss."

"We need your help," Abel said. "The Lord God His Own Self wants us to mate with our sisters and fill the world with single wide trailers."

"Doesn't sound like my problem. Besides, I like trailers. They're nice for sleeping under."

"We don't mind that bit. It's the sister bit," I said.

"We need girls," Abel said. "Ones we ain't related to."

"I don't make girls. I just get them to eat stuff." The snake slithered towards another rock. "You boys mind that sword, you hear?"

Here is where Abel pulled out the fat dead rat. He plopped it down in front of the snake. "We'll make them our own-selves. We just need you to tell us how."

The snake sniffed at the rat. "I might could help you out." It looked at us, its beady little eyes twitching. "You might could help me out some too."

"We gave you a rat," Abel said.

"I'm a vegetarian."

"What's that?"

"Greens."

I beamed. I grew the greens on our farm.

"Then what do you want?" Abel looked perplexed.

The snake waved its stubs around. "I miss my legs."

"We don't make legs." But just as Abel said it, I had me an idea.

"So if we make you some legs, you'll tell us how to make us some girls?"

I didn't know snakes could smile; this one grinned and extended one of its stubs. "Shake on it?"

So the snake told us what we needed to know. While it told us, I looked around for sticks that were just the right thickness while Abel pulled string from the hem of his cut-offs. In no time, we knew all about how the Good Lord made Pa out of mud and Ma out of a rib and the snake was tottering about excitedly on little wooden stilts we'd tied to its stubs. All in all, it was quite a satisfactory bargain on both sides.

"So we just need some mud?" I asked.

"Or ribs?" Abel asked.

"Not exactly," the snake said. "See that sword yonder?"

We both nodded.

"There's some trees there. One with red fruit and one with orange fruit."

We both nodded again. Bits of this sounded a little familiar. One of the stories Pa told on two six pack nights.

"Mind you don't touch the red, boys," the snake said as it practiced high jumping its former rock. "The Lord His Own Self gets rightly pissed about that one and I don't want to lose my legs again."

In the end, it just came down to who ran the fastest and who threw rocks the best.

Me, I'm slow as hell. But I'm a crackshot with a rock.

We lay in the bushes outside the clearing and watched the sword flash by like a gigantic hummingbird set on fire. The snake had told us what to do with the oranges. It hadn't told us how to get them. But again, Abel was mighty smart.

"You knock 'em down," he said. "I'll just run out and grab us some."

So I did, and he did. That boy sure could run. Whack. An orange fell. Whizz. The boy flew. Buzz. The sword spun and saw no one there at all.

I guess Bubba wasn't the only one dumb as wood.

Abel made the run three times and after that he was tired out but we had us five oranges on account of my excellent aim. I didn't think nothing of it when he tore one in half and handed it to me. I just sucked the juice out of it and he did the same. Looking back, that was a mistake of sorts but it saved our asses.

We figured we needed at least two more so I took aim at a branch and let loose with a rock after the sword passed. Whack. The oranges fell. Whizz. The boy flew. Oops.

Children, and you grown ups, too, listen up: When someone says to you that you oughta tie your shoelaces in the off chance that you might trip over them remember this bit.

Abel did *not* tie his shoelaces. No one had told him to before —

wearing shoes was a bit new to us growing up in a trailer and all. We actually didn't know what those strings were for.

Abel bent over the oranges, grabbed them up, and then went ass over teakettle as he tripped. He sat up with an *oh shit* look on his face just as the sword lopped off his head.

His head rolled to the side and he blinked at me.

There wasn't much blood but his clothes had caught fire. I sat stunned for a second until he said something.

"Ma's gonna be pissed," his head said.

I didn't know swords could look confused; this one did. Of course, only being four of us in the entire world, it hadn't lopped anyone's head off before. But I'm sure it figured that this was not how it ought to go.

I figured the same but then remembered the orange we shared. At least now we knew it really *was* the Tree of Life.

"Way I see it," Abel said (knowing I couldn't rightly talk without giving myself away), "we need a diversion."

I nodded to his head to show I understood. With that, his body lurched up and took off running through the trees. Even dismembered, that boy could run.

The sword gave chase and after they'd gone, I went out, scooped up the two oranges, grabbed another three just in case, and picked up my brother's head.

"Better get going," he said. "I'm pretty sure I can't outrun that sword."

"I grabbed a few extra oranges," I said. "Maybe I can make you another body."

"First things first. We still need girlfriends."

And so we escaped the Garden of Eden. The snake watched us zip past Bubba's sleeping form and waved its little stick leg at us.

"Way to go, boys," it said.

I waved because Abel could not and I did not stop running until we reached the river. There, I propped my brother's head up against a log and commenced to dig in the mud.

I decided to make Abel's girl first since he'd been cut up. I didn't know how exactly she should look so I kinda thought about Ma and all her curves. And I wasn't sure how the Lord God His

Own Self had come up with hair so I just took some grass and shoved it into the right places. All the while, Abel gave me pointers.

After a bit, I tore some oranges and squeezed the juice all over the mud girl. The snake had thought this would do the trick even though the Lord had just breathed on his creations to bring them to life.

It did not work at all.

About this time, I was feeling a might angry and sad all at once. I think Abel must've been feeling the same way because he started to cry.

"You're going to be in *so* much trouble," he said between sniffs.

"Me?" I asked. "What about you?"

"Ma will say you're the oldest and should've known better. Besides, I ain't got no body. That's punishment enough."

I thought about this. "Can't do chores with no body."

He brightened up somewhat at this. "I hadn't thought about that."

"Besides," I said, "If we get this to work, I done *told* you I'd make you another body."

Funny we was talking about bodies because at that moment, a loud sucking noise made us look over yonder. There, dragging itself through the mud and marsh grass, was Abel's body. Or what was left of it.

Now it was more like half of a torso and an arm. The rest had been cut clean away.

An idea struck me. My brother wasn't the only one with brains. "Hey," I said. "Maybe we *do* need a rib after all."

Suffice it to say that the rib did not work by a long shot. It was a disappointing setback given just how long it takes to cut out a rib with a pocketknife. And I broke the pocketknife all to shit, too.

So we just sat there, me and Abel's head, and stewed.

"We need us some help," I said to my brother.

"We had us some help," he said back. "It did not work."

I looked at his head, then at his cut up torso and at the bloody rib poking out of the mud girl. "No," I said. "It did not."

"Pa is going to kill us."

"Naw. He can't on account of the oranges."

We were quiet again. An old crow settled down and commenced to peck at my brother's eyes. I swatted it away.

"We need help," I said again.

"Maybe the Lord God His Own Self will help us," Abel said. And just as he said it, a big bug flew right up his nose and he sneezed mightily.

That gave me another bright idea.

In the end, near as we could figure, all we needed was a dead possum, Pa's razor, and one of Ma's old sheets.

I propped Abel's head up in the fork of a tree so as not to alarm our folks and headed back East of Eden and just a bit south.

"Don't be gone long," he said, looking out for other crows.

I found the dead possum right away. It was half squashed in the middle of the trail. For those of you who study such things, possums have been getting squashed in the middle of thoroughfares since the very beginning. I do not know why but I am glad because it saved my ass . . . sorta.

I helped myself to one of Ma's sheets, hanging on the line, and wrapped the possum up in it. I did not need to hide it though, or hide that I was covered in my brother's blood, because she and Pa were otherwise engaged when I snuck into the trailer. They had taken the Lord at his word it seemed and were making all kinds of hooting and hollering noises when I passed by their bedroom.

My stomach turned as I thought about the sisters to come.

I took Pa's razor and ran back to the river just in time to scare off another bird.

First, I hid my brother's torso under a pile of brush. Then, I shaved that damn possum bald and tossed it into the river. It floated a bit and then sank.

I put all that possum hair into my ball cap, set it aside, and commenced to digging in the mud some more. This time I built me a mud man (without his head of course.) Abel gave me some pointers, having felt his former body was deficient in some areas below the belt.

"This works," I told Abel, "And we can share the girl."

He would have shrugged but could not. "I reckon we done shared everything else. And it's better than a sister."

So, I put his head in the mud and covered over the two mud bodies with Ma's sheet. Then I stood back and admired my handiwork.

"Now I'm going to fetch the Lord."

Abel grinned up at me. "You sure are smart, Cain."

"Thank you." I grinned back. Then I went to see Bubba.

"Bubba," I said. "I need to call upon the Lord."

Bubba looked abashed. "He was just here and he was pissed."

Bubba then told me the tale. Seems someone had hit him on the head, stolen some fruit, tied legs onto the serpent, and left a goat's head calling card. He told the Lord it was most likely Beelzebub helping his boss out and winked at me as he said it. Somehow Bubba had hid those beer cans. Maybe, I thought, he wasn't quite dumb as wood after all.

"Well," I said, "I still need to see him."

"He's looking over the tree. I'll send him by."

So I thanked Bubba and went back to the river.

The Lord God His Own Self strolled by a bit later.

"Hey boys, you seen a big demon 'round here goes by the name of Beelzebub?"

"No," we both said.

"We ain't seen nothing," Abel said.

The Lord scratched his head. "What in tarnation are you two doing?"

"We're playing Genesis," I said.

"I'm Pa," Abel said and rolled his eyes towards the mud girl. "That's Ma there."

"And I'm playing you," I said, trying to look all humble.

The Lord looked rightly pleased.

"Maybe you could help us out," I said.

Now he looked even more pleased. More tickled than a girl on prom night.

"Way I figure it," I said, "This game is a way for us to tell our story to the generations to come after. We want to be historically accurate and shit."

The Lord nodded. "I like this."

I pointed to the mud girl. "Is this how you did the hair?"

The Lord came over, stooped down and looked real close at the mud girl's hair. This was my cue. I up-ended my ball cap onto the Lord's Own Head and all that possum fur and dander cascaded down.

For a moment, the Lord looked quite surprised. Then he sneezed mightily three times and ropy wads of snot shot onto Abel and the mud girl.

That mud girl started coughing and sputtering and the Lord His Own Self whipped back the sheet. Sure enough, it was a *real* girl, though her hair never was quite right on account of the grass I used. Sadly, Abel was still just a head. The body was just mud. I reckon him already being technically alive messed up our plan somewhat.

The Lord, he chuckled. "You boys done good."

That, of course, was a relative statement given my brother's predicament.

The girl sat up looking truly bewildered. She was the prettiest thing I ever seen and I named her Jenny right on the spot.

We all sat there a bit and just looked at each other.

"Ma's still gonna be pissed," Abel finally said.

The Lord looked at the brush where Abel's hand poked out. "I reckon she is," he said.

"What do we do now?" I asked.

"Way I see it," the Lord said, "There's this place called Nod out yonder. Room for a bunch of trailers there."

"What about Ma and Pa?" I asked.

The Lord looked very thoughtful. "You just hightail it and leave that to me. I'll think of something to tell them." And he did. Though it was not historically accurate.

So Jenny and me and Abel thanked the Lord kindly and I scooped up my brother's head. Then we left.

I started this out talking about two questions but there is a third that has made me famous. Am I my brother's keeper? I reckon I am because of his peculiar condition.

Me and Jenny and Abel, we had ourselves a long life on account of them oranges and shit. We experienced a lot of fine adventures, what with the Big Flood and the Ten Plagues and that one time when God's Own Son Himself hung out with us in the Orient for a spell. But those are all other stories.

Jenny is saying it's time for supper. Sometimes I miss supper with Ma and Pa and the Lord. At least there are still trailers.

"What are we having?" I ask her before I wrap this up.

"Meat," she says.

"And greens," my brother says.

"I'll grab us some beer," I say.

FEARSOME JONES'
DISCARDED LOVE COLLECTION

Fearsome Jones collected discarded love like some folks collected aluminum cans. He gathered its remnants to himself, finding it sometimes in the strangest places. A crumpled dinner receipt from the Rainbow Lounge on the steps of a posh apartment building. A wilted bouquet, it's "I'm sorry — Please let's try again" placard stained with rainwater or tears. A wedding band tossed from the window of a funeral bound hearse.

So when he saw the young coffee cart girl from the corner of First and Lenora leave the AlCom Building crying and clutching a bloody bundle of restroom paper towels, he followed.

The evening traffic had stilled, slipping into the routine of patrol cars and cabs, the pedestrians owning Seattle's night. Slinging his backpack of papers, he put her twenty yards ahead and kept her there.

"Gotta smoke, Fears?" Skinny smiled up at him from the hotel stoop.

"Later," he said, moving past.

"Hey — need some smoke, man?" Skinny sold him his weed each week.

"Later, Skinny. I'm onto something."

Skinny laughed behind him. Fearsome, eyes locked on the slouched shoulders, pressed forward.

She paused at the foot of a hill, looked around furtively, and started up. The park. He just knew it.

As she crossed the sidewalk and cut into the lawn, Fearsome dodged into the 7-Eleven to watch through the window. She'd slowed now, her head moving side to side, studying benches and bushes. A few small children played at the swingset while a mother stood protectively by. Fearsome saw the girl's fist move to her mouth as she watched. He couldn't see her eyes from this distance, but knew what was in them. Then, she turned away quickly, lifted the lid of the trash-can, and gently set the bundle down. After a moment, she left and Fearsome saw her eyes as she passed the store. Shame and despair, lines of tears, lips pulled tight with resolution.

As soon as she vanished around the corner he broke cover and made for the park. The bundle mewled pitifully as he lifted the lid and Fearsome scooped it up.

"Well, what have we here?" A bit of discarded love, a bit of someone else's life. Someone else's secret shame. Come to think of it, she *had* been wearing baggier clothes, moving a bit slower, smiling a bit sadder as she'd served him his one cup of free coffee each morning for the past few months.

He dug through the blood-matted paper towels, finding a foot and then a hand . . . both cold. "What has old Fearsome found?" He pulled away the paper like an excited Christmas morning child and gasped at the face it revealed.

"Goddamn," he said, his voice a whisper. "You are one *ugly* motherfucker, ain't you?"

The baby stared up at him, its face contorted and purple. Three eyes — black as a Republican's heart — blinked into the fading light and the misshapen mouth twisted and sucked at air. Fearsome realized he'd held his breath and let it out with a slow whistle. "Jeezuz Christ."

He covered the face back up, and clenching his latest bit of discarded love, he turned back down the hill to the Hotel he'd called home the past six years.

Fearsome poured himself a glass of bourbon, took a swig from the bottle, and fumbled the cap back on, his eyes never leaving the baby on the bed.

He'd cleaned it up and wrapped it in an extra pillow-case. The umbilical cord, he'd thought, would be a problem. But it had simply fallen off, leaving a small rosebud nub slightly higher than it should have been on the baby's belly. It was hung like a brother, but he couldn't quite see it as a *he* just yet. As he'd scrubbed it down, ugly had become weird and weird had become *different*. Other than. The ears lacked definition, the nostrils were too "flappish" and the eyes, boring into him with sapient expectation, ran ghost fingers down his back.

He drained the glass in one calculated gulp and set it down. Moving to the bedside, he shifted the pillowcase as a small stream of urine arched onto his large black hands.

"Shit. You already done pissed on me." He went to the window, groaned it open, and looked down. "Skinny," he yelled.

The young man stood and turned. "Whassup Fears?"

Fearsome dug the pack of Newports from his shirt pocket and dropped it down. "Wanna make a fast twenty?"

The street kid nodded.

"Good . . . come on up. Quietly."

He grabbed the baby and a pillow, setting it up in the scum-coated tub. He pulled the bathroom door shut as Skinny rapped softly.

"What you got in here?" he asked as Fearsome opened the door a crack, leaving the chain in place.

"Never you mind. And you keep quiet about this." He shoved a fifty into a scabby hand.

"I saw you come in in a hurry, man."

"Yeah. Got the shits eatin' your Mamma. Now get on up to the Rite Aid and get me some diapers."

Skinny laughed. "They don't make 'em in your size, Fears."

"Not for me, fuck-stick. Small diapers." He paused, hearing the strangeness of it all in his voice. "*Baby*-diapers."

"What?"

"Just get them."

"Why?"

He spun his lie fast as ever. Lies had saved his life as far back as he could remember. "My . . . uh . . . my grandson's gonna be staying with me awhile. Only we gotta keep it quiet. Ballsy'd have a fit he knew I had a kid here."

"Grandson? I didn't know you had a grandson."

Neither did Fearsome. At least not for sure – but he might. Standley'd be what? Twenty-one now? He shook off the math of too many years. "Just get the diapers for me, Skinny."

Fearsome shut the door and turned to the bathroom. Halfway back to the baby a word fell into his mind with the splash of a well-aimed stone.

Hunger.

"What the hell?" He looked around the room, sure of the tiny voice.

Hunger. Now.

"Holy shit on a poop-sicle stick." He yanked open the bathroom door, knees weak. Three eyes blinked up at him like midnight flashers. He jumped to the open window, hollering. "Skinny!"

The kid stopped, midway across the street. Fearsome ripped out another fifty from his wad, crumpled it into a tight ball of green, and pitched it to waiting hands. "Get food, too. And . . . a bottle."

"Food? What kinda food?"

"Jesus, Skinny, *I* don't know. Ask someone for God's sake."

Skinny shook his head and moved off.

As he shut the window, a yowling racket filled his head, punctuated again and again. *Hunger. Now. Hunger. Now. Hunger. Now.*

"God-Damn-Almighty-Fucking-Christ." Fearsome clawed at his temples and staggered to the bathroom. "I got it. I got it. Hunger. Now." The jackhammering subsided and the little mouth puckered into a grin.

Thirty minutes slipped by and Skinny returned, his arms full of Rite Aid bags. Fearsome had to open the door to get everything in. As he took the plastic sacks, Skinny pushed by before he could stop him.

"Grandson, eh? Fearsome, you old dog. Let's see the little tyke." Skinny looked around the room. "Had me a baby nephew once."

Fearsome intersected him at the bathroom door, torn between rooting through the bags and ousting his unwelcome guest.

"Yeah. That's nice, Skinny. Got my change?"

"Sure. But I wanna see the baby."

No believe me you don't, he thought. "Not such a good idea." He needed another lie fast. "He's . . . he's got birth defects."

"Doesn't surprise me. Genetics and all."

"Fuck you, Skinny."

Skinny handed over a mess of bills and loose change. "Already kept mine," he said.

"Good deal."

"So?"

"So what?"

"I wanna see the baby." His voice had that whiny tone to it.

Another voice dropped into his head: *Hunger. Now.*

Skinny's face nearly slid to the floor. "What was that?"

"I said: He's hungry now. Maybe tomorrow. And I'll maybe have another twenty for you, too. Lord knows what else I might need."

"I've fed babies before — "

Fearsome grabbed Skinny's arm as gently as he could and escorted him to the door. "Tomorrow. Maybe."

Skinny's eyes lit up. "Promise?"

"Yeah, yeah. Now let me feed this kid, okay?"

He pushed Skinny through the door and shut it, working the chain. Then as the clamor started up again behind his eyes, he rummaged through Pampers and Gerber jars until he found the bottles and formula. He dumped a can in to the tin coffeepot on his hot plate and waited, memory rushing in like a belated tide.

He'd met Marsha the week after he got out of the Pen. She'd been dancing her way through college at a strip-joint in Chicago's steamier downtown. She was a young, scrawny white kid and his two degrees and life of crime had mesmerized her.

They'd shacked up for just a few months when she announced the coming baby.

At first, he'd panicked, tried to talk her into an abortion, but as her belly swelled he'd settled in easy as sin. Held her as she cried after telling her folks he was black. Took a second job so she could quit dancing. Even gave up weed and booze, though he'd missed them fiercely during his twenty year "vacation."

He measured her labor by the three packs he'd smoked outside the hospital, and raced in stinking like Newports and two days of sweat to hold his infant son.

They named him Standley — the name that had been intended for him — and they settled into their one bedroom apartment in the Projects.

The itch came on him again, there, as the bills piled up. He started lifting cars again for easy money and when Terrence Champion went down, the bastard squealed and nearly took the rest of them with him. Fearsome lit out for New York in the dead of night, kissing his girl and baby goodnight and goodbye as they slept.

He never went back to Chicago again, but he called sometimes when he was too drunk or too high to stop himself. When he had cash, he sent it, and Marsha's Christmas cards followed him slowly around the country for twenty years, sometimes catching up to surprise him.

These days, from her last cards, she worked at some firm in Chicago. Marsha Jones, Attorney at Law. Never married, but she'd taken and then kept his name nonetheless.

Her cards had stopped mentioning Little Stan a long time ago.

Fearsome tested the formula on his wrist and winced. "Shit. Hot, hot, hot."

He ran the bottle under cold water and picked up the baby. Its eyes locked on his and it opened its mouth expectantly. It looked savagely triumphant. "Hold your horses, little man. Don't wanna burn yourself."

He picked his way across the room to a ratty recliner crowded in the corner. Cradling the baby, he put the nipple to its mouth.

After a few tentative sucks, the baby spit it out, its face caving in as it purpled a deeper shade. *Salt.*

Fearsome shook his head. "What?"

Salt. He remembered the chemistry courses he'd taken in prison on the path to his first degree. He saw the images forming in his mind: NaCl, like a movie from school.

"Salt?"

Salt.

Putting the baby in the crook of his arm he climbed to his feet and went to the dresser. He found three packets of McDonald's salt and tore them open, dumping them into the bottle and shaking it up.

Seated again, the baby drained the bottle and burped loudly as Fearsome patted its back.

"Good one."

Then, he taped on a diaper and tucked the baby into his bed. "You gotta have a name, baby. So what you like?" Two of the baby's eyes closed, the third blinked rapidly, struggling to stay open.

Fearsome ran his hand over the baby's scaly, bare scalp, rubbing it lightly. "How about Standley?" He smiled. "My little man Stan."

Curling up beside the newest piece in his collection, Fearsome fell lightly into sleep as the Seattle skies leaked rain onto the street outside his window.

*

His own mother had named him Standley before she died, but his grandmother had intercepted the doctors before they could complete the birth certificate. When they'd questioned her, she'd told him later, she'd put on her best "pissed off black woman" look, put her hands on her hips and told them: "The Good Lord done see fit to take my one baby and give me another. If'n I'm gonna raise 'im, then by the Lord's Mercy, I'm gonna name 'im, too." And so they scratched out Standley and wrote in Fearsome under her approving eye.

When he was six, she told him that story. Afterwards, she told him what his name meant.

"Fearsome," she said, "A name is a powerful good or a powerful harm. The Good Book says a good name is more precious than ointment. And the Book is filled with meaningful names."

They sat on the porch in her swing, rocking to the sounds of the "only white boy as could ever sing" Elvis Presley. She was ancient to him, larger than life.

"In life, boy, you gotta know when to be *fierce* and when to *fear*. That's what your name is. Don't forget it."

But by thirteen, he feared nothing. He started with cars, then petty B&E. The gig at the First National, at sixteen, was *supposed* to be easy. But it had all gone wrong and when the man at the door grabbed the barrel of the shotgun, Fearsome squeezed the trigger and skirted a death penalty by claiming tearfully that it had gone off accidentally and pleading the ignorance of his misguided youth. One of his many life-saving lies. His grandmother's heart attack in the courtroom hadn't hurt and he'd been given life.

Caged, he became fiercer but learned to dodge the Queens and the Klan. Got his degrees, put on a good show for The Man, and got out at twenty years, thirty-six and alone in the world.

Three times the voice blasted his head and three times he stirred awake and fed his baby. When he heard the pounding rain at six, he re-counted his cash and decided to skip the morning ferry terminals.

Real Change newspaper — produced and distributed by Seattle's homeless — had given him his break from crime. He made enough to stay in clothes, groceries, weed and booze. The hotel was almost as expensive as an apartment, but close to the swarming suits and skirts that provided his livelihood.

With Christmas nearing, he could miss a beat. People would give him twenties and watches at Christmas, a small price to pay for their white, middle class privilege.

He waited until nine, checked the sleeping baby and slipped down to the sloop. Skinny waited, his cup half full of coins. The coffee girl wasn't at her cart. No free coffee today.

"Hey Skinny."

Skinny grinned, his teeth yellow. "Hey gramps."

"Wanna make another twenty?"

"Diapers and formula?"

"Formula, toys and . . . salt. A big thing of it."

"Salt?"

"Don't ask." He shoved some bills into Skinny's cup.

"What about a binky? Babies love binkys."

"What the fuck's a binky?"

"You know . . . something to stick in their mouths to suck on. When they're crying and shit."

"Just take your faggoty ass up to Rite Aid before I put my size eleven in your mouth to suck on."

Skinny laughed. "Okay, okay."

As he walked away, a thought struck Fearsome. "Skinny?"

"Yeah?"

"Get the kid a pacifier, too."

Skinny crossed the street shaking his head and mumbling as he went.

When Skinny knocked an hour later Fearsome didn't have the heart to wake up little Standley. He cracked the door.

Skinny pushed the sack through, then the change. He looked nervous. "Some suits around the park," he said. "Lookin' for a baby."

This was one of those times to be afraid. Kidnapping was a felony charge and no one would see it any other way. "Suits?"

Skinny nodded.

"Cops?"

"I don't think so. They don't walk like cops."

Fearsome peeled off another twenty and pushed it through. "Just keep quiet about this, okay? It's my grandson . . . visiting up from Tacoma. Got it?"

Skinny hesitated. "I don't want your money. I'll keep quiet. Only . . . "

"What?"

"Can't I just see him?" Fearsome was a sucker for pathetic faces, and Skinny worked him over like a prison yard brawler.

"I don't think that'd be such a good idea."

"Ah . . . come on, you old fart. I oughta at least know *who* I'm covering for. "

"And you can keep your yap shut?" He was suddenly thinking of Champion all those years ago.

Skinny held up two fingers. "Scout's honor, dude. Swear to God."

Fearsome scowled, paused, then unchained the door. "Five minutes. And not a word, Skinny, or *I* swear to God I'll open you up in your sleep like a Santa Claus present."

Skinny's face beamed as he fell through the doorway. Fearsome stepped aside and pointed to the bundle on the bed.

"Oh what a cute . . . Holy-fuck-me-Jesus!" Skinny stepped back, and said it again, this time in a quiet voice. "Holy-fuck-me-Jesus."

"I know . . . he's no looker, that's for damn sure."

Skinny stared, mouth working for words.

"But he . . . well, he sorta *grows* on you. Isn't that right, my little man Stan?"

Three black dots flashed open on the baby's face.

"He's got three eyes."

"Yeah," Fearsome said. "The better to see you with." He laughed at his own joke.

"Genetics," Skinny said. "Figures an ugly fuck like you would have fucked up grandkids."

"Welcome's worn, Skinny. I'll need you tomorrow."

After Skinny left quickly, Fearsome lifted the baby and danced him around the room. He paused at their reflection in the bathroom mirror and he held the baby up so its grayish face partially eclipsed his own dark face. The scars, the broken nose from twenty years of prison life, juxtaposed against the baby's innocent, misshapen, three-eyed head.

"You're not so bad, my little man Stan. Not so bad at all."

*

The next day brought more cold December rain and Fearsome sent Skinny off for baby clothes at Nordstrom's. He'd already gone through his pocket wad and dipped into his rainy day wad, a rubber banded bundle of bills between his mattress and his box spring.

"Make sure you get him a stocking cap," he'd told Skinny.

By afternoon, little Standley was ready to roll. The stocking cap nicely covered the third eye and strange ears. The nose could hide behind the pacifier but could also be explained easier than the rest.

With the baby in his arms, the cash rolled in. Half the people didn't even bother with taking the papers, which kept him happy — he paid a quarter for each and every extra was one more he could sell.

He made rent in two hours. Groceries in three. Booze and weed money. He looked at the baby as they walked home, the sky clearing finally.

"Goddamn," he told the wriggling, hungry bundle. "No more weed or booze."

Midway to the hotel, the voice grabbed him again. He found himself getting used to it.

Feeer. Zum. Hunger. Now.

Pride flooded him. "Did you just say my name?"

The baby blinked up and him and mewled.

Feer-zum. Fear.

"Yeah, that's right, little man. Sometimes you gotta be fierce. And sometimes you gotta fear." He chuckled and the yowling started, louder than ever, dull butter knives grinding into his brain.

Behind the pain, he saw a black car, shrouded.

He looked up in time to see two dark suits hustling Skinny into an even darker sedan.

"Fear," he whispered, and dodged into the shadows, his brain furiously spinning lies and escape routes.

Back in the hotel room, he dragged his military surplus duffle from the closet. "I'm not giving you up, my little man Stan." He caught himself realizing how close he'd come to saying *again*.

Again. He remember the way his son had smelled the night he left Chicago but he could never remember what he looked like.

He dug the Glad Bag from beneath the bed. It was nearly full, his collection of discarded love. He knew he should clean it out, even leave it all behind. The baby was enough to take. But he couldn't and he opened the bag.

Propping Stan the Man up against his folded knees, Fearsome pulled each piece from the bag, the flowers, the ring, the cards, the poems scribbled on napkins, and passed them before the baby's three eyes for approval. He talked slowly in a low voice, explaining the meaning behind each bit from his collection.

The last piece he pulled out was a tattered picture. He held the photo in his hands like a wounded butterfly, then held it in front of the baby.

"My boy. My . . . other . . . boy."

The baby gurgled and cooed. *Feerzum. Good.*

Fearsome smiled. "Not so good, little man." He tickled the baby's chin. "Maybe finding you was the greatest good I ever done. Or the greatest good ever done me. I don't rightly know."

Ten minutes later, he headed down the stairs as quickly as an old man with an armful could move. Ballsy waited at the counter.

"You got rent for me, Jones?"

"Yeah, yeah." He shifted the open duffle bag so the baby, lying on top of his clothes, couldn't be seen. *Now you be quiet little man.*

Quiet, the baby answered.

"What was that?" Ballsy asked.

"Nothing dude." He peeled off two hundred dollars from his newly replenished pocket wad. "This should square us up."

"You moving out?"

"Yeah. Time to move on. Sister's in New York . . . think I'll head there. Haven't ridden a train in years." The lies rolled easily off his tongue.

"Well, best of luck to you."

"Thanks." He moved towards the door and opened it.

"Hey, Jones," Ballsy called out. "Hold up a second. Got something here for you." Ballsy came out from behind the counter, a bright red envelope in his hand. "This came for you yesterday." Seeing his hands were full, Ballsy tucked it into his coat pocket.

"Thanks, man."

"No problem. You take it easy."

"You too."

He moved through the door and into the night. The temperature had dropped but Seattle winters had always been mild. Christmas lights sparkled and shoppers moved towards crosswalks even in this part of town. Fearsome would miss it.

As he lost himself in the crowd, he saw a squad car and a black sedan slip past silently. He looked over his shoulder and watched them slide to the curb in front of the hotel. "Sorry Skinny," he said. "I knew you'd talk."

Talk.

He lowered the duffle bag enough that he could peek in on the baby. "You and me, we'll be just fine."

Jerry had been the best when it came to new identities. Fearsome had used him twice before age and honesty had brought him back to his real name. He'd retired to some small town outside of Medford but he was still connected.

Fearsome hitched his way to Portland in the night and fell into an Econolodge bed after feeding Standley.

A knock at the door awakened him.

Covering the baby, he went to the door. "Who's there?"

No answer. Then, the knock came again.

"Look, Goddamn it, I'm not opening the door until . . . "

But suddenly he *was* opening the door and stepping back as a man stepped through.

He could have been a movies star. Perfect hair, perfect teeth, piercing blue eyes, a deep tan and athletic build. He wore khaki slacks and a yellow shirt — summer clothing.

"Hello, Mr. Jones," Mr. California Sun Tan smiled and extended his hand. Fearsome tried to ignore it but found himself shaking it. Again to choose: Fear or fierce . . . which response? He felt both.

"Who the *fuck* are you and what do you want?" Only, he knew what the man wanted and Fearsome was already wondering if he could take this guy or not. He had youth but Fearsome had meanness.

"You have something of mine."

"I don't know what the hell you're talking about." He stayed between the man and the bed where little Standley slept.

The man's face suddenly turned inside out and went gray. Flappish nostrils flared and a third eye, black as spilled ink, unstuck its lid from the yellow ooze that coated it.

Fearsome felt a warm rush of thought streak through his brain towards the bed behind him. He heard a pleasant cooing and another stream of warmth, this one tenuous and less focused, returned.

"He is the savior of our race and the bridge between our worlds."

"Well if he's so damn important why'd she dump him in the trash?"

Mr. California Sun Tan's face fell back together with a white toothy smile. "She had no idea what he meant. We had hoped to intercept her but were . . . delayed."

"So now you're just gonna take him away?"

The man nodded slowly.

"I won't let you." He raised his fists. "I won't *Goddamn* let you."

The man blinked and Fearsome sat down heavily on the floor, suddenly out of breath. "Forgive my use of force, Mr. Jones."
The man stepped past him, gathered up the baby and headed for the door.

Feerzum. Good.

After they left, twenty years of tears broke through his head and he sobbed himself to sleep on the floor. He awoke in the early afternoon, stiff and sore.

He went to the bed and stared down at the empty pillowcase. "Left his pacifier," he muttered, picking it up. He took it to the Glad bag and tucked it inside carefully. Then, he dug through his collection, poking each bit with his finger until he found his son's picture.

Digging Marsha's card from his pocket, he ripped it open. Sure enough another business card, another hastily scribbled "Call sometime — let me know you're alive."

He sat on the edge of the bed, picked up the phone, and started pressing buttons. The tears started again but he grabbed hold of them fiercely and held them at bay.

Her secretary put him through without asking who it was. Maybe she knew or maybe it was the Friday before Christmas and anyone who called was somebody important just now. He coughed a little and sniffed when he heard Marsha's voice fill up the phone.

"Hey baby," Fearsome Jones said. "How you been?"

The line crackled in the midst of her hesitation. "Fears? Oh my God. Is that you? Where are you?"

"Portland."

"I haven't heard from you in . . . "

"Too long," he said, finishing her dangling sentence. "I know. And I'm sorry." He waited, letting the words soak in. He waited, hoping she would say something. She didn't. "Anyway, what with it being Christmas and all I was kind of hopin' you could put me in touch with Stan."

"I would if I could, Fears. He's gone. I have no idea where. Last I heard, he was in Atlanta." Her words tumbled out fast. "Fell in with a bad crowd and lit out one night. Sound familiar?"

Fearsome felt a second wave of loss roll over him. "Atlanta?"

"That was two years ago. He could be anywhere."

Anywhere. "Well, thanks, babe."

"Fears, I — " Her voice had that tone in it that said she wanted to talk more, but he cut her off in a quiet voice.

"Merry Christmas, Marsha." He set the phone down. Another batch of tears pried at his eyes, nose and throat. He coughed them back, running a hand over his face. Time to be fierce.

"Atlanta," Fearsome said to the empty room. Then, gathering up his things, he let himself out into the night in search of a train station.

THE DOOM OF LOVE
IN SMALL PLACES

We met at work.

She looked at me when she walked into the room and I was immediately untethered. Pretty brunette in a red dress who *knew* she was pretty, knew that the thigh-high slit along the side of her skirt and the haphazard plummet of her neckline were reefs where men could be shipwrecked. Her flashing eyes sang danger and peace in two-part harmony. Each step towards me delivered the unrelenting clip-clap, clip-clap of heels across a tile floor so brightly polished that it reflected back her matching red panties.

I held my breath and waited to catch fire from the sight of her.

"Central Supply," she said when she stood in front of my desk. Her voice melted the crystalline sugar on my glazed donut. I watched it puddle and pool on the paper napkin.

I swallowed. "That's me, Miss."

She smiled. "Just you?"

I nodded. Now my styrofoam cup started bending from the heat of her, tilting precariously. The coffee inside it bubbled. "Just me."

She leaned over my desk and bent slightly, tipping her breasts toward me. They hung, held in place by a red bra. "I need more love," she said. "We've run completely out on the fifth floor."

The hair on my arms curled in on itself, the stink of burning in my nose alongside her floral perfume and her peppermint breath. I forced my eyes to her face, squinting to see her through the haze of smoke.

"Are you okay?" she asked.

My tongue expanded in my mouth, swelling to block my words. I forced it back to normal size. "You must be new?"

She threw back her shoulders and tossed her hair. "Not so much." Her teeth shined now, fine and white and straight. "We just don't use a lot of supplies anymore on the fifth floor. I think the last person they sent down was Bill when they ran out of hope."

I remembered Bill. He'd dragged himself in here and died in the corner before he could tell me what he wanted. It wasn't the first time. Wouldn't be the last. "I remember Bill," I said. "Good chap."

"Dead chap," she said.

I shrugged and motioned to the chair beside my desk. "It happens a lot around here."

She sat and crossed her legs. The slit fell open like a theater curtain. Long, slender legs, white heat shimmering off them to singe my eyebrows.

"So you need some love," I said, opening my card file and thumbing through the microfiche.

She folded her hands in her lap. "Please."

"How much?"

"Well, as much as you can spare."

I slipped the flimsy plastic film into the reader and hit the switch. A blue field swimming with white letters blurred into focus with the turn of a knob.

I watched her out of the corner of my eye. She pulled self-consciously at her bra-strap and fidgeted. "Elevators still out?" I asked, trying to make small talk.

She nodded. "Board says they're not repairing them, either."

"Bloody barkers," I said. Of course, she had no way of knowing that I was the one who told them not to repair the elevators. Working elevators meant the rapid movement of supplies up and down the building. I'd sent the memo in, followed all the usual forms. Naturally, they'd listened to me.

They had to.

I moved the arm of the microfiche reader, sliding the film over the light. "Love," I said. "Any particular size or shape?"

"Love comes in shapes and sizes?" she asked.

"All," I said.

She answered me with a laugh.

"We're out," I lied. I had a smallish off-brand muzzled and leashed in the back of the storeroom that I'd left off the inventory. "But we could order some."

She stood, came around my desk so she could read over my shoulder. She leaned in to me and I felt her breath on my neck. "How long?"

I shrugged. "They'll send it through the canal. Drive it in by truck from there. Then there's the pass. Eight weeks maybe?"

"That long for something as simple as love?"

I swallowed and nodded, felt her press against my shoulder as I turned in my chair. "How much should I order?" I picked up a pencil and a requisition tablet.

Her eyes narrowed in thought. "I don't know."

"Well, is it a small space or a large space?"

She looked confused. "Pardon?"

"The space," I said, "where you need the love?"

"Oh. I don't know. Is it important?"

I nodded. "It is. Too much love in a small space, it'd drive you mad."

"Why is that?" she asked.

"I think it's because love rapidly expands, depleting the oxygen and eradicating all life but its own."

"But oh," she said, "what sweet madness it would be." She pursed her lips. "Eight weeks? It took me three to get here."

"Damned elevators," I said. "But you don't need to go back. You can stay here with me. I have an extra cot in the back office."

Clip-clap, clip-clap across the tile. Heat receded as she paced away. She laughed. "You're a troll," she said. "Why ever would I *stay* here with you?"

She had a point. I *was* a troll. Of sorts. Supplies or bridges, it matters little. Trolls guard. I thought about my donut. I thought about the love leashed somewhere behind me. I thought about the girl in red *everything* pacing the sub-sub-basement clerk's station at the foot of the storeroom doors, three weeks down the stairs and ladders of the Bureaucracy.

I grimaced. "I don't *know* why you'd stay here with me."

I snuck a glance at her. Creamy white thigh peeking out, smooth curves, legs scissoring. I stood up and lumbered toward the phone on the wall. I lifted the receiver and held it to my ear, ringing the crank. "Gallingwise Seven Six Three, please," I told the operator when I heard her cut in.

When Central Stores picked up, I read off the requisition numbers, ordering an abstract by numeric coding. They gave me release order numbers that I scribbled in blue pencil onto the requisition forms.

I tore off the sheets and gave her the carbon copies. "Eight weeks, they said, give or take. You're still welcome to stay. I've got running water, too." I sat back down at my desk, chair groaning beneath my weight.

Her eyebrows lifted. "Running water? Hot or cold?"

I smiled. "Both."

She tossed her hair again and struck a pose. "Do you have any idea how hard it is to get *this* look out of a bucket of secondhand washwater?" Or rusty water from a broken pipe, I thought. I'd watched her through my periscope that morning before she tackled the last half mile or so of her journey down, before I knew I was her destination.

I could have her, I thought. I could have her here for eight weeks with me only it wouldn't be because of me. It would be because of the makeshift tub, the series of pipes and tubes and hoses tapping into the central boiler. Little comforts I'd rigged to make my job more tolerable. But the *because* didn't matter.

"It's that bad up there, is it?" Of course, I knew that it was.

She rolled her eyes. "Fifth floor is a wreck. Frankly, none of the others between here and there are all that wonderful, either."

"But I'll bet the seventh floor is just fine." Of course, I also knew *this*. That was the Board's floor and I kept it that way just as I kept the other floors the way *they* were. Memos flying from my pen. Keep the Machine under a constant state of stress and alarm, taut with opportunities for improvement . . . just like the world beyond our little game of government.

"Have you ever been to the seventh floor?" she asked.

"Wouldn't want to," I said. "Incompetent gits, the lot of them."

A moment of fear washed her face and she blushed at it. She looked around slowly. "I can't believe you *said* that."

"Why? It's not as if they can hear." And, I told myself, it's not as if it weren't true. They *were* incompetent. That's why they needed me.

She paced some more. "Running water and a cot?"

"And donuts," I said, "Delivered every Tuesday." I paused. "I might even have some extra liquid hand soap lying about. Makes a passable bubble bath."

Her smile shown out not just from her face but from every part of her, beaming out from the tips of her fingers and the ends of her hair and the curves of her hips and breasts, the line of her legs and neck, the exhilaration of her eyes.

"I'll stay," she said.

"I'll call up to five and let them know."

"No need," she said. "The phones are out past the third floor."

"That's unfortunate," I said. But of course, I'm the one who kept them out. "I'll send up a memo then." I grabbed a memo form and rummaged through the box near my desk for an undented pneumatic carrier. "It'll take longer, though."

She curtsied. "Thank you, kind sir." She paused, her brow furrowed. "I don't believe we've been properly introduced. I'm Harmony Sheffleton," she said, extending her hand.

I shook it. Her hand disappeared in my own massive fist. "Drum Farrelley."

"Drum as in Drummond?" she asked.

I nodded. "Glad to know you." And I tried not to smile, tried not to show her that I was as excited about her staying as she was, though for different reasons. But I failed. I felt my fat lips twitch into a grin. "Let's get you that bath," I told her.

And that was how we met.

Time moved at measured pace as it does in all Bureaucracies. And here, in the tangled, loose ends of the Great Red-Tape Wrap-Up, there was really not much work to do anymore. Inventory and a bit of paperwork, filing and a bit of maintenance. Few came for supplies these days and I liked it that way. It gave me time to admire my guest.

Her first bath set the tempo for our time together. It quickly became a daily ritual for her to lay in the tub up to her neck in warm bubbles while I sat on the other side of the cracked door. We kept the door between us and we talked. Mostly about work but sometimes about life because the two were so intricately intertwined.

"My job is dull beyond measure, utterly uninteresting," she said during her third bath. "But yours is quite fascinating. Tell me more, Drum?"

And I did.

Our first week slipped past. On Tuesday, the Rationer came with his donuts, unlabelled tin cans and packets of instant coffee. He even had a few mealy apples that I swapped a case of obsolete toner cartridges for. Harmony clapped her hands with delight when

I showed her, then suddenly because serious as she lowered her voice.

"Won't you get in trouble for that?" she asked.

"For *what*?"

"Those toner cartridges — " she started.

"Were completely worthless and taking up valuable and much-needed storage space," I finished for her. "Just part of the job."

She raised one of the apples to her mouth. I watched her lips part, watched her shiny white teeth slide into the pock-marked red skin. It's my heart, I thought. She's biting into my heart and in seven weeks there won't even be a core to show it was ever there. The tube whistled and groaned, a battered carrier dropped into the cradle.

Harmony stepped towards it, setting the apples on my desk. "May I?"

I nodded.

She opened the carrier, pulled out the memo, unfolded it, read it. I watched her eyes move back and forth, her lips now tightly pressed together. She looked up. "They'll expect me back with the love once it arrives. Until then, I should make myself useful to you down here."

She crumpled the memo and moved towards the furnace.

"We usually file all correspondence," I said as she tossed it in.

"Sorry. I didn't think it was important."

"It probably isn't," I said.

She grinned. "So after my bath, I'll make myself useful to you." She picked up the apples, stepped closer to me. My size dwarfed her.

"Any good?" I asked.

She smiled and stepped even closer, now eclipsed by the shadow of me. I could smell Grundy's Liquid Anti-Bacterial Hand Soap rising from her skin in waves but it could've been summer sun on a field of roses. I could see the swell of her breasts as they struggled to fit a bra two sizes too small, the white skin disappearing into a trace of red lace. She lifted the apple, the meat glistening where her teeth torn into its skin. The apple rose slowly and I watched her wrist, her fingers, her arm as they traveled upwards towards me with it. She held it under my nose, near my snaggle-toothed mouth. "Taste and see," she said.

*

After her bath, she hung her clean clothes on the makeshift line by the boiler. I had rummaged an oversized jumpsuit from the janitorial supplies. She held the collar closed with one hand while she slung her clean dress, bra and panties over the makeshift line with the other. My own clothes from yesterday still hung there and I blushed when I saw her dainty scraps of underwear next to my tent-sized, tattered and stained boxers.

Four weeks had passed now. She'd taken twenty-nine baths. I'd sat outside the door each time, listening to the music of her movement in the water, listening to the wet slap of cloth on concrete on the days that she scrubbed her clothes.

"So what are we doing *today?*" she asked.

"Inventory, I think."

Her eyes lit up. "Can we do the abstracts this time?"

I thought about the love I'd hidden there and the small box of second-hand hope concealed behind row upon row of ennui, terror, despair and longing. I shook my head. "No, it's paper today."

She pouted. "But *I* want to do the abstracts."

I remembered the time I dropped a bottle of despair, splattering my boots with thick, black strands. I'd had to burn them eventually. "Trust me," I said. "You really don't."

"I *want* to do the *abstracts.*" She stomped her foot. Then, her mock anger collapsed on itself and she burst into a fit of giggles.

I chuckled at her. She offered a sheepish grin.

"Paper it is," she said.

The front office bell chimed and we went out, hoping it was the Rationer. He'd not shown up Tuesday for the first time in seventeen years.

Now he stood in the office, bruised and bandaged, on a Thursday.

"Black Drawlers on the stairs," he said, patting his sword. We made our trades. He threw in an extra can of potted meat as an apology and I threw in an extra box of Number 1 Pencils as a thank you. Keeping the Machine broken was one thing; Drawlers in the stairwells was another.

Harmony's eyes had gone wide. "Black Drawlers? Here?"

"Sometimes," the Rationer said as he hefted his pack into a battered wheelbarrow. "It's the season for them."

I looked at the calendar and flipped the page. He was right. After he left, his wagon wheels squealing on the tile, I looked up at her. "It *is* the season," I told her, dropping my fat finger onto the day after tomorrow.

Her eyes danced. Music thrummed from her muscles as they followed her eyes, dragging her body into a little jig.

"Do you celebrate down here?"

"Not usually. You?"

She shook her head. "We used to. I miss it."

So the next day, we made our little red hats from cotton swabs and construction paper and paste. She opened eight unlabeled cans, mixed the fruits with fruits and the vegetables with the potted meat and two fistfuls of rice. I took a screwdriver to the furnace grate and pushed the office's single faux-leather couch in front of it. We wore our hats and ate our rice stew while watching the fire sort itself out.

"Do you have a copy of the Cycle?" she asked between spoonfuls. "My mom used to read it to me every Dragon's Mass Eve."

"I know it by heart," I said.

Her eyes widened. "Drum, you surprise me. What's a troll like you doing with scripture rattling about in his head?"

I set my empty bowl on the small table between my massive feet. "I wanted to be a priest when I was younger. Spent a year in the seminary, then gave it up for all of this." I swept my arm wide to encompass our surroundings. I barked out a laugh. "My own kingdom."

She looked around. "It's a bit small." Her forehead wrinkled. "Why didn't you stay on with the seminary?"

"The world wasn't in a good place for it. Civil service seemed a better bet. Of course, this was thirty years ago. When I was closer to *your* age."

"I'm older than I look," she said. She wriggled herself closer to me. I looked down at her, inhaled the scent of her hair and skin. She put her bowl down, lay back and closed her eyes. She still radiated more heat than the fire but a month of life with her and I didn't have to worry about catching fire anymore. The deepest places in me had burned to the ground on that first day. "Will you recite it for me?" she asked.

"I haven't said it for a long time," I said.

"You'll do fine." She opened her eyes, trapped me in them briefly, then closed them again. "Please?"

I cleared my voice. "Muscles tire," I said, my voice rumbling low into the room. "Words fail." I paused to let the language set its own pace. "Faith fades." I watched her, watched her own lips moving to the words as mine did. "Fear falls." Her eyelids twitched a little. She was watching me watch her and a smile pulled at her mouth. I paused again, then closed my own eyes and gave myself to language and mythology. "In the Sixteenth Year of the Sixteen Princes the world came to an end when the dragon's back gave out . . . "

I recited it all the way through. Afterwards, we didn't speak. Together, we lit a candle for the broken dragon upon whose back the world languishes. Then, we turned towards the north, knelt on the floor with my hands swallowing hers, and whispered a prayer for the Santaman's second coming.

Later, we ate our fruit salad and talked.

"Do you believe in the Santaman?" Harmony asked between bitefuls.

I shook my head. "Not really. I did once."

"I don't think I do, either. If he were real, he'd have come back by now."

"Maybe," I said, "he's waiting for us to figure things out for ourselves."

"Or maybe our hearts are too small for that kind of love," she said. "Like you were saying when we first met: The doom of love in small spaces. Maybe if he *were* to come back now, we'd go insane from it. Maybe this broken world is opening us up somehow, making us really, really ready for him."

"I like that," I said. It reminded me of my job. Keep the Machine in disrepair and disconnect, keep the thousands of us in the Bureaucracy inches from disaster to bring out our best and finest effort. I smiled down at her. "It has a certain poetry to it."

She bit her lip. A devilish light sparked in her eyes. "Are you ready for your gift?"

"A gift? You got me a gift?"

She nodded. "It's Dragon's Mass Eve, Drum. Of course I did. You can't celebrate Dragon's Mass without gifts."

I sighed. "I didn't get you anything. I just . . . didn't think about it." But of course I had. I'd thought about it ever since the Rationer reminded me of the day. For something like thirty years, the only things I'd ever let loose from my supply room had been the scant little I had to in order to keep my job. Except for the seventh floor, but I told myself that was just to keep the Board greased up and pliant. Still, I'd walked the aisles of my lair looking for something, anything, to give the girl in red. I'd even taken down the small box of hope, shaken a bit into my big hand, before tipping it carefully back inside.

Harmony stretched herself up on the couch. "Well, I have an idea about that," she said.

"What's that?"

She drew her face closer to mine. I could smell pear syrup on her breath; it intoxicated me. "I'll give you my gift. And if you like it, you can give it back to me."

I frowned. "Shouldn't it be the other way around? If I *don't* like it, I give it back to you?"

She shook her head. Her hair flowed like liquid midnight when she did. "It's what *I* said."

"Okay. If I like it, I can give it back."

She pulled away, her face concerned. "Are you sure?"

"Yes."

She leaned back in.

Then she kissed me.

And because I liked it, I kissed her back.

At seven weeks, the phone rang when she was in the bath.

"I'll get it," I said.

After the call, I went back to my place by the door.

"Who was it?" she asked over the noise of the water.

I rubbed my face. I planned a lie, planned it well, then failed miserably to deliver it. "It was Central Stores," I said. "There's a bit of a problem."

"What's that? Truck break down?"

Worse, I wanted to say. Our world is out of love, it's on backorder. They sent the ship but the ship sank on a reef and the world's last love drowned in the hold. But suddenly I couldn't speak. Suddenly pin-pricks pushed at my eyes and darkness dragged at my heart. I thought about my secret stash and knew that soon I'd have to tell the truth. But for now, after a lifetime of success disappointing others, I didn't have it in me to disappoint her. "Nothing important," I said. "They're just running a bit behind. I'll send up another memo and let them know."

The door opened. She stood there in nothing but a towel that hid little. "How far behind?"

"A few more weeks."

"I'd like that," she said. "Besides, I still haven't helped you with the abstracts." She turned, poised on the tips of her toes, her dark hair plastered over her upper back and shoulders.

"Trust me," I told her. "They're pretty much the same as everything else." I snorted. "You've picked the rest of it up quite quickly. You could probably *do* this job when I retire."

She flinched; I should've wondered why.

"You're retiring?" She used the heel of her foot to push the door partly closed. From the corner of my eye, I saw brief flash as the towel dropped to the floor.

"Someday," I said. "Don't know what they'll do without me." But I *did* know. At least, I thought I did before Harmony walked into my office looking for love. Before meeting her, I'd known the place would fall entirely once I stepped down. I'd kept the Board distanced from the rest of the Bureaucracy. I'd sent them the cream and others the curds. I'd kept the Machine barely functioning but once I moved aside, our small space in the world would collapse in on itself. The other six floors would storm the seventh in a rage. But now I wondered. Maybe someone else could take my place, could prolong the inevitable until the world's groan wound its way north. And maybe — though I doubted it — maybe in the north, salvation would stir and a red-clad myth would strap on his sword, saddle up his wolf-stallion and ride south to find us and show us a new home.

My sudden collision with truth and passion unsettled me.

"What are you going to do?" She asked. Now I could hear her scrubbing her clothes. "When you retire, I mean?"

"I used have it all planned out," I said. "I was going to cash in my pension and buy a horse. Ride west."

"Why not now?" she asked.

"Epiphany," I said.

"No, *Harmony*," she answered. "I'm Harmony."

"No," I said. "I *had* an epiphany."

She laughed. "That's my sister's name. So when did you have this epiphany?"

A minute ago, I didn't say. "Doesn't matter."

The door opened. She stood in front of me, freshly scrubbed, wearing the oversized jumpsuit. She hadn't kissed me since Dragon's Mass Eve. And I hadn't tried to kiss her. But once in awhile, in the midst of our days, there would be a pause, a moment where we simply stood still and looked at one another.

We had our moment and then we went to work.

On the morning of the seventh day of our eighth week, she skipped her bath and wore her red dress instead of the coveralls.

"It's time for the truth, Drum," she told me, "no matter how hard it is."

She'd caught me. I didn't know how. Maybe she'd read it on my face all this time. I'd lived by lying my entire life but somehow she saw past it and knew me. I put my head in my hands.

"I'm sorry, Harmony," I said.

She looked surprised. "What are you sorry about?"

"That call from Central Stores last week. The shipment isn't running a few weeks late."

"Drum, that's not important."

"No," I said. "You're right. It's time for the truth. There's no love coming. There's none to send. The ship went down, all hands lost." I paused. More truth pushed at me. "But that's not all," I said.

Her eyes blazed at me. "I didn't come here for the love, Drummond."

And suddenly, I realized what she meant about it being time for the truth. Time for *her* truth, not mine. Time to uncover *her* lie and lay it out for me to see.

"I'm not even from the fifth floor." She waited. The fierceness in her eyes abated, became a smolder then ashes mixed with rain. "I'm from the seventh."

I growled. It started in my belly and worked its way into my throat and past bared teeth. "You lied to me. You're from the Board, aren't you?"

She nodded, her eyes wandered to the clock. "The memo should be here any minute." The rain drowned the ashes. Her lip quivered and she started to cry. Her shoulders shook.

I wanted to grab her and shake her, toss her about like the toy she made me feel like. "All that interest in my work? All that *making yourself useful?*"

She nodded. "I'm your replacement." She looked up, her face glistening from tears and snot. "When they ran the ad, I applied for it. I wanted to make things better. *They* wanted to make things better, too."

The pneumatic tube clanked and groaned. A heavy carrier dropped into the cradle.

I turned away from it. I opened the carrier and a battered gold watch fell out, far too small for my thick wrist. A card fell out, too.

I ripped it open and read the message. Gratitude of the Board and all that rubbish. Warmest wishes for a happy retirement. Utmost confidence in Miss Sheffleton's capabilities.

I looked over at her. Her dress rippled with her sobs.

She saw me looking. "I don't want it anymore, Drum."

I didn't say anything. I turned around and left.

She found me sitting in the back of the storeroom. I sat on the floor, stroking love's soft underbelly. It rolled its eyes at me and tried to lick its lips behind the muzzle.

I'd decided it wasn't so bad after all. I'd given my thirty years. I'd even decided that her betrayal was a blessing in disguise, jarring me out of a rut I'd lain in for too long.

I felt her hand on my shoulder. "Will you ride west?" she asked.

I shook my head. "I don't know."

"Stay with me," she said. "Don't retire. We can work it together." She waited. When I didn't answer, she added: "I want you to stay."

I scratched behind love's ears. "Would we keep things the same or let them fall apart?"

"Neither," she said. "We'd make them better. It's time to try a new way."

She knelt down, her own hands petting the love. It twisted to get more of her. "What's this?" she asked.

More truth, I thought. "It's love," I said. "I lied before about being out. I just wanted you to stay here with me." I looked at her. "I was tired of being alone."

"Imagine it," she said. "You and me. We fix the elevator and the phones, first. Get the supply chain running so that Facilities can take over the repairs. Before you know it, we'd have a different world."

"And," I said, "we'd have some love and a little hope."

She grinned. "You've got hope here, too?"

I smiled. "Only a little."

She kissed me for the second time. I kissed her back.

"Okay?" she asked.

"Okay," I answered.

I felt along love's muzzle and found its buckles with my fingers. Harmony reached over and slipped love from its leash.

SUMMER IN PARIS,
LIGHT FROM THE SKY

*Life is marked by intersections and measured by the choices we make at
each pause in our journey. I am fortunate to have made a good choice at
the right time but more than that, many before me did the same and so the
stones were set in the path long before the day of my birth. Will you not
come after me and walk the stones so many before you have helped to put
in place?*

>   —Adolf Hitler
>   Commencement Address, Yale University
>   School of Human Rights and Social Justice, 1969

Adolf Hitler came to Paris in June 1941 feeling the weight of
his years in his legs and the taste of a dying dream in his
mouth. He spent most of that first day walking up and down the
Champs Elysées, working the stiffness out of his bones and muscles
while he looked at the shops and the people. Some of the dull ache
was from the wooden benches on the train from Hamburg; most of
it was age. And beneath the discomfort of his body, his soul ached
too.

He'd never been here before, he thought as the Parisians slipped
past in the noon-time sun. He snorted at the revelation. A fine painter
you are, he told himself.

Of course, it was only for the summer. Then Paris . . . and
painting, he imagined, would slip quietly to the back row of his
memory. He would return to Berlin and take a job for the government buying supplies he would never see for people that he would
never know. In the end, he realized, he would become his father's
son and live out the rest of his days as a quiet civil servant.

Alois Hitler had been a hard man, even a cruel man, before the accident. But death up close can change the hardest heart and after nearly a month in the hospital, he returned to his family with a deep faith and a sense of compassion for all humankind . . . especially his children. He listened. He prayed. He studied St. Francis, St. John of the Cross, Meister Eckhard and even Buddha. He became gentle and warm toward his wife and their five children. Until the very end, he encouraged Adolf's dreams. And when he died, still working as a customs official for Napoleon IV's puppet chancellor, he left behind a small but sufficient inheritance to finance his son's art.

By living frugally and occasionally taking odd jobs, Adolf stretched it as far as he could. He'd even set aside a bit for his old age. But come September, he'd decided, it was time to put away the canvas and brush. Time, at fifty-two, to put away childish things.

Adolf sighed.

And then something happened. He stood in the shadow of the Arc de Triomphe, dwarfed by that first Napoleon's grandiose gesture of complete victory, dwarfed by the size of his own dreams in the shadow of over thirty years of failure. He stood, feeling his breath catch in the back of his throat and his eyes turning to water. And suddenly, he was no longer alone.

A girl — a pretty girl, a dark girl dressed in ragged clothing — separated from a crowd of passing students. She walked up to him without a word and kissed him hard on the mouth, pressing her body against him while she fastened a flower into the button-hole of his Prussian great coat. After the kiss, she vanished back into the crowd.

Adolf licked his lips, tasting the apples from her mouth. He took in a great breath, smelling the rose water from her skin and the sunshine from her hair. He listened to the sound of his racing heart and the drum-beat it played. He felt the warmth of her where it had touched him.

It was his first impression of Paris.

His second impression was the perpetually drunk American, Ernie Hemingway.

After a day of wandering aimlessly, as the sun dropped behind the horizon and the sky grew deep purple, Adolf found de Gaulle's and went inside because he heard American music.

Americans had always fascinated him. He'd met a few — not many because they tended to have little use for Europe. America was an entire continent without kings or emperors or royalty of any kind. A place where they selected their own President every four years and where any one of the ninety states from Brazil to New-foundland was a thriving nation in and of itself united by democracy, progress and freedom.

A middle aged man stood on the bar leading the room in a bawdy tune. He worked the song like a conductor, waving a pistol instead of a baton, and scattered drinkers around the room joined in the song. A man in a ratty suit crouched over the piano, mashing the keys with his fingers with a rag-time flair. Adolf watched and smiled. The man sang too fast and slurred too much for the lyrics to make much sense but the gestures and pelvic thrusts conveyed the gist of it.

When the song was done, the man dropped lightly to the floor amid cheers and brushed past Adolf on his way to a table at the back of the room. Adolf found an empty table near the American and sat down. The pianist launched into another song, this time in French — a language Adolf grasped better — and he blushed. Looking around, he was the only one who did.

"Are you a priest, then?" the American shouted across at him in English.

Adolf looked up. "I beg pardon?"

The American grinned. "You're blushing. I thought you might be a priest."

He shook his head. "No. Not a priest."

"Well then, are you a homosexual?"

The word escaped him at first, then registered. He blushed even more, looking around for a different table to sit at. He had heard that Americans were quite forward but until now had never experienced it. "I'm sorry, sir," he said. "I'm not liking men, though I am very flattered by your . . . " He struggled to find the right word, couldn't find it, then said the closest one he *did* find. "By your . . . love."

For a moment, he thought the American might hit him. But suddenly, the American started to laugh. The laugh started low and built fast, spilling over like an over-filled bathtub. Adolf wasn't sure what to do so he offered a weak, tight smile. The American leaped up with his beer in his hand, staggered a few steps and sat heavily in the empty chair at Adolf's table.

He leaned in and Adolf could smell days of alcohol rising from his skin. "Deutsche?"

Adolf nodded. "Ja."

The American stuck out his hand. "Ernie Hemingway."

He took the hand, squeezed it firmly and pumped it once. "Adolf Hitler."

Ernie waved to the bar. "Hey, de Gaulle!"

A slim man looked up. "Oui, Monsieur Hemingway?"

"A beer for my new friend Adolf Hitler."

The bartender nodded. "Un moment, s'il vous plaît."

Then Hemingway leaned in again, his voice low. "You got any money?"

Adolf nodded. The man's fast speech and unpredictable movements made him nervous. He found himself blinking involuntarily.

"That'll save us both a bit of embarrassment."

He nodded again, not quite understanding. The bartender arrived with two pints of light, foamy beer and Hemingway raised the glass. "To life, liberty and the pursuit of happiness," he said.

"To your health," Adolf said.

"I'm afraid it's far too late for that," another voice said. The pianist — finished with his tune — pulled up a chair, flipping it around backwards and straddling it. He was a short man, wiry with curly hair gone gray, blue eyes and a brief but contagious smile. "We just have to hold out hope that somehow he'll manage to pickle himself before he begins to decompose."

Adolf didn't understand but said nothing.

"Adolf Hitler," Hemingway said, "Old Mother England's wittiest bastard child, Chuck Chaplin."

They shook hands.

"Fresh from the train?" Chuck asked in perfect German.

Adolf nodded. "Yes. This morning."

"Looking for work here? It'll be hard. You're not Jewish are you?"

"No, not Jewish. I'm a painter."

Chuck nodded. "Are you any good?"

Hitler smiled. "My English is better than my painting."

The pianist returned the smile. "And your English is atrocious."

"Your German is quite good."

Chuck grinned. "Benefit of an English education."

Ernie looked perplexed, trying to follow the rush of German in his drunken state. "What are you two going on about?"

Chuck turned to Ernie. "Drink your beer, you silly sod." Then, back to Adolf in German: "Do you have a place to stay yet?"

Adolf shook his head. "I was going to ask after a boarding house or hotel."

"Nonsense," Chuck said, switching to English. "You can stay with us. At least until you find something more suitable."

Adolf looked around again, suddenly unsure what to do. He lowered his voice. "I'm not a homosexual," he said in a quiet voice, nodding towards Ernie. "Tell him for me? In English?"

"What's he saying?" Ernie asked.

"That he admires your mustache and the light in your eyes," Chuck answered. "Particularly the way you dimple when you smile."

"Bloody British fairy," Hemingway muttered into his beer.

"That's not," Chuck said slowly and deadpan, "What your mother said to me last night."

Perhaps, Adolf thought, Paris was a mistake after all.

Very little is known of his life before the Revolution. The records and recollections of those who might have known were lost in the heavy fire-bombings during the final days of the War for Democratic Change. And the man himself rarely offered up a personal detail, despite having given over five thousand documented speeches over the span of his life. In an early American lecture, he casually mentioned coming to Paris to be a painter. In a spontaneous speech at his son's wedding, he fondly recalled a kiss in the shadow of the Arc de Triomphe. We may never know more than these scattered references. But would knowing matter? Or would it merely add to the legend of this great but humble man?
　　　　—Nicholas Freeman, Editor
　　　　　Preface, *A Kiss in the Shadow:*
　　　　　Essays on The Pre-1942 Life of Adolf Hitler,
　　　　　Harbor Light Press, Seattle, 1986

By day Hitler wandered the city with his easel and stool and pallet and canvas. At night, he sang and drank with his new friends down at de Gaulle's. He never did move out. He slept on a cot in the corner of their large loft and tapped into what little remained of his inheritance to help with expenses. Ernie and Chuck took him under their wing, showing him around the city and helping him with his English.

The economy was struggling as a massive influx of Jewish refugees fled the Russian Civil War. The Empire was already stretched thin with footholds in Africa and Indonesia. There were quiet rumors that Napoleon IV was gradually losing his grip on sanity as he entered his eighties and even quieter rumors that his military advisors and generals had plans of their own.

Still, the summer was hot and bright and one afternoon in July, Adolf looked up from painting the Arc de Triomphe and locked eyes with the girl who had kissed him there over a month earlier. She was staring at him, a slight smile pulling at her mouth.

He licked his brush and tried to resume work, suddenly uncomfortable with her wide, dark eyes. She took a step closer.

"You're no good at it," she said to him in heavily accented French. "You've gotten the colors all wrong."

He shrugged, feeling a stab of annoyance though her voice was playful. "It's how I see it."

"Perhaps you need spectacles," she said, taking another step closer.

Adolf chuckled. "And this from a girl who kisses men old enough to be her grandfather?"

"You don't look so old," she said.

"Perhaps you are the one who needs spectacles?" He looked at her. She was tall, slender, with long arms and legs. Her breasts were small but high on her chest.

"How old are you?" she asked. When he didn't answer right away, she grinned. "I'm nineteen."

"I'm . . . old." He set down his brush.

She laughed; it sounded like gypsy music to him. Then she repeated herself. "You don't look so old."

He nodded.

She stretched out her hand. "I'm Tesia."

He took it, uncertain what to do with it. Finally, he raised it to his mouth and kissed it lightly. "Adolf."

"German?"

"Yes. You?"

"Polish."

"We're neighbors then," he said, not knowing what else to say.

She smiled. Her teeth were straight and white. "Yes." She pointed at the bench near his stool. "May I sit and watch?"

"May I paint you?"

She laughed again. "I couldn't let you. You'd get the colors all wrong and I'd be cross with you." She caught her breath. "I wouldn't want to be cross with you."

He snorted and went back to work. She was right, he realized. He could never paint her.

He painted quietly and she watched in silence. When it grew dark, he asked her if she wanted to have dinner with him and she said yes. He packed up his supplies and tossed his canvas into a nearby waste-bin.

"Why do you do that?" she asked.

"Like you said: I'm no good." He shrugged. "Sometimes I use them to keep me warm at night. They burn well."

"Ridiculous." She dug the unfinished painting from the garbage. "I like it." She tucked it under her arm.

They walked to a small cafe that overlooked the Seine. He went in first as she paused at the door. From inside, the smell of roasted rabbit, baking bread and fresh sliced onions drifted out. The waiter frowned when he saw them.

"No," he said.

"Pardon?"

He pointed to a newly painted sign near the door. "No Jews."

Adolf felt a stab of anger. It passed quickly. "Monsieur," he said in careful French, "I'm not Jewish."

"Not you," the waiter said, pointing at the girl. "Her."

Adolf looked. She blanched, her eyes a bit wide and her nostrils flaring. She clenched her jaw. He saw the band on her arm now. He hadn't noticed it before but why would he? He'd heard about the new laws but they had seemed far away to him. He shook his head in disbelief. "You are making a mistake."

The waiter said something under his breath that Adolf couldn't quite understand. He opened his mouth to protest but felt a firm hand on his arm.

"We'll go somewhere else," Tesia said.

They had a quiet dinner by moonlight. She stole two apples from a cart. He bought bread and cheese. After eating, she kissed him again, this time more slowly.

He pulled away. "I'm too old."

"Nonsense," she said and kissed him again.

Afterwards, he asked her, "Why did you kiss me that day when you first saw me?"

"Because," she said, "you were beautiful and you stood alone."

He walked her home. Twice, as blue-coat soldiers passed them on the street, she pressed herself closer to him, concealing the band on her arm.

"Why don't you take it off?" he asked her.

"I don't know," she said, standing on the doorstep of a run-down hotel. Inside, he could hear loud voices conversing in Polish and Yiddish and Russian. "It's against the law, I suppose."

"It's a silly law."

"Most laws are." She smiled, kissed him quickly and fled inside.

Whistling a love song he dimly remembered from his youth, Adolf made his way back to de Gaulle's and his waiting friends.

When he looked for her the next day and the next, she was nowhere to be found. When he returned to the old hotel, he found it somber and empty.

July slipped into August.

My father never talked about the events leading up to the war. He simply smiled, waved his hand and said it was unimportant. After he died, I found a photograph in his belongings. He and two other men sitting at a table in some nameless bar raising their glasses to the camera. He was gaunt, bearded and hollow-eyed, dressed in a tattered Prussian coat. The back of the photograph reads Summer in Paris, Light from the Sky, scrawled in his pinched, careful German script and it seems to have been taken at night, possibly in 1941, the year he met my mother. His companions, their connection to my father and their present whereabouts are unknown.

—Jacob Ernest Hitler
Memories of My Father: An Introduction to the
50th Anniversary Edition of Unser Kampf,
Penguin Books, New York, 1992

The explosion was all anyone could talk about.

On August twelfth a blast ripped through Notre Dame Cathedral as Napoleon IV knelt to receive Mass from his archbishop. Fourteen people were killed, including the Emperor and his young wife. Photographs of the bombers, arrested later that night, filled the newspapers. Four frightened Jewish youth. Hanging them, the generals now in command claimed, would not even scratch the surface of the conspiracy that threatened the Empire. Still, they hanged them quickly.

Hemingway threw down the newspaper in disgust. "Those sons of bitches," he muttered.

Chuck and Adolf looked up at him.

Ernie kicked the paper. "Do you believe this?"

He'd been drinking most of the day. At least once, they'd taken his pistol away as he waved it about. There were more soldiers in the streets these days and though the patrons of de Gaulle's little tavern thought their American mascot eccentric, the blue-coats might not be so inclined.

Chuck shrugged. "Name of the game, my friend."

"It's a goddamn travesty," Ernie went on. "They killed their own goddamn Emperor and then they blamed the Jews."

"It's just four," Adolf said.

Ernie pulled back one fist, reaching for his pistol with the other. "Four? It's not just four. Don't you see it coming? There will be more laws. It's a shell game, Adolf. They will whip up the people and keep them focused on their chosen scapegoat. They will move the Jews now to a separate place for their own good, to protect them from the angry mobs that they themselves have created. When the dust settles, there will be a lot of dead Jews and a new Emperor who is *not* a Bonaparte." He pointed to the picture of a French general in the newspaper. "Behold your new Emperor."

People were listening. They looked uncomfortable. Chuck lowered his voice. "That's enough, Ernie. You're making a scene."

Ernie jumped up, his chair tumbling backwards. "Someone sure as Christ needs to. What you people need is a revolution."

Adolf caught his sleeve. "Sit down, my friend."

Ernie looked around as if suddenly coming to his senses. He sat.

Chuck laughed. "You and your revolutions."

"It worked for us, didn't it?"

"If it worked so well," Chuck said, "why are you here?"

Ernie stole Adolf's beer. "Because I'm an American. I'm free to come and go as I please."

Adolf remembered stories about the American Revolution. He'd studied it in school, though his textbooks said little. No one really believed that the young nation of upstarts would live beyond its cradle. But Lincoln averted civil war over slavery and assisted the Canadians in gaining their own independence. Naturally, the grateful northerners joined the Union. And shortly after, the Spanish-

American conflict left the United States with an entire continent under its sway.

"A revolution would never work here," he told Ernie.

Chuck agreed. "He's right. The army's far too strong."

"Ah, but words are stronger," Hemingway said.

Adolf leaned forward. "Words? Against rifles?"

Ernie waved for another round. Suddenly, his eyes glinted with an almost savage intelligence. "Listen," he said. "I'll tell you just how I'd do it." The beer arrived, de Gaulle looking pained when Ernie waved the ticket away. "Later, mon ami. That's a promise." He looked around to make sure no one was listening. "First," he said, "I'd write a book."

Chuck laughed. "But you're a terrible writer. Your words stumble about on the page like drunken soldiers in women's shoes." He paused for dramatic effect. "And those were just your grocery lists."

Ernie pointed, eyebrows narrowed in a mock scowl. "You're quite the bloody comedian."

Adolf chuckled at his friends. "So you'd write a book?"

Ernie nodded. "Yes. A book about all of the horse-shit here. A book so passionate, so full of raw rage and sorrow that people'd sit up and take notice."

"And that would bring about a revolution?"

"In time it would. Yes."

"Nonsense," Chuck said. "Who'd read it? The Jews? The gypsies? The Marxist refugees? They don't have pots to piss in or blankets to sleep in. It'd do them more good on the fire, keeping them warm."

"Not the Jews," Ernie said. "The *Americans*."

Adolf sat up. "The Americans?"

"Naturally. You'd have to get them involved. First, with the book. Then with speeches. Maybe even a traveling troupe of the persecuted and oppressed. They'd eat it up for breakfast, lunch and dinner. And they've got the resources. Strong army. Strong navy. Airships."

Adolf swallowed. "Why ever would they be interested in a Frankish Revolution?"

"Two reasons," Ernie said, holding up two fingers. "One: A democratic foothold in Europe. Two: The liberation of the Jews."

"The Jews?" Adolf asked.

"Freedom for every race, color, creed," Chuck said in German.

"You saw what they did with their emancipated Africans. Liberia's doing quite well; shining that blessed light of liberty for all of Africa to see."

Adolf leaned in. "But most Americans are Christian, aren't they?"

"They are indeed," Ernie said with a grin.

"And?" Chuck asked.

"Jesus Christ was Jewish," Ernie said. "It's all a matter of perspective." He raised his glass. "To democracy," he said.

They raised their glasses, too. A boy who sold photographs to tourists pointed his camera at them and raised his eyebrows. Ernie winked at him.

A bulb flashed. A shutter snapped.

The next night, Adolf gladly handed over a handful of coins for the photograph and tacked it up on the dressing mirror in their loft.

He never considered himself to be a great man but an adequate man. He never considered himself to have made history but rather to have been in the right place and the right time to do his small part. Well-spoken but shy, intelligent but unassuming, he caught the public off guard with his dry wit, his careful words and his passionate commitment to human rights. For this reason, it is said that only Hitler could go to America.
—Dr. John F. Kennedy
*Out of the Ashes: A History of Modern Thought
from the French Revolution for Democratic Change
to the Re-Birth of the Nation of Israel, 1941 - 1952,*
Harvard University Press, Boston, 1971.

Throughout August, he kept an eye open for Tesia but Adolf was convinced he'd never see her again. She was a smart girl, he told himself. Smart enough to see the stirred pot start to boil. As badly as he wished to see her, he hoped he would not because that would mean she hadn't left this dangerous place.

There were more soldiers now and more laws. More signs in shop windows. Rumors flew of outlying rural churches desecrated by Jews. The local synagogue was burned to the ground by angry citizens while the police and soldiers stood by.

"It's heartbreaking," Adolf told Chuck one afternoon as they walked to de Gaulle's. They spoke exclusively in English now.

Adolf had gotten quite good at it.

Chuck kicked an empty can. "It is. Man's inhumanity to man, I think they call it."

Adolf stopped. "I think Ernie was right."

Chuck laughed and stopped, too. "About the book?"

"Maybe. About the Revolution. About the Americans."

"Perhaps," Chuck said, resuming his brisk pace. "But I don't think it will happen."

"Why not?"

He clapped Adolf on the shoulder. "Who's going to do it? Are you going to do it?"

"Of course not."

"Why not?"

Adolf opened his mouth. He started to say *because I'm not a Jew* and the realization of it twisted his heart in his chest. "It's not my line of work."

"Exactly," Chuck said. "This sort of work requires more than just a willing body."

"More?"

Chuck's hands moved as he talked. "Joan of Arc, King Arthur, Moses. What did they have?"

Adolf thought about it for a moment. "I don't know."

"God," Chuck said. "They had the voice of God, the vision of the grail, a light from Heaven. A power they could point to over their shoulder."

"A light from Heaven?"

Chuck pointed up. "Licht vom Himmel."

Adolf nodded. They stood outside de Gaulle's now, waiting to go in. He smiled at his friend. "And when they have that?"

"One spark to start the fire," Chuck said.

They walked in. Ernie waved them to their table. He was remarkably sober for the time of day. He grinned. "You're becoming popular, Adolf."

Adolf raised his eyebrows. "Yes?"

Ernie nodded towards the bar. "De Gaulle said a girl was in looking for you earlier. Said she'd be back later."

He coughed as a shudder passed over him. "Did he mention her name?"

"Foreign girl. Dark." He lowered his voice. "He thought she was Jewish; I assured him she was not."

Adolf took the meaning from his words and nodded. "Thank you."

He shrugged. "She's more trouble than you need, friend. These are bad times for love."

"I don't love her," Adolf said. "I hardly know her. And she's just a girl."

Ernie patted his hand. "That's what they all say." He opened his mouth to continue but the sudden opening and closing of the front door stopped him. A young man stood panting in the doorway and the room went quiet.

"They're relocating the Jews tonight," he said. "Outside of the city. For their own protection, they said."

"*Who* said?" de Gaulle asked.

"I heard it from a soldier. They're lined up along the Champs Elysées. Blue-coats for block upon block. They've even called up the reserves."

Ernie looked at Adolf. "For their own protection," he said quietly.

Outside, the shouting started. Whistles blowing, sirens wailing. Adolf hung his head. "They'll go, *won't* they? They won't fight back."

"They might," Chuck said. "But after a few of them are killed, they'll stop. They'll go like sheep and hope the butcher is a shepherd."

Adolf rubbed his eyes, disbelief gnawing at his stomach. "What do we do?"

Ernie looked up, his face pale. "We wait here for it to be done. Then we leave Paris."

The bartender dimmed the lights. He passed around shot glasses and bottles. The handful of men drank themselves drunk and fell asleep at their tables.

In a whisky fog, Hitler dreamed of another life, another time. A dark time, a time when a caricature of himself strutted about in uniform, barking out orders and gazing with pride upon a broken cross. And other men in uniform, men who saw the light from the sky spreading out behind Adolf like a halo, raised their hands to him and cried "Heil." And on the hands that they raised, blood shone out in that awful light. Blood of the martyrs, blood of the ages, and Adolf looked down at his own hands and saw that they were bloody, too, and he reached back to find some of his father's faith and compassion but found that in *that* life, in *that* world, there was nothing but rage and hatred to reach for.

Hitler wept.

He woke to screaming and leaped to his feet.

Ernie mumbled; Chuck stirred.

He heard the screaming again, distant from the alley behind the tavern. Either the others were too drunk to notice or too drunk to care. He moved quickly to the back door and stepped out into the night.

"Hello?"

The screaming stopped. Instead, he heard muffled, muted sound. He followed it.

Behind a pile of crates he saw two large forms crouched on the ground over a smaller bundle that bucked and twisted. As he drew closer, he realized they were two soldiers and a girl. One blue-coat held the girl down, a razor at her throat and a hand over her mouth. The other had pried her legs apart, his own trousers pushed down to his knees as he raped her.

"Wasn't enough to kill our Lord," one of the soldiers hissed. "You had to kill our Emperor, too, Jew-bitch."

Adolf stopped. His heart fell into a hole somewhere inside him. His stomach followed after. His eyes locked with the girl's and suddenly she stopped struggling.

She's waiting for me to save her, Adolf thought. He couldn't move. He stood transfixed while powerlessness and shame washed over him. Tesia lay still and the soldier thrust twice more before looking up.

"You there," he said. "You this girl's father?"

Adolf cleared his voice. "No."

"Then mind your business. You can come back for your turn later."

Something snapped like a guitar string in his spine. Adolf turned and fled for de Gaulle's, his feet pounding the cobblestones. Behind him, he heard Tesia struggling again, trying to scream but unable to do more than moan. He ran into the tavern, kicking over chairs and tables as he went, until he reached his own. He stood panting, sobbing over his friends, then bent over Ernie to frisk him.

Ernie stirred. "What the hell — "

Adolf found the revolver, yanked it from the pocket, and wordlessly stalked out of the tavern. Each step steady, deliberate, until he saw the soldiers. Until he saw Tesia beneath them. Then he stopped and looked down at them.

A blue-coat looked up. "I thought I told you — "

The pistol didn't roar or buck like at the cinema. It popped and shimmied just a bit and he thumbed the hammer and pulled the trigger again to be sure it had really worked though the soldier was already falling sideways, his mouth working like a landed trout.

The other soldier let go of Tesia and scrambled backwards on his heels and hands, fear white on his face. The revolver popped again once and he thrashed away, popped twice and he rolled over with a sigh.

Adolf, still clutching the pistol, dropped heavily to his knees. Tesia lay still, her dress and blouse ripped, her eyes closed. He reached for her, pulled her to himself and she fought him, kicking and flailing and growling low in her throat. He released her for a moment, then tried again. This time, she let him pull her in and he cradled her, rocking back and forth. He had no idea what to say so he said nothing and let that silence sweep him aside like a giant hand. After a few minutes, shouts from over rooftops brought him back from that quiet place he'd gone to.

He shook her gently. "Tesia, we have to go."

He stood, pulling her up and keeping her close. The revolver dangled in his hand and he looked again at his handiwork. The two soldiers were dead now or soon would be. They lay sprawled like cast away dolls. The realization of what he'd done struck him. Blood on his hands.

Hanging on to her, he bent as far away as he could and threw up on the ground. When he ran the back of his hand over his mouth he smelled whisky and cordite.

He heard a quiet cough and looked up. Ernie, Chuck and a few others from the tavern stood there watching him.

Chuck looked at the bodies and then the girl. "Adolf, what have you done?"

Ernie stepped forward, snatching the pistol from his hand. He tucked it into his waistband. "I think he did the right thing, Chuck. This is where it starts."

One spark, Adolf thought.

*

Were he alive today, he would say himself that this monument is not about one man's struggle but about the struggle of many. Our struggle, as he put it so well. From 1942 to 1952 — when the charter was finally signed — he struggled alongside us, raising support and awareness for our cause, never asking for anything for himself. With his wife and his children often by his side, he went from city to city speaking in any venue that would listen. And though originally published in his native German, his book was a shot heard 'round the world, translated into over forty languages within its first five years in print. I heard him speak shortly before his death: "Well-aimed words will always be more powerful than rifles," he said. And his words roused a slumbering giant, turning its head towards cruelty and oppression, towards a cry for freedom in a far away land.

　　—Rabbi Benjamin Levin
　　　Dedication Speech, Hitler Memorial,
　　　Jerusalem, Israel, 1992.

They told Adolf to take her to the loft and wait for morning. De Gaulle had a nephew who was driving to Calais the next day; they'd hide Hitler and the girl in the back of the truck and hope for the best. He ripped off Tesia's armband and tossed it away.

"Listen to me," he told her. "You are not Jewish. You are my daughter, Klara, and you are ill. We are looking for the hospital. We left your papers at home by mistake. Do you understand me?"

She nodded. Her eyes were red and she limped now, but she stood on her own.

"Good." They set out at a brisk walk. More shouting and sirens punctuated the night, suddenly joined now by occasional gunshots.

Along the way they saw soldiers running. They saw groups of men and women, some now fighting back. People called news to one another from their opened windows. Two soldiers had been killed raping a girl, someone cried. A band of drunks was storming the police station looking for guns, another shouted. Adolf heard it as if it were far away and kept pushing them towards safety, towards home.

He locked them inside. He took down half a bottle of schnapps from the cupboard and poured two drinks with shaking hands. Tesia did not speak and did not meet his eyes. He knew she was still in shock, the color drained away from her skin and her face slack. He tucked her into his cot, wrapping his great coat over her and when he pulled away, she clutched at him and mumbled something.

He bent in closer and heard the words. "You were beautiful," she said, "and you stood alone."

He held her as sobs racked his body. The world had never seemed so grim and despairing and he wondered if it had always been that way, if he'd just never seen it before. He felt the broken girl in his arms, felt her breath against his neck and smelled the sweat and dirt on her. Behind him, in the window, something like Heaven's light grew beyond his wildest imaginings, filling that cavity in the world's soul. His tears subsided; Tesia slept.

After an hour of holding her, he left her side to pack his things. He'd leave his paints, his pallet, his brushes. He knew he'd never use them again. But he did pack his suitcase with clothing, bedding and canned food. He also checked his papers and counted his money. Somewhere, he could buy her the papers she would need.

On a scrap of paper, Ernie had hastily scribbled a name and an address — a friend of a friend at the U.S. Embassy in London. Ernie had pressed it into his hand before leaving with Chuck and the others to storm the police station and start their Revolution for Democratic Change.

"Viva la France," they had said as they went racing down the cobblestones.

Adolf took down their photograph from the mirror. He looked at it and smiled at his friends.

If I'm to be a writer, he thought, I should write something about this place, this time. Something so I will never forget.

He found a pen, turned the photo over, and after a moment's thought, wrote on the back of it in his pinched, careful, German script: *Summer in Paris, Light from Heaven.*

Hitler weighed the pen carefully in his hand and wondered if one man could make a difference. He weighed his destiny carefully in his heart and wondered if the Americans would listen.

LAST FLIGHT
OF THE GODDESS

I shed no tears when I put the torch to my wife. I suppose I could have. Who would fault an old man his grief?

That morning, as Bambilo Broadback helped me strap on my breastplate, fasten my greaves, and put on my gauntlets, I thought about the crowd I expected. Old faces and nearly forgotten names representing a time that had moved on when I was a younger man. While he huffed and puffed to make those recently polished relics fit, I wondered who would attend. Surely the Crown Prince and his consort upon shiny white stallions and beneath purple and gold banners. And Azerminus the Mage, of course. And Fenruk Ironmauler and the three pretty, young prostitutes he passed off as his wives. The list marched on and on. We'd sent messenger birds everywhere.

But when the moment came it was a small gathering. Henry the Livery Man. Jacko and some of the old regulars from the tavern stood there in their Restday Best. Margi Fenroper and some of my dearly departed's other friends. And a priest older than I that stank of last night's beer. He said a few words. I said a few words. No one else spoke.

We'd dressed her in her finest silk robes. Bambilo's wife, Buckabith, had painted my wife's face and fancied up her hair.

In life, as the years crept on, we'd talked about death. I'd always said "Roll me to yonder creek; feed those damnable trout that have vexed me so long." No hero's send-off for me, though years back I bore the title. And she had always said "Give me back to the sky." In my mind, I'd envisioned my Luendyl on a pyre shining in her armor with Shymalius's twin scimitars clenched in her white fists and the Demigoddess Gladenda's Helm of Knowing masking her face. But retirement brings new priorities, and gradually all our glammered accouterments bought us a hearth, a home, a quiet place to raise our daughter. In my mind, I'd also envisioned a throng of grief-struck nobles, heroes, fans, and hopefuls.

In the end, a near dozen of us gathered around a pile of alder logs, and I set torch to the most beautiful woman I had ever seen.

She fell from the sky like a goddess. I remember it well. I was camped in the heart of the Blast-lands, the ruins of Ghul-Shar-Tov on the horizon painted silver by the rising moon. I heard a rustling in the air, followed by muttered curses, and then a yelp as she spun down and thudded into my tent, knocking it down and tangling herself in the canvas.

"Damn," the goddess said. "Damned damnable damnation."

She was beautiful. My first impulse was to laugh, but when the moonlight caught her long red hair, her face, her sleek form, her armor-entrusted breasts, my humor failed. And my words as well.

She stomped her feet, and I realized they were sparking and smoking. A pair of highly unreliable Oingeltonken's Flights of Fancy Winged Shoes fluttered and flapped their last. Finally, she looked up.

"What are you staring at, soldier?" Her hand moved towards the hilt of a scimitar at her waist. I remember thinking at the time that it looked a bit like one of Shymalius's fabled twin blades, but then her breasts distracted me again.

I shook my head. "Nothing," I said and thought better of it. "Everything."

She smiled. That's really all there was to it. It hooked me in a way my lures and worms could never hook the leaping trout of Brookwood Down.

Her eyes narrowed and shifted towards the ruined city behind me. "Here for the treasure then?"

"No. Renown. Prestige. You know."

"Nobility," she said. "How nice."

"And you?"

She sized me up. I was a pup then. I'd just slain my first giant the winter before. More an accident really — he'd fallen onto my lance and I'd then put my long sword in his ear. Still, it had netted me a reputation. I was wearing my lower-end Yorlund's Eye-Blinding Plate Mail Extravaganza. I filled it out nicely and had all my hair in those days. She must have felt whatever I felt, too, because her smile stretched across her face like a cool river. "I'll take whatever I can get," she said.

It started fast between us and lasted most of the night. In the morning, after we'd sorted out whose armor and undergarments were whose, we routed the beasts from Ghul-Shar-Tov and pillaged a small fortune from its catacombs and vaults.

It started fast between us. And lasted the rest of my life.

The tears came that night in the tavern. Slow at first, then an unstoppable rush. Only a few were there to see it.

"Andro?"

I looked up through water. "Yes, Bambilo?"

"It's okay to cry."

Halflets and Fey make lots of talk about being in touch with the child inside, about expressing your feelings and all that *Venison Stew for the Heart* crap. I subscribed more to Berserker Bronbur's time-tested wisdom: "When angry, smash stuff. When sad, smash more stuff." But the image of her pyre took the fight out of me. I pushed aside my empty beer mugs, hid my face in my hands, and just let loose with it.

Ten minutes or so passed. Bambilo patted my shoulder. "She was a good woman."

I snuffled. "The best."

"She was a strong woman."

"The strongest." I sniffed and wiped my nose on the sleeve of my tunic. I felt composure leaking back into me.

Bambilo sighed. "It's a shame Karysa couldn't be here for it."

And that started the tears all over again.

At first, I thought I hadn't heard her correctly. We were back to back under the torture dome of the Demon King of Zharid Keep. Blood made the floor slippery, but his minion Gibbers rushed on and we piled up their bodies around us. I brought Fangblade down to spark and split a Gibber helmet, dodging to the right to avoid being skewered by a spear.

There was a brief lull, and I glanced over my shoulder at her. "What did you say?"

Luendyl had both scimitars by now. We'd been together for nearly ten years. We'd slain fierce foes, rescued fair damsels and girlish princes, won and lost two kingdoms and a dozen fortunes. Those blades whirled and spun, limbs flying and blood splashing. "I don't want to do this anymore," she said again. "It's not good for the baby."

I took off a Gibber arm. "The what?"

Two more fell behind me, gurgling and kicking. "The baby, Andro. Our baby."

My sword arm came down and I turned to face her. "I thought you were using Azerminus's Egg Charming Elixir?"

She sliced through a Gibber as it lunged at me. "I was."

Another darted in, its eyes wide and its mouth gaping. I paused to run it through and turned back to her. "Then *what* happened?"

She shrugged, then brought both blades down on the Gibber Chieftain's skull-helmet. "Remember those damned winged shoes I was wearing when we met?"

I looked around. We were the only two left standing. "Yes?"

She smiled that smile that had hooked me a decade ago. "Magic can be a fickle thing."

I remember a hundred thoughts rushing me at once. Andro Giantslayer . . . a father. The deposed King Andro of Grunland . . . a father. A father. A father. A father. My heart caved in, then expanded. I sheathed Fangblade, that glimmering sword carved and enchanted from a dragon's tooth.

She sheathed her blades. Her blue eyes searched mine and began to twinkle. "Well?"

"Well." I scratched my head. "I suppose we could sell off some of our gear and buy that place near Brookwood you liked so well."

She threw herself at me. I can still hear the crash of metal today. I can still taste her mouth on mine.

After the kiss, she pulled back and drew her blades again. "Sell our stuff? Are you mad?" She pointed to the door to the Demon King's throne room. "Let's finish what we've started and buy the whole damned town."

"And the river," I said thinking about the fish I'd seen jumping there last spring. "I'm going to need a new hobby."

For the next two hours we savored every moment of our last

fight together. Of course, we had no way of knowing then that the Demon King had bankrupted his treasury the winter before.

I drank too much that night after the funeral but Jacko did not cut me off. He kept the mugs coming. He'd lost his wife the year before.

When it was down to just the two of us, I lunged to my feet.

"I've a cot in the back," Jacko said.

"I've a bed at home," I said. The room wobbled. Or perhaps it was me.

"Tomorrow then."

"Goodnight, Jacko." I left the tavern. Outside, the village slept as dogs barked beneath a starry sky.

I took the forest path along the creek and listened to the water dance across the rocks. Evergreen and wood smoke scented the night air. I reached our dark little house in the clearing and paused at the door, my hand outstretched towards the latch.

Turning, I made my way around the house and up the hill behind it. The fire had burned itself out. I walked to the center of the charred wood and piles of ash and sat down.

"Luendyl," I said. "I don't know what to do."

The tears came back and at some point in the night, I stretched myself out over her, and fell asleep. I dreamed about goddesses falling from the sky, and when the morning sun woke me up, I knew what to do.

I ran to the house, raced in and kicked aside my pile of armor from yesterday's service. I took down an urn from the mantle. It bore the crest of the Kings of Devyn, stamped into its platinum surface.

We'd never sold it, though we'd been tempted. We'd put aside plenty for our future, and when Karysa'd hit her stride, she'd started sending a bit home now and again. I took the urn outside to the creek and unscrewed its top.

"Sorry, Falgron," I said as I dumped its contents into the water. "You were a faithful steed to the last but I've no need for you any longer." I suppose I could have found another urn if I'd stopped to think about it. But I didn't.

I went back to the top of the hill. I scooped handfuls of my wife mingled with alder ash until the urn was full. I replaced the cap.

"Are you ready, Luendyl?"

Back inside, I set her next to my armor. Henry had used old bridle scraps to lengthen the straps. My broad shoulders and heavy chest had dropped closer to the middle now. My hands and joints ached from a hundred battles. Still, I managed to suit myself up without Bambilo's help. I pulled a tarnished sword down from the wall and buckled its belt around my waist. Nothing like Fangblade, but what blade ever was? Next, I packed my rucksack, nestling the urn down amid clean socks, a blanket, some rolled up clothes, a crust of bread, and a bit of cheese.

When I turned to the door, a boy stood there waiting.

He was maybe fourteen. Soft-faced and big-eyed, hair poking out from beneath a green cap. He had a lute slung over his shoulder.

We stared at each other and finally the boy spoke. "Are you Andro Giantslayer?" He was trying too hard to deepen his voice. That should have been my first clue.

"Yes." The weight of my armor, sword, and pack toppled me. I dropped to the floor and hoped it looked like I was just sitting down quickly.

"Exiled King of Grunland?"

I shrugged out of the pack. "Yes."

"The Finisher of Fang the Dread?"

"Yes."

"Founder of the Heroes League of Handen Hall?"

"Yes." I paused. "I had help."

"Father of Karysa the White of the West?"

I felt pride bloom. "Yes."

"Husband of Luendyl the Fierce?"

I swallowed. "And Fair."

"Huh?"

"Luendyl the Fierce and Fair," I said. "Yes."

"Is this a bad time?"

I looked at my pack, at my armored legs stretched out on the floor, the sword sheath pinned beneath them in an uncomfortable way. "The worst possible," I said. "What do you want?"

The boy blushed. That should have been my second clue. "I've come a long way. From Alderland through Mistvale along the Dragon's Spine Mountains."

"You're vexing me."

"Last month, the Emperor of Shaluzan announced a contest among minstrels. He swore by the jade throne that the musician with the most moving song would be granted title, land and — " The boy moved his hands in a wide, exaggerated arch. " —And vast wealth beyond anyone's wildest imaginings."

The way he moved his hands, the way he moved his hips. My third clue. I opened my mouth. Closed it. Thought a minute. Looked closer at his face and eyes. "Aren't you really a girl?"

"No."

"I think you are."

"I most certainly am not."

I shrugged, then climbed to my feet, leaving the pack on the floor. "Makes no never mind to me," I said. "Boy or girl, help a tired old man with his pack and I'll help you with your song."

"It has to be original," the girl said as she picked up my luggage. "And very moving."

"I'll see what I can do."

We walked out the door and into the summer sun. "And pretty, too," she said.

I looked down at her. I could see my daughter in her face now. The short, crazy hair underneath the cap. The awkward walk with my pack slung over her shoulder. I couldn't think of anything else to say so I repeated myself. "I'll see what I can do."

We were fishing, my daughter and I, up-creek behind the house. I remember it was summer then, too. I held my rod — an enchanted bit of bamboo that Azerminus had brought on his last visit — and watched the ripples in the deep parts of the water. Karysa poked at a rotten stump with a stick.

"I've been thinking," she said. She was fourteen I think.

"Yes?" I shifted my weight on the boulder. Even back then, my joints got stiff.

Her stick followed a beetle's scurrying trail. "I don't want to marry Bambilo's son after all."

Bambilo Broadback had settled in on the farm just the other side of town. He and Buckabith had a litter of Halflet kids and the oldest, Bondilo, had made our daughter his solemn quest to win. I'd never taken it seriously.

"Really?"

Karysa nodded. "First of all, I don't really like boys very much."

I grunted. "Because you're too busy trying to be one."

She ignored me. "No, I know what I want to do when I grow up."

"What's that?"

"I want to be a hero. Like you."

Since that day in Zharid Keep, I'd done the odd job here and there. To keep my skills and blade sharp, I always told my Luendyl. Karysa had grown up with it. "And your mother, too," I said. "She was quite the hero in her day."

"Was," Karysa said. "But she quit."

"Sure. To have *you.*" I reached over with my free hand and mussed her hair. "Trust me. No gibber, dragon, troll, or giant ever gave your mother half the fuss you have."

She laughed. I laughed too. I held my rod out to her. "Want to give it a try?"

She took it from me and stood up, her face serious as she watched the water. "I'll bet I'll be a great hero. The greatest. Why — "

But at that moment, a trout hit the line hard, and as she pulled it in, I knew she was right.

Someday my daughter's heroics would be legendary. Of this I had no doubt.

The minstrel girl and I walked all day. As the sun set over forested hills, we pulled aside of the King's Way and made camp. She'd carried her pack, my pack, and the lute all day and hadn't slowed down once. I had gasped and coughed and wheezed my way beside her.

"Should I build a fire?"

I nodded, winded.

"And then we can work on my song?"

I nodded again and waved her away.

Later, with the fire roaring, I shared my bread and cheese with her. "We'll hit town tomorrow and stock up," I said. After we'd eaten, she picked up her lute and tuned it.

"So where are you going?" she asked, her fingers moving across frets and adjusting knobs.

"I'm taking my wife out for one last adventure."

She wrinkled her nose. "I don't think we've known each other long enough for me to be considered your wife. Besides, you're too old."

"I thought you said you were a boy?"

"Oh yeah. I did, didn't I?"

I chuckled. "There's nothing wrong with being a girl. Gods know I've told my daughter the same thing a hundred, hundred times." I reached for the rucksack and drug out the urn. "Anyway, I didn't mean you. I meant my wife." I tapped the lid.

"You mean Luendyl the Fierce?"

"And Fair," I said. "Yes."

She gulped. "In there?"

"Yes. She passed three nights ago." I felt the tears coming but this time held them back. I could feel my lower lip quiver.

"You must be very sad."

I nodded. "More so than you could imagine."

"I can imagine," she said. "I'm alone, too, now. My folks passed about five years back. Troll raids in this little border town where we lived." She picked out a melody, frowned and twisted the knobs a bit more.

"I'm sorry to hear it." I threw another stick into the fire. The sound of the lute could not cover our silence. "Well, enough about loss," I finally said. "Sing me a song about life."

"And after, you'll tell me stories?"

"Yes. We'll start on that song of yours. Win you your title and land."

"And wealth," she said.

"Of course."

She closed her eyes and drew in a breath. The melody from her fingers grew louder; her voice lilted up and out, strong and sweet and clear as a brook. I'd never heard that tune before. Or if I had, I'd never heard it sung so well.

After the song, after the stories, I dreamed of Luendyl. She sat across from me by the fire and watched the girl sleep.

"She reminds me of Karysa," I said.

Luendyl smiled. It was a playful smile with a bit of sadness about the edges. "What are you doing, old man?"

"I'm taking you on one last adventure."

"You're crazy. You're too old to be out jollivating around in that get-up." In my dreams, I'm always wearing my armor and sword.

"You told me to give you back to the sky."

"And how do you suppose you'll do that?"

I shrugged. "I'll figure it out."

"One suggestion?"

"Yes?"

Her grin showed teeth this time. "Whatever you do, don't use Oingeltonkel's flying shoes."

I laughed. "No. I don't suppose I will."

Luendyl looked at the sleeping girl. "Andro?"

"Yes, my love?"

"It's been a whole day and you still don't know her name. You really should ask."

"Not sure she'll tell me. She thinks she's a boy."

Luendyl laughed. The music of it was quite like the song earlier. "Sounds familiar, doesn't it?"

It did.

A boot in my side brought me awake. Time was, not even a haunt could sneak up on me. Not so now. I jumped and sat up.

"What have we here? An old man and his granddaughter off to the fair?" A group of five men stood in the midst of our camp. They wore dark forest-colored clothes, bows slung over shoulders, and knives glinting in their hands. A pre-dawn gray wrapped the woods around us, and the road shimmered like white water.

"Perhaps," another one said, "'Tis no grandfather at all but a buggerly girl-grabber. What say you, girl?"

The girl sat up. She looked angry. "I'm not a girl. I'm not a girl at all."

"That doesn't make it any better," I told her. "Keep quiet and I'll handle this." I struggled to stand. Another boot tipped me over.

"Stay down, old man." This one was the leader. I could always just tell by the look of one. "If you cooperate, we'll leave you to your lechery. And if not — " he pointed his knife at me and etched a cross in the air. "No more girls for you."

Three days of grief washed out in anger. I can't remember

how long it had been since I'd felt a rage coming on. Years perhaps. Dozens of years more likely. I bottled it as fast as it built, stored it up, and felt around under my blanket for the hilt of my sword. "It's my coin you'll be wanting, I suspect."

The bandit leader laughed. "That too." He backed away, eyes never leaving me, and scooped up the urn. "Platinum, boys. Pure platinum like I said."

Purple spots crowded my vision. I tightened my grip on the sword. I'd learned years ago to never sleep with it in plain view or sheathed, a habit that had saved me more than once. I felt my muscles tighten, and the world slowed down around me.

"Let." My hand moved like water, sliding the sword out from under the blanket. "Go." My other hand flattened itself against the ground. "Of." My legs coiled and creaked beneath me as I pushed myself up. "My." The sword came up as the bandit, too late, tried to leap backwards. "Wife."

I could have taken his head off. Or at least partially. But at the last minute, I turned the blade and smacked him in the temple with the flat of my sword. He went over fast, dropping my wife as he fell.

The girl scrambled from her blankets to grab up his knife while I stood over him with the point of my sword at his throat.

He recovered quickly. "There are five of us and two of them," he said. "Don't just stand there . . . get them."

His four companions exchanged glances. Their faces were white in the morning gloom. They didn't look like they were in a hurry at all.

I grinned down at him. "I think your friends might be smarter than you." My anger burned out fast, replaced with surprise at how easy it came back. I hadn't moved like that in years. It felt good. I'd pay for it later, of course. "And if they're as smart as I think they are, they'll be leaving soon."

They turned and bolted. Most bandits are a cowardly lot.

"As to you," I said. "I'll be having *your* coin now."

He slowly untied the small purse at his belt and set it on the ground.

"And now, an apology for the girl and me."

"I'm not a — "

I turned my head and let her see my scowl. She closed her mouth.

"Apologies, Sir and Lady." The girl kicked the fire a bit, eyes flashing mad.

"Now off with you." He scuttled away from me like a crab, then stood and turned in the direction his friends had gone. "No, no," I said. "Not *that* way. The other way. You can find your friends later. After we've gone."

Something like gratitude mixed with a sneer twisted his face. He opened his mouth to speak, thought better of it, and ran away.

The girl stared at me. "That's going in the song," she said. "Definitely."

"You haven't seen anything yet," I told her. "By the way?"

"Yes?"

"My wife told me I should ask you your name."

She looked at the urn. Then she looked back at me. "No she didn't."

"Yes. She did. Last night."

"I think I'll leave that bit out of the song."

"Whatever you say. It's your song."

She started rolling her blanket, gathering her things, shoving them into her pack. I sat down, suddenly a bit shaken.

"Andrillia," she finally said. "My name is Andrillia."

"So you *are* a girl?"

She glowered at me. "Don't push it."

Time was, every village boasted two or three Andros or Andrillias. I think the first Andro I met was a boy of maybe four years. A pretty woman opened the door of her hovel and shouted as I was passing through her small town. Falgron was in his prime back then, massive and white, hooves striking sparks on the cobblestones.

"Andro, come in for supper!"

I reined in and dismounted. "That's very kind of you, Madam."

She looked frightened. A large armored man and a large armored horse towering over her on her porch. She started to speak when a small voice rang out up the street.

"Coming, Mom." A boy lightning-flashed by me and into the house.

By then, Luendyl caught up with me. "Are we stopping?"

"That boy has my name," I said, nodding to the house.

Luendyl smiled. "Sometimes you're quite oblivious. Do you know that?"

I frowned. "What?"

"We've passed through hundreds of towns and villages. There have been Andros and Andrillias in every one of them since that little bit with Charnak the Terrible and the Six Princesses of Arghulistan. I think it tipped the scales a bit on that prestige of yours."

"Oh. That." I smiled at the memory of it. "I had help." I looked at my wife, sitting high and proud and beautiful in the saddle. "And I haven't seen any little Lues and Luendyls scampering about."

She smiled and nudged her horse forward. "That's because I'm one of a kind."

And always will be. I knew it then. I know it now.

We bought a pony in the next town and tied our packs onto him. We also bought dried meat, more cheese and bread, and a few wineskins. When the storekeeper realized who I was, he threw in some spare socks and a wool cap for beneath my helmet. He warned me to keep my feet dry and my head covered. Andrillia had a purse of her own and bought more paper and ink.

We set out again that afternoon. The summer day held clear and warm. I thought about leaving off the armor but couldn't bring myself to do it. It rubbed my skin in places, it rode snug in others, and its weight pulled at me while the sun slowly cooked me. I left it on. Such journeys should not be comfortable.

"Where are we going?" Andrillia asked.

"North and then east," I said. "How did you get your name?"

"I think you saved my grandmother's life or something. I'm not sure."

"Probably did. I used to do that sort of thing a lot."

"I know. That's why I came looking for you. Only I didn't think you'd be so old."

I laughed. "I suppose I *am* old."

"You are," she said in a matter-of-fact way. "But that's okay. It'll make for a great song. Even if you die on the way."

"Thanks," I said.

"Don't mention it. Tell me about your daughter."

"She reminds me a lot of you," I told her. "But you like boys, right, even though you want to be one?"

I looked over at her. Andrillia frowned and thought about it. "Yeah. But don't tell anyone."

I nodded. We kept walking, and as we walked, I told her about Karysa.

I couldn't eat roast duck without thinking about her. Because when she showed up in our lives, the midwife who delivered Karysa stank of the roast duck she'd prepared for Restday dinner. And frankly, she was about the size of a roast duck when she came out.

She grew up too fast. We fought too much. We laughed a lot. We played a lot. We cried some. At fifteen, she learned the longsword. At sixteen, she learned the bow. The next year, we sold a few gems I'd plundered raiding a troglodyte lair and bought her that first suit of armor. Karysa had wanted to come with me but I'd refused.

"It's too dangerous. You could get hurt."

"So what?" she asked. "I'm not afraid of a couple of trogs." We were in the yard; she was practicing her dodge, thrust, and parry.

"A couple? Two dozen or more, most likely." I'd worked up a sweat as her sparring partner. She was good. "Out of the question."

I pressed her. She pressed back. Our swords clanked and clashed together.

Then I said it. Shouldn't have, but I did. "Maybe you should re-think this whole thing."

"What whole thing?" She still hadn't broken sweat. She had her father's height and her mother's looks. Of course, none of us knew where the white hair came from.

"The hero thing. It's really not that great."

"That's not how *you've* told it."

"Well, I was wrong. Besides, what about Bondilo Broadback?" Another dodge, thrust, and parry. "You could settle down. Get married. Have children." Our swords started to spark as she put more muscle into it. "It's quite rewarding."

She frowned at me. "Dad, I don't like boys."

I stopped, dropped my guard. "Don't like boys?"

"No. Never have."

"What's *that* supposed to mean?"

She stopped too. She shrugged. "I like girls. Just like you."

I didn't know what else to say so I said the obvious. "I only like your mother."

She sheathed her sword. "That's not what I mean."

"Oh." I just stood there and let it settle in. "Well, okay then," I finally said, "Bondilo has a sister, you know."

"Oh, Dad," she said and walked away.

A few minutes later, Luendyl came outside to see why I kept plunging my head into the trough and shouting curses at the horses. Her look alone was all the question she need ask.

"Our daughter likes girls," I said.

She cocked her head to the right and raised one eyebrow. "And?"

"That's all. She likes girls. Not boys."

Luendyl sighed. "Sometimes," she said slowly, "You are quite oblivious. Do you know that?"

I nodded. "I guess I am, aren't I? You've known for years, haven't you?"

She hugged me. My dripping head made her chest wet. "It's not the end of the world."

I stared at her breasts. I did that a lot, I guess. Armor, wet dresses, bare — it didn't matter; they fascinated me. "You're right. It's not. It's just not what I expected."

"Often the things we love best are what we expect least," she said. She saw where I was staring. "Remember that night in the Blastlands?"

"How could I ever forget?" I grinned, she caught my grin, and tossed it back. "Want to go inside or just do it right here?"

"Both," she said. And we did.

The next year, we bundled our little girl up in her very own suit of chain-mail and a shiny new sword and sent her off to make her mark upon the world.

We ran into a horde of gobbers on our third night under the stars. Actually, they ran into us. Gobbers are a bit shorter than gibbers but nearly as fierce and twice as stupid. Andrillia had just gone to fetch water when I heard the crash and crunch of many feet in the underbrush. I drew my sword.

They broke cover, shouting and shrieking, miscellaneous weapons gripped in their clawed hands. They poured past me as if I were a rock in the middle of their river. One of them took a half-hearted swing, putting a small dent into my side. I cut down a few, ran another through, and then they were gone. Behind them, I heard the baying of hounds and the crash of something even heavier moving towards us at breakneck speed.

Andrillia raced back into our small clearing. "What's going — "

A massive form hurtled towards us from the forest, interrupting her. It reared up, hooves flailing. Four large dogs blurred past, growling and howling, tearing up the ground in their pursuit of the gobbers. The dogs were my first clue. The smell of strong cologne, my second. I lowered my sword.

"Clovis?"

The hooves came down. "Aye. And who be you?"

"It's me. Andro."

Clovis sauntered forward. Centaurs as a whole made me uncomfortable. My head spun and my stomach lurched from their bizarre breeding tastes. Clovis was no exception. When Luendyl and I ran with him back in the day his eye went from human to horse to everything in between.

"Andro Giantslayer, by the Nine Hundred Toes of Erlik!" He towered over us, looking down, a bow and arrow held loosely in his right hand. "What in the Five Hells are you doing here?"

Andrillia spoke up. "He's out on one last adventure with his wife."

Clovis looked at the girl. He grinned. "A nice little filly. And where is Luendyl the Fair?"

"And Fierce," I said. "Luendyl the Fierce and Fair."

Somewhere over my shoulder, I heard gobbers screaming and dogs snarling. "It'll have to wait," Clovis said. "I've a-work to finish yonder." He reared again. The reek of perfumed oils filled the air. "But I'll be back shortly."

He slung his bow, drew two large axes, and galloped away.

Andrillia's face wrinkled and she held her nose. "He stinks."

I sheathed my sword and went back to building the fire. "You should smell him *without* the cologne," I said.

*

When Clovis returned, he hauled off the three gobbers I'd killed. "You're too old to be doing this," he said, slinging them over his back.

I didn't protest. The day's walk had worn me down.

Andrillia and I sat at the fire; Clovis stood at the edge of its light, shifting back and forth as the smoke changed course. He smacked his lips loudly. "And where's Luendyl?"

I nodded to the urn. I'd put her on the log beside me.

His face clouded. "She's gone then? Old friend, I'm sorry."

I felt loss in my throat again. It rose up from my stomach and closed off my words.

His large hand settled onto my shoulder. "She was a fine woman. A fierce warrior. A filly like no other."

I patted his hand. "She was indeed."

"And who is this? A granddaughter perhaps?"

Andrillia looked up from her script, her pen pausing between the paper and the ink bottle. "No. His daughter doesn't like boys."

Clovis arched his eyebrows. "Really?"

"Never mind, Clovis. She's a minstrel. She's tagging along collecting stories."

"Ah. Emperor Quon bin Jaheen and another of his damnable contests, I presume."

"And I mean to win it," Andrillia said. She went back to her writing. While she scribbled, Clovis and I passed a wineskin between us. His dogs hunkered down near the fire. Our pony worked at a bit of grass, a wide white eye turned in their direction.

"I'm truly sorry about Luendyl," Clovis said. "She was something to behold." He reached behind him, foraging in his saddlebags. "I have something that might help." He pulled out a tattered copy of *Venison Stew for the Heart* and offered it to me.

"Thanks, Clovis. It's not the help I'm needing, but thanks."

His eyes narrowed as he returned his book. "And what help *are* you needing?"

"The kind with wings."

Clovis chuckled. "Wings, eh? What are you up to, Andro?"

I shrugged. "A short flight. Over the Blastlands."

The centaur laughed. "They make those shoes, you know."

I shook my head. "I'm thinking something bigger. And more reliable."

He scratched his beard. Andrillia lifted her lute and began to pick out another melody. Clovis closed his eyes. "I'd start with the King of Grunland," he finally said.

"He's not a big fan of mine."

"No, no . . . not the father. The son. The dad died in a fishing accident years ago."

This piqued my interest. "I didn't know he fished."

"I think the fish had *him* actually. One of those saber-toothed pikes the size of a wagon. Snarf." He made a slurping noise and smacked his lips. "One bite and that was that."

"And you don't think the son would have a grudge?"

"They got their bleeding throne back, didn't they?" Clovis chuckled. "Besides, it was years ago. Years and years."

"True enough."

"They'd be the closest, I'd wager. Though Azerminus had a djinn at one point, I'd heard. That could work, too."

"I wouldn't know where to find the codger."

Clovis snorted. "Surely he came for Luendyl's send-off?"

"No. He didn't."

"Sent one of those singing scrolls?"

"No. He didn't."

I heard the growl and saw the eyes flash. "Why that Gods-damned fop! I'd be ashamed to show my head if I were him. What did the rest of the old gang have to say about that?"

I swallowed. "Nothing. The old gang didn't turn out."

Agitated, he pranced back from the fire, tore up some sod, and tossed his hair. "The old gang didn't turn out? For Luendyl the Fair's Farewell Pyre?"

"And Fierce," I said. "No. They didn't turn out."

I could tell he was working himself up to a lather over it. I couldn't think of anything else to say. "You know, Clovis?"

His voice bellowed out. "What?"

"You weren't there, either."

He stopped. He sauntered closer and yanked the wineskin from my hands, up-ending it into his mouth. Wine splashed down like red rain. "Bloody shame, that," he said. "Bloody shame."

*

Handen Hall at Godsfeast was a bright and merry place. We'd hired the few giants we hadn't killed to build it from old, old trees taken from the Elderwood. It was our last Godsfeast there, Luendyl and me. Her belly was swelling. She'd already sold off her armor and taken to silk robes. We'd just finished building our house on Brookwood Down.

Fenruk Ironmauler sat arm wrestling with Hamrung the Bold, an older hero of some renown who died not so long ago in the battle for Gremgol's Pass. Clovis the Hunter stood to the side, one arm draped around a mare and the other draped around a Bythulian dancing girl he'd recently rescued from some troll's stewpot. Dozens of others sat in various states of drunken recline. Azerminus the Mage brought the hall to order.

"Heroes League of Handen Hall," he said with a somber voice. "We come to the end of our feast and the end of an age."

"And the end of our ale," one of Dunder the Dwarf-lord's stepcousins added.

"Here, here," someone shouted.

"It gives me no pleasure to say it." Azerminus paused, then looked at Luendyl and me from beneath those jutting white eyebrows. "But Andro . . . Luendyl . . . you will be sorely missed."

"Here, here," a different voice said.

"Six years ago, we dozen heroes stood upon this ground, hallowed with the blood of our fallen, and covenanted together to build a hall to their memory that light would go out from this place into the lands." Azerminus was ever wordy and worse still when he had some wine in him. I can't remember the rest of what he said but there was much jest about the new adventure we stood on the edge of. At its conclusion, he gave Luendyl a satchel of magic diapers, and the roof rose with applause and laughter.

Luendyl gave him her sweetest smile. "They'd best work, Azerminus. For the years are creeping on you and you'll be a-needing some of these yourself before too long."

"And a pretty girl to put them on him," the stepcousin said in the midst of the uproar.

We stood at the front. We basked in the blessing of our friends. And after Clovis and his evening's work left giggling and pinching and neighing. And after Dunder gathered up his drunk friends to find a tavern. And after the hall lay quiet and stinking of alcohol, flatulence and cooked meat, the three of us sat down with a bottle Azerminus had managed to hide from the others. Luendyl waved off the wine in favor of some grazzelberry juice.

"I'll surely miss you," he said. He also cried easily and even more so with some wine in him. The tears coursed down his cheeks and into his beard, spattering his blue sequined robe. "I'll surely miss you both."

"But you'll come visit," Luendyl said.

"And go fishing," I added.

He nodded. "I will indeed. And I've heard of a magicker in Xantun who makes these amazing bamboo fishing poles."

Luendyl patted his hand. We drank some more.

"It won't be the same." He reached out a gnarled hand and patted Luendyl's stomach. "Still, what an adventure!"

We laughed. I caught her eye and saw the light dancing in it. I'd watched her decapitate hobgibbers in the White Wastes of Norlish. I'd seen her pluck the Crown Prince of Dervon from a giant's cooking pot. I'd raced with her through the skies beyond the Blastlands, arrows singing past us. But in all of the places, in all of the times, I had never seen her look happier than she was now. And I had never seen her look more beautiful.

"To parenting," Azerminus said and lifted his glass.

"To parenting," Luendyl and I said, and we all drank together.

The old wizard shook his head. "I still can't believe it."

Luendyl turned on that smile again. "Believe it, old man." She rubbed her belly. "I think that Egg Charming Elixir of yours needs a bit more work."

We said our goodbyes to Clovis that morning. Under protest, I finally let him slip the copy of *Venison Stew* into my pack. I'd decided at the very least it could come in handy if kindling ran short. We entered Grunland six nights later without further misadventure.

But misadventure met us at the border.

"Names?" the fat guard asked.

"Andro Giantslayer," I said. I held up the urn. "And Luendyl the Fierce and Fair."

"And Andrillia," the girl added.

He scratched his beard and opened a scroll on his desk. He scratched some more, then stood. "Wait right here."

I was tired. That's my only excuse. We'd walked long hours that day. When he returned with a squad of Grunland Elite I didn't even reach for my sword.

"Andro the Usurper?" the Captain asked.

"Andro Giantslayer," I said.

"You are under arrest for high treason." He looked at Andrillia. "And your cohort as well. She looks a dangerous sort. There'll be no insurrection this day."

Then they took the urn, my sword, Andrillia's lute, our bags, and Foster, our pony. They stripped off my armor and manacled my hands and feet. "This is ridiculous. I demand audience with Harvald at once."

The captain of the guard sneered. "What a coincidence. His Royal Highness demands audience with *you*."

I was King of Grunland for exactly eight days, three hours and twenty-seven minutes the year after I met the love of my life and the year before I married her. I met Harvald the Second on my first day as king.

I remember the disapproving look Luendyl gave me as I dangled the wailing infant heir by his feet. She only needed to say one word. "Andro."

I looked at her. "Yes, my darling?"

"It's a baby. Not a toy."

I shrugged. "They shouldn't have left it lying about."

She took him from me. "You were chasing them with a sword."

Harvald the First had been tied up in the Gibber War of Aught Three. His queen, Drusilda, was frolicking with a dwarven acrobatics troupe at the summer palace in Rhendlis. I'd seen an opportunity and taken it. I didn't realize they'd left their son behind in the care of overly anxious nursemaids.

I shifted my crown. It made my head itchy. "Well, what do we do with it?"

She made little cooing noises at the baby. Little Harvald (a terrible name if you ask me) sputtered a bit more, and then gurgled a laugh. Babies are fickle things. "Is baby hungry or . . . " Luendyl sniffed at him. "Baby is *messy*."

I often repeat myself when I don't know what else to say. "What do we do with it?"

She scowled at me. "We change him, silly."

With the baby under one arm, she rummaged through a massive oak bureau etched with carvings of nymphs and fawns. She pulled out a diaper and knelt on the floor.

I've seen many sights. Severed limbs. Ditches of blood. The leftover gobbets of flesh in a dragon's bone pile. And I've smelled many smells. Charbroiled flesh. Week-old entrails. The toe-nail clippings of giants. Nothing I'd ever seen and nothing I'd ever smelled quite prepared me for this.

I fought back the nausea. "Gods, woman, what are you doing? Put that back on. Quickly."

She laughed. "Don't mind silly Andro. He just doesn't understand." After wadding up the messy cloth, she tickled the baby's stomach. "Don't mind him at all."

She was enjoying this too much. A dire thought slipped into my head. "You remembered your elixir today, right?"

She frowned at me. "Of course I did."

"Good."

She looked back at the baby. "But I'm going to want one of these someday."

My brain stumbled. It must've shown because she raised her eyebrows at me, waiting for my response. I ran five possible answers through my head before replying. "Uh . . . someday. Of course."

"Andro?"

"Yes, dear?"

"I mean it. Someday." She fastened the clean diaper onto the little prince. "Hopefully, by then they'll have figured out diapers that change themselves."

"I'll speak to Azerminus," I said. "After all, I am a King now."

"You do that. How's the crown?"

"It itches," I said. "Don't know how much longer I can stand wearing the damnable thing."

I didn't need to worry about that, though. Eight days, three hours and six minutes later, Harvald the First brought his own and three neighboring armies to bear on my kingdom. And all for the sake of a baby who, frankly, seemed a lot happier when his parents were away. It would be a few more years before I understood that kind of love.

Parents are fickle things.

*

My first words to Harvald the Second: "My, you've grown."

He was twice as fat as his father. I wasn't exactly sure how he fit his behind into the throne.

He leaned forward. The massive oak chair creaked. "Andro the Usurper," he said. "We are pleased to see you."

I looked around. Other than the guards and the girl, we were alone in the throne room. Light poured in through high stained-glass windows that depicted his father in a more robust and heroic manner than was necessarily true. "We are?" I asked.

He smiled. "Yes, we are."

"It's been a long time, Harvald. Last time I saw you, you had no teeth and soiled yourself regularly."

"And now *you* are the toothless pantaloons soiler." He laughed at his joke. Personally, I thought it was terrible humor.

I showed him my teeth. "No Diamblestori's Mystical Masticators here. As to the other — well, you'll just have to trust me. I may be old, but I'm not *that* old."

"And this is your army?" He looked at the girl. "We are amused."

I tried to move forward. The manacles clanked and the guards held me back. "Harvald, I am not seeking your throne. I retired years ago. I've actually come to ask for help."

This time, his laughter exploded from deep in his belly. Waves of fat shook and rolled. He continued laughing until big tears streamed down his cheeks.

I grinned as he composed himself. I thought maybe his humor was a good sign.

"What help would you ask of us?"

"Something with wings. For a short flight." I decided to appeal to his humanity. "My wife and I would be forever in your debt."

"And where *is* Luendyl the Usurpress?"

"Fierce and Fair," I said. "Luendyl the Fierce and Fair."

One of the guards stepped forward, holding the urn. "I think she's in here, your Highness."

His beady eyes narrowed. "Is she?"

I swallowed. I felt grief rustling in my belly. "She is."

For a moment I saw a spark, some kind of connection. Maybe

some buried part of him remembered my wife's fond care. Or maybe we met on the even playing field of loss, his parents having both passed. Whatever it was, I decided to follow through.

I offered up my saddest smile. "Clovis the Hunter sent us. He thought you could help."

His eyes narrowed. "The centaur?"

"Yes."

The spark went out. His face went dark. He opened his mouth. "We'll not speak of him or the shame his cavorting caused my father." But then he did speak, the words tumbling over his fat lips. "To think of that beast and my mother rutting away in the stables. It broke my father's heart. He carried it with him to his deathbed."

I often say the wrong thing at the wrong time. "I thought your father died in a fishing accident?"

The gathering clouds on his face broke into a storm. "Enough." He muttered and blustered underneath his breath, shifting on his throne. He placed both his hands on his thighs and squeezed until his knuckles went white.

Andrillia stepped forward. "Your highness, may I speak?"

Harvald nodded.

She no longer looked like a girl pretending to be a boy. Instead, she was a young woman standing with confidence before the third most powerful man in the realm.

"Forgive my companion's insensitivity. Loss clouds his already questionable judgment." She bowed her head. "I beg your pardon on his behalf."

Harvald looked at her and then back at me. "Your daughter?"

I shook my head.

"Granddaughter?"

I shook it again. "A minstrel. She's gathering tales for her trade."

The storm passed. Interest replaced anger. "We would hear a tune, minstrel."

A guard pushed her lute into her hands. Andrillia offered a shy smile, swallowed, and began to play. The notes lifted into the high vaulted ceiling of the throne room, the stone walls throwing back the melody. When her voice joined the strings, it was like honeyed mead pouring over the tongue. She sang a song of famous deeds. The king nodded his approval. She sang a song of recent loss. The king wiped a tear. She sang a song of bawdy humor. The king slapped his knees and guffawed. And last, she sang their grand, sweeping national anthem "O Grunland Fair." It moved Harvald to his feet, his large body shaking.

Then Andrillia stopped, looked the king dead in his eyes, and bowed deeply.

"We are most pleased," Harvald said. He sat down.

"Thank you, your Highness." She handed the lute back to the guard and took her place beside me. "Will you help us?"

"They were good songs," he said. "It would be a shame to kill such talent." He turned to me. "Your companions have ever been your saving grace."

I had never heard truer words. I decided to keep quiet this time.

"Escort the lady minstrel to our guest quarters." Andrillia opened her mouth then closed it. She gave me a worried look but followed the guard out of the room. Harvald studied me as they left. "Our father had a dragon on contract."

"Of the winged variety?"

He nodded. "But she doesn't fly anymore. Not since her mate died. She doesn't do anything anymore. We send her cattle and gold. She does nothing. The bandits and gobbers run amok in our land, the peasants organize and protest."

"Perhaps I could talk with her?"

Harvald smiled. For a moment he slipped out of his royal plurality. "I think that could be arranged. I think perhaps you could even help her."

"I'd be happy to try. What do you have in mind?"

That conniving look was back now that Andrillia was gone. "Vengeance satisfied can be a great motivator. You see, our inconsolable dragon's mate was killed quite brutally some time back. His name was — "

Realization came home. "Fang the Dread."

He smiled. "Fang the Dread."

"What about the girl?"

"She'll be our guest. We'll tell her that we escorted you to the border and sent you on your way. Of course, you'll be dead by then. A bony, gristly meal I have no doubt."

Despite my sudden discomfort, I was impressed. "You've gotten quite good at this, Harvald. You wear the crown the well."

"Thank you." He shifted its weight on his head and scratched his scalp. "It itches."

*

You never forget your first dragon. I met mine on the day I asked Luendyl to be my wife.

Giants are one thing, all blunder and bulk, but dragons are lean, mean, liquid grace.

Fang the Dread was no exception. The first time I saw him, he was outlined against a full moon, hovering and preparing to dive on an unsuspecting village. I sat on a hillside, studying him while Luendyl slept. I prodded her.

"He's here, darling."

She stirred and sat up, the blankets spilling around her and the moonlight glinting off her armor. On work nights, she often slept ready for the fight.

Fang dove, disappearing behind a barn, then lifted with a bellowing cow clutched tightly in his talons. The dragon turned east. Below, lights came on and shouts were raised.

Luendyl wadded her blankets into a tight ball and shoved them into her saddlebags. "Let's go then."

I leaped onto Falgron's back, mentally checking off the list we'd created two nights before. "Follow him home. Take his head. Take his treasure. Collect our reward."

"Exactly." She surged forward. Her steed, Frazen, was considerably faster than Falgron. I pressed to keep up.

We tore across the fields and through copses of alder and beech, leaping streams and skirting ponds. We followed that damnable dragon for six hours. The sun rose on our pursuit, the sky moving from gray to mauve. The pounding hooves and flapping wings drowned out any birdsong.

Then he vanished behind a mounded hill.

I reined in. Luendyl, just a bit ahead of me now, did the same. "Do you think this is it?"

I shook my head. "I think he saw us."

She laughed. "That's impossible. He hasn't looked back once."

"Maybe he heard us. Or smelled us."

She sauntered towards me. "Andro, I think it's highly un — "

Did I mention lean, mean, liquid grace? Three things happened at once. Fang dropped like a heavy stone from nowhere. A large, bloody cow plowed into me and tumbled me to the ground. Luendyl lifted off her horse and into the air to race east in the clutches of Fang the Dread.

One word, bellowed gleefully as Fang hurled his dinner at me, reverberated in the morning air. "Virgin!"

I climbed back onto Falgron and spurred us after her. She had managed to draw one of her scimitars and hacked at Fang's ankle, raising sparks. Fang accelerated and increased altitude. I'm not sure if any words passed between them, but Luendyl suddenly stopped hacking and settled in for the ride. She'd always loved flying. Fang leveled out, descended a bit, and sped on. I tried to tell myself that she was screaming in terror. That's what she's always maintained. And though she denied it to the very end, I still think she was actually *laughing*. Giggling like a little girl.

"Hang on, love," I yelled after her. I doubt she heard. But I needed to say it more than she needed to hear it. I pushed Falrgon harder that day than any day before. We stayed a nudge behind the dragon's shadow as it coursed over the meadows and hills. Eventually, we hit the wall of an enormous cliff. Above, Fang scuttled three-legged over a ledge, careful not to bang or squeeze his newfound prize overmuch, and disappeared into the mountainside.

I dismounted. I stood at the base of the cliff and stared up, scratching my head beneath my helmet.

Personally, I thought Oingeltonken was a dangerous wizard and the only good that had ever come from his enchantments was my wife crashing down into my life years before. But in that moment, for the first time, I actually wished for a pair of those Flights of Fancy Winged Shoes. But in the end, I had to do it the old-fashioned way. I dug the rope and grapnel hook out of the bottom of my saddlebags, turned Falgron loose to graze, and started climbing.

Halfway up, dented and dusty, I paused to rest and re-set my hook. Sounds drifted down. Deep, rumbling noises from the cave entrance above.

The dragon, it seemed, was singing.

Love songs.

To my girl.

I climbed faster.

"Fair and buxom maiden show to me your wares," I heard Fang sing as I pulled myself onto the ledge. The large cave stretched back into the mountain, as dark and menacing as the beast's mouth. Piles of meat-laced bone lined the entrance. Remnants of cows, horses, villagers. The stink overwhelmed my nose and sent tears into my beard and down the neck of my chain mail shirt. I stretched out on the rock, catching my breath.

The deep bass voice paused, then shifted to cooing. "Such a sparkly, shiny virgin."

I crawled to my knees and drew my sword. I stood.

"Fang the Dread!"

The cooing stopped. Deep in the cave, I heard the rustle of scales on metal. Sword leveled, I entered the reeking lair. Odors shifted the further I walked. A touch of vanilla mixed with the rotting meat. Dim light flickered ahead. A voice bellowed out. "Who calls my name?"

I should've kept quiet. But I rarely do. "Your so-called virgin's man."

Fang lowered his voice. "You didn't say you were married."

Luendyl answered; I could tell she was amused. "Oh, we're not married." She raised her voice for my benefit I suppose. "Not yet anyway."

By now, I'd turned a corner and could see. The massive cavern lay in the guttering shadows of a dozen large scented candles. Fang the Dread crouched in a pile of treasure, Luendyl clutched loosely in a claw. His head weaved back and forth, one emerald eye watching her and the other watching the entrance.

I sucked in my breath. He made the giants look small and insignificant. Still, I strode into the candlelight and raised my sword. Fang watched me but kept talking to her.

"But you *are* a virgin?"

Luendyl shrugged. "Well. Not exactly."

Fang howled in agony. "Not exactly?"

I stepped closer. I couldn't help but grin as I thought about *how* 'not exactly' she was. "Not by a long shot," I said.

"Andro," she said, "You're not helping."

Fang's eyes narrowed. "What does *not exactly* mean . . . exactly?"

I think I saw her blush a bit in the candlelight. I watched her lips move as she silently counted off names on her fingers. Naturally, I knew we weren't one another's first. But I think every man wants to believe he's no more than second. Or maybe third. I made myself look away as she finished her first hand and started on the other.

"Um . . . what are we counting?"

Fang howled again. I suddenly wanted to join him.

Fang tightened his grip on her. "You are either a virgin," he said, "Or you are lunch. Which is it?"

"Oh. Definitely a virgin."

I'd gotten close enough that coins were clinking beneath my feet. Fang's head moved quickly until it was just a few feet from me. His eyes dilated. His huge mouth opened, easily the size of a small door. "And what say *you*? Do you concur?"

"I guess that depends," I said.

"Upon what?"

"What happens if she *is* a virgin?"

I had never seen a dragon shrug before. It is a terrible thing. Bits of gold flew up, the room shook. "I still eat her. Just more slowly. By candlelight." I had also never seen a dragon grin before. It's equally terrible. "With a bit of soft music and a vat or two of wine."

I moved to the left just in time. His snout came down, jaws snapping where I had stood. I didn't know what else to do, so I shoved my sword into his ear.

Fang roared and twisted, snapping off my blade at the hilt. He let Luendyl go and dug at the sword in his ear with a long talon. She scrambled to my side, drawing her scimitar. "Took you long enough," she said.

I tossed the hilt aside and looked around the treasure mound. I spotted a large axe and waded through the gold towards it. Fang thrashed, shaking the room, and I fell into the gold. Luendyl leapt aside, bringing her blade down on the dragon's neck. The enchanted steel sparked on his scales. "I don't think this is working," she said.

I grabbed up the axe and rolled as his mouth again fell. I heard a crunch as his fangs struck the hard stone floor. When his head came up again, blood and gold spilled from his mouth. I swung the axe up, driving it diagonally into his gums at the base of one massive tooth. Luendyl put her scimitar into his other ear, and though her blade held together, it was yanked from her hand as he jerked away.

Suddenly, the vanilla scent lost itself in the smell of hot sulphur. Smoke billowed from his nostrils as Fang snapped his mouth shut. "He's going to flame!" I shouted at Luendyl.

She moved. His tail whipped around and sent her into the air to land heavily on the other side of the cavern. She didn't move.

We'd fought dozens of battles together. We'd killed hundreds of foes. We'd faced danger and death at every turn for most of our three years together. For the first time, I realized I could lose her. Could have already lost her. Something broke inside me and my own roaring matched the sound of the flames blasting from the dragon's mouth. I raced towards her, a trail of fire chasing my heels.

"Luendyl?" I scooped her up and kept running. "Not this way," I said to no one in particular. "Not this way." Fire singed the hair on the back of my neck.

We left the cave and I laid her out on the ledge behind an outcropping of rock. Her eyes fluttered.

"Not what way?" she asked.

That was the first and last time she ever saw me cry. "We're supposed to grow old together," I told her.

The cavern was quiet behind us. I looked back over my shoulder.

"Well?" she asked.

"Wait here."

Dragons, ever the arrogant lot, never suspect that those who live to run away might return willingly . . . or in a calculated rage. Fang lay growling on his back, claws digging at the blades in his ears, long tongue licking at his wounded gums. He did not hear me. But he did smell me. He craned his neck and squinted into the smoke that still hung in the air.

"You're *back*?"

I said nothing. I hefted the axe and planted it in his open mouth. With my bare hands, I pried free the tooth I had loosened. He yowled, his claws rasping against the metal of my armor. I felt hot fire where they tore through and ripped my skin.

"We're supposed to grow old together," I told the dragon as I shoved his own fang deep into his throat. It pushed easily through the scales, and with a final roar, Fang the Dread jerked, heaved, and then lay still.

"We will, Andro," Luendyl said from behind me. I didn't realize she had followed me back into the lair. I turned towards her, my hands shaking, the giant tooth slippery with both my blood and Fang's.

"Promise?" I asked.

"Promise," she said.

I fell into her arms and she held me up. Looking back, I can see that she's always held me up.

She was frying dragon steaks on a small fire when I regained consciousness. I was bandaged and feeling better — it ends up that dragons keep well-stocked medicine chests.

Luendyl poured five hundred-year-old wine into diamond goblets and served up dinner on ruby-encrusted platinum platters. "I'm going to want a ring," she said.

I looked at the treasure mound. "I'm sure we can find something."

"And a *real* wedding. Handen Hall should do nicely."

"Whatever you want, love."

She looked at me carefully. The light softened her face, and for a moment she didn't look fierce at all, only fair. Absolutely the fairest. "Are you sure about this, Andro?"

"We're supposed to grow old together," I said again.

She nodded, sipped her wine, then pointed her fork at my plate. "How's your steak?"

"It's good," I said. "Tastes like chicken."

Breya the Dark's lair was nothing like her husband's all those years ago.

It was more a mud hole than a cave, set deep in the mountains on Grunland's northern border. The guards had hauled me there by wagon and deposited me, unshackled, at the mouth of a hole carved into the muddy clay. They gave me my pack and my wife and stood waiting, swords drawn, for me to go inside.

"Thanks, boys," I said.

They kept waiting.

"I can take it from here."

They said nothing.

Finally, I turned my back on them and entered the hole. Dirty sunlight followed me in, casting a gray gloom over the lair. "Hello?"

I heard something large stir. "Are you the surprise they told me about?"

"Maybe," I said.

"The one that's supposed to cheer me up?"

"Quite possibly, yes."

Again, the stirring. "Come closer then. I can barely see you."

I moved into the larger room. Breya coughed flame and a torch guttered to life. The room was sparse. The dragon lay along the wall in a trough roughly the size of her body.

"And who exactly are you? Another acrobat?"

"No," I said.

"A juggler?"

"No."

"Magician?"

I shook my head. "No."

"Good. Can't abide any of them. Ran the last one off with his robes ablaze." Her eyes moved over me. "Then what are you?"

I thought about lying but suddenly I felt tired of it all. No point lying to her or to myself. I'd come to the end of it and I would die on my feet. "My name is Andro Giantslayer. I killed your husband."

Her head came up fast. "My husband?"

I swallowed and closed my eyes, waiting for the fire or the teeth. Nothing happened.

"And they sent you up here thinking that would make me feel better?"

I opened my eyes. "Yes. I think Harvald said something about me being a gristly, bony meal."

Breya laughed. "Not even a meal. More like a snack. Still, there's one flaw in this plan of his."

"What's that?"

"My husband wasn't killed. He just got sick and died. Some giants we used to play Pillage and Plunder with buried him out in Alderland."

"Same as my Luendyl," I said. That hollow, empty space was back in my stomach.

"Your what?"

I sat down, cradling my wife on my lap. "My Luendyl," I said. "She just got sick and died."

Uncomfortable silence settled between us. "Well," she said, "What do we do now?"

I shrugged. "They're waiting out there for you to eat me or burn me or something."

"For killing my husband?"

I chuckled. "I didn't *think* Fang was marriage material. Not the way he went after the virgins."

"Tell me about it. Fang was . . . " She paused. "Wait a minute. You killed *Fang*?"

"Yes. Fang the Dread. Did you know him?"

"Now it makes more sense." Her head moved towards me, her glittering claws tearing into the mud. "Fang was my *first* husband."

I clutched my urn and waited. Again, nothing happened.

"Thought your wife was a virgin, I'll wager," she finally said. "Candles. Music. I know all about it. Certainly wasn't the first time. That's why I left the bastard."

I nodded. "We weren't married yet. But still . . . "

"But still," she said. "I remember feeling glad that someone finally put him out of my misery. Disgusting worm."

Silence settled in again. I leaned against the muddy wall, tracing the outline of the urn. Breya watched me. I've always disliked uncomfortable, quiet patches along the way but time and time again, my interruptions of those silences have taken me down difficult roads.

"The first year or two are the hardest," she finally said.

I looked up at her. "Does it get better after that?"

"No. Not really. You just get used to it."

"Oh."

"I suppose there are things you can do, though, to make it a bit more bearable." She snorted. "Not that I've had much use for that."

"Like what?" I asked.

"Oh, talking about it. Staying busy. And there are books out there, too."

"Well, I've stayed pretty busy." I dug around in my pack, pulled out Clovis's copy of *Venison Stew for the Heart* and held it up. "I'm not much of a reader, but a friend gave me this."

Outside, a horse neighed. Low voices conversed.

"Blast and bother," Breya said. "Are *they* still waiting?"

"I suspect so."

She stretched out, her neck twisting and extending down the passage. "Yes. Still waiting. We'll have to do something about that."

I put the book away, picked the urn back up. Strange to have so much of my life reduced to ashes and memories. During the long walk to Grunland, the conversations with Andrillia and the others, it had been easier not to think about it. "What do you have in mind?"

She snapped her tongue over her lips. "I think you should scream really, really loud."

I screamed. Breya thrashed her tail, sending mud and water down the passage. I kept screaming until she nodded for me to stop.

"There," she bellowed to the guards outside. "He's finished. You can go home now."

A few minutes later, I heard the wagon clatter away.

"So what now?" she asked.

I set the urn down. "We could talk, I suppose."

"Do you want to talk?"

"Not really. Do you?"

"No. Not really." She lowered her head back into the mud. "What about that book?"

"Fey and halflet bare-the-soul and talk-about-our-feelings crap," I said. "Anyone carting around a five-year-old in their head needs a walloping if you ask me."

She laughed. "Still, it might pass the time."

I pulled the book out. "Might be good for a chuckle or two, I suppose."

So I flipped it open, found a story and started to read.

The first one was about Pyflee the One-Winged Pixie who, despite her obvious deformity, still managed to win the Gildis Fairy Air Marathon pennant three times running.

"Ridiculous," Breya snorted.

"Preposterous," I added.

Then I read about Orgle the Obese, a troll with an uncontrollable appetite for pickled dwarf feet who, after falling in love with a dwarven princess, became a vegetarian, lost three hundred pounds, and founded a crutch factory.

"Who writes these?" Breya asked.

"No idea," I said. "But the crutch bit is clever."

Next, I read about a king who hated music and a minstrel who hated kings and how, after being stranded together in the belly of a lactose intolerant giant, they gained an appreciation of one another's jobs by trading places for a year. The king won Shaluzan's contest and the minstrel won three major wars and annexed half another kingdom.

"Well, that's at least plausible," I said.

"Barely," Breya said.

Last, I read about Gilda the Troll Wife, whose husband died in some silly, senseless way, and how she spent the first dozen years doing absolutely nothing and the second dozen years doing absolutely anything just to keep her mind off the big hole in her heart and —

I closed the book. "I think that's enough of that."

She sighed. "I think so, too. Silly, pointless book."

I tucked the book back into my pack. It was my turn to ask. "What now?"

She shrugged. "We should do something."

"Want to get out for bit?" I asked.

She stretched her wings and cracked her neck. "What do you have in mind?"

"I have an idea. Do you like minstrels?"

She shuddered. "They make me gassy."

"You'll like this one. She's a good kid. We'll just need to rescue her first."

She thought about it for a moment. "I've never actually been on the other end of the rescuing bit. Might be nice for a change."

I gathered up my wife and my pack. I climbed onto Breya's back. "Go easy on me," I said. "I've never flown dragon before."

She bucked forward, snaking for the entrance. "Well, you know what they say?"

Outside the cave, she unfurled the fullness of her wings and beat against the air. "No," I answered. "What do they say?"

She plunged upward, gravity pushing me down into her scales. "Once you go dragon, you wish for a wagon!"

I groaned. "We should send that one in. It belongs in the book somewhere."

"Hang on," she said. And I did.

And suddenly, I understood why Luendyl laughed so long ago and why she always said that I should give her back to the sky.

This is the part I don't want to write.

If you don't want to read it, skip on ahead. I'll meet you down the road.

Luendyl the Fierce and Fair, Fiercest and Fairest, went to sleep on Godsfeast Eve and never woke up.

She'd been sick. Coughing. Sore. Fevered. But she'd been all these things before. We'd decided that if she were no better the next morning, I would make the trip to town and see what the apothecary had for remedies. I made her some soup and sat with her while she ate it in bed.

"Still no word from Karysa?" she asked.

I shook my head. "She and the League went north. That Witch Queen in Nebios is acting up again."

She nodded, slurping at the soup. "Glad she got the League back together. I wonder what Ansabel is up to?"

Ansabel was our daughter's partner. Daughter of some duke or count that she had rescued from certain doom. They made their home near Handen Hall and talked a lot about adopting, though I suppose they could've charmed Azerminus into a revision of his Egg Charming Elixir.

I shrugged. "I'm not sure. She's probably with her parents for the feast."

She finished her dinner and I took the bowl away. I put it in the sink and went back to her. Coughing, she patted the quilt beside her. "Come back to bed, Andro."

I stretched out next to her and held her hand. "You'll feel better tomorrow, love. If not, I'll go see what Bremble has on his shelves."

"I might not, Andro."

"You will," I said.

"But if I didn't . . . "

I shushed her. Something she hated, but she didn't say anything this time. She drew in a deep breath. I heard the rattling in her lungs.

She was always good at figuring out how to say her piece. I think maybe that's one of the keys to a good marriage — knowing how to talk to the other person about something they don't want to talk about. "You haven't been fishing in a while," she said.

"No. Busy with other things."

"You can never be too busy for what you love," she said. "I want you to remember that."

I laughed. "Remember. Hell, woman, it's what you've taught me from the start. That night in the Blastlands? Danger lurking all about and me rutting like a schoolboy with a goddess who'd fallen from the sky?"

She chuckled. "That was a good time."

"They've all been good times."

"Or that time on the Grunland throne? And on Fang's treasure pile?"

I twisted and looked at her, squeezing her hand. "Not just those times. All of our times. Everything good and perfect in my life came from you."

"And Karysa," she added.

"Must I remind you where *she* came from?"

She snorted a bit. "No need. I remember that well enough."

"I rest my case."

She let go of my hand, then stroked it lightly with her fingers. "I need to rest mine, too," she said.

I kissed her cheek. "Get some sleep, love. I'll see you in the morning."

She smiled at me. Then she said the same thing she always said, whether I was staying up late, heading to town, or gallivanting off to do a hero's work. "Don't be too long. I'll miss you too much."

And I said what I always say: "Be back before you know I'm gone."

She went to sleep. She didn't wake up the next morning. Or the next. Or the next. On that third day, I shed no tears when I put the torch to my wife.

Ashes and memories.

No doubt, you've heard about the Rescue of Andrillia Songweaver from one of her own songs. Her exceptionally deft usage of poetic license is commendable.

It actually went something like this.

Breya and I crashed through the glass dome of Harvald's throne room, showering the room with a rainbow of glittering shards.

The guards scattered. Harvald jumped up, his behind catching in the throne and carrying it up with him. He toppled and fell over. Breya landed heavily in the center of the room.

"Where's the girl?" I asked.

Harvald lay on the floor, whimpering. I looked around. One of his chancellors cowered nearby, mouth hanging open. I pointed. "You. She's here in two minutes or my friend starts roasting."

The chancellor tore out of the room. I remember wondering if he really would find Andrillia or just keep running. It didn't matter. Andrillia arrived two minutes later. I pulled her up behind me and we were airborne again.

She grinned. "I knew you'd come back for me."

"Andrillia . . . Breya. Breya . . . Andrillia, the minstrel I was telling you about."

Andrillia clutched at my shirt. "This is *definitely* going into the song."

"You may need to dress it up a bit."

"Oh, I will. Don't worry."

We hit Breya's optimal cruising altitude. She whipped her head around to look at us. "Where to now?"

"The Blastlands," Andrillia said. "A short flight?"

I nodded. "Is that okay?"

"Yes," they both said. And we were off.

Just another push," the midwife said.

"I'm tired of pushing," Luedyl said through gritted teeth. "Get that baby out of me or I'll carve you in half."

Always helpful, I squeezed her hand. "We sold off the scimitars, love."

"Andro, you're not help — " The words were lost as her growl became a shout. Sweat poured down her face. I used my other hand to run the damp cloth over her forehead.

I looked at the hand she held. In her grip, the tips of my fingers were as white as her knuckles. "Sorry, darling."

"Just push," the midwife said again. "It'll be over before you know it."

"Then let's trade places, you gibber sucking rat licker." She roared again. I thought I heard bones crunching in my hand.

Azerminus poked his head into the room. "Is everything going — " His face went white. "Oh my. Excuse me." He disappeared.

I can't remember exactly what Luendyl said next, something about where she was going to put the next Egg Charming Elixir he concocted. It evoked a painful image.

Then a new voice entered the room. A high, warbling cry that I couldn't ever imagine growing to love as much as I did.

After, with the baby cleaned up and wrapped in a blanket, I sat with Luendyl and our daughter.

Tears ran down my wife's face. "Oh, look at her, Andro. She has your nose."

It was a lot smaller, but I could see it. I didn't know what to say. "She has your ears."

"No she doesn't. Those are yours too."

I laughed. "She's doomed then."

"Not if she has her mother's sensibilities."

"True. What do we call her?"

We'd never been able to decide. We'd tossed out Andro and Andrillia straight away. Dozens of other names I can't remember were also pitched and tossed over the months as we built our home and settled in to Brookwood Down.

Luendyl looked up at me. "What was the name of that princess?"

"Which one?"

"The one we went to rescue? The one that Duke What's-It hired those ogres to kidnap so he could force her hand in marriage?"

"Oh. *Her*?"

"Yes. *Her*." The baby made strange gurgling sounds.

"Why her?"

She shifted her bundle, baring her breast. "Remember? We got there and — "

I laughed. "And she'd somehow managed to take on the whole lot by herself. Asked us to take her straightway to Duke Grandor's hunting palace so she could take him on as well."

"Exactly. Left quite a mess of him, too."

I scratched my head. "I don't remember her name. Karyla? Karyna?"

"Karysa," Luendyl said.

"Karysa?"

She nodded. "That was a girl who could take care of herself."

I leaned in and kissed her. "So are you. Maybe we should call her Luendyl the Fierce."

"And Fair," she said. "You always leave that bit out."

"Sorry."

"It's okay." She rubbed the baby's chin with the tip of her finger. "Karysa. What do you think of that?"

"Ogres beware," I said.

"And dukes," my wife added, smiling down on the life we had made together. "Don't forget dukes."

We entered the Blastlands before dawn. The night had slipped past, Breya and Andrillia making small talk about songs and dragons and treasure while I kept quiet and thought about everything that had brought me to this place.

"You're terribly quiet," Andrillia said.

"Just thinking," I answered. The sky around us took on the color of steel. I was watching as the ground below grayed as well, scanning the horizon for the desolate ruins that had become the birthplace of life and love for me so many years ago. "Might turn a bit south," I said to Breya.

"Ghul-Shar-Tov, right?"

"Yes."

"It's not far." She banked a bit. Steel became deep purple and then pink. I looked over my shoulder to see the sun crest the Dragon's Spine Mountains. That's when I saw her, racing across the sky to meet us.

Luendyl, glittering in her armor, legs moving tirelessly to the beat of Oingeltonken's Flights of Fancy Winged Shoes. I opened my mouth and would have pointed if I didn't need to hang on.

Andrillia turned to look. "What is it?" But she couldn't see. Maybe the angle was wrong.

She moved across heaven, my Luendyl, her arms stretching out and her mouth opening. My tears made her glitter all the more. She drew closer and I heard her call out.

"Dad!"

Not Luendyl. Karysa. A spark, a puff of smoke, and the left shoe cut out. Oingeltonken's left shoes were ever his bane. She spun, trying to regain control, but at this altitude there would be no slowing the fall. And no tent below to catch her. She plummeted, hands still stretched out.

Now Andrillia saw her. "Is that — ?"

"Breya," I shouted, "Can you catch her?"

The dragon said nothing. She just spun and dove; we hung on as best we could. Air rushed past. I could see my daughter flailing below, digging frantically in her pouch for some bit of scroll or potion. Breya's mouth reached her before the rest of us. She caught Karysa in her jaws.

Andrillia and I cheered. "Well done," I said.

Breya made some muffled response.

"Don't talk with your mouth full," my daughter said.

We landed on the floor of the Blastlands. I slid down from Breya's back and hugged Karysa.

"Dad, what are you doing out here without me?" She looked tired. Her eyes were red and puffy. "Why didn't you wait?"

I felt my shoulders sag. "I sent the birds out. No one came."

"We were up north. Remember? Nebios?"

I actually had forgotten. Or not made the connections. Now I know it was just the grief. It clouds you. It fogs you in. But in that moment I remembered. "The Witch Queen? How did that go?"

Karysa looked angry and sad at the same time. "We'll finish up with her later. As soon as we got the message, we turned south."

"We?"

A large patch of carpet settled onto ground beside us. A wizened old man stepped off, followed by a grizzled warrior and a grouchy dwarf lord.

Azerminus walked quickly over and put his arms around me. "Old friend," he said, "I'm so sorry for your loss." Fenruk's large hand came down on my shoulder. Dunder stood apart, looking somber. Azerminus stepped back.

"We came as soon as we could," Fenruk said, joining the wizard.

"We had to fight our way back," Karysa The White of the West said. "Where's Mom?"

I pulled the urn from my pack. "She's here."

No one spoke for a bit. Finally, I said the right thing. "Karysa, I'm sorry. I should have waited longer."

She softened a bit. "You should have. But we all knew it could happen someday. And you really had no way of knowing when . . . or even *if* I could get back." She hugged me again. "At least we found you."

"Was I hard to find?"

"Not too hard," she said. "You left a pretty wide trail. That last bit with the King's Throne Room in Grunland . . . that was priceless." She looked up. I followed her gaze and saw the ruins on the horizon. "But I knew eventually you'd end up out here."

Azerminus conjured chairs for us. Breya stretched out in the sun. Andrillia sat wide-eyed and listened until someone called on her for a song. She sang. We ate and drank and told stories about Luendyl the Fierce and Fair.

When the moon rose over the Blastlands, Karysa and I climbed onto Breya's back. The lost city of Ghul-Shar-Tov shone silver below us as she lifted us into the air. She began to fly in a widening circle, wings stretched out in the moonlight. Laughing and crying at

the same time, Karysa and I opened the urn and gave her mother
— my wife — back to the sky.

Spring is coming on now. New life is showing in the leaves.
Brookwood Down is quiet these days, but for the birds and creek
and the occasional song.

Karysa and Ansabel informally adopted Andrillia. I guess that
makes me informally a grandfather. They've come to visit a time or
two. She always brings her lute and plays our song. Alas, Andrillia
did not win the Emperor's contest. But somehow, she did manage
to win the heart of one of his thirty-seven sons. I'm hoping it's a
long courtship, but her new parents will help with that.

The Broadback boys added on to my barn and now Breya comes
and goes as she pleases. She's started dating . . . something I doubt
I'll do . . . and she even went a few rounds with a certain perfumed
centaur acquaintance of mine. How they managed, I dare not ask.
Azerminus has been out at least a half dozen times and swears he's
hauling me up to Handen Hall for some kind of lifetime achievement
medal they're tossing about these days. I'll most likely go. And I'll
smile a lot and think about my wife and the times we shared both
there and everywhere else.

So why have I filled these pages up? I look at them, quite a stack,
though I'll wager nothing like Orvid and Drimbull's *Venison Stew for
the Heart*. What's it all about, really?

I think if I've learned anything, in the very end, it's this. The grand-
est adventures of our lives aren't about horses and swords and ghost
cities lost to time. They are the choices we've made and why we've
made them. And the greatest treasures in our lives aren't the sleeping vaults beneath moon-misted ruins or the treasure mounds of flam-
ing dragons. They are the people we have loved and been loved by
along the path of our choices. And the most sweeping battles we will
ever fight are not against gibbers, gobbers, giants, or trolls. They are
against other foes — any foes that stand between us and our true
treasures in the adventure of our living.

I've heard many good words along the way. You'll remember
these, I'm sure:

Often the things we love best are what we expect least. Your
companions will ever be your saving grace. You can never be too
busy for what you love.

And now my tale is done. By my own measure, I've had a great adventure full of unexpected wealth along the way.

Now those damnable trout are calling my name. Oingeltonken has supposedly perfected a self-casting rod. I'm going to try it out with some trepidation and some worms I dug out of the garden last night.

I've set the skillet out. I'm planning fish for dinner.

Afterword:
TEN YEARS LOGGING
THE IMAGINATION FOREST
Ken Scholes

Well, howdy!

If you've gotten this far into the book that's a good sign. Really, you can stop now if you want to. But if you're like me, you might like to know a bit more about the stories, how they came to be, where they first appeared, what Extremely Clever Things the author tried to do or wished he'd done or completely failed to do. So consider this our time for that.

Let's have a cup of coffee and talk. Tea's fine, too. Or whatever beverage you choose. Have a seat. Already sitting? Okay.

As I write this, I'm forty years old. I've just typed END on my second novel (*Canticle*— coming in 2009 from Tor books.) And I've undergone that wacky transformation that takes place when short story writers start writing novels, under contract and with deadlines. Which means, alas, less time for short fiction. For now, that is.

But from 1997 to 2007, I wrote a lot of short fiction and you're holding some of it in your hands right now. I enjoy the form — I like the challenge of fitting all that story into such an enclosed space. I like the wild ride of chasing down the various bits and pieces that become a short story.

These stories have appeared in various places at various times. Some have even shown up more than once. Some have had Very Nice Things said about them by reviewers and by readers who dropped me little notes here and there over the decade.

All of them are my paper children, strange products of my psyche and circumstances birthed through fingers flying over the keyboard. Old growth harvested from my imagination forest.

If you're like me, you listen to the commentary on the DVDs because you're just *always* curious about the story behind the story.

Got that beverage yet?

Here we go.

The Man With Great Despair Behind His Eyes

This story took longer than any other short story I've ever written. I started it in 1998 and finished it in 2004.

I've always admired Meriwether Lewis and I think I identified with him because of his struggle with depression — something I've wrestled with myself. It became the central conflict of the story.

As with many of my stories, it started with me playing "what if?" with circumstances. What if no one found D. B. Cooper because he fell back in time? What if Lewis and Clark found him as an old man in the woods? I jammed the first draft out over a period of a day or two. It was largely the same as what you've read — but with a much different ending. The ending I had just plain didn't work and I didn't know what to do about it. So the story languished until one day, I re-read it and instantly knew the right way to land it. I just had to wait until my writing muscles were bigger.

Easter eggs? Some Simon and Garfunkel references and my favorite bit: Man-from-the-River feeds Lewis his own last words, "I am no coward. I am so strong and so hard to die." There is some debate as to whether Lewis was murdered or finally succumbed to his depression and took his life. I suspect the latter is more true so I ran with that assumption.

This one is also known for the infamous "Seaman erupted from the underbrush" line that now has me reading my stories aloud to my wife before I read them aloud to the rest of the world. And don't go back looking for it — I cleaned that bit up.

"The Man with Great Despair . . . " first came out in *Talebones* in 2005. It was my first lead story in that fine magazine. Later, it was reprinted in the anthology *Prime Codex*.

Action Team-Ups Number Thirty-Seven

What happens when superheroes and supervillains retire? Where do they go? Do they ever *really* retire? This was the second humor piece I'd written. It was drafted a few weeks ahead of Norwescon 2005 for *Talebones Live!* — a big group reading that Patrick puts on each year. I try to write something new specifically for that event. It read well. Later, the story made its rounds and landed at *Shimmer* for their Winter 2006 issue. They even sent me into the studio to record an audio version — you can find it on my website if you'd like to hear it.

I intend (someday) to do more with these characters. Colonel Patriot actually shows up in a few other stories and NM is referenced as well.

Soon We Shall All We Saunders

Jay Lake is creatively contagious. We should just nail that fact down right now because several of these stories are connected to him in some way. This particular story was born on a Saturday morning in October 2005 during a chat session with Jay on AIM. We were talking about something (I don't remember what) and he said "Someday we'll all be Scholes's." And I typed back: "No, soon we shall all be Saunders with his greasy hair and his sweaty hands and his stink of onions and menthol shaving cream."

I don't know why I typed it. Leroy my inner redneck muse just showed up and wanted something to do, I reckon. After Jay and I finished chatting, I slid right into finishing this story about conformity and about everyone becoming the same, about the fear of becoming someone we don't like and then discovering that if we were them, we probably wouldn't mind so much.

I actually worked for a few years in a merchandising supply company and drew a bit from my time there (that's where the label gun repairman bit of my biography comes into play.)

Eventually, this was picked up by Deb Layne for *Polyphony 6.*

A Good Hair Day In Anarchy

One visit to Ed's Barber Shop — with a story due for the Swensons' writing class — and voila, another paper child was born back on Memorial Day weekend 1998. I'd read a lot of westerns as a kid and the notion of a space western was just too cool to pass up. Of course, it wasn't nearly as cool as *Firefly*, which showed up later to wow me.

"A Good Hair Day in Anarchy" is one of the oldest stories in the collection. It languished for a goodly while but eventually found a home with Lone Star Stories. Why did it languish? Because I didn't really think it was all that great a tale. Imagine my surprise when it was picked up for a reprint in Suddenly Press's *Best of the Rest 3: Year's Best Unknown Science Fiction and Fantasy.*

The lesson here? We're not the best judge of our own work.

Write it, revise it, submit it, and go write another. Let the editor decide what's good enough for print.

Into The Blank Where Life Is Hurled

I still owe John Pelan a beer for this story.

We were having lunch in the U-District (in Seattle) when he told me his next editorial project was going to be a tribute anthology to William Hope Hodgson.

Until then, I'd not heard of Hodgson but that was quickly remedied. I picked up *House on the Borderlands, The Night Land,* and several other books and started getting familiar. When the story hit, I felt it. My first glimpse of it was when I read about Hodgson's encounter with Houdini and suddenly, I knew they had to serve time in Hell together. I ran off to beef up on my familiarity with Houdini. I started the story in August 2000, wrote a few pages, and then bogged down into Life Stuff. But I read the fragment a few years later and became re-enthused. I went to Ellensburg, Washington, in 2002 for a conference and while I was there I decided to do some research on Hodgson in the Central Washington University Library. I wrapped the story in Fall 2002. After it made its rounds to the pro markets, my pals David Goldman and Damian Kilby urged me to send it to Writers of the Future. I won third place for my quarter and had my first pro-level publication along with the other perks of winning the contest, including an amazing workshop and a beautiful bit of art that illustrates the story (framed and on the wall of my den.)

"Into the Blank Where Life is Hurled" is one of my favorites among my paper children. Some Easter eggs, too. The code between Bess and Harry is real — it spells out BELIEVE. He'd promised his wife that he would get word to her if there was an afterlife and they'd agreed on that code. And the electric pentagram is from Hodgson's Great Carnacki tales. The title comes from Hodgson's poem, "Grief," at the end of *The House on the Borderland.*

The story has deep personal meaning for me as well: This was the third of my hell stories and the first in which our heroes escape to better things. In a way, it marks my own transition from a darker time in my life into a bright and shining season. The story originally appeared in *L. Ron Hubbard Presents Writers of the Future, Volume XXI,* 2005.

The Santaman Cycle

This, of course, wasn't a story. It was a writing exercise. Just ask John Pitts.

I'd written the first bit of this on a lark, experimenting with a different style of writing. I pulled open the file at a Crossroads Mall Writing Sunday one day while visiting the Pitts Family up north. I shared it with John and he raved about it. "You should finish it."

"It's not a story," I told him. "It's a Writing Exercise."

I will not type exactly what he said here but it was emphatic. He suggested (emphatically) that I finish it and show it to Jay for a second opinion. So I did.

Jay surprised me by immediately offering to buy it for his first solo editorial project, *TEL:Stories*. How could I say no? It was one of my faster sales.

This story plays further on my fascination with the Santa Claus myth. I imagined a world where his myth grew into messianic proportions and gave him the task of saving us all. This one also ended up as a *Talebones Live!* reading, though by then it had already been sold.

I'm told it's one of the shortest epics around.

Hibakusha Dreaming In The Shadowy Land Of Death

Jen and I were up to our necks in buying our new house and getting ready to move when I fell into an IM session with Sean Wallace. Sean's been a big supporter of my writing since reading "Of Metal Men and Scarlet Thread and Dancing with the Sunrise" and he asked me if I'd ever written any Japanese fantasy. Seems he was editing a new anthology . . . .

Of course, it was a terrible time to tackle a new story but I love a good dare. I scoured the internet for as much Japanese folklore as I could find, brushed up on my Japanese history a bit, and fell into the notion of Japanese folklore heroes and gods in group therapy in post-war Tokyo. I wasn't sure where it was all going until one day, I was chatting with Jerry at my day job and he brought up Ed Deming.

Suddenly, it all made sense and came together. Loss of identity in the face of cataclysm and I even worked Godzilla into it.

I wrote the story over a period of four evenings, hunkered down amid stacks of boxes in the new place, researching as I wrote it.

I really enjoyed blending mythology and Total Quality Management into this tale.

It appears in Prime Book's *Japanese Dreams*.

One Small Step

I don't typically write fables with an intentional moral but I got to thinking what would happen if talking chimps got ahold of *The Naked Ape* and the Bible — and what would we do about it? And I got to thinking about the moral of the story. "One Small Step" was the result. It was another one for *Talebones Live!* and when I finished reading it and got to the punchline, the room was so quiet you could hear hair growing.

At Worldcon a few months later, I dropped by the *Aeon* party and told Marti McKenna that I was due to submit something to them. She grinned and said, "Is it the talking chimp story from *Talebones Live?*"

I submitted it that night via email and the next day (on a panel of all things) Bridget McKenna announced the purchase. It appeared in *Aeon Speculative Fiction* #9 in late 2006.

I dedicated this one to my science teacher, Charles Stores, who planted those seeds of knowledge despite my fundamentalist leanings in those days, and whose honest questioning has taught me a better way of life than I ever imagined back then.

I still hope that someday we'll learn the moral of this tale in regards to exploitation and violence. Maybe we'll learn how to be better primates.

Of Metal Men And Scarlet Thread And Dancing With The Sunrise

Sometimes we write stories that change our lives and we don't even know it.

In early 2005, I was reading up on markets and saw that a small press market I was keen on had a call for stories about mechanical oddities. You've probably already read here that I love a good challenge story — I like to write on a dare. Part of the fun in writing is the game of finding some new, fresh way to meet the editor's guidelines and at the same time, tell a story I want to tell.

In this cause, I had a line leftover from that time when I was experimenting with Writing Exercises like "The Santaman Cycle." The line was: *Rudolfo rode to Glimmerglam in the Age of Laugh-*

ing Madness. It stuck with me and when I sat down to write a mechanical oddities story, it popped back into play. I wasn't sure where I was headed and I really didn't think I was on to anything terribly special. I wrote "Of Metal Men" over the course of several lunch breaks, sitting in the Big Town Hero sandwich shop in Portland, nibbling on tuna sandwiches while I cranked out this story about Androfrancines and mechoservitors and ancient spells and Gypsy Scouts.

I'd just won Writers of the Future and I was running giddy at the time.

It went off to the markets and became my second pro level sale when *Realms of Fantasy* picked it up. It picked up some nice recognition along the way, including some fan letters. But the most important thing that came from that sale is Allen Douglas's art — it gripped me, shook me, would not let me go. I saw in his painting of Isaak that there was far more to the story than the bit I'd written.

Eventually, this story expanded into my five book series *The Psalms of Isaak*, with the first volume — *Lamentation* — appearing from Tor in February 2009.

I felt my life change the day my agent told me Tor was taking all five books.

It was a nice feeling. I'm glad I listened to my Redneck Muse Leroy and wrote this one when the idea popped up and dared me.

So Sang The Girl Who Had No Name

This was another of those stories written for the Swensons' class — and my first Hell story. I wrote it in the summer of 1998. One of my favorite C.S. Lewis books is *The Great Divorce*. And of course, I'm fascinated by religion — leftover from my days as a preacher, I think, though I've changed a good deal since then. The notion struck me one day, after reading Lewis's book, that if free will were one of God's great gifts upon humanity, that it stood to reason that our free will should continue as long as we have awareness . . . even beyond the grave if there were an afterlife. So why not be able to choose? And in Lewis's book, he imagines a traveler going by bus from hell to heaven in order to be saved. Why not a traveler by bicycle in order to extend grace? In order to give a grief-struck trucker a song that made hell bearable to him and called down bits of heaven into it?

Somehow all of that processing became this story. It was the second story I ever sold (in 2000 to Twilight Showcase) — and then I sold it again later to Jeremy Tolbert at *Fortean Bureau* in 2004.

The shriekers and howlers all end up in "Into the Blank" of course. The song he sings — well, I drop enough hints there that you should be able to figure it out. It was my brother's favorite song — they played it at his funeral when I was a little boy. It became a comfort to me and remains my favorite song to this day.

It's seen me through some troubled waters of my own.

Edward Bear And The Very Long Walk

When I was in the first grade, my folks let my sister and me pick out one LP record each. I picked a pretty cool dramatization of *Planet of the Apes* and *Beneath the Planet of the Apes*. My sister picked an LP of someone reading a handful of the original Winnie-the-Pooh stories — not the Disney version but the classic. Oddly enough, it grabbed me more than my own record and I found myself listening to it over and over again. Eventually, I also read all of the stories Milne wrote about his "bear of little brain."

Flash forward to 2000. I had re-read the Milne books as an adult, fallen in love with his writing all over again and I suddenly thought there was a story in it. I'd read Waldrop's "Heirs of the Perisphere" and it had fueled my imagination a bit. I knew it could be done. So I set out to tell my little story about a toy bear stranded on a hostile alien planet, the sole surviving member of a colonization effort gone wrong.

In 2001, it found a home in *Talebones* — my second sale to that esteemed publication. When it came out, I dedicated it to Howard for showing me the way.

This was the first of my stories to get a bit of buzz. It landed me a great note from my TOC-mate, Jim Van Pelt, whose work had been knocking my socks off for a few years at that point. It also led to a rather stellar *Tangent* review that brought about one of the closer friendships I've ever had. Back before he was Jay Lake the Literary God, he was Jay Lake the *Tangent* Reviewer and Literary God in Training. He said nice things, I said "Thank you," and not long after, we met at a convention and a legendary friendship was born. The story went on to pick up an Honorable Mention in *Year's Best Science Fiction*, some scattered award recommendations, and then marched out again in 2002 (*Best of the Rest 2*) and in 2005 (*Revolution SF*). Most recently, it's landed in the audio world as a part of *Escape Pod*, read beautifully by Stephen Eley. It continues to be my most popular story.

I think it's because we all want to believe that the simple and ordinary can be heroes, too, if we answer the call.

That Old-Time Religion

I love writing challenge stories. Time allowing, it's a sure way to get a story out of me quickly. It worked on "Hibakusha Dreaming" and "Of Metal Men" and "The Doom in Love in Small Spaces." It worked on this one, too.

Another market popped up — they wanted short stories featuring the Ten Commandments. I got pretty excited, this tying in nicely with my former occupation and all. Fortunately, they listed some of the stories they weren't seeing enough of and that one about idolatry and jealousy made the list. I had this idea suddenly and went off and cranked out this bit about the end of the world as we know it.

Then, of course, I re-read the guidelines just prior to submission and my heart sank. They wanted stories that were more in keeping with modern day Christian interpretations. I think they used the words "uphold biblical values" somewhere in the small print. Suddenly, I realized that though idolatrous orgies, insecure deities and faithless followers were all extremely biblical in the truest, most honest read of that collection of scattered writings, these were not the biblical values they were looking for.

So it never got to them. But it eventually landed at *Weird Tales* and that was a high point. Most of my heroes were published there, and the day I picked up my copy I got quite twitterpated seeing my name in that fine magazine.

East Of Eden And Just A Bit South

Remember how I said Jay Lake is creatively contagious? This story is how I learned that great lesson. We were at Norwescon in 2003 at the beginning of our friendship and I first broached the subject of writing something together. He gave me a title: "The Boy's Own Guide to Dating Outside the Gene Pool" and turned me loose to start a story that he would later finish.

Of course, loving a dare, straightway I bent my mind towards his clever title and started running through exactly what kind of scenarios would require such a guide. First, I dabbled with aliens but that seemed too obvious. And then, that age old question dropped nicely into my brain somewhere between Seattle and Longview on I-5: Where *did* Cain find his wife? And it was as if the writers of the *Dukes of Hazzard* decided to try their hand at the Book of Genesis.

I got home, sat down, and wrote the first half of this story. I sent it to Jay for him to finish. Then realized out of the blue that I knew exactly how it needed to end, finished it off that night, and sent Jay a note apologizing profusely for bungling our first collaboration. He was kind and told me I could keep the title but in the end, it was too cool of a title for me to take so "East of Eden and Just a Bit South" took its place. I'm still looking forward to seeing what Jay does with his title. It'll be awesome whatever it is.

I remember back in my preaching days that there were several answers to the age-old question of where Cain got his wife. I like the one I came up with. And of course, I wrote this just a week or so after a certain redhead landed in my life. On one of those first dates, she was complaining about her hair not doing what she wanted it to. This is the first time Jen debuted in my fiction but it surely wasn't the last. There's quite a trail of amazing redheads running through my fiction now.

"East of Eden" appeared in *Aeon Speculative Magazine* in February 2006. Trailers, Yoohoo and angels named Bubba. It's a world I hope to return to someday.

Fearsome Jones' Discarded Love Collection

When I lived in Seattle, I knew a man very much like Fearsome. He made his living selling a newspaper for the homeless and he was just chock full of character. I had this image in my head of a down-on-his-luck homeless man who collected bits of discarded love. And somewhere in the midst of it, I heard yet another story of a young girl leaving her newborn infant in some place where one ought not to leave their new little person. I found myself thinking about the circumstances that could bring something like that about and I wondered what would happen if the baby were half alien.

Voila. Another story came together. This one eventually landed at *Fortean Bureau* back in July 2004.

Ken Scholes

The Doom Of Love In Small Spaces

In January 2005, I started working for a government agency and, being a writer, my brain is always looking for story. There, tangled up in the red tape of procurement and contracting, I've had the opportunity to see Bureaucracy at work. It's no surprise that it bled into my fiction since all of my fiction is fueled by living with my eyes wide open. Back in 2006, when I decided to try my hand at a spicy slipstream story for an anthology I wanted to break into, I fell into this little tale about a world short of love and a supply troll who worked to keep things broken so he'd be needed.

This story surprised me when it showed up and when I got to the middle, I was ambushed yet again. I had no idea that this was a loose sequel to "The Santaman Cycle" until I found myself writing the Dragon's Mass scene and discovered that that little epic of mine had become the gospel of that post-apocalyptic world.

Lately, Drum and Harmony have been on my mind. I'm wondering if that means I'll be visiting them again soon?

This one was published in the April 2008 issue of *Realms of Fantasy*.

Summer In Paris, Light From The Sky

I think if I've ever written a story that could be misunderstood, this is it. I've been told that it's even a *dangerous* story. I suppose perhaps it is, in a way.

It was August 2005 and I was getting ready for my Writers of the Future workshop in Seattle. The weekend before, my pal Ken Rand came to Portland to teach at the Willamette Writers Conference. Because he was staying with us, Ken arranged for Jen and me to attend his class at the conference. He was teaching from his book *From Idea to Story in 90 Seconds* — definitely a book you'll want if you're a writer. One of the many exercises he taught us was one where we took three randomly generated words and brainstormed a story verbally with our partner in ninety seconds. My three words were Hitler Leads Whiskey and I brainstormed a tale where Hitler went to work for a distillery outside Paris and led a resistance movement against a Totalitarian French regime. The next day, the story was still brewing and I knew I would need to write it.

I wrote the quotations first — arranging them in such a way that they would tell the second half of the story in a kind of order that gradually revealed what happened *after* Hitler left France for America. Then, I wrote the connecting narrative. I started it on a Monday and finished the story on the train to Seattle the following Friday. It doesn't really follow the conventions of an alternate history but it wasn't intended to. And though some have expressed concern over my choice of a protagonist, I think I needed it to be a monster everyone could recognize.

Why? Well, because I've unfortunately known some monsters and they're not always so easy to recognize. And at some deep, under the surface place, I was exploring these monsters and the circumstances that brought them about. I think our monsters are made more than they are born. I think that our environment and our upbringing can bring about great good or great evil. Who can know if Hitler would've taken a different path if he'd grown up in a different Europe or if he'd had a different relationship with his family of origin? Could an evil mass-murderer be a human rights activist? I think this is the best short story I've ever written. It may be the best I'll ever write. I weep and watch the goosebumps rise every time I read it.

I hope it continues to be taken in the spirit with which it was written. Early indicators are that it will be. It's to be my first work of fiction translated into another language — Hebrew, of all languages — for a leading science fiction magazine in Israel. And it's the first of my stories to rack up a sizeable number of Nebula recommendations.

It originally appeared in *Clarkesworld Magazine* in November 2007.

Last Flight Of The Goddess

Jay Lake called this a love letter to my wife as well as Gary Gygax in his introduction to the original hardcover that Fairwood Press put out in 2006. He was right, of course. I was sad to hear of Gary's passing this year — he changed my life with his little game — and this is as much a tribute to Dungeons and Dragons as it is to my amazing wonder-wife, Jen West.

I was playing Fable, a video game that actually aged your hero and allowed him to marry, when this story showed up on my lap during the winter of 2004. It was reminding me of my Dungeons and Dragons days as a kid. I had the first line and then after that, I just ran to keep up. This is the first time I remember a character seeming to dictate to me rather than simply being the subject of my authorial manipulations. I let my fingers fly while Andro told me his story. He broke my heart and then filled it.

This is about love and life and loss and what treasure and adventure are *really* about. And like all of my stories, it's a metaphor of something deep at work inside of me. In this regard, the discovery of family and a love deeper than any I've ever known. I could not have written this story if I'd not married Jen just six months before.

And it unfolded organically — the scenes laying themselves out with our hero and heroine sharing their lives together amid swordfights and magic diapers. And even Jen was hooked right away — she kept asking me when I was going to finish and she would have me read each scene as I wrapped it. It was a big hit, especially with her.

Of course, the market for novelettes is pretty thin and it was too tongue-in-cheek for many of the bigger magazines. So I thought it would be doomed to languish. This is actually it's third appearance in print.

The first time, it was a single run hand-bound copy made by the ever-generous Stephen Stanley — complete with a Stephen Stanley original cover — so that I could give it to my wife for Christmas 2005.

And that gave me an idea. So in 2006, I sent Patrick a note asking him who he knew out there that might do a good job with a chapbook. He asked why. I told him I had a novelette that no one seemed to want. He asked to read it and then, voila, it hooked him, too.

He then designed a stunning cover and put together a beautiful little limited-edition hardbound and it became my first stand-alone title. It was released at World Fantasy Convention 2006 and did very well with reviewers and readers.

I think Jim noted at the front that this was the right closer. I think so, too. I think it says everything there is to say about what is important to me.

As always, it is dedicated to the Fiercest and Fairest of them all. We've adventured together these last five years and the treasure I've amassed is sizeable. Thank you, darling.

Well, there you have it. A little bit about each of these forays into my imagination forest. A lot grows there. The alligators I'm wrestling. The lessons I'm learning. The notions I'm exploring. Most of the time, it's beneath the surface and it only bubbles up into my awareness after it's found its way into a story. I wouldn't have it any other way — it makes the process more meaningful, I think. One the reasons I've dedicated this book in part to John Pitts is because he told me, back in 1998, that I should write from my own biography and not be afraid of that. It changed how I wrote. It led to these stories, all of which have had John's eye upon them over this decade of brotherhood and writing. (Thanks, pal.)

And the other person I dedicated this collection to? My high school English teacher, Joan Owens. J.O. was the first person beyond my family to recognize my knack for storytelling and feed that muse inside me. She took me to hear Vonnegut speak. She took me to hear Angelou speak. She made me write, write, write some more and encouraged me to submit. She helped get me into the Young Author's Conference and the Centrum Art Camp at Fort Worden. She read my stories and loved them. Of course, I left writing behind me for about a decade but when I came back, I dropped her a note along with some of the earlier stories in this collection. She was delighted that I'd finally come home to Story. Alas, I tried to find her again in 2006 but she'd left the party before the punch was served.

I think she'd be tickled to know that an English teacher (Jim) wrote the introduction to this book and an English teacher (Patrick) wrote the preface and published it. It's a serendipitous honoring of her influence — and the influence of all teachers — on the lives of the young.

Well, time to say thanks. Thank you, John and Joan. Thank you, Patrick Swenson and Jim Van Pelt. Thank you, Jen. Thank you, Jay. Thank you, Howard. Thank you, Writers of the Future contest, and thank you, Miscellaneous Editors, who first brought these stories into print. Also, thank you, Lynne, for those magical proof-reading eyes.

And last but certainly not least: Thank you, Dear Reader, for giving your time to this book. I hope you've enjoyed it and I hope you'll come back to visit me in other books as I keep logging my Imagination Forest for stories to tell.

Ken Scholes
Saint Helens, OR
June 24, 2008